Pardners

by
Dave Lloyd

ISBN-13: 978-1493673353

Other books and short stories
by Dave Lloyd

Fiction

Outlaw
The Pistol

The Montana Saga
The Rebels - book one
Pardners - book two
T.S. Grounds - book three
Home Ranch - book four

Riverboat Trilogy
Fort Sarpy - book one
Upriver- book two
Captains - book three

Books of Short Stories
Tales
Arikara and Lord Guest

Sharpshooter Trilogy
Sharpshooter
The Hunters
Legacy

Non-fiction

History of Early Rosebud

DEDICATION

My historical fiction series is respectfully dedicated to my grandmother, Catherine Barley Lloyd, my father, William James Lloyd, and my mother, Winnifred (Jaastad) Lloyd. They all grew up in Rosebud, Montana, or across the river from it. It must have been a nice time and place to have been young.

These books are memorials to those Montanans who served in the conflicts depicted herein in defense of their homes and country. Any mistakes I have made in them are mine alone.

I would like to acknowledge Rigg's Camera and Gifts of Miles City, Montana, and the now closed Coffrin's Studio for many of the photos I was allowed to use in this book when I first published it in 1989. The Huffman pictures are now owned by Huffman's Wild West Gallery in Bozeman, Montana. To me, the Lady Cameron and Huffman pictures are priceless windows into our past.

PARDNERS
by
DAVE LLOYD

PART I
DAYS OF THUNDER

Chapter 1

Miles Town, Dakota Territory

Wheels crunched on gravel as the bay team pulled the incline up the north bank of the Yellowstone. The ford was downstream of Fort Keogh and looking back from the wagon seat, the boy could just see the early morning smoke of cook fires beginning to rise above the cantonment.

There was a low hanging mist on the river. Coming across, it had swirled around them like the water had eddied about the wheels of the wagon. Pulling out from the fort in the dark, they had run into its grayness at the same time they had encountered the cottonwood trees which stood sentinel along the river's south bank. October's chill had begun to litter the ground with bright colored leaves.

The bay team, reluctant to leave their corral with its crowded warmth, moved slowly in their harness, pulling the haltered saddle horse tied behind them in a shuffling head-down walk.

Like the horse, the boy at the old man's side was sleep-groggy and fighting morning cold, his ears tucked below the brown blanket coat's upturned collar.

Speaking with a soft lisp, the old man urged the team on up the draw, topping out onto the bluffs which leaned over the north bank, expertly working the lines. The wagon, heavy loaded and tarped tightly overall, creaked and rocked on the uneven path.

The old hunter had shaken the boy awake in the dark and with no words being spoken, they had made ready to pull out. The boy had done his early morning business, washed his hands from a wooden bucket hanging from the wagon side, then started breakfast.

The old man came to the fire and picked up his cup, holding it out for the coffee the boy poured. While the boy had remade the fire, put on the battered coffee pot and fried bacon and potatoes in a blackened fry pan, the man had nose-bagged the team and hitched up, his hands sure and gentling in the morning dark. The saddle horse came nuzzling in when it heard the bays crunching oats and, head through the corral bars, begged the man for some, too. The other horses in the corral had mostly all shied from the activity stirring just outside the railings, but the horses of the man and boy, dog gentle from countless grainings and handlings, came eagerly for their morning feed.

Rays of dawn spread across the eastern sky, tingeing the hills about them with red, turning the thinning mist pearl-white. The boy felt a talking mood coming on as he saw the sun's rim begin to show above the rugged sky line off east and down-river to them. "Will it live, do you think, Matthew?"

"Made it through the night. My guess is it will," the terse reply came. Matthew Ground's voice, lisping soft and pleasant sounding, carried easily above the noise of wagon and horses.

"It lost a lot of blood before you got him all stitched up. I wasn't sure" The boy glanced shyly at the man riding next to him." I didn't mean to get you in trouble with the law."

The pale blue eyes swung up to the boy, piercing him now as they always did when the man looked full at him. "See you learn a lesson from it, son. A man looks for trouble, he always finds it."

Abashed, the boy nodded. He looked back at the dog lying atop the tarp towards the back. Its coat was short-haired and brindle colored, seamed in places with stitching which showed the man's handiwork. It had a huge snake-like head, swollen just now 'til its eyes were nearly shut, from the savage beating it had taken. Seeing the boy's attention, it slapped its tail a few times on the canvas.

"I wonder what its name is?" the boy said, putting his eyes back on the road ahead.

"I'd say it's your dog now and your job to name it." The man smiled with the words, and passed the boy the lines. Toby's heart lifted. It was going to be all right now, he knew. Matthew wasn't mad at him.

Other than his partner, Frank, Matthew didn't seem to be a man who liked people around him. He didn't come right out and say it, but Toby could notice him begin to tense when they came into contact with others. The old man would become even more alert, if that was possible. His right hand, too, Toby knew, would be free always and close to the holstered pistol at his side.

He was like the white headed eagles they saw occasionally, the boy thought. Same eyes, long white hair falling back over his collar from under the low crowned hat, a thin, hooked nose. He was spare and lean but thick about the shoulders with work-ridden muscle. His hands and wrists showed strength yet, too, though here and there across their backs could be seen red age spots. Rarely did he let his beard grow, preferring instead to shave every other day or so. Which was curious, Toby often thought, for it would have covered the old wounds which showed so on his face.

The sun began to warm the day. Both stripped off their coats and stuck them under the tarp cover. The man settled back, his pipe going steady now, eyes moving like always, relaxed on the wagon seat. The boy was good with the horses, a teamster now with years of experience at the lines. Both rifles rested between them on the seat loaded but uncocked. Twin belts loaded with cartridges lay by their feet on the wagon floor. The two rifles were Henry repeaters and it was all Toby could do to lift one, carry and shoot it. As often as not his target practice took the form of meal getting. Usually it was small game: prairie chicken, jack rabbit or young sage hen. Most were head-shot by the boy with rifle or pistol, for, as much as he hated to kill, it early had been impressed on him that one must do so to live himself, and the head shot was a mercy shot.

Mid-day found them far out from the river, threading their way through chest-high greasewood and sagebrush and moving in a northwesterly direction. Antelope bands were nearly always in sight, first stalking towards them in curiosity, then stretching themselves in swift flight away. Several times also during the morning they had sighted small groups of buffalo out on the prairie grazing head-down but wary.

In the tall buffalo grass were a myriad of small scurrying animals that never failed to fascinate and amuse Toby. Rabbits, the big jacks and smaller bunnies, bounded away from the wagon path as they went along. Flocks of large, slow walking sage hens and the smaller prairie chickens scattered before them, ruffling their feathers at the indignity of having to move out of the way. Occasionally a badger was glimpsed, a skunk, or a rattlesnake sunning itself. Meadowlarks trilled, and in the distance, mourning doves could be heard cooing their haunting refrain. The boy took it all in with a concealed delight, for he liked the wild things, the animals, and dreaded the time when he had to help kill them.

3

All combined to bring a sense of peace to everything, affecting both man and boy alike with a sense of quietude as they rattled along.

They stopped for noon on a small rise so they could watch the country around. Toby built a small fire and put on the coffee like always—one large scoop of Arbuckle's to the pot of water from the cask strapped to the wagon. The man slipped the bridles on the team and hobbled them so they could graze a little. He did the same with the saddle horse. Toby, meanwhile, brought the dog a drink. The animal lay still after taking a little water but his tail thumped the tarp in gratitude.

They brushed each other off before Toby poured the hot, steamy coffee, the rich tan dust smelling of sage and grass. An hour before Matthew had told the boy to get his little plinker, a single shot Remington .22 carbine he had bought for him from a trooper at the fort. The soldier had sold it for five dollars and hurried off to Miles to meet his friends in a bar. Matthew had sent Toby with a silver dollar to the trader's store in the cantonment where he'd gotten several boxes of the little shells. The boy had been delighted with it and Matthew had helped him sight it in behind the cantonment. "It'll save lead and powder and your shoulder, too, lad. But keep up your practice with the others." The little gun had proven accurate to the old man's satisfaction and Toby had used it to shoot some prairie chickens for the noon meal right from the wagon, the horses used to the sound of gunfire.

The fry pan was sputtering with bacon grease and Toby rolled the cut-up chickens in the top of his flour sack then laid them piece by piece in the hot pan. Next he sliced some potatoes into another. They'd bought a hundred pound sack at Leighton's, as fried spuds were a favorite.

They were just beginning to eat from laden tin plates when the horses swung their heads to the east and a party of four riders topped the ridge several hundred yards from the camp. Matthew watched them come for a moment, then set his plate to the ground and pulled his rifle from the wagon. He motioned to Toby to gather the stock to the wagon, where the boy tied them tightly. Then he also got his rifle from the wagon seat and stepped behind to watch with the man as the riders came up.

"Not too friendly a reception there, mister!" one of the men called to him from where they were walking their horses in. He'd seen the rifles, noted as did the others, the wariness.

4

"It's not a friendly country. Hold it right there!" The soft lisp had a steely ring to it that halted the group about twenty-five yards out, their pack horses behind jostling into the riders.

"Now mister!" one of the riders began in an angry tone, only to be interrupted by the taller, older man flanking him.

"We're peaceable, sir, and merely after a cup of that good smelling coffee and maybe a little information on some horses we're looking for. May we come in?" The rider leaned on his pommel and motioned to the fire.

"You may. The rest may keep to their saddles 'til we've talked. Come ahead. Watch the others close, lad, I'll talk to this one."

Matthew stepped around the wagon. The dog raised his head as he passed and slapped his tail briefly.

The old man kept to the side, his eyes taking in the man walking to the fire and also the three riders behind him. "Cattle drovers," he thought, relaxing a little.

"Well now, sir," the taller man began, stepping down. "My name's John McLean. These riders are mine. Chipper Bowe, Dutch Henry and T. J. Roberts. We're hunting strayed stock, horses, sir, with an MC brand on the left hip. You wouldn't have seen any? Twenty head from our remuda came up missing three days ago. We lost their trail because of buffalo, but they were heading towards the river."

"No. We're just out of Fort Keogh this morning. Haven't seen them. Pour yourself a cup and we have some grouse here if you'd like some. Toby and I have already filled our plates."

He turned to the riders, satisfied they were what McLean had said. They had the unmistakable stamp of working cattlemen.

"Step down and come in." The riders gratefully did so, one of them getting cups and plates from a pack horse." Toby, you can pour for 'em. And cut some more spuds up." The boy obediently leaned his rifle against the wagon and stepped to the fire to comply.

Later, the men sat by the fire, smoking and sipping coffee, the horses grazing close by.

"I'm bringing a herd up from the east to Fort Benton. Been a hard trip. Lost both stock and men. Indians, stock thieves and weather have all been bad, "McLean rolled another smoke and seemed disinclined to leave now he'd eaten. He glanced again at the stern faced old man across the fire from him. And at the boy, a slender towhead about eleven or twelve, sober and quiet but very attentive to the white haired man.

Though tan and smooth-faced, the old man had puckered scars on each cheek, an apparent old bullet wound. "Ah, well," he thought. "Many men could show scars from the war." Come to that, he could himself, thinking of the leg which still bothered him when he'd ridden as he had these past months. Still, the man across from him was singular, a man to respect, he felt, never mind his apparent age. A man he'd like to know and ride with, sometime.

"Well, Toby, you have the touch of a good cook. Wouldn't like to hire on my outfit, would you? The boys are about to hoorah the one we got out of camp. His biscuits are like rocks, I swear."

The one called Dutch Henry assented with a grunt. "That's so, Boss. The boy here could cook rings around old Gravy boat. How's about it, son? Want to pitch in with a tough cow outfit?" He smiled through his cigarette smoke at the boy doing up the remains of the meal.

"No, sir, thank you, though, I better stay with Mr. Grounds." He knew the men were funning him, started to smile, then realized with a pang that he'd let the old man's name slip from him. He couldn't stop a glance at the man sitting motionless at the wagon wheel, puffing his pipe.

"Grounds?" The name ran through the minds of the men by the fire. They said nothing, however, of it then.

"Well, sir, we should travel on and I guess, let you do the same. I see you have a bad hurt dog there. Is he going to live?"

McLean stood and walked to the rear of the wagon, looking at the motionless dog.

"I think he might make it now. He's made it through the night," Matthew remarked, standing also. "Would you be needing some food or coffee to take along?"

"Oh, I don't guess so. Thanks. We'll head into Keogh and pick some up. May hear of our horses there. "The riders mounted and came forward. "Thank you for your hospitality, sir. We may see you again. So long. Toby, you keep pitching those biscuits!"

"I will, sir, good-bye." The two stood and watched as the group rode south toward Miles town.

"Toby"

"I know, sir." The boy looked down in misery.

"It's alright, lad. Let's move on." The man turned to hitch up.

Chapter 2

Sunday Creek, North Side of the Yellowstone.

Night found them on the north fork of Sunday Creek. It no longer was flowing but retained some shallow pools of good water, though muddied from buffalo, deer, and other wild game. A hole dug in sand on the shore and bailed a few times brought clear enough water for Toby to fill his coffee pot and water the horses.

While he was at it, he dipped some for the dog, too, who thanked him with his tail and lapped greedily, holding up his massive head with a little more strength. Later the boy spread a saddle blanket over the dog against the fall's evening chill.

"Take your roll over by the creek and don't forget your guns." The instructions were puffed out around the stem of his evening pipe. The man himself also slept away from the fire each night with gun in hand and rifle close. With his other precautions, it had gained him his old age. A dubious reward, he sometimes thought.

Next day brought with it a weather change, a cold wind which presaged the fact that it could be a short autumn. Mid-afternoon they pulled down into a grove of cottonwoods clustered round a hot springs. A cheery fire flickered by a deep pool and Toby pulled the team into a spot close to it, in front of which a tall, thin, stoop shouldered man stood. A roan saddle horse nickered in the grove and the team answered.

"You're early! Didn't expect you 'til tomorrow or the next day! Hiyah, Toby! Catch any dance hall girls in town?" The deep southern voice didn't match the thin man it came from. "Did you'all get my chew?"

"Sure did, Frank! We got everything!" Toby replied eagerly as he jumped down. Matthew followed and began unhitching.

"Hmm. See you brought a dog critter back, too." The thin man had sauntered to the wagon and caught sight of the dog still in his place at its rear. "All beat to hell, looks like."

"He was beat bad, Frank." The boy glanced at Matthew. "Matthew stopped it."

"Hmmm. Yes, I bet he did."

The thin man, hands resting on a heavy gun belt, spit a stream of brown from pursed lips. "Damn it, Matthew! I don't know if I can take another month of your being down because some son-of-a-bitch got in your gun sight!" The words were drawled through a half-smile, but serious, nonetheless.

"Don't worry, Frank. This one won't bother me. He was beating on Toby when I came up."

Both men turned as one and walked to a camp table. On top of it a chess game, hand carved from bone, horn and wood, was set up and showed a match in progress. They sat in canvas folding chairs and Toby brought the coffee in each man's favorite mug.

"Supper'll be ready soon. Frank, you have to see my new gun! It's a little .22. Shoots dead on." He brought the weapon over to Frank, who looked at it with exaggerated admiration, then went off to see to supper.

Around the cottonwood grove came the sounds of a myriad of songbirds: red-winged blackbirds perched on the cattails surrounding the larger warm springs pool warbling their melodious call, meadowlarks and thrushes adding their music to the chirping of sparrows and numerous small yellow canaries. To it all, the boy listened contentedly as he went about his evening work. His world was at peace. He couldn't think of another place he'd rather be than with the two old men and the animals he loved around him. He hummed a little as he worked and the dog, hearing, thumped his tail on the hard ground. The men sipped their coffee and studied the chessboard.

"I scouted farther northwest while you was gone. Lots of buffalo and I heard some gunning down the one draw about ten miles out. I didn't go see who it was. Didn't want to spoil a stand. Howsoever, I also run across some old Indian sign. And this far west it could be Blackfeet. More likely Sioux, though. Jackson smelled 'em before I saw their tracks. That horse's a caution, I tell you. It can smell Indians farther than Toby's young eyes can probably see them." Frank's lean jaws worked rhythmically as he prepared to spit again.

"Well, that means we better work within range of each other. And Toby should come with us. The camp'll have to look after itself while we're out." Matthew moved his rook.

"I got $240 for those we took in. Supplies came to $40 or so. Here's the bill and your half." He reached in his left vest pocket, drew forth a lading receipt and some bills. "Took paper. It's easier to carry," he said.

"Yeah, I like the precious metals myself, but they do weigh you down. Knew a man once to drown because his money belt was so heavy. And he just wouldn't unbelt it," Frank reminisced. He moved a piece on the chess board, "There. That ought to do for your knight."

"Supper's ready!"

Toby called and the men got up to fill their plates at the fire, then sat back at the table, the chess pushed aside so the boy could sit with them. They sat in silence while Matthew said grace.

"Oh Lord, we thank you for our safe return. We thank you for the good dog you have seen fit to provide us. May he be a protector to the lad. We ask that you forgive me for taking a human life and lastly, Lord, we thank you for our daily bread, the food we have before us. Amen."

The others echoed the 'Amen' and the meal was eaten silently.

Later, Matthew went to check on the livestock. Toby and Frank took up the supper dishes. As usual, Toby washed and Frank wiped, then put the things away in the cook box.

"Alright, Toby, let's hear it. You know Matthew isn't going to say anything. What happened in town?"

The boy handed him a soapy plate, which he dipped in hot water.

"Well, we got to the river at sundown. The hides were heavy and Matthew took it easy on the horses. Next morning we pulled over to town and Matthew sold the hides at Leighton's. Then we loaded up the wagon with supplies, or Matthew did. He gave me some money for candy, and I walked downtown to see what it looked like.

There was a crowd in front of Chinnick's Saloon. They'd built kind of a cage there and there was a bunch of badgers in it, most of 'em dead, and the dog. There was a badger hanging from his leg and wouldn't let go. Finally the dog killed it, but it hurt him bad. Then this man came in and started whipping on the dog and swearing and cussing. Nobody else seemed to care so I ran up and grabbed his arm, asking him to stop, then he took in on me." Toby stopped and showed

Frank several welts on his body where the quirt had landed. Frank looked grim.

"So then, some of the men jumped in and stopped him and about that time Matthew came."

The boy's eyes glowed as he again remembered it, how the old man had suddenly appeared, how the men had released the swearing man. Matthew had faced him, saying nothing to him but asking Toby if he was all right. When Toby had said 'yes', Matthew told him to go get the wagon for the dog.

At this, the man had shouted more obscenities, saying the dog was his, if he wanted to kill the damn thing, he would. Toby had obediently started for the wagon, but stopped at the edge of the crowd when he heard Matthew's reply, "No, the dog isn't yours."

"What's that, what do ya mean, you old bastard, that dog is mine!"

"Dead men don't own dogs."

At this, the crowd seemed to see Matthew for the menace he was. His right side turned slightly to the man at his front, his right arm down by his low swinging gun. The crowd scattered from around them.

The man, too, seemed to register a dawning awareness of the peril facing him.

"Well, now I know, it isn't a killing matter over a damn dog, I guess. A few dollars."

"And beating on my son with a quirt? Oh, yes, to me it's a killing matter!" The steel in the soft lisp spread the crowd out even further.

"Well, hell, if that's the " The man had broken off to draw his pistol, a cross-draw from his left side.

The gun had come out of the holster when two shots had struck him down. The old man had fired and put his pistol away before the other had slumped to the ground, hit twice in the left shirt pocket.

Directly after, Sheriff Healey had come and taken Matthew away. The coroner had come and picked up the body. With help from a bystander, Toby had got the dog up into the wagon, had taken it out to the fort and washed and bandaged it as best he could. Later, Matthew had come back and sewn some of the larger cuts together. They'd left the next morning.

"Well, Sheriff Healey is a good man. I'm sure he let him go when he heard the facts," Frank remarked, soberly. He seemed deep in thought.

The dishes done, the men settled down in their canvas chairs for a little more chess before dark. Toby drifted off with his new little gun to try for some prairie chickens coming in to water. Presently, the men heard the plink of the small calibered weapon.

"Toby sure likes that new little popper you bought him," Frank ventured.

"I bought it from a private at the fort after we got in. He wanted some drinking money. Shells are cheap and it doesn't make much noise."

"What about the dog?"

"He's a fightin' dog, a pit bull. Born and bred to kill. He probably won't make much of a pet for the boy. I've seen those kind of dogs fight and it's usually to the death. There's no quit in 'em and they're usually vicious."

"If he's no good, a bullet would be a mercy compared to what he's suffered so far."

For a while they discussed the hunting, then Matthew commented, "What we need to do now is get ready for winter, get some hay put up, some wood stacked. By the springs here is a good spot. We can cut those meadows below. I brought a couple scythes, a rake and another pitchfork."

"What about a cabin this year?" Frank asked, "I hate a dugout. Dirty, stinky, you're always cold. Trouble is, cabin logs are pretty scarce out here on the North Side."

Matthew moved his castle. "How about an Indian lodge? We've both wintered in one before. They're not bad. We could have a big canvas four poler made by the Nez Perce´ that Miles has penned up at Keogh."

Last year had seen the Nez Perce´ flight to get out of the country. After several hard battles, the army had finally caught them before they'd reached Canada and they were being held at Fort Keogh under guard.

"Well now," Frank pondered, "that sounds good, if they'll do it, and we can get it up here. Druther have buffalo hide but I s'pose they couldn't tan 'em in time."

After Toby got his dishes put away, he had gathered up his .22 and some shells. He'd counted out five from the box of fifty, and walked down the coulee away from camp. Frank and Matthew would

11

talk and drink coffee and play chess 'til dark and he knew that it would be okay if he went for a short hunt for tomorrow's pot.

The water took its time going down stream through the coulee and there were cattails where the small pools collected and eddied by the side of the banks. Once he saw a turtle duck its head under and he startled several ducks, who rose squawking and quacking angrily at being disturbed.

Toby drew the gun's breech lever down and stuck a shell in after looking through the bore to make sure it was open. The lands and grooves shone brightly as he held it up to the sky. The men had cautioned him about this several times, citing instances of people hurt when they fired a weapon with an obstructed barrel. "It don't take but a second to make sure she's clear. You don't want to ever forget," Frank had cautioned. His own brother had been injured with an eye put out back in Texas where he'd grown up. Toby knew the men watched him constantly about being gun safe so he was careful now.

Farther down the creek was a grove of stunted cottonwoods. Toby came to their fringe, then settled in behind one with a view to an area which looked like it got some use from game as they came for water.

In that rich wilderness he didn't need to wait long for the parade to begin. First came a mother skunk with some half-grown young ones who wanted to play and wrestled with each other until one fell in. The mother skunk fished her youngster out and scolded the whole bunch back up the bank. Then, in rapid succession, came badger, fox and a wary coyote. Not 'til nearly dark did the birds begin flying and walking in to water. Toby sighted carefully and got three, all head shots at about twenty-five to thirty paces.

"Good shooting for the dim light," he thought proudly. He took a piece of twine from his pocket and tied their legs together, then slung them over his shoulder. The birds and the gun made a satisfying weight for the walk back to camp.

"Three shots. How many birds?" Frank asked as he saw Toby appear in the dusk. "Just three, I couldn't get them to line up or I'd of gotten more," Toby cockily replied. The old man grunted a half-laugh.

The boy put his gun away and went to clean the birds.

"I hardly heard that little popper go off, it's so quiet," Frank commented to Matthew. "Nice gun for the boy, alright."

They sat a while longer and finished their smokes, then headed for their bedrolls.

* * *

The boy was up the next morning as dawn began to tinge the sky red with the promise of another beautiful fall day. He started the fire, put on the coffee and cut bacon for frying. Later, Matthew appeared, poured a cup, then, carrying it, went to take the horses to water. Frank showed up and also poured his morning cup, then started peeling spuds for frying.

Breakfast over, the dog fed and watered, they saddled up and then hitched the team to the wagon. While Toby followed up in it, the men took their Sharps rifles, bandoliers of ammo and canteens, and headed for the killing grounds north of them. Hides were not yet prime, wouldn't be 'til late November, when they would make good robes. Before then they were shot for leather only.

Now came the part that the boy hated and the men also viewed with distaste: the wanton killing of an animal who really had no defense. The men, and even Toby, understood that it was the extinction of a species. They also knew that the Indians depended on the buffalo for their life's food and had legitimate cause for hatred of the white hunters who killed for hides only. Still, it was making them a living and a stake for the future.

The high greasewood and sagebrush forced them to pick a crooked trail for the wagon behind. After a half hour of travel in a northward direction the men halted behind a small butte for Toby to come up to them. When he did, Grounds told him to hold there until he signaled him, or Frank did, then the two rode out and around the butte.

A flat beyond held buffalo grazing which spooked at sight of them back to a larger bunch beyond. The plain behind had groups of the dark shapes scattered over it.

"I'll pull a sneak down this way if you want to go around, " Frank offered. Neither had to go into detail. They had hunted together for too long. Matthew headed off to the left and Frank guided his horse down into a coulee that went in the direction he needed to get in range. Several hundred yards on, he stopped, took a hackamore and lead rope from a saddle bag and secured his horse to a sturdy growth of sagebrush. The sorrel was a five year old, but late broke, and still a mite skittish of gunfire. He took the heavy canvas bandolier filled with .45/120 shells over his shoulder, picked up his rifle, cross-stick and a canteen, and started on up the narrowing coulee.

Once at the crest, he hunkered down, took off his hat to put his empties in, set up pointed cross-sticks and checked the wind with a little dust. It was still blowing lightly towards him. He dropped the breech of his Sharps, glanced through the bore, then inserted a shell and levered the breech home. He set the heavy barrel in the V of the sticks and raised the back sight to the 200 yard notch, the distance his experienced eye told him was between him and the small herd slightly below and to his right. He set the back trigger, took a dead aim at a likely bull and dropped him like he'd been hit by a giant hammer.

The workday had started. Across the flat to his left he heard the sound of Matthew's rifle come back at him like an echo. He rapidly levered the case out, threw it into his hat and stuffed another in the breech. A large cow, hopefully a dry one, came before his sights to sniff the dead bull and he laid it down with another center shot. He was on today, he could feel it. His shoulder, where he'd been shot in the war, wasn't bothering him, and hence his normal flinch from the heavy recoil was missing. Also, his shooting eye seemed a lot clearer, though maybe it was just a trick of the light.

More and more, he was aware physically of good days and bad days—the bad, unfortunately, outnumbering the good too often. It was a sign of age, he knew, and suspected the same was true for Matthew, but they seldom discussed it.

He levered out the case and chambered another shell, picked his targets sparingly and in an area about an acre square, dropped seven buffalo. Then he quit, though the making of a stand was there, the creatures standing dumb and almost resignedly waiting for their bullet. The easiness of it always offended him and, he knew, also bothered Matthew. Thus, they shot only what they could surely handle, and no more. A half hour or less of killing. A half hour, with the boy's help, to skin each buffalo and do it well. Then, at camp, another half hour a hide to spread, stretch, peg, and scrape each one. It all took time and the hides were heavy. The work was hard, with a lot of it on your knees, a bad position for men no longer young. However, well cared for hides, liberally rubbed with alum powder to preserve them from bugs and rot, brought another fifty cents apiece, at least. To increase their production they needed skinners, something Matthew was going to check on in

14

Keogh but didn't get to do. But then, skinners meant more men to feed and bother with.

A good skinner, though, young and active, could handle another twenty hides, which meant eighty dollars or so. They could pay a dollar a hide and still make money. They could also hire a bad one and have more trouble than they cared for. 'Better not to bother. We're making enough as it is,' Frank thought. Both Grounds and he had full money belts and quite a bit more in a tin box strapped to the underside of the large freight wagon where it was out of sight. Would it be enough for their old age and the education of the boy, was the question. Frank doubted it. What they had talked many times of was a horse ranch somewhere. Both he and Matthew could then take their ease and make some money messing with something they didn't have to shoot or skin.

'What's more,' Frank thought longingly, 'horses had a good clean smell to them, a consideration, given the business they were in now. Why is it a man gets himself wrapped up into doing things he detests?' He was tired of killing things: the Rangers, the war and now this.

The last buffalo to go down to Frank's rifle was a big cow. He went back down the draw, collected his horse and rode out on the flat to it, seeing Grounds come forward at nearly the same time. He went to the cow, got down and cut its throat to bleed it, the knife, though razor sharp, dragging in the burred heavy hide. The cow's meat would be choice, much better and more tender than a bull's. Then he mounted and went to the ridge to signal the boy, who, hearing the shooting quit, had already started to come up.

They were half done with the skinning when Grounds looked away toward the south where he could see a little dust rising.

"Get up on the wagon, Toby, and see if you can tell what that is coming."

The boy jumped up on the wagon seat and peered southward, where far out he could see the dust Matthew had spotted.

"Looks like a jerky, sir!"

"That'll be the Sheriff," remarked Frank. "Probably coming to put you both in irons."

Matthew merely grunted and turned back to his skinning. Frank, getting no encouragement to quit and gab a while, did the same. Toby went between each of them, helping turn the animal, sharpen the knives, hoist the hide into the wagon after folding it, or pour the ever-present coffee from the little fire he'd made from chips immediately after driving up onto the flat.

Presently the buckboard, with two men in it, pulled through the sagebrush, down the dry wash and up onto the flat where they were working.

"Howdy, boys, nice day for a buffalo slaughter!" The large man driving hollered as he brought the rough looking big buckskin around close to the bull Grounds was working on. The horse ruffled his nose and turned skittish at the sight and smell of the bloody carcass.

"See you've got the coffee on." The man climbed slowly and stiffly down from the vehicle, went to his horse and snapped a tie rope onto a heavy bit ring, then tied the rope to a sagebrush. "Come on down, Jason, and we'll grab a cup of coffee from 'em here."

Without waiting, he went to the back of the buggy, came up with two enamel cups and stumped to the fire where he poured out two cups of the dark fluid, hot and steamy. One he handed to the silent Jason, who took it eagerly. He was clearly chilled from the long ride in the cold clear air.

The sheriff was a big man, made taller yet by a huge snow white Stetson riding back on his nearly bald head. His mustache, which was tipped with white, rode out and down over his mouth, sticking into his cup as he sipped and slurped.

"Ow, ow, damn good and hot—just the way we like it!" Healey exclaimed, "Sure could use some cream, though." He rummaged around in the wagon and came up with a fruit jar of cream, opened it and poured some in his cup.

"Anyone else care for a dopple of the good life? How about you, son?" Toby eagerly took a generous portion in his own cup then added some more coffee to it. They stood by the bloody carcass and sipped for a while in silence.

"Well, boys, my manners need some close work. This here's Jason Wheeler, an English boy straight from the old country. He's going around with me to visit some of the outfits, see if he can't find work. He's been staying with me and the missus and I'll vouch for his honesty and his being a good worker. He's also a nice boy, his folks raised him right, by jingies. If you can use him, I think he'd work out. Jason, shake hands with two old Texas Rangers and their boy, Toby. Matthew Grounds, Frank Shannon. They will do to ride the river with,

16

as I know. We rode up from Texas together through a storm of Indians, by jingies."

Frank was pleasantly surprised at the straight look and firm grip he received from Wheeler. The young man was short but stockily built, with black wavy hair and a wide forehead which seemed to denote intelligence. His voice was deep when he spoke.

When he shook Toby's hand, he smiled and said, "Howdy, there, as they say out here. I am very pleased to meet you." They all noticed the English accent.

"How do you do, sir." The boy responded with manners ingrained by the two old men who'd brought him up. However, he was subdued around strangers, seeing so few people as he did. Like Frank, he was taken with the pleasant, straight look he received from the man.

"The Arbuckle's tastes better from over a fire, that's a fact, by jingies." The sheriff was talking to Grounds who was folding the bull hide. Together, they hoisted it into the wagon. "Say, Matthew, remember what Captain McCormick used to tell us about stomping snakes? Pull up your boots and watch your backsides? Well, Matthew, beware the dog beater's friends. He has some nasty ones. I just wanted to tell you," Healey said with a sober look.

"I've heard that they've sworn to get you. Their new leader shot old man Riggs to get the Kingship and he was a rough old cob. His name's John Stringer. Stringer Jack, they call him. Good looking, dandy dresser, real polite, hard gambler, never seen him drunk. He's left-handed, Matthew, remember that. Wears a cut-down .44 in a cross-draw holster."

Matthew cleaned his knife and said shortly, "I'll keep it in mind, Tom." He poured his coffee and refilled the sheriff's cup. "Who is doing all the talking? This Stringer Jack?"

"No, some of his crew, I think. They're hunting on the Musselshell, I hear. The one you put under has a brother named Lucas. Lucas Baker. He's probably the one shooting off his mouth. He's a knife man, a skinner, cut up several of his acquaintances, but I haven't heard of him killing anyone. Well, Frank, how's the shoulder been?"

He turned to Frank, who'd been listening nearby.

"Pretty good today, Tom. How's the foot?" The sheriff squirmed at this. Years back he had shot some toes off while practicing his quick draw. Frank liked to tease him about it as Tom was vain about his neat, small feet. He kept them cased in beautiful custom-made boots from McDonald's.

"Well enough," he replied, with a glare at Frank.

Frank smiled. "When you going to clean the riffraff out, Tom? They're filling up the country."

"Oh, it'll happen in due time, boys, due time. Well, I'd better skip along. Are you going to hire my boy here?" He put a hand on Wheeler's shoulder.

"What do you think, Matthew?" Frank directed his question at the stern old man he'd partnered with for many years. He gave a little nod and Frank nodded back. "Yes, we can use you, Wheeler, if you'd like to hire on. Skinning's hard work, though the pay is good. Fifty cents a hide is what we'll pay a beginner. Later, we might double it."

"I'd like to go with Sheriff Healey to visit some of the other camps, if I might. Then when he comes back, if I'm still with him, I'll stay and work for you." The deep bass voice, like his appearance, was pleasing to the ear. "The money sounds all right. That's not a problem. I just want to see some of this vast country. It's exciting!"

Healey laughed. "Son, it's more of the same as right here, though if you'd like to come I can use the company, by jingies. I'll tell you, Jason, that these two here can teach you more about living in this country than anyone I know. If they will take you, I'd work for them."

"That's okay, Tom, let the boy go with you. It'll give him some idea of what's out here." Matthew moved to tighten the cinch on his saddle horse then he swung into the leather. "See you bring him back in one piece. Frank saw some old Indian sign over west."

"Bye the bye, Tom, don't you want to fill your waterbag before you head out?" Frank suggested. The sheriff glared at them all as he turned the buckskin away. "No, damn you, I don't want to fill my waterbags! See you boys tomorrow or the next day."

The buckboard wheels spurted a little dust as he slapped reins and the buckskin jumped into a trail eating trot towards the west. A series of creek drainages, some dry, some running, some pooled here and there, lay in this country north of the Yellowstone, south of the Missouri and east of the Musselshell River. The country thus bounded was called the Big Dry or the North Side: a land of bare buttes, buffalo grass, sagebrush and greasewood. Wild plum and chokecherry thickets lined the creek bottoms, with some cottonwood trees here and there where sufficient water allowed them life. In the draws and along ridges some juniper and cedar trees, along with a few pines, survived, but mostly the land was open and a person could see for a long way. Colors of silver sage, lime green of cactus, tan of grass and sandstone rock and the black-brown of buffalo mingled and merged to a harmonious blend of pastel coloration that pleased the eye. Smells, too, were present: the sharp, pepper-smell of the sage, the musty smell of the dust and the buffalo's tangy scent were a not-unpleasing combination that complemented the sweet smell of plum, chokecherry and cactus blossoms in the warm months. In after years, Toby could instantly be transported back to that place and time by a smell of sage or other familiar scent.

Watching the wagon bumping away over the flat, Frank laughed and slapped his leg. Toby did the same and even Matthew grinned. For a moment, the flat, filled with dead carcasses and startled magpies, echoed to their laughter.

"Biedler said he could follow Tom's trail all the ways back to Keogh by the shit stops he took."

The water on the north side of the Yellowstone River was for the most part full of alkali and if drunk in quantity, became a powerful emetic, and the springs they were camped by were the worst. About the only way it could be used for human consumption was in coffee where the alkali boiled away. Frank had made sure Tom had filled up on the water the first time he'd come out to visit. His sudden attack of acute diarrhea had gotten him some intense ribbing from his friends and Tom had heard all he'd wanted about it by now.

The skins loaded, they pulled back to camp and commenced the job of stretching and staking them out. At dusk the messy job was completed and the two men went in to the smell of buffalo loin chops frying in bacon grease, with biscuits rising in the 'side kick', the collapsible tin oven.

"Toby, if we didn't teach you anything else in this life, you could always get a trail job running a grub wagon," Frank commented. Matthew had told him about McLean's offer.

While they ate, Toby asked them if they thought Wheeler would come back.

"We'll see, son. I think he will, though," Frank replied.

"Why, did you like that pilgrim?"

The boy replied thoughtfully, "Yes. Yes, I did. He sure had a deep voice, didn't he?"

"Well, look who's here." Matthew pointed to the dog that had come crawling out from under the nearby wagon, the smell of meat cooking to much a temptation.

"Here, boy, come here!" Toby called. The dog made it slowly over to the table and lay quivering. Toby scraped the plates onto one and set it in front of the animal, who nosed it and began to eat. "You know, Frank, I think he's getting better." After eating a little more, the dog crept back under the wagon.

The next day Frank's shoulder was paining him and he stayed in camp while Matthew and Toby went out to reconnoiter. Through the night a bank of racing clouds from the west had brought some sleet and the ground was white and wet in places where it had piled up. Frank fed the dog who seemed even better, watered the stock and did up the dishes. Then he fixed some harness, made up some bullets and chopped some wood. About mid-afternoon, his sharp old eyes noticed a flicker of movement at the lip of a coulee about six hundred yards to the west of camp. With no apparent haste he checked his rifle and pistols, put out ammunition in easy reach and went to secure his horse, tying and hobbling it, for his hunch was Indians.

A minute or two after he'd secured the camp, a dozen Indians came up out of the defile, quirting their horses, howling their war cry. Frank lay beside the low wood pile by the dog. His buffalo gun was propped over a bedroll and he held the .44 Henry ready. His pistol was unholstered and on his other side where his right hand could reach it.

"Come on, you bastards. Come on!" Unconsciously he was muttering, and the dog, hearing his voice, moved closer to him and became more alert as he sensed the tension in the man beside him.

At two hundred yards the warriors, spread out as faster horses took the front, passed a white rock. Seeing this, Frank opened fire. The rapid firing with the repeater put down two horses and three of the hard-riding warriors before they passed a second white rock at a hundred yards. The others sheared off, the hooves of their horses throwing dirt clods up and over their heads as they went past the camp. Frank swung on a big buck riding a dark bay. He killed the horse and rolled the rider fifty yards to his front, then made a head shot on the muscular warrior as he raised himself from the ground.

Beside him the dog growled, the sound deep in his chest. The old man looked at the dog and the big scarred head was turned to their rear.

20

Frank grabbed his pistol and turned to engage three Indians who'd entered the rear of the camp. Had the dog not warned him, they'd likely have made him into mincemeat. As it was, their leader raised his rifle, a trapdoor Springfield. Frank threw up his Colt and fired into the muzzle flame of the Indian's rifle. The big .45/70 slug whizzed by his right shoulder. His gnarled hand re-cocked the gun in recoil and sent off another round into the chest of a heavily painted brave advancing in spite of the fact his leader was down, shot in the face. The third, a young boy about sixteen, stopped in his tracks, frozen, then came on, raising his gun. The old man shook his head and shot. The youngster slumped.

A flurry of hoof beats and two shots in back of him made him whirl. Matthew was coming in a hurry out by the hundred yard rock, his sorrel lathered. Without stopping, he raised his Henry and shot rapidly twice more toward the rear of the camp. The war party was in full retreat to the south.

Matthew made a circle of the camp to see if there were any hold outs, then rode in. He stepped from the heaving horse and looked at Frank, who was sitting on a stump.

"You all right, pard?" Matthew put a hand on his shoulder in concern.

"I'm fine, thanks to the dog here. He warned me. These here were pulling a sneak on me." In the center of the camp lay the three Indians. The first had been shot in the left eye. The implosion of the bullet in the skull had bulged the right eye out from the head. He lay on the long infantry rifle he'd fired. The boy was head shot also and lay as if asleep. The second warrior was shot in the chest and shuddered out a death sigh as they stepped over to him. On the horizon to the north, the wagon with Toby driving topped out the ridge and started down the slant into camp. It slowed as he drove by the dead braves on the flat.

The first lay twined with a dead pinto horse. A rawhide rope was wrapped several times around the barrel of the horse and the legs of the dead rider were stuck in and under this rope. There was a chest wound on the horse but none on the Indian. He'd broken his neck when the pony fell and rolled. Arrows from a quiver lay scattered close by and the rider still clutched a bow. Like the others, he wore paint in streaks and blotches on his face and body. A red hand print over his mouth caught Toby's eye as he passed and he quivered.

The other warriors were shot in the chest or head and the boy turned his head as he passed them, their wounds making him feel queasy in his stomach. The scene in camp didn't help.

Matthew and Frank were standing together, talking about the incident in seeming unconcern. They watched him pull up.

Toby couldn't take his eyes off the dead Indian boy. Something must have shown in his face because Matthew gathered him up and walked him out of camp.

"Son, you know life out here is hard. The Indians hate the whites because we're killing off his food supply. That Piegan war party was out to kill all the white hunters on the north side, if it could. You can bet there's some dead whites on its back trail and sure that youngster took part in it. Like it or not, it's kill or be killed out here."

Matthew put his hand on Toby's shoulder and continued.

"Now come over here. I want to show you a little about Indians."

They'd walked out of camp to the south. Now Toby saw that another Indian lay face down on the prairie where Matthew had downed him as he'd raced into camp. They approached the body warily, as the old man instructed, "If you aren't sure of a killing wound, you mebbe better put another in him to make sure." So saying, he brought up his belt gun and matter-of-factly put a round in the head of the dead warrior. Toby flinched and started to look away.

"Now, youngster, what I'm telling you might save your life. Are you going to listen or be squeamish about it?"

"Yes, Sir I'll listen."

With a boot, the old man turned the brave over. A ghastly painted face came into view. Matthew holstered his weapon and knelt down.

"Now, Toby, see here. This war paint all means somethin'. The red chin signifies he's out to kill his enemies. These plains Indians also paint their ponies up. Stripes on the front legs show he's counted coup, that is, done a brave deed. A red hand print shows an enemy killed. Each of these feathers has a meaning. I know the split one tells he'd been wounded in battle. The rest tells of some of his other deeds. This little bag here around his neck is where he packs his sacred good luck charms. They didn't help him today. Look at that necklace—see these things here?"

He pointed to some tanned leathery objects strung on the leather thong between beads and colored quills. With a sick thrill, Toby saw they had nails. They were fingers, six of them strung together.

22

"He took them off his enemies. Here on his leggings these tufts of hair are most likely scalps. They string 'em around their war shield, too, and paint them up with sacred totems and such.

"See this bracelet?" Matthew pulled it off the dead wrist."Finger bones hollowed out and strung together. Powerful medicine. I've seen 'em with dried noses, ears, even hands cut off and strung up. This is a warrior, Toby, and he doesn't show mercy to his enemies. With them, it's like I said, kill or be killed."

Matthew handed the grisly objects to Toby, who gingerly took them. Matthew picked up the Indian rifle, a Spencer. Together they walked back to camp.

Frank had walked out in the opposite direction to check on the braves who died there and pick up the horse that had stayed by his dead master. He met them in the middle of the camp.

"Well, pard, you've got a nice war horse there," Matthew commented. The small wiry buckskin had a rawhide noose tied to its bottom jaw in typical Indian fashion for a rein. As Matthew had mentioned, he was painted up in grand style, with a red hand print pointed down on his chest.

"What does it mean when it goes down like that," Toby asked, and Frank replied, "Well, son, that means the owner was on a death mission—do or die, like. This print back here on his rump tells what warrior clan he was in. A warrior group, like a certain army regiment. These feathers and bag in his mane are big medicine—shows the horse was a real war horse. He fought right alongside his owner. He's yours, boy. But be careful of him. You'll have to mount wrong side for a while."

The horse seemed dog gentle but a little spooky of the white smell. Almost speechless with the gift, Toby took the braided rein and led the little buckskin to the grove, where he hobbled him with the others.

When Toby came back, Matthew had unsaddled his horse and instructed Toby to rub him down with a gunnysack and blanket him. Frank threw his leather on another horse and dropped his lariat. Matthew looped the legs of a dead brave and Frank pulled the body out of camp and down the creek to another cottonwood grove below. He came back for another, his horse spooking a bit at the death smell.

"Toby, come here." Matthew called the boy over and they looked at the boy Frank had shot. Matthew had turned him over and had seen

23

that his body had fallen on a cut-off Springfield carbine he'd been holding. His hand was still curled around the stock. What Matthew had wanted to show Toby though, was another necklace draped around the dead boy's neck. Like the first brave they'd examined, it had fingers enmeshed in it.

"This kid was no amateur at the killing game, either, son."

The boy shuddered.

They stripped the body of weapons and ornaments, then Frank pulled it down the draw to the cottonwoods with the other. Later they went out to bring in the other ones to the north of camp. One of those on the flat particularly caught Toby's interest. He had green war paint smeared over the top of his chest and his head was all green, with white lines running down his face either side. He wore army trousers as leggings, the seat cut out and a breech clout substituted, instead. One hand had two fingers cut off.

"Why has he got some fingers gone?" Toby asked in wonder.

"They cut 'em off when they lose someone in their family, sometimes," Frank remarked.

"It's supposed to remind them of their sorrow. Guess it would."

This brave had a tack decorated .44 Henry and, like the horse, they gave it to Toby.

"You're getting together an outfit compliments of the Piegans, Toby," Matthew commented as Frank pulled the last one down to the cottonwoods. The dead horses went there, too, and they lifted Toby up to help tie a series of dead limbs together between tree forks to make a platform. Then, they hoisted the dead Indians to the aerie they'd made for them and went back to camp.

That night was a little windy, and with the cloudy sky, dark enough to make Toby's exhausted mind almost feverish with tension and fear. He listened to the nightly coyote chorus, the hoot owl down in the trees by the Indian bier, and the sighing of the wind flapping an untied tarp on one of the wagons and shivered in his bed roll until finally he couldn't stand it anymore. He got up and built up the fire again. There was coffee left in the pot and Toby was pouring a cup when a cold nose thrust up behind his neck and he nearly jumped out of his skin.

"You dog, you scared me stiff!" he hissed at the stiff legged form wagging its tail beside him. He gave the big head a cautious pat.

Then Frank appeared. "Couldn't sleep, young'un? Wal, I was rolling around some myself. Another cup of your coffee sounds good. Any left?"

They sat in their chairs by the fire a while, listening to the night sounds when Matthew came out of the dark to join them. From his duffle in the tent, Matthew had brought out a bottle of brandy and poured a generous dollop in each of their cups. Frank was beginning a story about rangering in Texas when the dog raised his head and growled. Toby had no more chance than to turn to the sound the dog had heard, when he saw that Frank and Matthew were gone. Then he identified the rattle he'd heard—a buckboard was coming. He looked for his two companions but they were lost in the night's darkness. The dog stayed by him, growling a continuous rumble in his throat. Toby thought to pick up his new rifle which he'd filled with .44 shells, and hold it in his lap.

Soon the wagon came up to the fire light.

"Hello the fire, it's me, Tom. Can I come in?"

"Come ahead, Tom. You're traveling late," Frank called. He and Matthew appeared with their rifles.

"Hey, Toby, you waited up for us, by jingies!" Tom laughed. "I brought your skinner back, boys. Indian sign about so we thought to make your camp tonight rather than lay out." Tom spotted the lance leaning by the wagon.

"What the hell!"

"Yeah, Tom, we had a visit from the redskin brigade today. They left some calling cards." Frank threw him the larger finger necklace.

"Whoee, that's something." Tom handed it to Wheeler, who gazed at it in fascination. They settled in and Toby cooked for the two hungry men. While they ate, Frank told them what had transpired. Tom spoke around bites,

"You are damn lucky, Frank, besides being a hard man to kill. This is what I was telling you, Jason. They're old hands at staying alive. I was on the flying squad of Nelson Story's trail crew with them. Story brought a herd through the whole Sioux nation slick as you please to the gold fields in '66. He told off half a dozen of us better hands with a gun to be a roving squad. When the Sioux would hit the herd in one place, we'd ride like hell to get over there and help out. There was thirty men on that trip, all good hands, but you know the best ones are sitting right here: Matthew Grounds and Franklin Shannon—and me, of course."

Toby felt better after cooking and cleaning up. He went to his bed, the dog coming with him. Together, they snuggled in the blankets against a night that somehow wasn't so haunting and lonesome.

* * *

The next morning dawned crisp and cold. The boy woke to find the dog gone from his side. The fire was sparking and the coffee pot bubbling. The dog was watching Matthew cut off some strips of bacon from the slab out of the meat locker. Abashed at being a slug-abed, Toby threw the covers back and scrambled out. After the chores were done and the breakfast eaten, the men sat around the fire visiting and coffeeing up. Tom told them about his circle around the buffalo range.

"Jason and me worked our way to the west through a lot of buffalo, boys. Grass and water is good this side of the river this year and the buffs are sure crowding in. Lots of calves these last few years. No matter which direction you looked, you could see buffalo. Over on Dry Creek we run into the young McNaney brothers and their outfit. They got a skinner name of Lamb who sure is no sheep when it comes to skinning. Young Jim told me this Lamb skinned sixty buffalo in one day! They seen some Indians but haven't had to fight, yet, they told us.

Then, I hate to tell you, but John Stringer and his outfit are located over between the middle fork and the South Fork of Lodge pole Creek. He's got another shooter and some skinners. Baker and a hardcase named Carl Rigney. Didn't like their looks. Some were out hunting with Stringer. Those in camp was drunk. Some whiskey peddler from Benton had come by and sold 'em a bunch of booze.

Sam and Bill Stone and LeValley's outfits are over closer to the Musselshell. Bill mentioned having some hides stolen, claimed it was Sioux. He and Sam traded some long range shots with 'em, he said, and Sam got hit in the arm. He's okay, though, the bullet never hit a bone. George Outhwait's over on Calf Creek. He's a real rimrocker. Told me he had some horses stole, trailed them and stoled his back plus he got five of theirs, too! Quite a trick, huh? Two of the horses were branded 'US.' I s'pose they came from Custer's troops. I told him to bring 'em in to the fort when he came and turn 'em in to the Fort." He got up stiffly.

26

"Any more of that coffee, son? How's the dog? He's pit bull, ya know. If you don't kill 'em, they usually heal up okay. Better than his ex-owner, ha!" Toby filled his cup again.

"They's probably some other outfits out there I missed. I know McNaney's mentioned that they heard shooting over north of them. Didn't know who it was but they were going to go check. Lots of hides but what a waste of good meat! No wonder the Indians are boiling mad. Since Custer went under, the Sioux and the rest of their friends been running amok all over the country. Guess they think winning that battle won 'em the war. They're gonna lose it, though, 'cause when the buffalo go, the Indian tribes up north here will be just like those down south—dependent on the white man for their food. It'll happen. But in the meantime, some blood's gonna spill. Look out it ain't yours, boys. Now, me, I'm gonna stay here 'til dark, then I'm heading back to Miles. The old pony knows the way back to his oat locker. He'll get me home." He poured some cream into his coffee.

Toby helped Jason Wheeler get his war bag and gear out of the wagon.

One piece of equipment was a rifle case. When Frank asked about it, Jason proudly pulled out a Sharps Business Model .45/70 to show them.

"Good caliber, Jason, but looking at that barrel, I'd say it's shot out," Frank said after a critical once-over of the weapon. He handed it to Matthew, then to the Sheriff, who peered down the barrel.

"Damnation, Jason. I should'na let you go buy that on your own, I guess! Thought you knew about guns. I'm sorry, boy. You better let me take that gun back for you and trade it for another. Next time you get to town you can pick it up at the jail, or I'll send it out."

"Won't I need it before then?" Jason inquired anxiously. He was on edge from all the Indian talk.

"We've got several you can use," Frank commented dryly. "Now, Tom, take this gun back for Jason along with this," he indicated a lance and one of the finger necklaces, "And trade 'em for a .45/120 Sharps. Might as well have the same caliber as ours. An 'Old Reliable' is what he wants for out here. Get him a long range back sight, too. Do it right."

Tom exclaimed, "Say now, those Indian trinkets are bringing plenty money in town! I bet I can get a new rifle for the necklace alone. I'll see how I can do, by jingies. What about that other stuff, want me to take it along, too?" Tom was enthused about the prospect of doing some trading.

"Sure, might's well, unless Toby wants any of it." Frank's manner indicated a willingness to get rid of it all, get it out of his sight.

"I'd like to have just the one war club if I could," Toby answered. He pointed to a stone headed club that had caught his eye earlier. The head of the club was ground to a dull point on either end, about six inches long with a smooth groove worked around its middle. This groove held the rawhide wrapping which attached it to its handle, a springy piece of ash. It had been fire-dried and likewise wrapped with rawhide, which, when dried, shrunk and turned hard as iron. It was decorated with dye and sported two trimmed eagle feathers appended to its handle. It was a lethal looking weapon.

"Go ahead and take it, son. We'll let Tom take the rest in and get rid of it," Frank urged. Two of the rifles had their stocks cut off. Frank had said it was because the Indian used them to hunt buffalo and they were easier to handle that way on horseback.

"Take these sawed off guns, too. They're no good to us. And, Tom, take a hind quarter of buffalo and give it to the Nez Perce' at Keogh. Tell them we want them to make a teepee for us, will you? A big one about twenty feet across on the bottom. Take the stuff, sell it, and use the money to pay for it. You can have what's left."

That evening, Tom pulled out for Fort Keogh. The next day they hunted buffalo. The days and nights were getting cold and hides were beginning to come prime. Jason went with Toby on the wagon and they tried to leave the dog in camp but it persisted in following the wagon, limping along. After a half mile, Toby relented and they stopped and hoisted it into the box. Thereafter it rode wherever they went, much to Matthew's disgust.

"Some camp-watcher it turned out to be," he snorted.

Frank took the dog's side, as he had ever since the Indian fight.

"Aw, Matthew, maybe it'll scout for the boys, keep watch for 'em. He's still healing up, anyway."

When Jason got out to the killing area, he threw on a leather apron, split up the middle and fixed for ties behind the legs. He took two knives from a case he'd brought with him from camp, jumped down off the wagon and started in to skinning. In no time, it seemed to Toby, he had the skin off and heavy as it was, hoisted into the wagon with little help from Toby, then went to the next.

Frank and Matthew had shot their usual number, thinking to work Jason into the skinning job easy at first. However, Jason was done by ten o'clock and asking for more.

"I can see we hired a go-getter, he's really something with them knives!" Frank commented in admiration. "Guess we'd better shoot a few dozen more for him or he'll get bored and leave us."

The coming week saw a repetition of that day: Jason was a top notch skinner. By himself, he could handle all they could kill. Frank's problem was his bad shoulder. Some days he could barely raise his arm from the recoil of the big gun. He finally took his jacket, stitched a leather piece on the shoulder to take up the kick and stuck some hair from a bull's head in to pad it. This helped, and Frank then could keep up with Matthew, most days.

Often, too, Frank would keep Toby back and together they would go down with the crosscut saw and cut down some of the dead cottonwoods for firewood. Several times they followed the creek down to some of the bluestem meadows and using the scythes, cut a load of hay. They brought it back with the wagon and stacked it by the south end of the corral. Neither of these activities seemed to hurt Frank's shoulder like the gun kick did, so frequently, Frank let Matthew and Jason do the hunting. Jason used Frank's Sharps and Matthew taught him to shoot it. However, he was a far better skinner than a shooter.

* * *

Around the first of December, G. W. Baldwin showed up with a freighter outfit to buy hides. He was a genial older man, full of fun, and the men and he were old friends.

"G. W., you old skunk. It's good to see you again," Frank hollered when they pulled in. "When you going to pay us all the money you owe us?"

"Soon as horses grow web feet, you old outlaw! I see you've been lazying around again, getting Matthew to do all your work, as usual. And here's Toby, growing up like a weed," Toby came up and G.W. gave him a silver dollar. "Here's something for your old age, son. Don't put it in a bank, they might lose it."

"Gee, thank you, sir!" Toby ran to put it in his war bag. G. W. drew Frank over to the lead wagon to introduce him to his crew. "Heard you had a visit from the Red Brigade, Frank."

Pretty soon, Matthew and Jason showed up. Frank and G.W. and the freighters had been talking while Frank showed G.W. the hide pile. In between wrangling about price, G. W. had mentioned the incident Matthew had been in at Miles.

"It's all over the territory what happened, Frank. Stringer Jack's crew has sworn to get Matthew. Did you know that?"

"Well, it's about what we figured, and yeah, Tom Healey was out and told us the same thing. We'll be alert. We've been through it before, or some like it. You know that, G.W."

"You bet I do, Frank, but these scum are getting organized, it seems like. Reminds me of Plummer's crew in the sixties up in the gold diggin's."

When Matthew and Jason stopped their team by the horse corral the men gathered around to help them off-load.

"Hello, G. W. You finally pried yourself away from the saloon, huh? What happened? You hit a streak of bad luck at poker, needed some more ante money?" Matthew grinned, as they shook hands. Frank led Jason up to introduce him.

"This here's our new man, Jason Wheeler. Meet G.W. Baldwin, poker player and part-time hide buyer. Jason here is a premium skinner, G.W."

"Now, Matthew, you know that poker part ain't true. Why, I hardly go near a poker table anymore, I'm too busy chasing you hunters down so I can keep you in coin." He introduced his freighters and they went to the fire. Toby had a fresh pot on and they coffee'd up. The freighters drew up logs and stumps and a poker game started.

"Damn, she's getting nippy out these days." G. W. shivered. Even in his buffalo coat, he could feel the cold seeping through. "Reminds me, we got an article on for you. Wagon number three. Nez Perce' teepee. Tom Healey bought it and sent it out to you. Says to tell you he still owes you some money."

"Thanks, G.W. I wonder if you'll take some meat in to them when you come back through if you have a little room. I 'spect they're starved for buffalo."

"Oh, I don't see why we couldn't handle some, if you'd get it ready for us. They can damn sure use it. We should be back in a week or so. Where do you want the lodge? They didn't have any poles to send along, but the squaw Tom got it from sent these thongs along and said to cut dry poles to their lengths. "

The teepee, as rolled out by the men and spread in the grass, was a big canvas four poler like Frank and Matthew had wanted. Unlike most of the lodges Toby had seen, this one was plain and unmarked, except that the door flap showed buffalo falling, some with legs in the air, all with red wounds on their sides. A couple of the dead ones looked skinned, but still had calves trying to suck the milk from them. Toby noticed that both Frank and Matthew were upset by the pictures. Neither, however, said anything. Later, they changed the door flap to a plain one.

After the freighters left, the tempo of the camp settled back into its well regulated rhythm. With the proper poles a necessity for erecting the teepee, Matthew and Jason took the wagon west to the Bull Mountains to find a patch of lodgepole. They were back the third day and Jason had an Indian story to tell.

When they had reached the Bulls late that day, they soon found a nice patch of pine to work the poles out. They quickly cut and trimmed 25 poles, each one about 25 feet long. Driving back the next day, they'd spotted a white horse motionless on the prairie, out by itself. Coming up to it, they saw it was held by a stout lariat rope looped around its neck and tied to the wrist of a dead buck Indian. Turning him over, they saw he'd been shot in the side. Perhaps after stealing the horse, he'd been shot, then gotten away only to die on the prairie. They'd brought the horse in with them.

"That's the way a lot of these prairie Indians do, especially the Sioux. They take off walking with a lariat to find a horse, steal it and ride it home a big man. They do love a horse thief, if it's one of theirs!"

Frank said while he looked the new addition over. "Lots of times, they just carry a little pemmican, some spare moccasins and a knife. Isn't anybody can live off the country like an Indian can. And the Sioux are better than most." He walked around the pony.

"Nice horse, no brand, no identifying marks. No sign of ever wearing shoes. Shies when you try to get on him from the left. Shows he's Indian raised. Got a deep barrel and sound legs. Let's mark him MF and turn him in, Matthew. We can pay Jason ten dollars for being there when you found him. Or, if he wants, he could pay us and we could mark him what he'd like and he can take him." He looked at Jason and Matthew inquiringly.

"I've never had my own horse. Would you mind if I have him, Matthew? I'd pay you for him. You could hold it out of my wages." Jason was eager to keep the horse, Toby saw, and didn't blame him. It was a better horse than most Indian ponies Toby had seen.

* * *

Frank and Matthew helped Jason work his horse through the phases of becoming a good saddle mount. Jason took their instructions seriously and intelligently. Both horse and man learned from excellent teachers. Jason finally settled on a simple JW branded on the left hip. Frank showed Jason and Toby how to rig a soft rope so as to lay a gentle horse down, then tie it before branding it. "Then you're not running such a chance of hurting it or it hurting you. Everything's nice and easy. Horse hide's thin compared to a cow. You don't need as big a brand or as hot a one for a horse. Specially a white one. Anything you put on will show up good. Indians even use weed juice like milkweed and such to mark 'em.

"How long did you live with the Indians, Frank?"

"Oh, guess it was three-four years altogether. Lived with the Kiowa for a time when I was a lad. Then, after Matthew and I came up the trail with Story's outfit, we worked the gold fields a while, then lived with the Nez Perce´ and sold meat to the miners for a time. Good people, the Nez Perce´. Real clean, real smart, good with horses. They raise appaloosas, a spotted horse. The Nez Perce´ treated us real good." A look of far-off times and happenings clouded his eyes.

"Wouldn't be some half-white kids running around their lodges up there, would there, name of Shannon?" teased Jason.

"Now you hush up that kind of talk! Especially around Toby!"

The lodge poles had to be peeled and dried before using. It took time from their hunting Matthew cut a bunch of ash pegs for the lodge pinnings and they had the lodge raising close in by the corral and their wood pile. First they cleared the ground of sagebrush and rocks and cactus, then they laid four of the bigger poles out, bringing their small ends, which they tied together, to the center. These were raised spaced out so they'd stand and the other poles laid carefully in around them. Then the heavy rolled canvas was laid against the supporting poles and unwrapped around them until the back met the front, where it was pinned with the ash pegs. Small cross poles were tied on to two poles making a ladder up so that Frank could pin the two ends as he came back down.

"Okay, now these poles go into the smoke flap pockets."

They worked together and managed to get those poles standing, then adjusted the others all around until the teepee was tightened over its entire circle. The canvas, though 10 ounce duck wagon covering, was much thinner than buffalo hide and couldn't be pegged down in the usual Indian way. It needed small round rocks pouched into the canvas at intervals around its bottom, then stout cord wrapped around them and used as ties for the pegging down. This way, the fabric wouldn't tear. The door faced southeast, as the prevailing wind was usually from the northwest.

After a lot more adjusting and time spent than any two squaws would have needed to erect the lodge, they had it squared away and pegged down properly to Frank's instructions. He next had them scrounge the area for fire rocks to lay the inside fire. Then the lining was hung around the inside to keep the constant condensation that occurs in a tent from dripping on them. Afterwards, the fire going and their gear stowed away, they hung a lantern from one of the poles and surveyed their new home.

"Cuts the wind, don't it?" Frank asked, pleased as punch and proud of their new possession. "She's a real beauty, right, Matthew? A hell of a lot better than a dirty cutbank any day. Look how good the smoke draws. Boys, we got us a real home!"

"We'll still need to stand watch, Frank. You know, a good place would be the top of the haystack out of the wind, I think. It's a little higher, too, so you can see a little farther."

Frank rubbed his leg where a pole had bumped it. "Yeah, I wouldn't put it past the Blackfoot to come back after us. They're hell for revenge, weather don't matter."

* * *

No sooner was the camp battened down for winter, than the first of three storms hit. The wind, which had been light but steady at times from the west, veered around and came straight down from the north.

It brought a heavy snowfall which kept them in camp and off the hunting grounds for a week.

The snowfall acted as insulation around the lodge, making it more snug and comfortable, if possible.

"Can't see why we didn't think of this before, Matthew. Sure is nice."

Frank reached up with a pole to start a large buffalo hump turning again in the smoke hole. Around the interior was piled in orderly fashion the weapons and gear of the outfit. The lantern cast a flickering rose of light as it swayed on its perch. Hides were spread on the ground to act as a buffer from the dirt and cold. Wood was stacked to the left side of the door. Withal, it was quite a livable existence, even to Jason's pilgrim way of thinking. Toby, having been with the two old men for several years, thought it was the lap of luxury. When out and away from the lodge at night, it glowed cheerily with a rose light through canvas and snow, which in the darkness of the winter made it homelike and inviting. The men occupied themselves with making willow backrests and other little knickknacks to add to their comfort.

When the weather moderated, they came out to a morning brightness that hurt the eyes. Everything was covered with a thick white blanket. To get wood or throw hay to the horses, they had to paw off a foot of snow. The smaller tent was partially collapsed under its weight and all the miscellaneous gear they had scattered about the camp was hidden and had to be scratched up from memory. It was an effort for the hunters to gather their gear for the daily hunt.

Matthew saddled up and directed Jason to hitch up the team. Frank and Toby stayed in camp along with "Cappy," as Toby had named the dog.

A half mile from camp the hunters had luck. The buffalo were plentiful as yet, though their numbers seemed thinner than before the storms.

"Buffalo will head into a storm, when everything else will drift before it. A lot of them probably went north," Frank pronounced.

Buffalo that Jason and Matthew saw now were nearly white from crusted snow matted in their hair. It didn't seem to deter their grazing. They swept the snow from the grass with methodic movements of their shaggy heads. Their breath and body heat hung over them like another blanket in the cold air.

Matthew put seven down close together and with the team pulled them down close to the hide area, where Jason could peel the hides and work them as best he could. It was cold, hard work and seven of the big animals in a day were enough to mess with.

After skinning the animals, they cut a lot of the meat away and hung it up in the trees along the creek from a pole between two tree crotches, then threw a piece of canvas over it to keep the magpies and crows off it.

Jason wondered what had happened to the hide buyer's outfit.

"Aw, they're holed up with McNaney's or Stone's over on the Musselshell, for sure," Frank thought. "They'll be along if we get a chinook and some of this snow leaves the ground."

*   *   *

Another week passed.

One evening Toby, just about to head for his bed, went out to the privy, and from long habit, scanned the twilight-tinged landscape. The setting sun had flooded the snow covered hills with redness but out towards the west Toby saw specks of movement and an instant later thought he heard a shot.

Evidently Cappy, the dog, thought so, too. He came from the lodge with a "whoof," then stood with Toby, staring off west.

"It looks like men. Is it Indians, Matthew?" Toby asked when he roused Matthew and the others from the lodge.

Matthew had his binoculars. "It's G. W.'s crew, I think. Looks like him in the lead."

He handed the glasses to the boy. "I'll saddle up and see what's going on."

Frank had them gather up their rifles, half-convinced that it was an Indian trick. Shortly, Matthew rode out and was soon back.

"It's Baldwin's outfit, alright. They're bogged down six or seven miles out in a big coulee. Horses played out. We'll have to go help 'em out tomorrow." He unsaddled and Toby took the horse back to the corral with the rest. Pretty soon the four men Toby had spotted came in, red-faced and blowing from their long walk in the snow.

The boy had fired up the coffee again and the men skinned out of their buffalo coats and leggins and stood close to the fire to warm up. Matthew did the coffee honors then topped off their cups with some frostbite medicine. "Well G. W. here's a go. Not often do we get to see

35

you using 'shank's mare.' Usually you're wedded to that saddle horse of yours."

"And here's to you boys. Thanks for putting us up." The men around the fire nodded likewise and the coffee mix went down in a hurry. Baldwin told them what had occurred.

"Things went pretty well away from Stone's until we started hitting some crusted snow out on the west fork of Dry Creek. We cut some hides up for leggins for the horses but they played out on the Sand Creek crossing. Too deep."

"We unhitched and pulled the horses out and set up camp. Then I thought we'd better come in here to see if you wouldn't break trail and help give us a pull in."

"Sure. You can bed down and we'll head out in the morning."

The freighters bustled around the warm spacious lodge, disturbing Cappy who let out a low growl that backed the men off in an instant.

"Say, that big monster would sure take a hunk out of a man if he got hold of 'em, huh?" one of the teamsters observed.

Next morning, they hitched up the team, cut leggins for them and tied some hides on behind to serve as sleds for the men to be pulled on.

Roughly six miles out on the men's back trail to the west, they came over a rise and dropped down into Sand Creek.

Smoke curled above the cook fire the other teamsters had going to brew up their breakfast. Their teams were harnessed but not hitched to the wagons.

With boisterous greetings and more coffee doled out to the incoming party, they hitched the horses into one continuous jerkline, then, one by one, pulled the wagons up out of the deep snow-filled coulee bottom and over the rise on to the long flat.

It was afternoon when they hauled into camp. Toby and Jason had whipped up a huge bean pot, baked some biscuits and were ready to fry the buffalo steaks when they arrived. The teamsters drew in and around the camp in a defensive circle, unhitched, watered and fed their weary stock, then put on their own feedbag.

After the meal, cards and whiskey came out. The freighters had already started their game again and had talked Jason into joining their circle around the blanket. Matthew looked at G. W., who shrugged as if to say he couldn't control them.

"Haw damn it, whoever said this pilgrim skinner could join in?" growled the freighter Toby had heard them call Dry-Axle Bill. "He's ruined my streak."

"Aw, Bill, you just thought you had a streak going."

"Maybe so, but I was coming back. Now, I'm down twenty dollars already. See your dollar and raise two."

The game went on.

Watching the play in the flickering light of the lantern, Matthew could see a fascination take hold in Jason's face. His eyes shone and eagerly followed the fall of cards on the blanket. He roared in his deep voice when he won, nearly cried when he lost. The freighters were enthused, too, but not with the same intensity that was working in Jason. They laughed at his antics.

The old friends sipped coffee, talking in a murmur drowned out at times by the sigh of a west breeze which fluttered the lamp, the stamp of a horse from the corral, the laughter and rowdiness coming from the group about the blanket.

"They worked hard these few days," G. W. remarked apologetically. "They deserve a little break. Hell, so do I. Come on, let's all set in!"

Matthew turned away and went to help Toby clean up.

"Aw, loosen up a little, Pard. We all need something else to do for a while." Frank's voice was already slurred from several heavy drinks. He and G.W. had passed the bottle back and forth while out on the trail in to camp. Matthew just shook his head. Presently he brought out his bullet mould and went to building bullets at the fire.

Frank and G. W. went over to the game and sat in. The teamsters were working on a second bottle and the stakes in the pot were getting high.

Three hours later, Toby, by that time in his bedroll, woke when he heard things get quiet.

"Listen, Greaser, I told you once to quit calling me 'Old Timer' and I'm fed up with your bad memory on the ante. The rest of us don't have no trouble, only you." Frank's voice rang in the arrested silence of the moment's tension.

"You old son-of-a-bitch! I don't need a grandpa to remind me to ante!" The teamster, a half-breed Mexican, looked daggers at Frank, dropped his cards and started what looked like a move for a weapon.

"Hold it." With the swift words came a click which signified a cocked six-gun. Eyes turned in the dim light to a darkened part of the lodge. Matthew spoke again.

"Now, boys, you're disturbing mine and Toby's sleep. I suggest you play a round of high card for the pot, then turn in."

"Hell, Matthew, I can take him, you know I can!" Frank was determined to make a fight of it.

"Don't matter. The boy's in here and bullets don't play favorites. You men want to fight in the morning, walk out a ways and go to it. Right now, I'm tellin' you all, the game's over."

"You're right, Matthew." G. W. raised his voice in authority. "Now the game's finished, boys. Let's hit the blankets. We gotta move out tomorrow."

The game broke up. Toby laid back down but sleep was a while in coming. Next morning the teamsters loaded up and started for Keogh. G. W. lingered behind.

"Too much booze, Matthew, but you know men. They will have their game and drink. If I tried to stop it, they'd quit me."

"No harm done, G. W. We'll see you in a month or two." Matthew, now the teamsters were gone, was willing to let it ride, as was Frank, who stood shamefaced at the lodge's entry.

After G. W. left, Matthew went to the corral. Toby went into the lodge. Frank stood by the fire looking miserable. "What's wrong, Frank?" Toby was bewildered by the behavior of his two old men.

Toby was uneasy but was remembering some past trouble because of this kind of thing. He brought the coffee pot over to Frank.

"Well, son, you oughta know that I broke my promise. Matthew was gonna quit me before if I didn't quit the booze. I promised I would, now here we are. I s'pose I should have left with G.W." Frank despondently held his cup out for Toby to fill. Jason, alarmed, made himself scarce, going to check his gear.

"I'll go talk to him, it'll be all right, Frank." Toby, his world the two old men, was desperate that it shouldn't fall to pieces. He loved them both and couldn't stand to see either hurting. Frank just shook his head.

Matthew always stood by me. But after I well, he said that was it. Either I swore off or he left. He'd a done it, too. Caught him saddling his horse like he's probably doing right now. Told him I'd never touch any booze that he didn't pour me. Up to now, I never have." He put his head in his hands and knelt before the fire. Toby ran to the doorway.

Sure enough, Matthew was horseback, heading out from the corral. Toby screamed, "Matthew, wait, please wait!" He ran through camp and came up to Matthew, who had reined in when he'd heard Toby.

"Matthew, don't go, don't go, please don't go!!" he sobbed as he came up to the old man. He grabbed the stirrup in agitation as if to physically prevent his leaving.

Matthew swung from the saddle and shook the boy by the shoulders.

"Son, what's wrong! I'm not going anywhere, just up on the ridge to see if the herd's close by." The boy sobbed and threw his arms around his neck.

"Frank said he'd broke his promise and you were leaving. Don't go, Matthew, please!"

"Why, boy, I wouldn't leave you. Always know that. I won't leave you." He patted the sobbing youngster with an awkward hand. "Frank and I are pards. We'll work it out. You tell him I'd like him to come with me to check the herd," He gave the boy a push toward camp and after a pause, wiping his eyes, Toby went off to deliver the message. After a little, Frank came out, went down to the corral and saddled up. Together the two old-timers headed for the ridge. When they topped it, they sat there for a while. Both Toby and Jason watched them from camp as they went about their chores. Presently, the sun coming up, they saw the two men turn and lope off the hill back to camp. Neither of the men mentioned what was said on the ridge.

* * *

The winter dragged by. They hunted when the weather was favorable, stayed in camp when it wasn't. The lodge fire usually was simmering a buffalo stew in the large cast iron kettle suspended over it. Overhead a lantern swung from the lodge poles beside a couple buffalo hams turning in the smoke.

In February, the temperature moderated and one evening Jason raised a holler when he saw horses churning through the snow towards camp.

Matthew came from his lodge with his binoculars and raising them, grunted "White men." The men and boy watched as three men rode up, pack horses behind them. When they got close to camp, they reined in and the lead man, heavily bearded and with a rifle cradled in his arm, gave greeting.

"Howdy the camp! Is this the two-ring circus outfit of Shannon and Grounds?"

Frank laughed. "Hell, it's John Leasure. Come on in, John!"

The three came forward and dismounted. The bearded man, John Leasure swung forward and shook hands with Frank and Matthew.

"Been a spell, boys, since Bozeman. How you been? This here's Howard Eaton and Captain Borden. Thought we'd head for the Musselshell, visit a few camps and do some hunting. How's it been?"

Frank introduced Jason and Toby, then proceeded to fill the Leasure party full of talk about the great hunting to be had in the area while they coffee'ed up.

"Better stay a few days and we'll take you out from here. The hunting won't get any better further west and the company won't, either."

"Well, Howard and the captain here are after a trophy bull or two and a cow to eat. But we also wanted to make a circle over west to see the country," Leasure remarked. The others nodded assent. Leasure was an older man in his late fifties. A life spent on the plains showed in his seamed tanned face.

"That's so. I'd like to get a big bull and send the head and horns home to the family in Connecticut," Eaton asserted. "The captain here wants to do the same. John finally agreed to take us out."

Eaton was the typical eastern businessman, full of bustle and ideas straight from the comforts of a society as foreign to the frontier as a country in Europe. His red round face was already wind burned and chapped from the cold. The army captain, though, showed durable service in the country's military arm on the frontier. He gimped from a bad leg and doubtless could show other scars from long years in army harness.

"Then, too, Miles asked us to come out and take a look around, do a little scouting for him," Leasure explained with a wink. He took his seat with a stifled groan.

"Aren't you hunting this year, John? Matthew asked. He handed Leasure a cup.

"Haven't felt good for quite a while. Got shot in the head in the war, you know, and wasn't supposed to live, but I wanted to spite the doctors, so I did. My head bothers me a lot, though. Aches so that sometimes I can't hardly stand it. Worse in cold weather. Last week or so it's been a little better, though." He sipped his coffee.

"Heard you had a run-in with some redskins, Frank."

"No, thing was," Frank drawled, "They was out of tobacco and wanted some of mine. Just couldn't persuade them I didn't chew their brand!"

The Captain and Eaton chuckled. Leasure grinned. "Some Indians are hard put to take 'no' for an answer. Mind a time we were down at Custer's lookout. We were running Pawnees, then. Remember, Jim?" Captain Borden nodded.

"I surely do. Lieutenant Crowell got his that day."

"That's right," Leasure agreed. "We buried him in that alkali on a butte a couple miles from the one they call 'Custer's Lookout.' A year later, when his relatives came to bring his body back we took them up the butte and dug him up. He'd petrified somehow and weighed about three times what he did alive. It's a fact, but hard to believe." He tamped his pipe and Toby brought a burning sliver to light it.

"I've heard of trees and plants petrifying. Don't believe I ever heard of a body doing it," Frank said doubtfully. "Have you, Matthew?"

"I guess it could happen. I've never heard of it myself, either," Matthew admitted.

"I saw the corpse and it's a true fact," Leasure asserted. The smoking and talk lasted several hours and Toby finally nodded off until Matthew shook him awake and pointed him towards his bed.

* * *

Next morning Toby and Matthew hitched up and went with Leasure's party out to the hunting grounds. The Captain and Eaton were in high spirits. "What a life, eh, Captain? Hunting all day, outside. I envy you and these hunters. Back home I slave in an office, and sometimes I don't see the sun all day. Right now I don't want to go back. It's great to be out here."

"This life has its moments, Eaton, but I'm sure we'd all trade places with you at times. Not right now, though."

Toby held back with the wagon while the men went on ahead. When they reached the edge of the grazing herd, Matthew directed them to spread out but Eaton objected.

"No, no, Matthew. We don't want to shoot from cover. We want to run them like the Indians do!" Matthew and Leasure were both doubtful.

"If you don't have an experienced horse that knows what he's doing, you could get hurt, Howard, " John protested.

"He's right, boys, that's a risky way to do it." Matthew supported Leasure.

"Nonetheless, we want to kill in fair chase." Eaton was adamant but Borden didn't look so sure.

While they were talking, the herd drifted away, like eddies from a thrown rock in a pond. Suddenly Eaton shouted.

"Look there, by George, there's a head for us!"

Out a ways, about seven or eight hundred yards, was a monstrous bull that had come out of a coulee to see what was going on. A magnificent specimen of the species weighing probably 2400 pounds or more, he had wicked horns tipped with white ivory that curled inwards. With a shout, Eaton spurred away from the group, the Captain after him an instant later.

"Oh, Hell!" Leasure pulled his rifle out of its scabbard and slapped his horse on the rump with the barrel. It jumped into a run. Matthew sighed and spurred his sorrel, following him.

When Toby came up, the whole caboodle was over the next ridge. He drew up and sat a while but they didn't come back, though shots were heard.

"We better follow 'em, Cappy. They'll probably be waiting for us." Toby slapped his lines on the team's rumps and got them moving in the direction the other men had taken. The next ridge, however, disclosed no horsemen, nor did the next.

Down off that ridge, he hesitated, then turned the team into the wide coulee below. The team was about to pull up the far side when a buffalo bull came loping over its edge. At sight of the bull, its bloody flanks heaving and eyes red-rimmed, the team spooked and attempted to turn out of its path to the right. The bull came on and hooked first at the terrorized horses, then at the wagon, which, caught teetering in its turning, went over with a crash. Toby and the dog were thrown clear. The panicked team dragged the wagon on down the coulee. With a shuddering snort, the bull turned on the boy dumped nearly into his path. With a sweep of his huge head he lifted and threw the boy twenty feet, then started for him again.

At that time, when the boy rolled over and saw the bull heading for him, horns lowered to catch him up again, he felt no fear, only a resignation that his life was over too soon. Then a hurtling something hit the bull square in its snout and clamped itself fast to that snorting, bellowing nose. In squalling rage, the bull flung its head up and over, the dog appended like a leech, keeping its hold.

The animal's attention turned, Toby stood cautiously, feeling himself over to see if he was hurt. He wasn't except for bruises and a torn coat. The bull, unable to dislodge the dog by tossing him, went to his knees in an attempt to crush the life out of him. Seeing this, Toby screeched and cast about, looking for his rifle from out of the wagon. He found instead a knobby stick. He charged the bull, screaming as he went, and swinging mightily, fetched him a whack in the ribs that landed with a "whomp" and made the dust fly. The bull grunted and continued grinding his head, trying to kill or dislodge the tenacious dog locked into his nose. The boy struck again, still screeching at the top of his lungs.

Suddenly Matthew was there. His rifle spat fire. The bull, hit by a bullet at the base of the neck, dropped like a chopped tree partially onto the battered dog. Matthew dismounted and together, he and Toby managed to turn the bull off the dazed pit bull.

The dog still lived.

"Feels like he's got some broke ribs, but he's got more lives than a cat. Now, how about you, youngster?" Matthew took in his bruised face and ripped clothes at a glance. "Did he hook you?" he asked anxiously. Leasure came pounding up then, with Borden close behind.

"I thought I saw him come down the coulee! You all right, lad? What happened?"

Breathlessly, Toby told how the bull had taken the team, then hooked the wagon and came after him. How the dog had bitten and held on the bull's nose. Then Eaton came up and he had to tell it again.

"Why, John, it's the very bull we were after!" Eaton exclaimed after a closer look at the dead plains monarch.

"Yes, it is and now you see why it can be so dangerous. These buffalo *aren't* cattle. They're damn mean when they have their blood up. We're lucky the boy wasn't killed," This with a glance at Matthew beside him, still looking grim. It crossed Leasure's mind suddenly that his two companions were somewhat responsible for the bull taking the boy. And that both old men could have been very hard to deal with in the event the boy had been hurt or killed. As it was.

"Let's get the wagon, boys." Leasure rode off down the coulee after the team, the other men with him.

Matthew asked again, "You sure you're okay, son?"

"I'm fine, sir. What can we do with Cappy?"

"Well" Matthew knelt by the dog and felt him over again."We need to wrap his chest, keep the rib ends together. Unless he's hurt bad inside, he should heal up.

When the others had turned the wagon up on its wheels and straightened the harness out, they brought the outfit back. While away, Leasure had lectured both of his friends on their actions. Eaton particularly, looked chastened.

"Do any of you have something we can use to wrap the chest of this dog? He's got busted ribs," Matthew asked.

Without a word, Eaton reached into his saddle bags and pulled out a clean shirt. Matthew looked at him, and taking it, tore it into strips. He wrapped the dog's chest securely, then lifted him into the wagon. "This is getting to be a habit, son," he remarked. The boy agreed.

* * *

They skinned out the bull, caped it as best they could and took the hide and head. It took them all to get it in the wagon. There they spread it so the dog had a bed and headed back to camp.

In the lodge that evening, they listened again as Toby told them what had occurred that day. When the dog heard his name in the story, he thumped his tail. From that story the evening's discussion went on.

"You know, we put two or three rounds apiece into that bull. He just wouldn't go down," Eaton exclaimed from his seat by the fire. He was taking his ease, pipe in one hand, coffee cup in the other after a fill of buffalo stew.

"That's because you're using too light a caliber and the bullet wasn't placed well," Frank drawled.

"Why, I'm using a .38/55. It's killed plenty of deer, even elk!" Eaton retorted.

44

"Too light for buffalo, though. Way too light. Buffalo are hard to kill, as you've seen. Their hide is an inch thick in places, with matted fur making it even thicker. Add mud and they have almost an armor on 'em. Then, their life organs are built low into their bodies. Everyone shoots too high at 'em when they first start hunting them. The heart is protected by their foreleg joint. It's hard to hit. And you can forget about shooting the head. Almost impossible to hit the brain because of all that hide and bone."

"Well, do all you hunters use cannon?"

"Just about all use the big Sharps. There's some Springfields and Remingtons. And most use the .45 caliber now, with a heavy soft bullet and a heavy charge behind it. .45/120 is about right. It'll drive a five hundred grain bullet clear through a bull and make a large wound channel doing it." Matthew handed his buffalo rifle over to Eaton, who examined it and handed it to Borden.

"Well, why is it you carry a repeater, too?"

"Firepower. An Indian charge could run over you if you were shooting single shot. Ask Frank."

"It's the pure truth," Frank stated solemnly. "The .44 Henry packs a good punch and a lot of shells in the magazine. It doesn't pack the wallop of the Sharps but for Indians and light game like deer it doesn't need to. I've killed buffalo with it, too, but they'll run a long ways, usually. Can't reload the Henry shells, either, like you can the Sharps."

Toby listened to the hunting talk until he began nodding off. Then Matthew sent him to his bedroll. The dog lay close by and the boy stopped to pet its ugly, scarred head. It wagged its tail and licked his hand.

Later Matthew remarked to Frank, "Strikes me the dog paid the boy back today. He saved his life, I'd say."

"Seems so. The bull wouldn't have gone under but for you, though, Matthew."

"Oh, I don't know." He chuckled, "The way he was going, he might have whacked him to death with that stick."

"Where did the boy come from? If I'm not being too curious," Captain Borden asked.

Frank answered, "His folks were part of a train that got jumped by Sioux out of Fort Ellis. The train fought 'em off but his folks were killed, along with some brothers. His little sister and him got took and far as we know, the sister's still with Little Wound's band. Matthew and I saw the young'un here at the fort when we were in trading one day. He wasn't s'posed to be seen, I guess, but a squaw sent him for water.

When Matthew saw him, we was able to trade for him. Then the Fort Commander wanted us to give him up to the army, but the boy wanted to stay with us. Even then, we left him there because the army was going to try to get him back to some family he had back east. Well, we left him but he snuck out an' come up on us a day out of the post. Seems like we didn't never go back. He's been a good boy. We had 'im about five years now. Got real attached to the little tad, but he's a problem sometimes. Gettin' to be a help though, lately." He got up and put some more wood on the dying fire.

"I wonder about his sister. Did they ever find her?" This came from Eaton.

"No. We never heard about her. 'Course Little Wound's band has been running wild. Still haven't come in, far's we know. Maybe when they do we'll hear something."

"What a way for a young white kid to grow up. With a bunch of redskins."

"Well, the Sioux are like most tribes, they treat kids pretty well, all kinds, even whites. It could be that she's alive still. She'd be eleven or twelve, now."

Borden shook his head, "I've seen 'em come in. The captives. I was through the Minnesota uprising in the '60's. I saw 'em come in at New Ulm and later on the Republican. It was pretty bad both times. Mostly the women and kids had it real hard. They were treated like slaves." He rummaged in his gear, brought out a bottle. "Let's have a nightcap." He handed it to Frank. Frank held it for a second, and handed it on to Matthew. Matthew looked at him, tipped it over his cup, then Frank's. A look of gratitude lit Frank's face at the gesture and he saluted Matthew with his cup.

"What are you going to do when the buffalo are gone, boys?" Eaton abruptly asked.

Frank was silent. Finally Matthew spoke. "When the buffalo are gone, we'll decide. But Frank and I will most likely start us a horse ranch around Keogh. The cavalry always needs remounts. Hay, too. Those bluestem meadows along the Yellowstone raise some beautiful horse hay."

While Matthew talked, Frank closed his eyes and nodded his head, running the fantasy through his mind: a snug ranch house, corrals full of horses, haystacks. A spring flowing cold water. He and Matthew and Toby. Together. Matthew and he would make a real horseman out of the boy. He had it in him to make a good one with horses. Animals liked the boy. At his age he could handle the big team, even to harnessing them. He sighed and took another nip of his brandy.

Eaton rose and slipped the lodge flap aside to go relieve himself. Outside the night air was cold, crisp, and the wind was kicking up. It sifted the snow through the sagebrush and bent the cottonwoods along the creek bank with a rustle. The stars shone as from a dome of darkness. A coyote chorus was tuning up down the creek. Gazing around, he stepped back into the soft interior of the lodge. He shivered as he took the new cup of coffee Leasure handed him. Jason and Toby had hit the blankets, Frank was nodding at his place by the fire. The rest sat half-mesmerized by its flickering heat.

"Damn cold out there, like to froze it off. Reminds me of a painting, Goya's *Winter*. Same cold colors and desolation." Eaton threw a robe over his legs to warm up.

"Still, Goya couldn't conceive the depths of a Territory winter." This from Matthew, who responded to Eaton's statement in an almost dreamy undertone.

Taken back, Eaton asked, "You're familiar with Francisco Goya, the Spanish painter?"

Matthew raised himself from his reverie. "I studied his work once in what seems another life, yes."

"And what about his *Colossus*?" Eaton was enthused at finding a student of the arts in a teepee on the Dakota frontier. "How do you interpret the giant in that painting?"

The gray eyes of the old man lifted and met the eager blue younger ones across the fire. "A symbolic figure which lends itself to various interpretations. My best guess is that it represents the specter of war. Napoleon was invading Spain at the time. I've often thought of that painting."

Both Borden and Leasure were surprised at the turn the conversation had taken, but not unduly so. The west had a cross section of men from all walks of life. They listened idly.

"And the closed eyes?" Eaton prompted.

47

Matthew smiled, "Now you're testing me. Goya painted closed eyes on his subjects to signify ignorance. War is ignorance. He carried the theme forward in his work called, I believe, *Disaster of War*. Many of the subjects had closed eyes."

"Very interesting, Matthew. May I ask where you studied?"

"Harvard, class of '53."

"Harvard. Way out here. 1853. The year I was born."

"It happens. And you?"

"Yale. Class of 1874."

"And the hand enlarged in the '*Hobgoblins?*'" Matthew smiled.

"Why, I believe I'm being tested!" Eaton was delighted at the exchange. "Probably it shows the grasping avarice of the church in those times in Spain. Goya hated what the religious and political systems were doing to Spain. Do I pass?"

"You pass and I'm heading for the bedroll." Matthew got up and walked stiffly to his bed and turned in. The others went, too. Frank opened his eyes with a chuckle and followed the rest.

Chapter 3

Musselshell River country, Montana Territory

Sixty miles west and north, a thin column of smoke threaded upward in the night. The smoke rose from a dugout which was one of several that had been shoveled into the side of a cutbank. The front had been framed up with crooked cedar poles and hides thrown over them and pegged down. A hide also served as an entryway. The dirt floor inside was covered with hides except for the fire hole in the middle which just now was throwing light for a poker game going on near it.

Seven men were grouped in a circle playing cards with a greasy deck. The men, with one exception, were heavily bearded and long haired. An eighth man lay huddled on a pile of hides in a corner of the cluttered dank interior.

Glancing toward the motionless form, one of the players, a tattered balding man with a running eye socket missing its orb, remarked in a low tone, "He ain't moving, Stringer. Reckon you killed him." He looked at his cards. "I'll bet two bits."

The one addressed as Stringer, the only one not wearing a beard, was a well-built man with burly shoulders and auburn hair. His complexion was fair and just now very wind-burned from the weather. His green eyes, set back under a somewhat heavy brow, were narrowed as he responded, "Call you two bits and raise a dollar, Weepy. The son-of-a-bitch should be. I hit him in the shirt pocket. Sam, get us some wood? The fire's going down."

Stringer directed his request at yet another man sitting behind and out of the card game. This worthy, a small lean wiry individual with a short salt and pepper beard, got up and strode from the dugout.

Outside he took a leak, then went around to the rope corral holding the horses and checked that all was well. Then he returned, going to a woodpile thrown against the side of the cutbank and gathered up an armload. He brushed the hanging hide aside and dropped the wood down beside the fire. One of the men in the game picked up a couple of the cottonwood chunks and placed them on the fire.

"How's the horses?" This from the massive shape seated next to Stringer Jack, a bull of a man named Paddy Rose.

"Fine, Paddy. You want me to get him out of here?" The man named Sam indicated the dead man lying on the hide pile.

"Sure, pull his ass on out, his lack of conversation was beginning to bore me." Stringer looked up and over his cards.

"And, Sam, I want his pistol." The green eyes glowed in the flare-up of the fire.

"You bet, Stringer, I'll get it for you." Sam McKenzie scurried to the dead man, and, lifting him, took a long barreled .45 Colt from the dead fingers. The gun was unfired. He handed it to Rose, who passed it over to Stringer Jack. He laid it on the hide in front of him. "Come on, boys, I'll ante this up. Throw in a dollar and we'll play for it."

Eagerly the men assented, each throwing a silver dollar beside the weapon gleaming in the firelight.

"How about me, Stringer, can I play, too?" Sam had pulled his burden out the door by the collar, throwing the body over into a snowbank. He'd re-entered as the others were anteing up.

"Sure, here's an eagle. That's 160 dollars now." Stringer tossed him a ten dollar gold piece. McKenzie caught it and tossed it into the pile, dragging silver dollars back. "Pot owes me," he said eagerly.

"Run 'em, Joe," Stringer directed. The man he spoke to, Joe Varner by name, was distinguished only by his crossed eyes, a handicap that caused him to keep his head cocked over to the side to see. He began to deal a hand of five card stud. The others watched tensely. The dead man's gun was a good one and they all wanted it. Forgotten was the quarrel and quick temper of their leader, John Stringer, the man known as Stringer Jack, who'd killed one of them over a breach of poker etiquette.

"Hey, hey, looky here!" exclaimed Rose who watched the up cards come around the circle and saw an ace of diamonds land on his down card.

"Ace bets," Joe intoned.

"Bet a buck for Lady Luck." Paddy Rose's huge spatulate fingers flipped a silver dollar onto the pot. He'd peeked at his hole card and knew it was another ace, the ace of hearts.

"I'll call." Brocky Gallagher, an older, sandy-haired, lank cattle drover with freckled skin and sparse blonde beard threw in his dollar. His alert blue eyes, erect posture and bow legs proclaimed his past calling, that of a working stockman. His slow speech was that curious drawl which brands one a Texan. He seldom took his eyes from Stringer Jack.

"I call." Another dollar went in the pot. Billy Downs, a whiskey peddler who liked his wares, was a sour individual who bragged as often as anyone would listen of how he cheated, robbed and killed the Indians he attracted as customers.

The others, Narciss (Weepy) Lavardure, a French breed, and Lucas Baker threw in their dollars, followed by Stringer Jack, Varner and McKenzie.

"Pot's right. Roll 'em." Stringer directed.

Varner began a slow careful deal.

"Pair of aces showing, Paddy. What are you betting?"

Rose pondered, then threw in a small gold piece. "I'll bet a fiver."

Varner picked his down card up then flipped them all over disgustedly. "Shit. I fold," Lavardure, the one-eyed French breed, did the same.

The bet came around to their leader. "I see your five and raise it two."

"Awful proud of them queens, huh?" Paddy grinned at his boss, whose up cards were a pair of cardboard ladies. He threw in another two dollars in coins. The rest grumbled and followed him, except Gallagher who folded.

"Cards, boys." Varner spoke and dealt.

Rose was disturbed because he'd been dealt a ten, but still, he had the best hand showing. "My bet. Another five." McKenzie looked at his hole card, an eight of spades, his up cards, a seven and nine of spades, then his last, a four of diamonds, breaking his small straight flush. "Damn it, I'm out!" His luck had run poor all evening.

Stringer Jack called but was pretty sure that Rose, who could be read like a book, was holding three aces. He himself had three queens and a jack.

Baker, his black eyes so close together they seemed like one, peered at his cards. What showed was all clubs.

"I'll call you but give me a club, damn you, Joe!"

51

Downs, drunk as he was, peered at the cards. Rose was probably holding three aces, Stringer three queens, and Baker a bunch of clubs, hoping for a flush. Downs' up cards were a pair of deuces and a king. He had the other king in the hole. He was beat on the top but if the draw, which looked favorable seeing the absence of kings and deuces showing, went his way he would have a full house. The odds were good, he thought hazily.

"I'll call, and Sam, you want another drink? Go get a bottle of joy juice out of my wagon, will you?" Sam got up and stumbled from the dugout again.

Varner said, "O.K. Pot's right. Here comes the last card," He began his slow deal around the circle.

Rose looked at his hand. He'd missed his ace but so had his chief missed his queen, drawing a four of spades.

Baker cussed, "God damn, there goes my flush!" He'd been dealt a small red card.

Stringer Jack merely flipped his cards over. "Hurry up with that bottle, Sam, it's getting dry in here." He shouted toward the entryway. A muffled shout from outside came back.

"Oh, hell, guess I'll see what you got. What's your bet, Paddy?" Downs acted beat but secretly he was elated. He'd gotten his king, making it two pair showing. The down king made his full house.

Paddy squinted blearily at Downs' hand. "What in shit do you have that beats three aces showing, Downs? I can't see your hand in here, damn it."

"He's showing two pair, Paddy, kings and deuces," Varner replied. His eyes, if crossed, were still sharp.

"Hell, I'll bet ten dollars. Put up or fold your ass," Paddy muttered uneasily. He had a sneaking hunch the whiskey peddler had him beat.

"I'm gonna have to call your ten dollars and raise you back ten!" Downs cried triumphantly. He was sure now Rose had only the three aces.

"You son-of-bitch! What you got? You got a house, don't you?" He reached over and turned Down's bottom cards over. Sure enough, there was the third king.

Downs whined, "Damn it, Paddy, you shouldn't do that. You're not playing fair poker when you do that. Hell, Stringer shot Carl for less than what you just did." He reached down to rake the pile in, the pistol with it.

"You want to try me, you son-of-a-bitch?" Rose asked him belligerently, half rising. Right then in the close confines of the dugout, it looked like more blood would be shed. Downs had the pistol in his hand but was afraid of the man moose confronting him. Rose could kill with his bare hands.

Stringer's voice cut through the tension. "Settle down, Paddy. It's hard to take but Billy won it square. Sam!! Where's that bottle?" He hollered the last.

Sam entered, carrying a bottle in his one hand and gripping the arm of a young Indian girl in the other. She struggled silently against the wiry little man's strength.

"Caught this little bitch trying to steal a horse. I don't know how she got loose! I thought you'd tied her tight, Baker." He threw the girl, a youngster about twelve or thirteen, into the corner where the dead man had lain.

"Here's your rot-gut, boys. Who won the pot?"

He sensed then the tension still rippling the atmosphere in the dugout. "What's wrong, Stringer?" He handed the bottle to him and Stringer pulled the cork with strong, even teeth.

"Nothing, Sam. Paddy's just pissed because three aces doesn't beat a full house." He took a swig, then passed the bottle to Rose, who glowered at him, then took a swig and handed it on."Ahh, go ahead, Billy, and take it. Guess we should thank ya for the booze and the girl. What is she, Sioux?"

"Nah, she's a stray Nez Perce'. I traded a Cheyenne out of her over at Benton. Cute little thing, ain't she?" Downs stashed his winnings into a pocket of his coat which was, like those the others were wearing, made out of buffalo skin. He stuck the pistol into another pocket.

"You want to play for her? Ante up ten dollars and I'll put up the girl, if you're of a mind to play some more." 'No sense upsetting his best customers,' he thought.

One by one, the men in the circle threw their ante in. Sam went to each, asking for a loan and being turned down by all. He turned away with a curse and grabbed up the bottle. His hands were killing him, frost boils showing on their backs, the fingers and joints swollen from working in the extreme cold. The whiskey helped numb the pain. He looked over at the girl lying on the hides. While he watched, she seemed to convulse then grow still, a sigh escaping her. He suddenly was suspicious and, striding to her, he turned the little form over. A skinning knife protruded from her middle and blood soaked her buckskin dress and the hides beneath her. His hand came away bloody. He stared.

"Aw, shit, boys, look at this. Our little playmate up and did herself in."

The men, with the exception of Stringer Jack, all crowded around Sam's discovery. Stringer sat silent by the fire, then pulled a watch from his vest and peered at it abstractedly. Its hands showed 12:20 but the time didn't really matter. The watch, an expensive gold Elgin, had, along with the gold chain and fob, been a present from his father the day he'd matriculated at Yale. That had been in another life. A proud moment for his family. Then he'd failed in his studies, cheated to catch up, and been expelled. He'd been conscripted and served through the last of the great slaughter under Sherman, marching through Georgia with "the Butcher", as the gray bellies bitterly called him. The watch had gone with him through it all, his only reminder of the life he'd known before. The inscription:

To our beloved son
John T. Stringer
on his entrance to Yale
September 4, 1863

pained him so that he had considered many times just throwing the watch away or gambling it. He never had. It was a last tenuous link.

He barely heard the profanity and loud discussion of his companions in his abstraction. This present life was a shadow life, without substance. He couldn't attach any importance to it. The before-life was what mattered, the life he could never go back to. He sighed, snapped the watch closed and, getting up, went out of the dugout to check on the horses. It smelled a hell of a lot better in the corral. He passed the still form in the snowbank without a glance.

Chapter 4

Sunday Creek, North Side of the Yellowstone

Another winter evening, a cold one with the lantern hissing from the lodge poles, its light flickering. The men, comfortable from an evening meal ala' Toby and his little popper, were as usual, coffeeing up. The dog was lying in his bed and twitching from time to time in his dreams. He was getting a little fat. Though still wrapped, his ribs had nearly healed and the animal could eat as much as a man.

Frank was expounding on the buffalo.

"You know, boys, in my life I've seen hundreds of thousands of 'em, probably millions. I don't know how many buffalo there are, the whole west is their pasture. But this northern herd is only a tenth, I think, of what there was." He stopped to bite off a chew, then resumed.

"It's a funny thing about the buffalo. They never mate during daylight. I've never seen a bull cover a cow and neither has any other hunter I've visited with about it. They mate at night. They have a calf every other year. Mate one month and calve a year later."

"Where did you see the most buffalo, Frank?" Captain Borden asked idly, puffing his pipe.

"The most I saw was on the Arkansas River. They were so close down there it was like riding through a loose herded bunch of cattle. It went on for miles and miles."

Eaton remarked, "You know, Matthew, the slaughter of the buffalo deserves a painter of Goya's stature. I wonder if one will come forth here in America."

Matthew sipped his coffee and considered the question. "Maybe. I don't think any back East painter could do better than what some Nez Perce' did on our teepee flap, though."

To that, the men all agreed.

"The bull," Frank resumed, "will walk a guard circle around the cows when they calve. They literally walk themselves into the ground.

55

You look, you can see these little circles all over the range." He went to the door flap, untied it and spit outside.

"What can you tell us about the buffalo, John?" Eaton asked Leasure. The old hunter pulled his pipe from his mouth.

"Wal, Frank knows more about the buffalo than I do. He's been around them since he was a youngster. The animal, though, is a funny built one. They got a lot of covering up front: hair, hide and bone. They will always face a storm where cattle and horses will drift before it. I've thought about that. Seems to me that drifting with a storm would keep you in it longer, where, if you faced it, you'd be done with it quicker." He puffed on his pipe.

"You asked the boys once what they were going to do when the buffalo were gone. It's a hard question. We're too old to be drovers, too tired to be miners, and too blamed honest to be outlaws. There's nothing on the frontier for men our age." Behind the pipe smoke Leasure's eyes held a somber view of their future.

Eaton stirred. "I don't agree with you, John. The West needs men like you, Frank and Matthew. Men who are wise in years, experienced, and steadfast. It won't be long before the buffalo are gone like you say. Then get yourself some land along the Yellowstone and hold on to it. It'll be worth some real money before too long. Or, you could start a freighter business. You men know horses and the country. I hear they're charging half a dollar a pound for delivered goods in Benton. If it takes some capital, I can maybe help you when the time comes."

"Thanks, Howard, if nothing else we appreciate your kindness," John remarked. The others heartily concurred.

The next day they said 'so long' to the Leasure party, as Captain Borden was due back at the fort soon and wanted to continue the circle they had begun. Toby was sorry to see them go as he'd gotten to like them and enjoyed listening to the evening's conversation.

* * *

Winter passed and one day Toby woke to the sound of geese heading north. He jumped up and ran from the lodge, the dog running happily at his heels. Except for a limp, it had healed of its wounds in the cold cleanness of the country. Above them, long flights of geese were strung out clear to the horizon, heralding the coming of spring.

The sight was one to thrill the heart, even the dog seemed affected for he ran about the camp uttering hoarse 'woofs' 'til Frank hollered at him from the Lodge. Toby slipped in with a coffee pot full of clean creek water.

"Frank, you should see all the geese. There's thousands of 'em flying right over us."

"Don't you think we can't hear 'em, youngster?"

Indeed, the air was full of the cacophonous calls of the flocks overhead, their numberless V's stretching from horizon to horizon.

"We're out of coffee, Frank. What'll I do?"

"Boil the water anyway, son. It'll take out the alkali." Frank struggled out of his bedroll. The Leasure party had been gone for weeks and the days had been filled with nothing but work and weather. The camp was ringed with hide piles and Frank and Matthew had remarked several times about Baldwin's nonappearance on the hunting grounds.

"Matthew, it looks like G.W. isn't coming and we're out of coffee and flour. Looks like one of us is due for a trip to Keogh for supplies. I think it should be me 'cause you get in too much trouble when you go in. I'll take Jason with me. He needs to take a break, don't you think?" Matthew was sitting up, leaning back on a willow rest that he favored.

"We've talked this out before, Pard, and either way is dangerous. Two men on the trail alone, Toby and I here alone. It's a bad deal and I don't like it. We can handle being short for another week. Let's wait that long, then I'll agree to a trip if Baldwin or someone else doesn't come by then." Matthew got himself up stiffly. The winter had taken its toll on him to an alarming degree. Unlike Frank, he never would spare himself.

"Alright, alright. We can wait a week, I guess. But we're not only out of coffee and flour, I'm out of tobacco, too, damn it!"

"I know how it bothers you, but I've saved a little something here that should tide you over." Matthew's voice was sympathetic as he rummaged in his warbag. He came up with an object and threw it over to Frank, who caught it against his chest.

"Why, damn me, pard, thank you!" The object turned out to be a carton of chewing tobacco. Frank opened up a package and happily bit off a chunk.

Two more days went by and spring was surely in the air. A warm chinook had taken the ice off the creek down below and the ducks had settled in the next day. The air seemed full of their cackle and the whistle of their wings. Soon, Toby knew, the other birds would return. He'd already seen a meadowlark or two, and prairie dogs were running about on the flat. The only bane was the foul stink of buffalo carcasses brought by the warm wind. It was an offensive smell that wouldn't let them forget their guilt for the wanton slaughter.

The growling of the dog woke the lodge the third morning.

Toby whispered in the direction of Frank's bedroll across the fire. "Frank, what is it, did you hear anything?"

Cappy was keeping a continuous buzz saw growl going deep in his throat. He stood spraddle-legged facing the lodge's entryway, head down, a menacing figure.

Suddenly, Matthew flipped the hide door back and the dog raced out. Matthew and Frank followed with their rifles ready. Then Toby saw Jason up and peering out the door with his rifle in his hands. He too, bent and stepped out cautiously. Belatedly, Toby scrambled around and found his rifle. He ran out.

The men were down at the horse corral. Frank was circling on a trail out about fifty yards, trying to read sign. Matthew was forking some of the last hay to the horses that were left. When Toby came up he saw that his buckskin and Jason's horse were gone. Jason was holding Cappy back. Matthew leaned his fork against a tree and said in his soft lisp, "Had a little visit this morning from the Redskin Brigade. They took your hay burners, boys."

"And you're just going to let them go?" Jason was red-faced and angry. He had grown inordinately fond of the white horse.

"Well, don't get your back up. First we see how many we're up against, then we decide."

Matthew returned to the lodge and came back with his coat and gloves. His pistol was strapped on and he was carrying Frank's gear. He dumped it on the ground, got a length of rope from one of the wagons and tied the dog to a wheel. Frank came in then and they had a war council.

"I reckon we should have started posting guard again this last week. Relied too much on the dog, I guess." Frank commented.

"How many?" Matthew asked.

"I make it just two. Course that's all that's snuck up to the corral. Probably joined with a few others over the hill." Frank strapped his pistol on and got into his coat.

"What do you think? Is it worth running after them? I hate leaving Toby and Jason here alone."

"Let me go with one of you," Jason begged. "It's my horse they took."

"And mine," Toby said eagerly. "Take me, too."

"I'll take Jason, Matthew, and we'll run 'em 'til it looks like we better turn back."

Matthew's scarred face looked dubious but he nodded assent.

Toby turned away in disgust. "Aw, I never have a chance to do anything around here but work. It's 'Toby, cook this; Toby, pour up the coffee; Toby, wash these up.'" The only reason you want me around is to do the chores." He went to the dog, Cappy, and put his arms around the scarred old head.

Matthew ignored him for the moment and helped Frank and Jason get ready to move out. After they'd swung up, Jason on Matthew's big bay, and Frank on his sorrel, Matthew handed up their rifles and a sack of hard tack and jerky.

"Take care, pard, no horse is worth your scalp."

"Will do." Frank looked at Toby but the boy remained crouched by the dog.

* * *

They galloped out of camp on a trail that headed north. Matthew then walked over to where the boy was sitting dejectedly by the wagon, petting Cappy's huge head. He squatted by them and for a while was silent.

"Son . . . it's certainly true you've been pulling your weight around here, especially lately. Frank and I don't seem to be getting any younger, and we've sure come to rely on you. Too much, I guess. You've sure been pullin' your weight. But this country is no place for a boy. Frank and I believe that what's best for you would be to send you to school back East. That's why we've been taking such a run at this hunting business. We'll have enough to do that if Baldwin gets here to buy these hides and the price is still up. I've got a sister back East that I've written to. She'll take you, I'm sure." The white head looked away toward the trail Frank and Jason had taken. "Course, you know, son, we both will miss you."

Matthew looked back to see the boy's face streaming tears that the dog licked anxiously.

"I didn't mean to complain, Matthew. Please don't make me leave you and Frank."

"Well, son, it's just that we're thinking what's best for you. Don't you want to go to school? Learn to read better and write a good hand? We've talked about it before." The old man's voice was even more gentle than before.

"But I thought we were going to get a horse ranch? Sell horses to the Cavalry?" The boy wiped his tears away with the back of a hand, pushing the dog away.

"Well, we've talked about it, yes. Maybe we could do both. You could go to school and come back in the summer to help us on the ranch. What do you think of that?"

"Maybe. But let's get the ranch first and get it set up, then we think of me going away. Please?" The boy's eyes were pleading as they locked into the old man's gray ones.

"Well we just will have to see, I guess. Let's go put the bacon on." Together they got up and walked to the lodge, the man's hand on the boy's shoulder.

All that day, the old man and the boy worked around camp, doing a number of chores that needed done. One of the bay team, Boxer, had a loose shoe. Matthew got a cotton rope from the lodge and haltering the big horse, they led it out and tied it to a tree. Matthew took his cotton rope and tied it about the forefoot. He lifted it and Toby tied it in place to work on. The gentle horse stood quietly while Matthew pulled off the shoe, worked the hoof a little and nailed the shoe back in place. Then he dropped the leg and checked the other shoes. Toby led the bay to the corral and put him back with the rest. Together, they went ahead and cleaned the lodge and reset some of its loosened pegs. Matthew sat out in the sunshine and worked up some shells for the buffalo guns, while Toby took his little gun and the dog and went down the creek for some ducks.

Meanwhile, Frank and Jason rode hard on the trail north.

The next day, after a night which had seen Toby standing guard for several hours, Baldwin's outfit showed up. His train was many wagons longer than he'd come with before, more men, all armed to the teeth, it seemed.

"Hello, there, Matthew, Toby. Where's Frank and your skinner?" G.W. greeted them when he rode in. "You've grown, Toby. Getting some muscle on you. Here's a dollar." He flipped heavy silver coin in the air and the boy caught it with a subdued 'Thank you.'

While the freighters set up the hide press and began working the hides through it, Matthew went down to the horse corral and began saddling Frank's sorrel. G. W. gabbed at him the while, sipping on a cup that Toby had brought him.

"Lots of news, Matthew. Sorry we couldn't make it earlier. Ice jammed up the river and flooded town. We couldn't get over 'til it dropped this week. Been waiting for a while. I know you hunters were getting low on supplies. Tell me what you need, we got it with us. What you doing? Where you goin'?" He asked plaintively. Matthew finished saddling and turned to him.

"Frank's out there running horse thieves. I couldn't go with him with Toby here and all. Now you're here, I'm heading out." Matthew took his rifle and stuck it in its scabbard. "I want you to take the hides and Toby and the dog with you. Take good care of them. We'll catch up to you along the trail."

Baldwin took his cap off and scratched his head. "Well, sure, Matthew, we can do that. Hope Frank and your skinner are all right. We can lay up here a day or two, though, and press your hides while we're waitin'. Fact is, I've got a couple good men I'll send with you."

"No, I'm heading out right now. Don't need any help." Matthew threw a long lean leg over the leather and hit a gallop in three jumps. Baldwin and Toby watched until he was out of sight.

* * *

Frank and Jason were in a shallow cut miles to the north. Frank's 'Jackson' horse was dead some yards from the lip of the draw where they were lying and the horse Jason had ridden was down from a merciful bullet from Frank's pistol. It had been gutshot earlier when the ambush had occurred. Jason's teeth were chattering and a suspicious stain on his pants front attested further to his fear. Frank, however, seemed philosophical about their position.

"All we have to do is save our shells and wait for Matthew. He always shows up when powder's burning. You'll see. Pisses me off about the stock, though. Trained that horse up to ride myself. Also, I'm about out of chew." A puff of smoke from a bluff about two hundred yards distant and a kick of dirt above his head made Jason's body jerk.

"Not so eager to catch a horse thief now, eh, boy?" Frank chortled. They had dug deeper in with their knives and were under good cover, but had no water.

"I make it about ten or eleven Sioux. I'm gonna see if I can get a line on one." Frank squirmed around and poked his head up quick, then back down. A late shot blasted. Jason's body jerked again. He took out his knife, his teeth chattering, and deepened his hole a little more.

Several hours of fast riding on an easy followed trail brought Matthew into the sound of gunfire off to his right front. He abruptly slowed and checked his rifle and pistol. Then he went forward at a cautious trot. Then, ahead of him, a brave broke from cover. He brought up his rifle.

In the draw Frank was suddenly listening. "That last shot sounded like a Henry, didn't you think, Jason boy?"

"I don't know." Jason muttered. He was in a funk. He knew they were going to be killed. Would they be tortured first, fingers cut off like he'd seen on the necklaces? Maybe he should just shoot himself now. He trembled. Toby's Henry was in his hands but he so far hadn't even let a round loose.

Another shot. Frank let out a whoop.

"That's Matthew's gun. We got to give him a little help. I'm going down the draw and try to cut around the right. You go left. Now, damn it, get up and go! You ain't dead yet."

He cuffed Jason 'til the young man made an effort to get away from him and scrambled up the draw, then Frank skittered like an old spider the other way.

Matthew had gotten a good view of the battle and pulled back a ways, then circled on a lope around to the Sioux's rear. He'd come up on their horses tied below a low bluff and cut them loose. Then he'd run them back toward the south trail. Returning, he'd pulled a careful sneak on the war party, attempting to get them all in sight. The best he could do was five or six, all strung out slightly above and in a partial circle around Frank's position, all absorbed in closing their trap.

His first shot was a careful one that lifted the warrior farthest left up on his knees, then flattened him. Powder smoke obscured his vision straight to his front and he rolled right to get around it. Coming up, he caught a warrior in mid-stride that had left his position. The rest went into cover, leaving two of their number down.

Knowing they would check the horses, and fearful they'd get his, he worked back as swiftly as his stiff old legs would take him to where he could see it. It wasn't an instant later, he heard Frank's gun sound. It brought a wave of relief. His pard was still alive. When an Indian slipped across the sandrock edge of the bluff towards the sorrel, Matthew put him down with a head shot, then changed position again. The horse was nervous, rolling his eyes and seeming to scent the dead warrior or another live one close to him. Matthew waited. While he did, he heard another shot, then Frank's Henry again. Then three pistol shots. It was hard to wait but he managed and his patience was rewarded. Another warrior came stealthily along the bluff, heading for the sorrel. Matthew sighted carefully and shot him in one of the white circles he'd painted on his chest. The brave spun and fell. The next instant a shot burned into Matthew's shoulder. He rolled instinctively to cover behind a sandstone ledge, banging his shin heavily as he did. Another shot came searching for him, powdering the rock face close by. Then it was still. He groaned. "Too damn old for this," he thought. Blood seeped down his coat front.

He listened a while, then rising, scrambled up and over the bluff edge behind him. He began a careful sneak as best his battered leg would let him. Halfway around, he stopped as another shot sounded, then Frank hollered. "Alright here, Matthew, there's a couple moving off north, the rest are down."

Still careful, Matthew edged back to his horse, checking to make sure the dead Sioux were still there. They were. He managed to mount and, galloping to present a tougher moving target, reconnoitered the area. He passed around Frank as he went, and Frank gave him a wave. Presently he came in.

"Looks like five or six down, another crawled off somewhere. You okay?"

Frank nodded. "Thanks for coming, Pard. You were better than the cavalry." He glimpsed the blood on Matthew's coat. "Hey! You hit?"

"Grooved the shoulder, is all. Where's Jason?"

"Down in the coulee there. Don't say anything, Matthew, he was pretty scared, "He went over to his dead horse. "Poor old boy, he was a good 'un, Matthew, wasn't he?" He reached down and gently took the bridle off its head, then undid the cinch and stripped the saddle off. "Well, she's a long walk back."

Frank and Matthew turned as Jason came up. The young man was still trembling and trying to hide his soiled front.

"Maybe not." Matthew slid off his horse and handed the reins to Frank. "Try for some of their stock I run off."

He sent Frank back over the hill south. Slipping his rifle in the scabbard, Frank took down his rope and made for the distant horses grazing head down a mile or so away. He kept his eyes peeled.

By the time Frank returned, Jason had stripped off Matthew's coat and they'd managed to plug the wound with a scarf. Matthew was sitting on Frank's dead horse when Frank rode up with four horses. One was Toby's little buckskin, walking lame, and another was Jason's 'Whitey.'

"Couldn't catch up to the others." He dismounted and went over to Matthew, pulled the shirt away and peered at the wound. Then he looked keenly in his friend's lean face.

"You've had worse, pard. Here, we'll tie up your front paw there." He took his neck scarf off and fashioned an arm sling for Matthew, then slipped the coat over and buttoned it up.

"Jason, throw the leather on your and Toby's horses."

Frank worked his saddle off Jackson, and approaching an Indian buckskin, he attempted to throw it on its back. It snorted and backed off, unfamiliar smells making it skittish. Frank cussed and dropped the saddle. Suddenly, he was blazing mad. Why, he couldn't have explained. It was just a combination of circumstances that always seemed to work against the pair of them. Fate, Matthew called it.

"Alright, you son-of-a-bitch, have it the hard way."

He caught the trailing head rope and pulled the horse close, and calling to Jason to throw the saddle on it, roughly eared the horse down. It snorted and tried to rear but Frank clamped tighter on its ear. Working together, they got it saddled, then helped Matthew climb on his sorrel.

Then Frank swung aboard, the Indian horse crow-hopping with him before he managed to pull its head up. Jason hopped up on his white horse and they started out, hazing the other horses in front of them down the back trail.

* * *

When, late that night, they reached the camp, Baldwin's wagons were still there. Frank, by then, was riding behind Matthew to keep him in the saddle. Together they got him down off the horse and into the lodge, Matthew trying weakly to help them, but his legs just not carrying him.

Toby had been in a nervous fluster ever since they'd been gone. Mostly he had just kept the fire going and the coffee pot on for Baldwin's outfit, which was finished pressing and loading the last of the hides. Knowing something was wrong, the dog hovered about him. Finally, he sat on his bed.

When one of the freighters, a hulking, bearded dirty individual with a huge chew in his jaw growled at him,

"Come 'ere with that coffee pot, pup."

Toby glowered at him and refused to budge. The freighter started for him, stopped when Cappy began his buzz-saw noise, then pulled his pistol from his belt.

Baldwin intervened, stepping in front of him. "I wouldn't mess with them, was I you. The old boys he belongs to are pretty touchy and you wouldn't want to piss 'em off. Here, I'll pour the coffee."

"So what's a couple of old farts gonna do?" the freighter belligerently inquired.

"Put so many holes in your hide you wouldn't hold water. Tell him, boys, about Grounds and Shannon. The one killed a man last year in Miles over that dog, and the other stood off a Blackfoot war party by himself this winter. They're out right now after some horse thieves and I'm betting they come back with their horses." He picked up a tin cup and handed it to the burly freighter, then poured him some coffee and splashed some more into his own cup.

"I knew 'em down South. They're a couple old gun hands. Warred together, rangered together and drovered together. They came up the trail with Story. They've about done it all and I can tell you they can make a pistol or a rifle play "*Dixie*." The boy is special to 'em so

65

I'd just leave him alone." The big freighter snorted and turned away, clearly unimpressed.

G.W. shook his head. 'Damn dumb whistlebellies,' he thought. 'Nothing but trouble.'

When, hours later, Frank and Matthew showed up with Jason and the horses, Toby's relief poured out. When he saw Matthew's condition, he turned to and made up the fire, put on water and got out an old shirt from Matthew's warbag for bandages. Baldwin came in and helped as Matthew's wound was cleaned and inspected, then bandaged. The wound was ugly and likely to get infected, G.W. knew. Any gunshot was dangerous. And, too often, it took the cloth deep into the wound where it festered and infected the injury.

"I think he should go in to the doctor. Girard at the Fort is damn good with bullet holes," Baldwin commented. Frank concurred.

"I think you're right, G.W. We'll let him sleep tonight and get going tomorrow." Frank clearly needed the night's rest also, showing the strain of the last two days in his stubbled face.

* * *

Next morning a spring dawn turned the hills a rose hue. Frank directed Jason to hitch the wagon up. Together, Toby and he got Matthew up and into a chair by the fire. He looked pale and wan, almost feeble in the early morning light. Toby had half-expected him to protest their ministrations but he assented to everything they did for him almost meekly.

The freighters were hitching up preparing to move out. Baldwin came over while they were cleaning up after breakfast.

"We're about to pull out, Frank. I wanted to pay up for the hides. You'll take a draft on Wells Fargo at Milestown, won't you? How are you today, Matthew?" G.W. sat down and let them fill his cup. "I guess I can handle one more cup. Thanks, Toby."

"There's a bank already at Milestown, huh, G.W.?" Frank asked. A few hours of sleep had perked him up.

"That's what I was going to tell you boys before you went chasing off after horse thieves. There's lots of things going on in Miles. There's about twenty saloons now, a newspaper called *The Yellowstone Journal*, a couple of stage lines, a dozen 'parlour' houses, dance halls, barber shops, you name it, boys, it's coming to Miles. Why, the General even has a talking metal line they ran from the telegraph station over to

66

the Fort and on into his office. He can talk over it to the telegraph operator from right there."

Seeing the incredulous looks on the men's faces, he insisted,

"I'm telling you boys the truth!"

"C'mon, G.W. You're blowing smoke again." Frank laughed, "It's more'n two miles between 'em!"

"Fact, boys. You'll see when you get in." G.W. was solemn as he pulled out his checkbook.

"962 hides at four dollars a hide. I'm giving you twenty- five cents more a hide than I do most of the rest. Comes to $3,840.00. Guess I'll throw in the coffee Toby got and, if you're going in anyway, you'll want to stock up there, save the freight."

He handed over the check to Frank, who took it and stuck it in his shirt pocket without looking at it.

"Jason, saddle your horse and turn the rest out after you halter 'em. If you let the halter ropes drag you won't have no trouble with them. If we leave 'em here, we'll never see 'em again. Come here, Toby, and help me."

They got Matthew up into the back of the wagon and comfortable, then put their camp gear and all the weapons in and started for town. Jason lined the horses out behind them.

Bison wading the river

Chapter 5

Miles City, Montana Territory

Early next morning, when they topped the bluff over the river, Frank whistled in amazement. The town had moved in to the east bank of the Tongue River and doubled in size. And the cantonment had moved out farther to the west. A company of cavalry was exercising maneuvers on the flat between the Tongue and the cantonment, and Indian teepees dotted the landscape all around. Puffs of smoke and the muted banging of muskets to the west pinpointed the rifle range where infantry were firing. Two steamboats were tied up to a landing a few hundred yards up from the mouth of the Tongue River. The scene from the bluff was overall one of tremendous activity.

When they reached the ford up river from the Tongue's mouth, Frank and Toby saw a ferry push out from the far side towards them. Frank decided to wait rather than drive over the bumpy rocky ford and further jar Matthew suffering silently in back. Several times Matthew had urged them to let him get out and ride but they had persevered and he'd resigned himself to the wagon. The collarbone was broken, he now felt, and the bullet hole was inflamed. He was lightheaded and feverish and knew he probably couldn't sit a horse, anyway.

Midway across, the ferry runner hailed him. "Ho there, you want the ferry?"

"Sure do," Frank hollered back.

The big planked contrivance edged across. When it reached the north shore, the man dropped the hinged front down onto a log bunker set in the mud. Frank drove the wagon up and into it without difficulty after they set some planks.

"Let's wait a while. We got some horses coming behind."

"Fine, we got room for 'em. Fifty cents for the wagon and a dime apiece for the loose horses, though." The ferry runner held a gnarled dirty hand out and Frank fumbled in his pocket for change.

"Say, isn't that pit dog the one Anson Baker used to have? Used him to fight badgers and such." He peered at Frank again. "You're not the one killed him, though. The old boy did that had white hair." He hadn't seen Matthew lying in the back of the wagon. Toby looked uncomfortable.

"It's the boy's dog."

Frank volunteered nothing else and Jason coming up with the horses about that time, they got busy bringing them on the ferry. When the horses were snugged to the rails, they pushed off with poles and Jason helped the ferry man work the cable.

"Good God," Frank breathed as they neared the south bank.

"What is it?" Matthew asked weakly from the wagon box.

"Haven't seen so much hustle and bustle going on since boom times in the gold diggins." Frank turned to their hired man.

"Jason, you take the horses over to Broadwater and Hubbell's stables and put 'em in the corral. Then either wait for us there or come on out to the Fort. We'll probably be at the infirmary out there."

When they landed, Jason gathered his little bunch and headed for the town. Frank drove to the cantonment and got directions to the infirmary.

"You wait, Toby, and I'll see if Girard will take him." He clambered from the wagon and walked up the steps into a frame-built structure with a sign on its front which proclaimed it was the "Fort Keogh Infirmary."

Inside, an orderly asked him his business.

"My pardner's got himself a bullet hole in him. I'd like the doctor to look at him."

In another room through an open doorway a deep voice boomed, "Tell him to take his friend to the horse doctor over at Johnson and Ringer's Livery. He works on civilians. I'm busy with army patients just now!"

Frank could hear him telling an unseen orderly in the next room that, "These coffee-cooling civilians are always cutting or putting holes in each other and expecting the army to take care of them when they do. I'm tired of messing with them."

Despite the orderly's protests, Frank pushed into the room and confronted the army doctor, a deep-chested side whiskered older man with a dark complexion. He was working on the leg of a private, the

69

faint young man holding tightly to the table as the doctor expertly and quickly bandaged the limb.

"There, son, the orderly will give you some crutches. Stay off that leg for a week and next time, watch yourself. Mule'll kick your fool head off." He turned to Frank and appraised him warily. "What may I do for you, sir?"

"My pardner out in the wagon's been shot by Indians. You're the doctor hereabouts, I understand, that knows gunshot wounds." Frank looked grim and dangerous.

"I've been known to treat a few in my time." He looked Frank up and down, then sighed, "I can tell I'm not getting any peace until I see this man. Orderly! Get a stretcher-bearer and bring him in."

When Matthew was placed on the table, the doctor peeled the coat back and gently separated the blood soaked rags from the wound. A groan escaped Matthew's tightly compressed lips.

"I'll clean him up and examine him. Why don't you wait in the orderly room 'til I get done?"

When the doctor came out, Frank and Toby were standing in a room filled with army, Indians, and civilians, all waiting to see the doctor. As he stepped into the room a clamor rose.

"Come with me, sir."

The doctor gestured at Frank to step into his side office.

"Orderly, take names and conditions. I don't see anyone here that looks terminal." He closed the door and turned to the anxious pair.

"Now, sir, your friend is being made ready for surgery." He stepped over to a skeleton hanging in the corner. Toby's eyes bugged at the apparition.

"I find it convenient to explain using this graphic example." Girard turned the articulated bones and pointed with a finger.

"Now this is the collar bone, called the clavicle. Under it is where the bullet went, grooving and breaking the bone as it passed. Then it hit the sub-clavicular vein, hence the heavy bleeding. Coming out the other side, it broke through the upper portion of the shoulder blade, just here. The problem is that cloth was intruded into the wound, the vessel is ruptured, the two bones broken with fragments thrown into the meat on both sides. And there's already some infection." He dropped his hand, "I must operate immediately."

"Sounds like it's serious, right, Major?" Frank asked gravely.

"It is, and his age and the length of time getting him here all combined to make it worse. We'll do what we can. It'll be at least two hours, maybe more, before I finish. He'll be moved to the ward afterwards and you can come see him in the morning."

He turned and they headed for the door. Girard, seeing Toby's downcast expression, asked, "Is he your grandpa, son?"

"No, Sir," Toby said shyly. "He's my step-father, like Frank is."

Frank looked at him oddly and they went down to the wagon.

"That was a good answer you gave the doc, son."

"Isn't it the truth, Frank?"

"I guess so. I just never thought of it, is all." He pulled the team around and they headed for town just as a hail from the door of the Infirmary caught them.

"Hey, there," a plump orderly hollered, "He wants to talk to you."

Frank turned back and followed the orderly in to a room where they had Matthew lying on a cot. Matthew lifted up his head when he saw Frank. "Here, take my pistol and my money belt."

"Sure." He awkwardly patted Matthew's good shoulder. "Don't worry, Pard, the Doc's a good one. We'll see you in the morning."

Since the Tongue River was up, they waited in line at the river bank above the ferry landing for a ride over to town.

"What's the name of that one steamboat, Frank? I can spell it: 'E- C- L- I- P- S- E-' but how do you say it right?"

"I don't know, lad. I never learned to read or write," Frank muttered. He clucked to the team as Toby turned to him in amazement. In the five years he'd lived with the two men he had never tumbled to the fact that Frank had just admitted to him now. In some way it diminished the old man in his mind, and he didn't like the feeling. To him, both men had always been bigger than life. Now, his world was in a tumble. First Matthew getting shot, now this.

After they crossed the river, they were almost immediately onto the main street of Milestown. "Miles City," the residents were calling it. "Old Milestown" was the original site a mile or so to the east.

Frank dejectedly pulled the team into Broadwater and Hubbell's livery stable. Jason came out of the dark interior. "Is Matthew going to be all right?" Frank dismounted stiffly.

"Don't know, he's worse hurt than we thought, but the doctor out there, Major Girard, is a good one, I guess," Frank morosely replied. Together, the two opened the big doors.

Toby pulled on through to the wagon yard beyond, parked the wagon and unhitched the bays. The livery hand took them in hand, saying he'd take good care of them, then Toby and Jason followed Frank out into the broad dusty street. They stayed close as he headed up the street, passing Indians, army men, bullwhackers, hunters and the like as they headed to Leighton's store. The store, too, was crowded but when Leighton saw them, he came over, wiping his hands on his apron.

"How do, Frank. And here's Toby and the young man from England. You stayed at Healey's for a while, didn't you?" He shook hands with them all. Toby noticed that behind the soiled white apron the handle of a pistol protruded. Frank unbuttoned his shirt pocket and pulled out Baldwin's check.

"He's turned into a derned good skinner, Leighton. Wonder if you'd cash this so we can pay him off, then put the most of it back in your safe. We'll be in later and stock up."

Toby, intensely curious, was already wandering away to gaze at the mountainous piles of stacked goods everywhere. He was growing so fast lately his arms and legs stuck out of his clothes at both ends and he hoped Frank would remember to get him some new ones.

"Sure, Frank, but the town has a bank now. Maybe you'd want to shift your money business with them," Leighton was saying.

"Nope. If it's all the same, we'll just keep on with you. Never have trusted banks for a long time. They always seemed to lose my money, then charge me for doing it." He handed the check over to Leighton who took it to his office. A huge safe dominated a whole one wall of the cluttered room. Leighton sat at the desk and endorsed the check with Frank's name, then had him put his brand on it.

"How much do you want to draw, Frank?"

"Well, we bin paying Jason 75 cents a hide and room and board. G.W. said we had 962 of them he took. Guess that makes $722.00, if my figuring is correct. Take this safebox and we'll put it all in there with Matthew's money belt and his gun belt. Give me the $800 odd to pay my skinner and get by for now." He sat while Leighton stuffed everything, including Matthew's rifles and his pistol, in the crowded safe. Leighton glanced at the somber figure as he counted out the money.

"What's wrong, Frank? Looks to me like you had a dern good winter."

"Aw, Matthew's hurt bad, Leighton. We had a run-in with some Sioux horse thieves over on Lodge Pole Creek. He took a bullet through the collar bone. We got him out at Keogh and the doc's probably operating right now. It took a couple days to get him here and I'm damn worried about him. We been pards for twenty years and you couldn't ask for a better one." He got up slowly. "I guess we'll be back and stock up after we find out about Matthew tomorrow. Thanks for stashing our plunder."

"It'll be here, Frank. Sorry to hear about Matthew. He's a good man." Leighton chuckled. "He sure set the tough element back on its heels last fall when he killed Anson Baker. I didn't see it but folks who did told me it was damn slick."

"There isn't no back-up in Matthew, that's for sure. Be right back."

Frank went out the store front where Jason and Toby waited.

"Alright now, boys, it's pay day. Jason, we owe you for 962 hides. That comes to $722. Here's $750. You done a good job, lad, an' deserve a bonus. We'll have to see if Matthew's going to be able to hunt again this year, so I don't know if we're going back out again or not. Some advice if you want it, is to get your outfit bought before you see the town an' leave it with Leighton. Then you'll have it if you go broke." He grinned a little. "That's experience talkin'."

"Thanks, Frank. I'll be around to see how Matthew's doing tomorrow. See you later." He hurried out, stuffing his money into his pocket.

Frank turned to Toby. "Well, son, lets buy us some new duds, then go get some grub."

"Could we go back then and see how he's doing, Frank?" Toby asked.

"Doc said tomorrow, but maybe we could ease out there this evening. We'll see."

They rummaged through Leighton's shelves with his help and stocked up some clothes: from new underwear to a new wool vest for Frank.

"I'd buy a watch but I never learned to tell time, neither," he confided to Toby. "Guess it never mattered so long as Matthew was there to tell me if we needed to know. Maybe we'll get you one, instead, son." The boy picked out an Ingersoll for $1.50 and delighted in the setting and winding of it.

They bundled up their old stuff and told the clerk to throw it away, all except for Frank's old Stetson which he wouldn't part with. Toby himself sported a new silverbelly straight brimmed Stetson.

"We'll go over to McDonald's and get us some new boots after we eat."

They walked across the street to a cafe, Merritt's, and being early for supper, found an empty table in the corner and took a seat.

A fat man in a greasy soiled apron came over and asked for their order.

"What you got?" Frank asked him.

"Well, by golly, we got eggs today. Mrs. Bender's flock is starting to lay again. How about some hog steak and eggs. Just picked up half a pig at the butcher. I know you hunters like something besides buffalo when you come in to town. Coffee? Got some milk, too, if you want some."

"Sure," Frank waved airily, "Give us the works."

After they'd eaten a pretty good meal, the cook brought them over the house specialty. He sat it down with a flourish. "Raisin duff with cream and sugar. Most of the hunters would swim the river for it." It was delicious and they both decided to have seconds.

Afterwards, stuffed, they headed for McDonald's and outfitted with new boots, belts and a collar for Cappy, who'd followed them quietly from store to cafe, plopping himself down by the entrances with a familiar air.

"Couldn't we go out now and see how Matthew is?" Toby couldn't wait any longer, and truthfully, neither could Frank. They headed out to the fort, their new boots hurting their feet, causing them both to eventually change back to their old ones.

* * *

"Well, he's resting now," the orderly said. "The surgery went okay.. Still asleep from the laudanum. He'll come out of it and be sick for a while, but he should be able to see you in the morning.

He shuffled some papers on the desk, wanting them gone so he could go take a short snooze himself. The Major was a hard taskmaster. After the surgery, they'd cleared the waiting patients in short order and Girard had gone to his quarters for a lie-down.

When they made it back to town, it was nearly dark and the saloons were all doing a brisk business. A fist fight was going on in a vacant lot, cheered on by some drunken soldiers and a hunter or two. Several Indian braves were passed out in the grove of trees by the ferry landing and the shuffle and stomp of some whooping customers in a nearby dance hall came to them as they passed its doors. The stores were still open, too, with customers going in and out.

"Guess the town goes day and night," Frank commented wryly. "Seen a time when I'd go with it. But not now. I'm too worried about Matthew. Guess we'll go bed down in the livery."

Next morning early, they rolled out of the sweet smelling bluestem horse hay piled back of the livery. When their morning business was done and their beds rolled, they went back to the cafe where they had eaten the night before. The cafe was busy though the sun was just barely over the horizon and the same fat cook with the same greasy apron came to take their order.

"What's the menu say today?" Frank asked.

"Got some lamb chops if you're so inclined. And Bender's chickens have started laying again." He peered at them a little closer. "But I guess you were in last evening and heard me say that, didn't you?"

"Lamb chops? It's been years since I've had some of 'em. Who brought the sheep in?" Frank asked curiously.

"Old John Burgess just brought 'em in from California. Took him two years." The cook laughed, his belly jiggling. "Good country around here for sheep, he claims. Want any or not?"

"Sure, bring 'em and some eggs, coffee and milk, too."

After breakfast, they collected Cappy and, going back down to the livery, they saddled up Toby's little buckskin and Frank's Indian horse. The saloons they passed were still doing business, though not so brisk as the night's had been. Along the boardwalk fronting the various buildings were placed cottonwood logs with their length squared off to make some comfortable benches for idlers to take their ease.

As Frank and Toby passed by with Cappy following, a loiterer turned to the one seated next to him and remarked,

"Say, isn't that the pitdog Anson Baker used to fight?"

The other opened a hung-over eye and gazed out into the street where Lavardure indicated. He started: "Damn sure is. I won a lot of money off that dog. Got a bite on 'im like a damn bear. Wonder if that's the old man killed Anson. I thought they said he had long white hair."

"Suppose that's the boy got Anson killed. Wonder where they're headed." Billy Downs watched them as the trio headed toward the Tongue River ferry. "Guess we could follow 'em and see if they're partnering with the white haired gent. Find out where he's at. Lucas'll want to know."

"You go. My head's killing me this morning. Take my horse if you want, but I'm headin' in for a drink." Downs lurched up and went through the door into Tate's. Lavardure thought a moment, his own head pounding from last night's carouse, then he got up and headed for the livery.

Matthew opened his eyes when he heard the orderly bring Frank and Toby in. The two sat on the cot opposite his bunk and Frank broke the silence.

"How's it going, pard?"

Matthew's eyes circled the room. Though mostly the beds were filled with army blue, surprisingly, there were two with Indians in them. "Scouts," he thought.

"Old bones take a while, pard, but I'm all right. The doctor's a good one." The eagle eyes closed, "How's Toby? Taking in the sights in the big city?" His voice, though faint, was stronger. Some color had returned to his face. The boy sparkled at the attention.

"You'd never believe it, Matthew. We ate sheep this morning- - lamb chops. We had eggs yesterday, and cream. There's some farmers here now. Boy, that cream is tasty! Last night we had raisin duff with sugar and cream. It was so good!"

The boy rattled on and the two old men smiled, listening, content in each other's company.

Through the door was heard Major Girard's strong voice. He was starting his rounds and came in on them.

"Here we all are! My old buffalo hunter is awake with his tribe gathered around him. Ho, tribe! Good morning. Your chief is much better." He was in a good mood, rare for him. Normally the orderly privates were scurrying under his ceaseless commands. Keogh was to him the end of the earth for a duty station and he counted the days until his date of transfer.

"Howdy, Major. We all thank you for what you've done for Matthew here. How bad was it?" Frank shook his hand.

"The clavicle was broken, as I thought. I cleaned a lot of debris from the wound: bone slivers, cloth and bullet fragments. However, he's back in one piece now and after a month or so, he'll be ready for light duty. He shouldn't be moved from here, though, for," He raised a pair of expressive eyebrows. "We'll say, five days. He lost too much blood and needs some peace and quiet, to build his strength."

"Major, we'll pay you for your trouble. Be glad to." Frank was adamant, dipping a hand in his pocket.

"I had a visit with Colonel Miles this morning at mess. He feels that since you were hurt while engaged with hostiles, we won't worry about payment. Doing our work, so to speak." He lifted the blanket, took the gnarled hand and looked at the cuticles. "Circulation seems good. I was a little worried about the artery, but it apparently wasn't damaged, "He replaced the hand under the blanket and looked at Frank.

"Let's leave him heal. He needs rest right now. Come in here and we'll talk." He stood and gestured to Frank towards his office and they walked away.

"Toby." Matthew whispered, "Lean over here." When Toby came closer he said, "I want a pistol, Toby. Tell Frank."

"Sure, Matthew, I'll tell him." Toby was suddenly apprehensive, thinking how helpless the old man was, weak and defenseless as he'd never seen him before. It shook him.

Outside later, after Frank had done visiting with Girard and they were heading back towards the ferry, Toby told him what Matthew had said. Frank promptly turned back to the infirmary.

The plump orderly was surprised to see them back so soon.

"I don't think you should see him again so quick."

Frank spread his thin arms. "I'll only be a little, son. Be right back." He slipped around him before the man could protest further. As the man started to follow, Toby came in crying.

The orderly swung back.

"What's wrong with you, sonny?"

"I fell off my horse. I think my arm's broke."

"Where's it hurt? The orderly took the arm Toby held out and manipulated it gingerly.

While Toby occupied the orderly, Frank slipped in and knelt by Matthew's bed. His partner's eyes fixed on him.

"Forget to say 'so long,' we'll be back tomorrow for sure." As he spoke, his hand slipped under the blanket for an instant.

"Guess I'll mosey, then." He got up and went out. Matthew closed his eyes, a faint smile on his lips.

"How's the arm, son?" Frank watched as the orderly worked on the boy. "It hurts bad, Frank." the boy grimaced, his eyes screwed tight shut.

"I don't think it's broke, anyway. Maybe a sprain or a muscle bruise. Did you land on a rock when you fell?" The orderly was like most men on the frontier, he liked kids.

"No, sir. You know it's feeling better now. Maybe you're right. It was probably just a sprain or something." He got up and followed Frank from the infirmary, the orderly's puzzled gaze following them.

* * *

Lavardure returned to Tate's a couple hours later to find Downs well into the day's drunk. He pulled him over to a plank table and began talking in a low voice.

Frank and Toby went to Leighton's where Frank decided he needed a new belt gun. "Hard to get a pistol to feel as good as the old Colt Army, but this .45 5 1/2" here has a nice pull to it." He bought it for fifteen dollars.

"I want this little .41 Remington derringer, too, Leighton." He bought it for twelve dollars.

"I never figured you for needing a hideout gun, Frank," Leighton remarked as he looked for some ammo for the second one.

"Never know, Leighton. I'm seeing the country cluttered up with some nasty characters. They're all congregating here, seems like." He loaded it and slipped it in his vest pocket.

"How's Matthew?" Leighton asked.

"He's gonna be fine. That army doctor, Girard, is a good one. Says Matt is gonna need a month or more to rest, though. Guess we'll camp out along the river somewheres close for a week or so 'til he can come back with us, or we figure what we're gonna do."

"You could stay here, Frank. It'd give me a chance to go home nights and sleep easy." Leighton's voice carried a sudden enthusiasm as he thought of the advantages of having Frank there in the store for security.

"No, Leighton, sorry, but I'm not wanting to be responsible for your store. You might sleep, but I wouldn't."

"Well, think about it. I'd even pay you."

* * *

"No, no, no!" Downs was saying, "If we go into the cantonment and kill him, we're in trouble with the government. We'll have to wait 'til he comes off the fort. I don't want any fuss with the army."

"You're right," Lavardure admitted, "but we can put the other one down and get Baker's dog back for him."

"Yah, we could do that." Billy was thoughtful as he poured another drink for them. "Wonder if this one is a gun hand like his white haired pard is."

"Well, maybe somebody knows 'em. Let's ask around. They're hunters so the hide freighters should know 'em."

Lavardure pushed back from the rough plank table and went over to the bar. He returned with a check-shirted, burly bearded individual who sat with him and Billy, lolling back in his chair. Billy explained, pouring him a drink.

"A boy, a pit dog and a couple old men? Sure. Matthew Grounds and Frank Shannon. Can't remember the boy's name, the little turd. Why?"

"The white haired pilgrim killed Anson Baker. He was a friend of ours."

"That's right, I remember hearing about it." The freighter took a drink. "Rough old cobs," G.W. said. "Rangered some, I heard. Harvey Lopez had some words with the other one over cards out north. He was goddam pissed about it."

"Lopez?" Downs was eager now. "Where's he at, would you know?"

"Try Chinnick's. I saw him there last night, I think. He's a half-breed Mex. Good with a gun. Killed a couple, three men, I heard,"

* * *

79

Frank left Toby and Cappy in front of Leighton's and hopped his horse. He cantered east, passing saloons and cabins, stores, liveries and dance halls. All the structures were cottonwood log or wagon canvas. He pulled up in front of a long log building and knocked at the door.

At his knock, the door swung open and a pretty, stout buxom woman stood there, a pale cast to her face. She stared, then spread her arms: "Frank! Come in!" Her English was so guttural, it was hard to understand.

"Hello, Gertie. It's been a while. Leighton told me you moved up here, thought I'd drop over for a cup of coffee." Wordlessly, she grabbed and hugged him.

"Come in, come in." She moved aside and swung the door wider to let Frank by. He stepped into a parlor area that was half waiting room, half bar.

"Pretty nice setup, Gertie. Lots nicer than Hays City or Dodge." Frank looked the setup over with an experienced eye. Even a piano, he saw.

"Come on through to the kitchen, we're just eating some breakfast." She bustled on through a narrow corridor with rooms leading off on each side and into a large kitchen and the chatter of six girls and a couple of men, one a hulking Negro who worked as bouncer and handyman, the other a piano player. The talk stilled as Frank entered behind his old friend.

"Mistuh Frank!"

The bouncer recognized him, though it had been quite a while. "We heard you was hunting hides up here." He got up and offered his hand. Frank took it. "Hello, Reuben. Good to see you again. Remember Hays City? We had a couple good times there, didn't we?"

Evidently the Negro thought so too, for he gave out a laugh that sounded like someone beating on a wash tub. "Hee, hee, hee, that we did, Mistuh Frank. And Mistuh Matthew is all right? We heard you brought him in to the fort wounded,"

"We had a run-in with some Sioux horse thieves and Matthew took a bullet in the shoulder. The army doc fixed him up good, though." Frank sat down and Gertie poured him a cup of coffee. He looked the girls over. Their hair in various stages of disarray, they were lounging in flannel wraps and gowns in the warm kitchen. They stared back with a hard disinterest for the most part. Most showed the effects of heavy drinking. He could see in their eyes a distant contempt for the old man in front of them. It would have bothered him even a year or two ago, but now it didn't. He ignored them and his eyes swung back to the madam.

"Gertie, you're looking real good these days," he drawled, sipping the hot drink.

'Gravel' Gertie, as she was sometimes called, smiled a smile that amazed her girls, and gave them an item for gossip for weeks to come. One by one, the rest took their coffee and headed for the parlor or their rooms 'til Frank, Gertie and Reuben were finally alone. They sat for a while in companionable silence, then Gertie asked. "How is he really, Frank? Tell me the truth now." Her hand, a beautiful long hand that Frank remembered, even dreamed about, came up and covered Frank's. It trembled slightly.

"He's fine, Gertie. Oh, he took a bullet but he's tough, even if he's old. We're all getting old," he said somewhat bitterly.

"Sure we are, Frank, but we haven't reached the end of the race yet, have we?" She patted his hand. "When you and him getting that horse ranch you always talked about? And what's this I hear about a boy tagging you around?"

Frank told them Toby's story while they sat at ease in the kitchen, the wood stove popping and snapping occasionally.

Reuben got up and poured their cups full. "Does you want a snort in that, Mistuh Frank?"

"No, thanks, I'm on the wagon. Matthew said we were quits if I ever drank again without his pouring it. Said he knew when I should stop, if I didn't. It's hard, but I been lettin' him pour ever since." He didn't mention his recent run-in with the freighter.

"That's good, Frank. Matthew always knew what was best. You stick with him." Gertie patted his hand, "Reuben, get those rolls out of the warmer. I bet Frank'll have some."

"Guess I'll have to say 'no' again, Reuben. We just ate down at Riley's. Had lamb chops, even. Haven't had 'em for a lot of years. And eggs! Toby and me put quite a feed on. Really should be getting back. I left him at Leighton's." He got up to go.

"I'll be sure and come back while we're around, Gertie. Fact is, we're talking 'bout a little horse ranch right here around Keogh. Thinkin' of staying here yourself?" Gertie and Reuben got up and walked with him to the door.

"Might as well." she smiled a bitter smile. "The fort is here and now we're going to be seeing the trail herds comin' up as soon as the buffalo go. I talked to a trail boss last fall, a man named McLean that said there was a lot of interest down south among the ranches for this north country grass. They think if it fattens buffalo, it'll do the same for cattle. Long as there's lots of men around, we'll stay." She patted his shoulder.

"See you're still ridin' dem big horses, Mistuh Frank. You always liked 'em," Reuben remarked as they stepped out.

"Yep. Had a big one that I sure liked that the reds killed. This one here is shaping up fair, but I doubt it'll be as good," He swung up, a lean man of a breed the southwest was producing that was beginning to make its type felt in the country's history.

"Give our best regards to Matthew, Frank." Gertie gazed up at him with genuine concern in her eyes.

"That I will. I'll bring the boy, too, maybe, so's you can meet him. He's a fine one. Reuben, take care." He swung the big sorrel around and started back to Leighton's.

Riding along, Frank marveled again at the changes he saw in the area. Establishing a permanent cantonment at the mouth of the Tongue had caused a major influx to the place. First came the contractors supplying the army's needs, from paper to bullets by the case. Bringing supplies in meant freighters and steamboats. Steamboats needed wood for fuel and woodhawks to cut it. Laundries for uniforms, usually run by enlisted men's wives and hanger-ons, sometimes Chinamen, then cobblers and harness makers for equipment. Blacksmiths, gunsmiths, saloons, and parlor houses, even breweries and bakeries came, too. They were all here, Frank saw, and more. Even banks and a newspaper. It was getting to be a fair town, maybe one with a future in the territory. Certainly it seemed that most of the residents thought so, plus a whole pile of the usual element Frank had seen in every boom town he'd ever been in, from Texas on up the trail to Kansas and railhead: gamblers, thieves, whiskey peddlers, pimps, the whole gamut of low life that Frank and Matthew, from their rangering days, had come to despise. He saw it again here and he didn't like it. These towns were inevitably a blot on the countryside.

As he came to the intersection of Sixth and Main where Savage and Sons had their general merchandise store, he was hailed by an army sergeant on the boardwalk. He hauled up and the army man, a burly ramrod figure in blue, came up to him. A corporal followed behind.

"Goddamn, Frank Shannon! I thought it was you sitting that horse!" He stuck out his hand and Frank reached down and grabbed it.

"How do, Macintosh. Good to see you again!"

"Frank, meet Corporal Weatherly. He's the bane of my life just now. The colonel thinks he should make a sergeant out of him if I can just shape him up some." He spat a brown stream from under a great brown mustache. Weatherly grinned. He was a pleasant faced redhead, freckle faced and small against the sergeant's greater bulk. The sergeant squinted up at the mounted man.

"Matthew Grounds still partnering with you?"

"Yes, we're hunting buffalo up north when we're not fighting Indians. Matthew's laid up over at the fort hospital just now. Indian bullet."

"The hell! We'll have to stop in and see 'im. Hope he's not too bad hurt." Like Gertie, the sergeant was genuinely concerned.

"Well, the doc over there seems a good one. You boys in blue are lucky on that score."

"Huh!" The sergeant's tone was scornful. "'Bout the only thing. Colonel's been killing us off at a rapid rate, what with the Sioux and these winter campaigns. He's damn set on that star and looks like he'll get it, to me." The sergeant spat again, looking down the street. "Ever see so much trash on the streets of a town, Frank?"

"I was just thinking the same thing." Frank threw a leg over his horse and stepped down. "Wonder why it is."

"Last of the buffalo out there. Lots of grass opening up just like it did in Kansas, you remember, and right here'll be another Abilene, with trail herds and the railroad all pointed this direction. Makes for a real piss-cutter of a town, it does. Right now, she's wide open and flapping her wings."

They talked some more and agreed to meet again later, then Frank stepped aboard and continued down Main. The two army men watched him go.

"Weatherly, there goes a real man. I knowed him in the war, when I fought for the gray. He and Grounds were as good as we had. Then I saw 'em later in Kansas. Good men." He turned and walked away, Corporal Weatherly following as usual.

When Frank got close to Leighton's, a crowd was gathered at its front. Riding up, he saw a knot of men and boys mixing it up and another snarl of dogs tearing into Cappy. Cappy was certainly holding his own or better, but was that Toby wrestling a boy there on the street? He stepped off his horse and waded through the crowd of loafers and bystanders to reach down and grab up Toby.

"Whoa there, son, a man could ruin his gun hand doing that. Get up here." He held the two boys apart, though both had their mettle up and wanted to wade into each other again. Then Toby spotted Cappy mauling one of the curs that had jumped him. The rest were on the run except for a couple that lay still.

"Cappy, dern you, come off 'em! Quit now!"

He broke loose from Frank and ran to grab Cappy's legs, trying to separate the dogs. Frank held onto the other boy, who commenced wriggling.

"Let go o' me, dern you, you old goat. My pa'll whup you, you don't," he snarled.

"Well, now, I think we need to sort this out first, young 'un. Settle down." He started to turn to the rest of the donnybrook, which he saw involved Leighton and one of his clerks against some other pilgrims. Suddenly he was on the ground. A large man had come from out of the crowd and put him down with a blow to the side of his head.

"Leave the kids fight, you old bastard. Mine was winning." He started to come forward then stopped stock still. Frank, on the ground, was holding a cocked six-gun leveled at him. The fierce eyes were straight and unwavering.

"I'm way past hand-fighting and I don't take to being mauled, " Frank came slowly, stiffly to his knees, then to his feet, still holding the pistol. No one seeing him doubted he could use it. "Now hop over and use some of that muscle to stop that 'un."

He gestured with the gun and the man, stepping carefully, grabbed down and came up with Leighton and his opponent. He shook them, threw them into the crowd, then grabbed the others and separated them. When they started to struggle, he smashed them together and threw that two into the crowd also. That done, he dusted his hands and turned back to Frank.

"You gonna shoot me, mister, make it a good one." He spit tobacco juice in the dust. His eyes couldn't quite come off the gun holding straight at his middle.

84

Frank snorted. "Hell, guess a man can expect that a father'll back his kid," He holstered his weapon, walked up to the man and offered his hand.

"Frank Shannon. This here is Toby, our stepson." The man looked his relief and took Frank's hand, "Silas Nickerson. This 'ere's my kid, Dee. Sorry I whopped you. Saw you holdin' my kid and it made me sorta see red."

The crowd started drifting off. Leighton came up, dusting his apron and himself off, his eyes twinkling. "Now damme, Frank, We had a good row going here and you went and spoiled it!" Leighton was feisty yet, and enjoyed a good battle when he could find it.

"Get back in there, Carl, and make sure they're not stealing us blind," The clerk, nose bloody, hurried back into the store.

"What went on here, Leighton?" Frank asked, fingering a swelling bruise on his temple.

"First I heard was the dog fight, then I came out and the boys were in it. When I tried to stop it, I got jumped myself." He felt a cut lip and wriggled a front tooth. "We give 'em what fer, though, that we did! Damn pilgrims! He looked full at Nickerson as he said it, then stalked back into the store.

"Well, Toby?" Frank prompted.

"Frank, I was just sitting on the log, petting Cappy when this one," he pointed at the other boy,"came up and wanted to fight dogs. I told him no, but he kept after me 'til finally he sicced his dogs on Cappy."

"Sounds like your boy got a little pushy, Nickerson. And pilin' on don't seem fair, either." Frank looked grim. And suddenly Silas Nickerson knew this to be a lucky day for him, a day that he'd hit death in the face, like, and lived to tell about it. He'd hit the old duffer a good lick up the side of the head, expected him to go down, maybe stay. But it hadn't happened quite that way. The old man had rolled in the dirt and when he'd stopped, had his gun in his hand. It made him remember this country wasn't Missouri, but gun country frontier.

"Well, sir, believe this boy of mine needs a butt-paddling. With your leave, I'll take him back to the wagon and perform that little job. I'm glad to've met you." He grabbed Frank's hand and pumped it, then took Dee by the collar and dragged the boy away.

Frank went to his horse. He petted its neck.

"Proud of you, Buck, staying ground hitched like that during the ruckus, with all that noise and people swirlin' around,"

He set Toby up in the saddle and they walked down to the cafe, Cappy strolling behind with an air of swagger in his limping walk.

"Your head's all swole, Frank." Toby was looking at Frank's temple as they sat at their usual table.

"Yeah, he fetched me a good one. I near shot him before I thought." Frank sipped his coffee. "Wasn't worth killing for, although I might have, when I was younger. See some knots on your head, too, youngster. Did you give as good as you took?" He grinned.

"I hope so. I didn't want Cappy to get hurt."

They both looked at the dog, and he, seeing their attention, gave out a "whoof".

"Well, Cappy gave a little better than we all got, that's for sure."

"Frank, I don't like town. When can we leave?"

"Easy, son. Matthew's hurtin' yet. We'll go out pretty soon and see how he is."

"There's Jason," Toby pointed. Their English friend had come in the cafe, looking about him. Seeing them, he came over, a curious downcast expression on his normally cheerful face.

"Well, son, you seen the elephant yet?" Frank asked, his lean face creased in a smile. He figured from Jason's expression that he knew what was bothering him.

"Aw, Frank, I didn't see any elephant last night, just too much whiskey." He sat at the table with them. "How's Matthew?"

"He's doin' fine now. The doc operated yesterday and cleaned up the wound. We're going out there, want to come along?"

"I guess not." He hesitated. "Frank, I did what you told me not to. I got in a game and lost all my money. They cleaned me. Can you loan me some more against my wages?"

"Did you buy your outfit yet?" Frank was sure he knew the answer to that, too, but he asked it anyway.

"Not yet, but I will."

"With what, son? Your good looks don't buy much out here." He got up, them trailing, and after paying at the door, they followed him out to where his horse and Cappy waited.

Frank untied the buckskin from the hitch rail. "Tell you, son, with Matthew hurt bad as he is, I'm not sure what we're gonna do yet. We need to get out to our camp and gather all our gear before it gets stolen. Why don't you go down to Leighton's and tell 'em I sent you to get an outfit. We'll be back in later and see you there." With that, he headed down to the livery.

Toby stayed put. "It'll be alright, Jason. He'll give you some money, you'll see."

"I suppose so, but now I have to wait. I'm afraid the game will break up and I won't get back in." He put his hands to his face. "All my money!"

"Well, I could loan you some. He gave me twenty dollars." Toby fished a ten dollar gold piece and five silver dollars out of his pocket. "You should be at Leighton's when we get back, though." He handed it over to Jason, who took it eagerly.

"Thanks, Toby! You're a real friend. I'll pay you back tonight." He hurried away in the direction of Chinnick's.

* * *

At the infirmary, Toby and Frank tied their horses and bid Cappy stay put. They went in and waded through the usual clamor of people there to see the doctor, walked on back to the hospital where Matthew was lying. The plump orderly called after them that Matthew had just asked about them.

"How do, Matthew." Frank pulled up a straight back chair to the bed. Toby stood by the side. "You're lookin' better." Truly, he had some color and looked rested. His eyes widened as he took in their assorted lumps.

"Both you boys look like you need some hospital time yourselves. What happened?"

"First, how are you coming along?" Frank insisted.

"Doctor tells me it'll be a while before I use my left arm, but I'll heal. See if you can find me some reading matter. I'm here for a while."

Toby started in and told Matthew what had happened, with some help at times from Frank.

"Well, son, you look well turned out, today, despite the scrap. See Frank got you some clothes that fit. Have him buy you a watch. Tell Leighton you want a good one."

Toby pulled out his Ingersoll and showed it to Matthew. "Frank already thought of it."

"I see." Matthew said, not looking at Frank, who spoke up.

"Long's we're talking money, you should know I put everything in Leighton's safe. Your money and gun belt's there and I paid Jason up out of my belt. Gave him 750 dollars. He went out and lost it just as soon as he could, in Chinnick's. Come down on me at noon asking for more against his wages. I told him I wasn't sure just what we were doin' yet. What'd you think?" He reached in his pocket for a chew and bit a healthy hunk out of it.

Matthew thought a while, his scarred face turned toward the window. "I can't see either of us hunting much more, though next year looks good for buffalo, I think. I'm more for locating that horse ranch we've talked of. Get the jump on people. We could squeeze through if we can buy our mares right. Why don't I talk to Colonel Miles if I can, and we'll head that direction. Suit you?"

Frank grinned and Toby let out a squeal of joy. "No more killing and no more dirty hides. Yay!"

"Then maybe we better cut Jason loose. He can hook up with a good crew if we vouch for 'im," Frank commented, "I'll send him out to get the rest of our gear and pay him 50 dollars more when he gets in, if that's alright."

"Be fine with me. Give him one of the Henrys or buy him one. He'll need it out north. A belt gun, too." Looking around to see if anyone was watching, Matthew snaked Frank's belt gun out from under the covers and traded it for the one his pard had bought.

"We get our gear in, I think the boy and I will set up camp down along the river aways. Neither of us are towners." He grinned at Toby."I'll see if I can scare up some books for you, Pard. Brought a paper, though." He pulled an issue of the *Yellowstone Journal* out of his back pocket and handed it to Matthew. The orderly came in, then, and said they'd visited long enough.

Back at Leighton's, Frank and Toby waited around its front for a while, watching the constant eddy and flow of people and horses by the store front and thinking Jason might show. After the recent set-to, Frank was averse to leaving Toby alone while he cruised the bars looking for the young man.

"Guess we'll go visit with Leighton a while." They got up and went into the large store. Leighton, his glasses askew on his round battered face, looked up with a smile when he saw them.

"Been out to see Matthew?"

"Sure have. He's perking up fine. Be up in a few days, I think." Frank's spirits had risen, seeing Matthew on the mend, "Say, Leighton, we left some gear up north. I wanted to send Jason and someone else out after it. Got any men around you trust?"

"Surely. Can they use your wagon?"

"Yep. It's at Hubbell's. They can take the lodge down and the little tent and bring it in for us. Want to give you fifty dollars for Jason to outfit with. He blew his poke the other night and never bought a lick of stuff he needs. Also, I need another Colt. A short one like I just bought." They headed over to the gun case.

"Seems like you're going through a lot of belt guns, lately," Leighton commented as he unlocked the case.

"This one's for Jason. We're gonna cut him loose and we want him outfitted right."

"What do you mean?" Leighton was startled, "You and Matthew quitting? Next year should be a good 'un."

"Wal, I think Matthew and me had a belly full of killing and skinning!" Frank's eyes glowed, "We're goin' after that horse ranch, Leighton!"

"Why, man, I'm glad to hear it!" The storekeeper shook hands with Frank, recognizing his friend's emotion. "Where's this horse ranch to be?"

"Haven't decided yet. Somewhere on the south side of the river, though. The water's better over here."

Leighton sold them a used .44 Colt for a good price and threw in some ammo. Frank told him to keep it for Jason when he showed up and Toby and he went for the door. Just as they reached it, Jason came in, breathless as though he'd been running.

"Frank! Toby! Good, I didn't miss you!! I won some money back. Here, Toby, here's your fifteen dollars." He poured out the coins in the boy's hands. Frank looked at Toby but kept quiet.

"Frank, I made almost two hundred dollars back!"

Frank looked at the young man's flushed happy face. He put his hand on Jason's shoulder.

"Son, we all have something we have to fight inside us. Call it what you will, the devil's work or whatever, I don't know. I do know strong drink seems to be mine. Looks like yours is gambling. I'm sorry, son. It's a tough one to battle, too."

He stumped on out of the store with both the others following. At the hitch rail he turned.

"Matthew and me are quitting the hide business. Shame in a way, 'cause next season should be a good one. We're gonna try for the horse ranch both of us been talking of. Miles will need remounts and the government pays well for stock. 'Fraid we won't need a skinner, but we could use a hand for the summer, getting corrals and cabins built if you want to stay with us. Otherwise, 'bout the only work we can offer right now is to get someone to go out for our gear. Do you want to do that? Like you to start right now or early tomorrow." He looked at Jason, thinking he knew the answer.

"Well.guess not, Frank." He looked down."I appreciate your helping me and advice, but I need to go my own way, I think."

"All right, youngster. You're old enough to plow your own furrow. I left 50 dollars with Leighton and a pistol for you. The money's for your outfit when you come to buy it. Remember, Leighton will treat you white." He shook hands."Good luck to you."

Toby stood by, miserable."I wish you'd come with us, Jason. We need you." Jason shook his hand, too.

"No, Toby, I want to see that elephant some more. When you get my age, you'll understand, "With money in his pocket, he was fairly dancing to get back to the game.

After Jason left, Frank went in and made arrangements with Leighton for a couple of his men to go for their gear, then they went down the street to the livery to put up their horses.

* * *

Going by Tate's, a one-eyed lounger on the boardwalk took notice and went into the saloon. He went to a back table.

"Billy, he and the boy just went by again. Looks like they're headed for the livery."

Downs looked at the dark faced man seated at his table.

"Well, Lopez. You still up to it?"

"Damn betcha I am." The freighter was half drunk from the whiskey Downs had been buying all day. He didn't need the brave-maker, though, when he thought of the old man who'd braced him up north. He knew he could kill him and he needed to. Nobody called him 'Greaser' and got away with it.

90

"Let's go." He lurched up from his seat, Downs and Lavardure grinning at each other, and they went out into the street.

At the livery door, Frank and Toby heard a loud voice giving someone hell.

"Damn you, Sam, I told Hubbell I'd pay him when I got to town and I will, just give me some time!"

"Now, Janey, the boss told me you didn't get any more time 'til you paid your bill."

"Ow!"

A loud crack was heard by the two listeners outside.

"Sounds like Sam needs a little help!" Frank grinned to Toby. They stepped in.

"Now, Janey, don't hit me again! Ow!" The livery hand was back in the corner of a stall trying to defend himself against a bulky figure swinging at him with both hands.

"Here now, what's the trouble?" Frank began, then whooped, "Calamity Jane, I swear!" The bulky figure swung around, to disclose a chunky built slab faced woman dressed like a man. She whooped likewise.

"Frank Shannon! You old horse turd! What in hell you doing here in Milestown? She rushed at Frank and nearly crushed his ribs, giving him a bear hug.

"Well, let me go, dern you, I'll tell you." Frank squirmed in her strong arms as the livery hand got out of the stall and made to get away. She swung around, Frank still in her grasp.

"Stand still, you son-of-a-bitch! I'm not done with you by a damn sight yet."

"Oh yes, you are!" Sam grabbed up a pitchfork and backed away defensively.

"Hold on, both of you!" Frank broke her grip and pushed her back. "What's the problem here now?"

"She owes a nine dollar livery bill, that's what, and Hubbell says to keep her outa here 'til she pays!"

"Well, I think that can be taken care of, easily enough." Frank pulled a ten dollar gold piece out of his vest and flipped it to the hostler. "There, now can we have some quiet so I can visit a little with an old friend?" Sam backed off and went to the office, mumbling.

"Now, Frank, you shouldn't be paying my bill," Janey protested weakly. "I was goin' to scare up the money today."

91

"Well, now, you can pay me back when you want to. That makes it easier all around, "Frank turned to Toby, who was taking it all in with round eyes.

"Son, this here's Janey Canary. Everyone calls her 'Calamity Jane,' for reasons you sure can see. Meet Toby, Matthew and me's boy."

She shook Toby's hand. Her hand was hard and calloused like a man's.

"Where's your pard? You and him still traveling together?" Janey asked. She followed them in to the livery's dark interior and they unsaddled Frank's horse.

"Yep. He's hurt just now from an Indian run-in out north. Gunshot. Doc's taking care of him out at Keogh." Frank drawled.

"You and him been in harness long time now."

"Yep, we have. Since before the war."

"Well, let's go get us a drink, talk about old times. Wild Bill's dead, you know." She snuffled a little. "Can't hardly talk about him without a tear coming, damn it."

Toby, listening, realized the woman was half drunk.

"Yeah, Janey, I heard about it." Frank patted her shoulder. "About the drink, though, I've sworn off. Matthew thought it was best I do."

"Since when did Frank Shannon let somebody tell him what to do, damn it!" Her dark eyes snapped as she stepped out into the sunlight from the dark interior of the barn. Frank and Toby followed her and all three nearly collided with a group coming in.

"Well now, here's the old son-of-a-bitch didn't like the way Lopez anted! Remember me, old man?" Lopez, his eyes glazed, came into a crouch, his hand close to his gun.

Frank shoved Toby away and stepped aside, clearing his field of fire of Canary who'd been in front of him. Though taken by surprise, he was instantly ready for action.

"Said it then, and I say it now. Don't call me an old man!"

"Hold it!" Billy Downs stepped between them. "I know you boys are ready to fight but you best walk down to the river to do it. That chunk of ground is off jurisdiction to the army and to the law here in town. Won't be no law trouble then."

"Who the hell are you?" Frank flicked his eyes away from Lopez and took in Downs and Lavardure, standing grinning behind.

"Just friends of Lopez, is all," Downs answered casually. "Why don't you wait 'til evening and you can try each other out down there, then."

Before Frank could answer, Lopez sneered, "Fine with me! See you then, you old fart, if you can make it that far, that is!" He turned and the other two fell in behind him. They headed back toward Tate's.

Canary breathed a sigh of relief. "Jesus, Frank, of all times for me not to have a gun on me. I thought all three were going to take you. Not that I was worried, mind!"

Toby asked anxiously, "Frank, what are you going to do? They might all three come tonight!"

"Well, I imagine they will, son. Don't worry, I've handled worse." Frank seemed unconcerned as he led his horse out to the corral.

Coming out, Frank looked at the sun. "About three hours yet to sundown. Let's go back to Leighton's." The three walked back up the street.

Passing Tate's, Toby could see the one-eyed man following their progress, standing at the window. "They're in there, Frank," he whispered.

"I can see 'em, son." They walked on by.

At Leighton's, Janey refused to go in. "I'm real thirsty, Frank. Think I'll go down to Charlie Brown's. Sure you won't come?" Her brown eyes looked at him in concern.

"No. Got business with Leighton. Might see you later, though. Oh, here's that ten dollars I owe you." He slipped a gold piece in her pocket.

"I don't remember you owing me, but I'll take it anyway. That makes twenty I owe you." She swung off the boardwalk and headed for Brown's.

"Hard to believe, son, but there goes a good woman. Least I guess she's a woman. Know one thing, she's a good nurse. Helped me and many another out when they needed it. And by the way, about Jason." He swung to Toby.

"I know, Frank, I shouldn't have loaned him money." Toby looked down at Cappy crowding his heels.

"No, son. It was right you did loan him. A friend always shares with a friend. Been upset if you hadn't." He tousled the head of the troubled boy. "Now don't you go worrying 'bout me. I've had a lifetime of dealing with things like this." He went on in the store.

"Why don't you go hit the candy counter? I got some talking to do with Leighton."

* * *

Back at Leighton's office, Frank asked, "What do you know about a freighter name of Lopez?" They sat at their ease both watching Toby up front, having a heyday at the candy.

"Nothing much, I guess. The rest of 'em stay clear of him. He's got a little reputation as a tough one. Been in a few bar scrapes."

"Know a tubby boozer and a one-eyed gent that might be traveling with him?" Frank bit off another great chew as he talked.

Leighton thought a little. "No, but I can ask around if you want. The one sounds like Lavardure. Does his bad eye drain the socket?"

"Yep."

"Well, then, it's probably 'Weepy' Lavardure. He's one of Jack Stringer's crew. Been in town a while. Think he came in with Billy Downs, a whiskey trader from Benton. He's got a whiskey gut as big as a barrel. A real booze hound, he is."

"Jack Stringer's bunch, eh?" Frank mused.

"You in trouble with that outfit?" Leighton asked. "Course, guess you would be, since Matthew killed Anson Baker last year."

"Nothing I can't handle, Leighton, but here now, if something happens to me, you should know everything I got goes to Matthew and Toby." He took off his money belt and took fifty dollars in gold from it before handing it to Leighton. "Put that in with the rest for me, for a while."

"I'll do it, Frank, but you better amble down and talk with Irvine at the jail. He's sheriff now."

"Oh, the hell. What happened to Tom Healey?" Frank wondered.

"He got a bad case of lead poisoning from a gambler off the *Eclipse*. Didn't make it."

"Where's the gambler got off to?" Frank asked idly. He'd liked Tom, for all his bluster.

"Well, the boys took him out and decorated a cottonwood down by the river with him. We don't take to our sheriffs getting killed," He smiled. "Tom liked you and Matthew. I just remembered Irvine has some of his stuff for you and Toby. Go see him."

94

"I will this afternoon, Joe." He stood and shook Leighton's hand. "Thank you."

One of Leighton's clerks knocked on the office window and Leighton slid it aside. "What is it, Elmer?"

"A couple of steamers just got in, sir. The *Western* and the *Josephine*. Want me to run a wagon down?"

"Yes, you'd better. We should have some stock on one or both. Hope those spuds came in."

Frank walked out and gathered up Toby, his cheeks bulging with hard candy.

Outside the store, the street had become filled with a bull-train, a long string of wagons pulled by oxen urged on by bullwhackers, as the men who ran the trains were called. They stood for a while and watched the train pass. As one of the triple-hitched teams went by, a whacker hailed them.

"Hey, there, Frank, is that you, by God?"

He was a towering man, so big Toby had to look way up even standing on the boardwalk. "By Gosh, if it isn't Big Sandy Lane," Frank exclaimed, pushing out his hand. The near-giant grasped it eagerly. "Damn it, good to see you!" He looked down at Toby from his height.

"Who's this, Frank, one of your ranger recruits?" The man laughed.

"This here's Toby. Son, meet Big Sandy Lane, the best bullwhacker ever lived. He hauled a lot of hides for Matthew and me down on the Arkansas."

"That we did. How's your pard doing? I heard he'd been shot by the Sioux."

"Yeah, he's out at Keogh doing just fine. Him an' me quit the hide hunting, Sandy. We're going into horse raising around here."

"Glad to hear it. Should be good. The Cavalry need remounts all the time, I know. I've got to get on. See you later, alright? Bye, Toby." He hurried on to catch up with his team, taking strides that caught him up without effort.

"That is a big man," Toby breathed.

"Yes, son, and his heart is just as big."

"You sure seem to know a lot of people, Frank."

"You stay on this earth long as Matthew and I have, you get to know a few. Good and bad. Come on, son."

Down at the log jail, they stepped in to see several men grouped around a table in the office, drinking coffee. Toby looked around and saw a rack of rifles on one wall, a big stove set back in the middle of the room. A counter inside the door kept people from coming further in. They stepped to it as a man with slightly slanted gray eyes and a short, trimmed dark beard asked, "Can I help you, sir?" Toby could see a silver badge hanging on his shirt.

"Might be you could. My name's Frank Shannon and I come about some stuff Healey left. Leighton sent me over."

* * *

Sheriff Tom Irvine, he of the dark beard, looked at the two just come in and saw a tall, spare lean-faced older man with a drooping brown and white-tipped mustache and washed out blue eyes. He had beetling brows and a stern solid look about him that Irvine, a keen judge of character, instantly liked. A Texan, from his speech. He had too, the look of a stockman about him, though not the jingling spurs and accouterments of the cowboy. The Sheriff noted, also, the belt gun he carried with such familiarity on his right side. The boy was likewise a little better dressed, with riding boots, wool vest and new hat, than most boys around town. Irvine rose and held out his hand.

"Healey spoke of you. You were hunting with a partner, Matthew Grounds out north, am I right?" Frank shook the offered hand. "I'm Irvine."

"Howdy. Yes, Matthew and me are pardners. This here's Toby, our boy."

"Hello, son." Irvine shook with Toby. "Want you to meet some friends of mine." He turned to the group sitting around a small table, who stood and came forward to shake hands also. "This is Fred Whiteside, he's been hunting over east this last season. Bill Bullard, an alderman and the town's brewer. Used to be a deputy under Tom. Granville Stuart, a friend from up west who's out here looking at range possibilities for cattle. Jay Strevell, one of our lawyers here in town and Jim Conley, one of my deputies."

"How do, men. Stuart, I remember you from the gold diggins," Frank remarked as he shook his hand. Stuart was a slender bearded man with a twinkle in his eye and a large gold watch chain hanging from his vest.

96

"Yes, I remember you, too. You and your partner lived for a time with the Nez Percé, if I recall, back of Nevada City."

"That we did, and liked it, too. I'm ashamed of the treatment we whites have given some of the tribes like the Nez Percé. They never asked for anything but to be our friends."

"Come in, won't you, and have a cup with us?" Irvine opened the gate and led Frank and Toby back to the table where more coffee was poured, "Need to make a fresh pot," Irvine remarked.

"I'll do it, sir," Toby offered eagerly.

Irvine raised his brows.

"Go ahead and let 'im. He makes a good pot," Frank smiled.

Irvine handed the pot over to Toby, who took it to the water pail and began filling it.

"Well, Frank, how's your partner? We heard the Sioux and you boys had a run-in over some horses." Strevell asked.

"He's doing fine, though he was hit worse than either of us thought. Broke his collarbone and knocked a piece off the shoulder blade. But Major Girard's a good surgeon. He cleaned out the wound just fine. We were just out there. He looked to be on the mend,"

"Girard's a good doctor. I've had occasion to use his services myself," Bullard laughed. He was big and hearty, a western man who fit in well with these others of strong character and experience.

"Grounds had a run-in last fall with a man named Baker. Killed him," Strevell mentioned, sipping his coffee.

Frank looked at him over his cup. "Yes, Baker used a quirt on Toby. He found out it wasn't the thing to do. We're both like fathers to the boy."

"We heard that, too. And you should know, I'm sure Tom told you, that it was written up as self-defense, so Matthew will have no trouble with the law," Irvine interjected, "You know, don't you, Frank, that Baker was one of a pretty rough crew? They could give you some more trouble."

"Tom Healey mentioned it his last trip out," Frank said dryly. "We'll be careful. We're not exactly babes in the woods."

"Someone said you and Grounds were once Texas Rangers, if I'm not being too personal." Irvine's tone was conciliatory. He was going into a man's background, a perilous thing on the frontier. Frank, feeling he was among friends, relaxed and sat back.

"Wal, we were. Rangered under Captain Kinney for seven years or more. Went through the war together, too." Frank sensed that the conversation had deeper undertones than casual range gossip.

"Can we ask what you and your partner's plans are?" Stuart inquired cordially.

"I'm glad to tell you that we're quitting the hide business and going into horses. Think we'll locate near Keogh and sell to the government," Frank stated. "Been on our minds for quite a while."

"Sounds like a promising undertaking," Irvine thoughtfully commented. "You'll need a good hand or two. Too bad the army shipped off the Nez Perce', they were damn good horsemen."

Granville Stuart said nothing, but looked grim. Frank remembered then that Stuart had married an Indian and was respected by the tribes. His wife, it was said, was well treated by Stuart and considered a respectable woman by all who knew her. Certainly Stuart would have a measure of sympathy for the plight of the Nez Perce'.

"Know any likely men we could use, tell 'em about our plans," Frank said. He held his cup out to Toby, bringing the pot over, for a refill. "Son, you want to see my pet bear?" Irvine asked the boy.

"Yes, sir. You got a bear here in town?" Toby asked doubtfully. Most western men were great teasers, he knew, and this could be another trick.

"Sure do. Helps us with the prisoners out back. Conley, why don't we go check on 'em? We'll take Toby with us, introduce him to Stonewall."

Toby followed the men out the back. Through the open door, Frank glimpsed a tall stockade with a chained black bear pacing around by one wall. He looked hungry.

"Sorry for the questions," Bullard remarked. "It's just that with all the riff-raff coming into the country, we're trying to get a line on the people we can count on. Your names were mentioned,"

"Matthew and I have always tried to stay clear of trouble. Haven't always been able to, though." Frank changed the subject. "Last I heard of you, Stuart, you were mining with your brother up west."

"Yes, but stock raising's always been in my blood, like yours, I suppose," Stuart remarked. Frank liked the looks of this man. A lean straight-backed military figure, strong willed but gentle voiced. He knew Stuart had a good reputation as a solidly honest man of good temper, though a hard business man at times. He, like Irvine, wore a trimmed beard and was well-dressed. His boots were soft black calfskin and the watch chain was draped with gold nuggets, one very large.

"I was sorry to hear about Healey. He was a good man. We was friends." Frank remarked to Bullard, "Came up the trail together when Story brought a herd into Bozeman in the spring of '66."

"Heard you did," Bullard nodded, "He mentioned you and Grounds were on Story's flying squad, fighting Indians all the way. Must of been quite a trip."

"Did he tell you the time the boys roped the bull elk over by Bozeman?" Frank grinned, in his element now, telling stories he liked to remember.

"Believe he did, but tell Granville and Fred here," Bullard chuckled.

By the time Irvine and Toby came back, Frank had the others laughing.

Toby interjected, "Frank, you should see the black bear! Sheriff Irvine is the only one he lets near him. Conley says he eats a deer a week."

"'Spect he does, son. We'd better be going now." Frank stood to leave.

"Just a minute, Frank. Tom left something here I was s'posed to give you." Irvine went to a small safe in a corner and twirling the dial, swung it open.

"Here you are. His belt gun and wallet. He said for Toby to have it, the watch, too." He handed over a holstered .45 Colt Army, with ivory grips and a Waltham pocket watch and gold fob. The wallet contained $265."He wanted Toby to have it all, or give it to him later, he said. Poor man didn't have any kin."

"Toby, you're getting quite an arsenal together. Got more guns now than I do." Frank chuckled.

"He left his Henry for you, Frank, and this fifty from before, he said he owed you." Irvine handed a .44 Henry to Frank, and the money.

"Did you make him a nice gravestone?" Frank asked, folding the money into his pocket.

"Already been taken care of by the town," Bullard remarked, "They put up a nice one. Gambler that shot him paid for it before we hung him. Least he could do, he said, "

As they headed out, Stuart detained Frank to tell him that he would be interested to see how the horse business came out. Maybe he could help with it in the future.

Walking back to Leighton's, Toby asked, "Didn't you tell them about Lopez, Frank, and about those other two?"

"No, son, they have enough to do. <u>Said</u> I'll take care of it," Frank said shortly.

* * *

Janey Canary, meanwhile, was visiting in Brown's Saloon about Frank's coming meeting with Lopez. One of those listening was a redheaded army corporal. He finished his drink and headed for the fort. Another was a short little parlorhouse piano player, out for a stroll before business began that evening. He likewise finished his drink and left the saloon.

When Frank and Toby got back to Leighton's, Joe Leighton met them at the door.

"Frank, it's all over town you're meeting Lopez tonight at the river. What's going on?"

"There's three of them, Mr. Leighton. And Frank wouldn't even tell the Sheriff about it!" Toby shrilled, his concern for Frank overriding his reticence.

"Frank, is that true? Good God, man, you're not a rip-roaring youngster anymore! What the hell's got into you? Three of them!" He glared over his spectacles. Frank glared back.

"I'm tired of people telling me I'm old, Joe! If I'm so old that folks can just run over me, I'm better off dead, so don't rag me about this!"

Frank's set face, his voice, put Leighton off and no more was said. Despite Toby's protests, the guns and money from Healey went into Leighton's big safe. Then Frank set him down and spoke to the boy directly.

"Now, son I told you before I'm used to handling things like this. Don't fret. But if it should happen I don't make it, you go out to Matthew. He'll know what to do." He hugged the boy, who broke into tears. "Now you stay here. I'll be back for you in a little while." He went out into the busy street. Toby sat for an instant, then jumped off the stool.

100

"Mr. Leighton! What are we going to do?" The boy's voice was nearly a wail.

"Son, don't worry. I'm heading out right now to the Sheriff. You stay here! Elmer, take care of things!" Leighton ran out the back door.

Toby sat for a second, then got up and pulled on the big safe's door. It refused to budge. He ran down the length of the store and looked in the gun counter. He had enough money for a pistol but didn't feel sure enough about using one like he might have to. Elmer, the clerk, came over.

"If you think I'm going to sell you a gun and have Leighton fire me, I'm sorry, Toby, but 'no' is the answer," he said. He took a rag and started wiping the counter top.

"Course, Broadwater and Hubbell have a nice gun selection down the street."

Toby hollered his thanks as he rushed out.

Running hard, Cappy following him, he made the three blocks and turned into Broadwater and Hubbell General Merchandise store. He literally flew down the aisle and screeched to a stop at the gun section. He rapidly scanned the shelf and immediately spotted a Henry rifle among the gleaming Winchesters. It showed some use, but looked serviceable to him.

"Quick, sir! How much for the Henry?" He pointed at the .44. The clerk ambled over and lifted the repeater from the shelf. "Twenty dollars. Good rifle. Want to look at it, kid?" He opened the breech and handed it over.

"I've only got eighteen dollars! Would you take that?"

"Nope, don't think so." He started to put it back on the shelf.

"Wait! How about a good watch, too. I've got some more money, I just can't get it right now!" He pulled out the Waltham and the gold chain and fob. "I'll leave this for the rifle and some shells, and come back later with some more money!" He dumped a ten dollar bill and a five dollar gold piece, along with three silver dollars, on the counter. The clerk picked up the watch.

"Believe that's Sheriff Healey's watch! Remember him carrying it. Where'd you get it?" He looked inquiringly at the boy.

"He left it to me when he died. Please, sir, will you take it?" Toby was in such a hurry he was dancing.

"Believe I will. Think I know who you are." He handed over the rifle and got a box of .44's down from the shelf, pushed them over the counter.

"Always throw in some shells when we sell a gun." Toby grabbed the gun and shells and ran out.

* * *

Gertie listened to Warren, her piano player, then turned to Reuben. "Get your ten-gauge, Reuben, and go on down there. Make sure they don't back-shoot him, will you, Please?"

"Yes, Missus. I'll sure see it don't happen." He reached behind the door and took an old Greener shotgun from a peg, checked it to make sure of the loads, and dumped a dozen rounds in his coat pocket.

Out at Keogh, the plump orderly had just finished telling Matthew about his partner and a man named Lopez. "Supposed to meet down at the river tonight, I hear. Hey! What are you doing?" He froze as a hand filled with a revolver came out from the covers.

"Believe I'll head down to the river and get a breath of fresh air. Loan me an arm to get on my boots, will you?" He struggled up, with the distressed orderly's reluctant help, to dress.

In the barracks, the big sergeant listened to the redheaded corporal's story, then turned to his locker and took down his holstered Colt. "Think I'll go over to town. See a man about a dog."

The corporal snorted. He went to get his gun belt, too.

Sheriff Irvine listened to Leighton as he poured out his story. He shook his head.

"If they're meeting down at the river strip, Joe, I'm out of jurisdiction. Town limit doesn't go that far, you know."

"What'll we do, then, damn it?" Joe questioned intensely. "We can't let that crowd murder a man like Frank!"

"Guess I won't need a badge for this." He took off the badge and laid it on the desk, took down a shotgun from the rack and put some shells in his pocket. He handed a loaded Winchester to Leighton. "Keep an eye on things, Jim." They went out and down the street.

Big Sandy Lane was in Charlie Brown's listening to Janey. "Well, hell. What are we waiting for? Let's go down there. Frank and Matthew helped me one time down on the Arkansas, here's a chance to pay him back." Janey borrowed a gun from Brown and followed the freighter.

Downs and Lavardure were sitting in Tate's with Lopez, who'd been joined by another freighter, a hard-bitten customer named Harry Dyer. Downs poured another drink from a bottle almost empty.

"Alright, then, Weepy. We'll go down early and get ready. You take the right side, use the Sharps. I'll take the left with my Winchester. Lopez, you and Harry brace him when he comes. You bring your hand up to your belt. When you do, I'll shoot him. You boys put a round in him, too, just to show you fired, 'case you're asked about it later." He stood, swaying unsteadily. "We get this one out of the way, we'll take the dog and the kid out north. Paddy Rose likes kids. Weepy can stay and wait for the other one to come off the cantonment. We'll come back then and get him, too." They filed out.

Tate looked after them with distaste, then came from behind the bar. Those sonsabitches were up to something nasty, but he wasn't sure just what he should do about it." Jackson, hand me that sawed-off," he asked the bartender, who tossed him a shotgun. "Think I'll trail those boys. They're up to no good, I'm damn sure."

* * *

Frank came down Main Street to the river at nearly sunset, a beautiful red sky with ducks and geese overhead almost constantly, flying up and down the river. He didn't think about death particularly, really wasn't even concerned about it anymore, except for Matthew and Toby. The boy had somehow become a large part of his existence. A good boy. A good pard. For the most part, a good life. Maybe too long a one, though. His shoulder ached, as usual, and his feet hurt in his new boots.

As he reached the edge of the river, he turned south into a grove some of the towners were calling a park. Usually, it was dirty and littered with drunk Indians and tramps. Just now it was nearly deserted.

"Over here, old-timer." He looked west and saw Lopez standing with another man by the river edge. Tall cottonwoods stood all around and some sheep wandered through, keeping the brush and grass eaten down somewhat.

"Well, Lopez, the master poker player. Is this your partner? You better hope you boys are better shooters than card players." He strode over toward them, alert to either side. Was that movement to one side of a tree? No more than he expected— a cross-fire. Then he stared.

Moving in on either side of the men facing him were others: Big Sandy Lane, Janey, Sgt. O'Brien and his redheaded corporal. Sheriff Irvine and Leighton were there, both with shotguns. They poked a man in front of them, the one-eyed customer he'd seen at the Livery. On the other side, he looked and there was Toby with a rifle. Standing by him with a hand on his shoulder was Matthew, looking damn weak. Reuben poked another man with his shotgun, the tubby individual who'd also been at the Livery, too, looking terrified. The saloon keeper, Tate, was there too, a stubby shotgun on his shoulder.

"Just a few friends here, Mistuh Frank, makin' sure they don't back-shoot you," Reuben called, poking Downs so hard in his fat gut that he bent over from the blow.

"Thanks, Reuben. Now, boys let's get to it, you're keeping us all from our supper." Frank called to the men in front of him.

Lopez gave a snarl and pulled his belt gun. As he came up with it, Frank's hand blurred down and coming up belt level with his pistol, fired. He cocked it back on the recoil, shifted and fired again at Dyer, who'd grabbed his own gun and had it coming up and forward. The round took him high and pushed him back, dropped him onto his knees.

Frank crouched as a shot came back at him. He shifted, fired again at Lopez, who lay propped up on an elbow trying with waning strength to bring up his pistol to fire another time. "Tough one," he thought, and aimed carefully, then shot a third time. Sometimes even a heavy .45 bullet wouldn't keep a man who was hard and tough down if he wasn't hit just right. This time Lopez was, a head shot. It destroyed the body's will and ability to function, better than a heart shot.

He walked forward, then. Lopez was dead, Dyer also, hit at the base of the throat. He holstered his belt gun and checked himself unobtrusively to see if he'd been hit. He was just fine, the evening was fine. It was good to be alive and with friends. They crowded around him. He looked at them, tried to thank them, but they weren't listening.

Janey turned and kicked Lavardure between the legs, putting him on his knees gagging. Reuben whacked the ten-gauge across Down's back, slamming him to the ground. Sandy Lane kicked the fallen man with a heavy boot, making the fat flesh quiver. It started a general melee that involved even Toby, who cracked Lavardure over the head with the barrel of his Henry. Matthew pulled him back and Frank came to stand beside them.

"Pard, you're up out of bed too quick, but thanks, anyway." He pulled his gun and replaced the empty shells. Matthew leaned on the boy. "Maybe we are getting old. You let that one get a shot off." He grinned a weak grin. "Aw, Matthew, the light was a little bad," Frank objected, "Age had nothing to do with it."

"Come on, people, the drinks are on me!" Tate hollered. There was a general surge back uptown. They left two groaning men and two bodies behind in the gathering dusk.

* * *

Midway up the street, Matthew slumped abruptly down and big Sandy and the sergeant carried him on into Tate's.

Tate roared when they came in: "Jackson, take the bung starter to these loafers and run 'em out. This is a private party! Army, you and Big Sandy help any that Jackson has a problem with! Here, boys, it's on the house, tonight!"

He slapped glasses on the bar, took a bottle from beneath it and ran it down the line without tipping it up. He pushed a soda pop over the bar to Toby.

"Everybody grab a glass! Now I want to propose a toast. He lifted his glass and everyone scrambled to grab one from the bar. "To Frank Shannon!"

They drank, all but Frank who stood by Matthew, who was seated at a table, Toby with him. Matthew reached over and clinked Frank's glass. "Drink up, pard. Some times are special. He chuckled, "Did you see Toby there, packin' a rifle?"

"Come to mention it, I did, " Frank looked at Toby.

"How'd you get your hands on a rifle, son? I thought I'd put all the guns in Leighton's safe?"

Toby muttered, "I bought it at Broadwater's."

"You bought it?" Frank laughed, a joyous sound of mirth. "Matthew, this boy has more guns than you and I put together! Leighton can't hardly close his safe door anymore." He drank his glass off. "Here, Tate, fill 'em up. I have a toast to give myself." Tate filled the glasses. Frank raised his and they all lifted theirs, too.

"To good friends, the best a man can have. Thank you all!"

* * *

The sun was streaming into the livery when Frank woke. It took an effort to open his eyes."Dern it, I'm sure now that on the wagon is the best place for me. I can't take the hangovers, anymore." He sat up , displacing the blankets that had been lain over him.

Toby was there, offering a cup. Good coffee smell filled the livery. "Here, Frank. Sam just made a fresh pot for us."

"Thanks, boy. What happened last night? Did Matthew get back to the hospital?" He grimaced as the hot coffee hit his lips.

"The sergeant and the corporal got him back fine. You really didn't drink so much, just you hadn't eaten anything. They put you in your bedroll and I stayed up a while here to guard,"

"You really buy that rifle, son?"

"Yes, sir. But I still owe some money on it. The clerk took Tom's watch 'til I brought him two more dollars." Frank tried to laugh but contented himself with a chuckle. "Guess we better go pay it up and get your watch back." He struggled up out of his bedroll.

"Saddle the buckskins, will you? I don't feel good enough to walk today."

While they were at breakfast, Sheriff Irvine came in and sat with them for a bit. He grinned when he saw Frank's condition.

"Don't feel all that chipper myself this morning," he stated, but he did order a meal when the greasy cook came over.

"Say, Frank, the boys got together a collection last night to bury Lopez and Dyer. I sent the undertaker down to pick 'em up this morning. He said Downs and Lavardure were gone and so was Lopez's and Dyer's guns and any money they had on 'em. Even their boots. No matter, the boys got up enough to put 'em under. I came over to see if you wanted to take in the church services this morning. Brother Van's holding forth over at Brown's and I thought you and Toby might like to come. It's Sunday, you know." Irvine, for all his toughness, was a good churchman, believing implicitly in the good book.

"If I can get my chin up off my chest, Tom, we'll come with you. Just so long as nobody sings too loud. Brother Van always holds a good service," Frank said. Matthew, Toby and he had heard Reverend W. Van Orsdel several times before and counted him a friend. Frank liked to listen to a good sermon and Brother Van was always guaranteed to provide that.

After the service, they headed out to Keogh to see Matthew. As they went into the infirmary, they could hear a deep voice holding forth, which wasn't Major Girard's.

"And damn it, if they didn't have the impertinence to name the scum-hole after me: Milestown." He snorted.

"Contractors preying like leeches on me, steamboats that wreck, freighters that never get the goods to me when I need them. I get moldy horse feed, hard tack with weevils in it, some of it left over from the war, ammunition the same, and all of it at three prices! Then they expect me to defeat as good a mounted cavalry as the world will ever know with raw recruits." A soft murmur told the listeners that Matthew was replying, then the booming voice resumed.

"Well, I've proven a winter campaign is the way to win out against them. Their horses are weak then and in poor fettle because of no feed, and dismounted they're easier to defeat. However, these northern winters will try one's soul."

Frank and Toby entered the ward then, and saw General Miles seated beside Matthew's bed along with Major Girard. They all were drinking coffee. The Major waved them in.

"Come in, come in, we were just in conversation with your friend Matthew here. General, meet Frank Shannon and their boy, Toby," the doctor urged.

The General rose and shook hands. In appearance, he was of burly athletic build. He showed an aggressive character, heavy brows, hook nose, a firm mouth and chin. Like most of the men of the day, he sported a thick mustache.

"Well, General, congratulations," Frank said. "Last we heard you was a colonel."

"Yes, the Army finally saw fit to recognize my field success," the General stated seriously. He gave Frank a penetrating look.

"You're the man who eliminated a couple of undesirable elements last night? We heard about it this morning. Good riddance, I say. The country is overflowing with this filth. I'd do a greater service to the frontier by campaigning against them." He emphasized the point by slapping his leg with a big capable hand.

Abruptly he changed the subject. "Now, Grounds, you asked about selling me remounts. I can tell you that I am in the market for horses all the time. What I want, though, are horses that are acclimated to this north country, besides meeting army specifications. Right now those are hard to find. Any others just die in the winter. They're needed badly. By all means, start your horse ranch. I'm sure the Army can make it a profitable business for you."

"General, soon's as Matthew is up, that's what we plan to commence on," Frank stated. An old enlisted campaigner himself, he was nervous around field-grade officers.

"Good luck to you, then." The General rose to go. The rest rose also, with the exception of Matthew. "I'll be back before you're discharged for another visit. I enjoyed this one. Carry on, men." He stumped out, Major Girard behind him.

"Well, pard, that sounded promising," Matthew remarked. He looked better, rested and shaved, sitting up in a chair, his arm in a fresh sling.

"What's this, Matthew?" Toby asked. He'd spotted a dutch oven and three leather cases by the bed, "Open 'em up, Toby. Reuben brought them this morning," Matthew told him.

"My goodness, look at this!" Each case contained a razor, a strop, a soap cup and a comb and brush with silver backing. "Those are toiletry cases. Haven't seen one for quite a while. Gertie sent them up for us, along with soup and prairie chicken pie," Matthew explained, waving at the offerings with his other arm.

"She's a good sort," Frank judged. "She's always liked you, pard, for sure."

"I always thought it was you," Matthew teased. "Nice gesture, anyway. Tell her thanks for me if you see her." His gray eyes twinkled, and Toby and Frank seeing it, were heartened. It signaled the return of Matthew's health. He brought his coffee cup to his lips and sipped.

"All right, boys, we need to make plans. Now I feel we should sell whatever we don't need, maybe even some of Toby's gun collection," he teased as Toby reddened. "Turn everything into cash we can—lead, powder, caps, skinning gear. Leighton would probably take the most of it back, I think. It should give us nearly $7000. all total."

"More, Matthew. Healey left three hundred to Toby."

"And I want that to go into the pot, too," Toby firmly stated.

"Healey was a good man. I see you're wearing his watch, son," Matthew said. Toby nodded.

"Soon's as I'm up, I'll head east on a horse buying trip. I'll be strong enough for that, anyway. Frank, you should hire a couple good hands. They can help you boys build a headquarters until I can bring some horses to you. Then we'll close herd 'em to keep them from being rustled. Getting good help is a key. We need a rider or two who can shoot. It'll be a while before Miles gets the country cleaned of Indians and we'll probably lose some horses 'til then, but the market's there at the same time. If we close herd in a couple separate bunches, we shouldn't ever lose them all."

"That's thinking, but where do we locate?" Frank wondered.

"Remember up-river a ways? Thirty miles or so? The south side, just this way from Rosebud Creek. There's another creek that runs north from those south buttes. Custer had a signal outfit up on one of 'em before the fight. The creek runs to the river, but a short ways up it, I remember there's a real good spring. Sweet water, if no one's taken it, I think it would be a good location. Good grass, water, a day's drive into Keogh and close enough to the river so the boats will stop." Matthew's voice was enthused as he talked about it. The spot had been in his mind for some time, weighing it against other places.

"You go and nail down the location. Build a working corral, a good cabin, check the range out. See if you can find some close hay meadows and put up some hay. Leighton'll sell you some hay equipment."I'll head east, hit the railroad at Bismarck and comb the country for horses. The army'll only take unblemished solid colored, sound winded horses. You know the kind: good height, good mouth. They'll have to pass military inspection. I should think from visiting with Miles that we can see a price range from $125 to $175 apiece, the upper, of course, for officer's mounts. I'll bring back what I can, unbroken or broke, and we'll work 'em out, then bring 'em in when we have a bunch to sell. I'll also look for a good stud and put together a band of mares for us, if I can."

"Sounds real good to me, Matthew. We'll go see Leighton today." The others in their hospital beds looked curiously at the enthusiastic three as they huddled together, making their plans.

Courtesy of the Library of Congress

Chapter 6

South Side of the Yellowstone

A week later a wagon pulled by a bay team topped the ridge and headed down into Graveyard Bottom, following a blurred set of wagon tracks that wound around clumps of sagebrush, sandstone ledges and deeply eroded little cuts in the rusty colored soil. A boy was driving it, doing a creditable job considering the rough terrain. Behind the heavily laden wagon came a little band of horses, pushed by a spare rider on a buckskin. On the far side of the creek, the west side, a log cabin sat, a small corral close by its north end. A wagon was behind it. A thin line of smoke rose from a crude chimney on the south end of the cabin. The day was turning out to be warm with a light wind blowing and the smoke trailed off into their faces.

When they got closer after crossing the creek and pulling the far side, the boy hollered, "Hello, the cabin. Anybody home?"

A loud female voice called back through the open door,

"Come ahead! Glad to see you, Toby! How do, Frank, how are you?" Janey Canary appeared in the opening, a flour sack apron around her middle. "Light down. The coffee's on. Put the horses in the corral here. I'll open the gate." When Frank ran the little band in, she closed the gate on them and came over.

Frank stepped down and tied the sorrel to a corral pole, then followed Janey into her home. Coffee smell hit him at the door and started his taste buds working. The cabin was surprisingly neat and homey.

"Well, see Lopez's friends ain't put you under yet. Was wonderin' how you and Toby were doing. How's Matthew?" She took some cups down from a wooden box cupboard nailed on the log wall by the fireplace, pulled the coffee pot out of its niche in the fire, and poured three cups out. Toby came in from tying the team.

"Hello, son, how are you?" She tousled Toby's head, making him grin.

"Just fine, Ma'am."

"Oh, don't call me ma'am. Make it Jane or Janey, suits me fine. Here's some canned cream I got in Miles. Near as good as real. How's your pard?"

"Matthew's fine, Janey. Went east to buy us some horses. Going to ride the railroad, he says." Frank slurped his coffee noisily.

"We're looking for a place, Janey, the horse spread I was telling you about. Matthew had it in mind to locate on a spring west of you a ways, over on a creek. Do you know if anyone's taken it yet?" His blue eyes squinted anxiously.

"Nope, not that I know of. It's not far off Rosebud Creek. Come to think, it'd be a good place! Matthew's thinking right." She stirred the fire, thinking. She seemed sad.

"What are you doing here, Janey?" Frank asked gently.

"Ohhh got plenty to do, plenty," she muttered.

"Guess I can't hire you to help us put up a headquarters, then?" Frank rejoined.

"Well sure, I could help you boys, if you want me." She looked down at her hands, rough and calloused like a man's. "Not many do . . . anymore."

"We could use you, for sure. Tried to hire a couple hands in Miles but everybody's workin'. We got a cabin and a couple working corrals to build, if the land's still open. I'd like to get a little barn up, too." Frank set down his cup. "Why don't we just trail on over and see?"

"I'll get a horse up," Janey said eagerly.

Two hours of easy traveling took them across several small ridges, a cottonwood flat and up a draw that headed onto a plateau a couple miles wide. Though grass was high, the coulees were waterless and dust rose from the wagon wheels at times. The rim of the plateau stopped the wagon for a minute and the little band of horses crowded around it. Frank came up beside them. On their right and below them the river angled. They'd been close to it most of the day. To the south lay a jumble of buttes. From the tallest, one of Custer's scouts had signaled back to his commander when they were out against the Sioux. North and west across the river about ten miles rose a single table-topped hill, a lone open butte which pinpointed the mouth of the Porcupine creek emptying into the Yellowstone River.

"See that grove up the crick there?" Janey pointed. "Trail goes down along here and follows the bluff after it crosses the crick. The spring's in the grove against the hill. Don't see anybody there. Looks like we made it in time."

The spring was in a bend of the creek, some few feet up the hill. It percolated down, forming a small marsh that drained its way into the creek. Seeing them coming, a little flock of ducks got off the water and headed for the river. Toby liked the place immediately. Frogs and cricket noise greeted them as they pulled up and he could see animal tracks all around the spring. No one was there, but on the little flat beside it, they could see the remains of fires and past camp sites. A good spring on a trail saw lots of use.

"This looks damn good! Matthew picked right." Frank exclaimed. "Clean out and rock that spring, build a corral down here and run the spring water through it. Build the cabin right over there. Hot damn! Let's get to it."

* * *

A hundred miles out of Bismarck, Matthew's stage met the railhead, laying track at a furious rate westward. "They keep laying track so fast, we'll see 'em in Miles this winter," one of the other passengers, a Lieutenant Simms, remarked. He was going back to the states, he'd confided to the other passengers, to be married. Matthew assented absently, watching the work from the window of the rocking stage. "Civilization is coming to the frontier," he thought. "But do we want it at the price it's costing us?"

* * *

At the spring, Frank was trying hard to keep from groaning.

"Must be a different set of muscles a person uses buffalo hunting than using a crosscut saw. Invention of the devil." Toby came over with the pot and refilled Frank's cup.

"You all right, Frank?"

"Sure am, youngster. Why do you ask?"

"Oh, Janey and me thought we heard you groaning, is all," he mentioned mischievously.

"Why no, son, must have been the wind. Sounds like it's coming up. Or maybe Cappy dreamin'." The old man slurped his coffee, wishing as usual for a drink. Just one.

They had shoveled into the hill for two days, making a dugout pantry and a hideaway to build the cabin over. Then they'd taken the wagon and gathered flat sandrock for cornerstones and walls. Janey had proven to be the strongest of them and a tireless worker. After fighting her skirts for half a day, she'd disappeared in the brush and come out with a pair of man's pants on. "Easier to work in," she remarked apologetically. Frank had said nothing, but Toby had been scandalized.

"Frank, she's a woman and she's wearing pants!" he whispered fiercely when he had a chance alone with the old man.

"Don't never mind, son. She's doing the best she can." Having seen her in work pants and boots before, he was not so unnerved as the boy.

They'd shoveled the cabin site clear of rocks and cactus, leveled it, then set the cornerstones. Down close to the river, they found a sandy bank and brought a couple of loads up by the site, then went back to a small hill where Frank had seen some good pea gravel. While they were shoveling, they heard a "hoot, hoot," and looking up, saw a steamboat nosing towards them from downriver. They stopped their shovel work, all of them glad of the diversion, and watched as the boat came gliding into the bank a hundred yards from where they stood. Toby broke, then, and ran like a deer down to the river edge. Smoke poured from the twin stacks as the captain held her in close to the bank, which at that particular spot, made an almost perfect landing. A couple of hands slid a gangplank out and came over to throw a tug-line around a nearby tree. Frank and Janey walked to the river edge. The boat, they saw, was the *Far West.*

"How do, Grant," Janey called. Like everyone on the frontier, she knew the *Far West's* captain.

"Jane Canary, how are you? And Frank Shannon, am I right? They said at Keogh you were along here somewhere." The short, stubby captain, the man whose boat had taken the wounded from the Custer-Reno battle down to Fort Union in record time, waved his cigar at them in good humor. "Supposed to be a woodhawk or two along here, Wheeler and Smith. Know 'em, Calamity? Need some wood to get on up to Fort Custer."

"Yeah, but you missed Wheeler. He should be just below here a mile or two. Smith, I'm not sure of. He could be closer to the Rosebud aways." She bit the end off the cigar Marsh had thrown her, then lit up, handing the other cigar to Frank. Toby looked wide-eyed.

"You interested in selling wood, Shannon? We'll be up quite a lot, running supplies to Pease Bottom, Fort Custer and Coulson's Landing, and could use it, if you are."

"Could happen that we'd be selling some wood, Captain. This is a good landing. We're putting up a cabin at a spring just above here. We're goin' into the horse business."

He puffed on his stogie.

"'Preciate the cigar, Cap'n. Next trip, bring up a couple thousand feet of two-by-sixes. We'll pay cash."

"We'll hoot when we come by. You ever need us to stop, tie a rag in the tree limb there and we'll pull in. Guess we'll back down and see where we missed Wheeler. See you folks again."

The two hands pulled the gangplank back and the steamboat made an expert turn in the river, backing around and upstream, then heading back down.

"Seems like they'd wreck on some gravel bar or run into a log somewhere," Toby remarked as he watched the boat move swiftly down river, aided by the fast current. Calamity snorted.

"Huh! Son, that Captain there is the best there is." Janey stated.

"He knows the rivers and their channels like a bear knows her cubs. He saved a lot of men's lives after the mix-up on the Little Bighorn. He ran this river in record time." She turned and trudged back to the wagon and began shoveling again. Frank took a rueful look at his hands and pitched in again, too.

Three days later they'd managed to mortise together a crude sandstone foundation and a stout root cellar hideout. Then they'd headed south to the pine hills just in sight on the skyline for cabin logs. Janey had also proven to be a good hand on the other end of a crosscut saw and successively worked Frank and Toby right into the ground. Toby, however, being young, was quick to recover. Frank took longer to harden in.

They camped in the hills not far from Signal Butte, a high scoria hill capped by a sheer rock parapet. "Toby boy, keep sharp watch all the time and heed that dog. We're in Indian country yet, son. They're

115

not all in Canada by a long shot," Frank cautioned. Even working in the woods, they all, including Janey, wore their belt guns.

Frank and Janey were old hands at cabin building and the log walls went up in good time with the help of the team, which Janey could expertly handle. Frank proved a top hand with an adze, a tool he confessed to having had a long acquaintance with in his youth.

He had brought some small windows and door lumber in the wagon from Miles and with those they fashioned doors, windows, and shutters for the cabin. They decided to wait on the roof for the cut lumber, then cover it with tarpaper and dirt.

"We get the floor in, I can use this new plane you bought, Frank, and make it smooth as a baby's bottom," Janey remarked, fingering its sharpness. "Gonna be a real neat cabin, we get done. Sure did a nice job on those windows and doors, didn't we?"

"You're a good craftsman, Janey," Frank assured her, "Or should I say craftswoman?"

"Call it what you want," she muttered, "I still enjoy working with wood. Shoulda been a carpenter, I guess."

They were settled around the fire outside the cabin. The horses were in a rope corral tied from cottonwood to cottonwood close in to the spring by them. Off to one side, a little tent sat with their perishables and gear stacked in it.

"Too bad we never got our lodge back, Frank, and all our tarps.. We could sure use them now." Toby remarked. The men Leighton had sent for their gear had come back empty handed, reporting the lodge and all their gear burned or stolen.

"Never mind, son. We got what we need right here." He sighed contentedly, always a man of the present, happy to live for the moment, especially when it involved coffee, tobacco and good talk. Janey, in this, was a kindred soul, though Frank could see a restlessness in her, which he correctly identified as a craving for whiskey, that vice he knew well.

They were putting the finishing touches on the fireplace at the cabin's south end of a morning, when Frank looked up to the east across the creek and saw a flowing white wave come pouring over the rim of the facing bluff.

"My God!! Sheep, a big band of sheep!"

They all left work to stare at the oncoming animals, herded by three men and a half dozen barking shepherd dogs. Cappy rose from beside the cabin wall and started for them, but sank down again at a word from Toby. One of the men rode splashing across the creek and up to the cabin.

"Hello, people, was looking to water here, if you don't mind?"

"Appreciate if you'd water down below or at the Rosebud. Never cared for the smell of sheep." Frank tried to keep the distaste from his voice, but didn't altogether succeed.

"Takes some getting used to, I admit," the other said cheerfully. He was a tall man of clean, open countenance, Frank saw, as he watched him swing down in front of them.

"Well, herd 'em down below us, at least, so you don't foul the water, and come up for noon meal with us. Toby, put the water on, son." He headed for the spring with the sheepman to water his horse.

"Howard's the name." He held out his hand and Frank took it."A.D. Howard. Don't want to crowd you. We heard at Miles you men were starting a horse ranch here. Thought we'd move up the Rosebud and locate some range there. Do you know of any outfits that might object?"

"No, but then we've been busy here and haven't made too big a circle yet to see just who is in the country. Janey thought that a man named Smith had located this side of the Rosebud's mouth, but I don't think he's a stockman." Frank knelt down beside the horse and washed himself in the clear, cold water. "Course, the Reds might have something to say. The country south is still Indian country, pretty much."

After supper, the other two men, Howard's herders, rode off back to the band. Howard, himself, was in no hurry to leave and made himself comfortable by the fire. Cappy, sensing a man who liked dogs, crept close for some petting. Howard obliged. Frank stoked his pipe and leaned back in full contentment as the daylight faded.

"You've been in this country long, Shannon?" he asked as he stroked the massive dog's head.

"Yes, even before Custer, it was. In '74, the spring of the year, me and Matthew was at Bozeman when a man named of Vernon come into the camp. Claimed he'd been with a survey party down here and they'd found some gold up Rosebud Creek. Well, some of the merchant folk there at Bozeman also were interested. They wanted to run a road from the Tongue on up the Yellowstone back to Bozeman, they said. But, really what they likely wanted was just to stir up the Sioux and the

Cheyenne and cause some Indian trouble to get the guvvement to step in and settle the hostile question once and for all. Guess you might say that it was the start of what got Custer killed, finally, right back here along up the Rosebud," He blew smoke into the crisp air above his head, watched a star fall across the horizon.

"About then, me and Matthew was pretty content to just stay on with the Nez Perce´, but that wasn't to be. The Bozeman crowd got up a strong expedition: one hundred fifty men, twenty some wagons, a couple pieces of little artillery with a couple hundred rounds for 'em, and plenty of horses. I remember one store there gave us a wagonload of ammunition. The men, most of 'em, was war experienced and good fighters. But they couldn't agree on a leader until Matthew's name came up. They came and asked us to take it on, Matthew as captain, me as his lieutenant. Matthew and I turned 'em down the first time and they came back an' finally talked us into it. Bill Cameron, who'd been an officer in the artillery during the war, they drew on as chief gunner. They called the outfit, as I remember, 'The Yellowstone Wagon Road and Prospecting Expedition.'

"A prestigious name," Howard murmured, "Did the expedition live up to it?"

"Well, you'll have to judge for yourself."

Frank continued in his soft drawl, and the rest settled down for a long story.

"We formed up the middle of February at Quinn's place just out of Bozeman. Too early, as I remember, for our stock was winter-weak and about the time we pulled out, the weather cooled down again bad. But the boys was chomping at the bit and wanted action. We had to keep the stock moving at night so they wouldn't freeze and I remember several of the men ended up frost-bit. We moved on down from the Sweetgrass to the Yellowstone, fighting snowdrifts most all the way. We had a shovel crew out in front, and on the hills it'd sometimes take fifty men on ropes to get the wagons up and over. We averaged about ten miles a day the whole trip but sure didn't start out that fast. Matthew and I wanted the boys to dig breastworks when we stopped because there was Indian sign around. But the ground was still froze in places, and this wasn't a popular pastime for 'em. There was a lot of bitching."

Janey got up and threw some more wood on the fire, then poured some more coffee. "Wasn't French Pete on that trip, Frank?"

"Yes, he was, and he did some fine fighting, too."

"When we reached the Porcupine flat, we laid up a while and let the stock get some grass in their bellies. Hunted some buffalo, too. Last of March we headed south and crossed the Yellowstone on the ice. The Sioux were probably watching us all the time because we landed in the thick of it soon's we made the crossing." He paused and relit his pipe.

"You know, we rode with good men, if hard ones. Most all of them were after gold, really. The road, anything else, could go to hell. Vernon's story, a lie somebody put him up to, we later figured, had fired 'em up. Many of 'em had been on quite a few gold runs. We were all willing to believe another one in the Bighorns. Especially deep in Sioux country where few whites had ever been. Hell, most was willing to wade through the whole Sioux nation for a chance at a gold strike. And, you know," he paused, "that's just what we did. Waded through 'em, anyway. Right away we hit an Indian trail heading for the Rosebud and we started in following that. A couple of our young men—we had about thirty young ones with us who hadn't fought Indians before, and were continually taking chances, anyways, a couple of 'em got out ahead of our advance guard, and suddenly they got charged by about a dozen stripped-down Sioux. Well, our advance flankers on the right saw 'em comin' in and made a rush for the Indians' gear and blankets. They got 'em gathered up and turned to the Indians, giving 'em hell. We wounded some and sure left some naked in the cold.

"Then, next day we camped early and some four or five of us rode on ahead to scout the trail out. Sure as hell, another bunch jumped us and we put 'em off, as we did all through the trip, by charging right at 'em instead of running. This was hard for 'em to understand, because we were usually out-numbered more than ten to one. This time one of our young ones, a boy named Bostwick, went out after a horse the reds left for a decoy and he was wounded several times, shot right off his horse. Then they rode up and commenced countin' coup on him by beating him with their coup sticks and quirts. They was so busy with him, we rode up and scattered 'em with our belt guns, getting a couple, as I remember, and saving the youngster, who later got well. Plus we got the horse, too! An Indian, you know, purely hates to lose a horse. Loses face, then, also, you see. That night the Indians tried to surprise our pickets but our men got in the first shots and drew blood again.

Next day we crossed the Rosebud and came up on a big trail. Four or five hundred lodges, <u>fresh</u>! Right then, there was some coffee coolers that were pulling their hair and wondering what they was doing coming along!"

He chucked softly and slurped his own coffee, took another puff of his pipe.

"Not boring you, am I?" he asked.

"I'm certainly not bored with the tale, go ahead," urged young Howard. Toby, too, had never heard the story detailed so accurately before, and was also interested. Janey, herself, had heard the story from several others but was always ready to listen to Frank's reminiscences.

"Wal, we camped on the east side of the creek on a bench and dug in. There was a coulee some yards below us and we dug a couple of picket holes out about thirty yards and stationed two men in each hole to cover that coulee. Another picket hole covered the creek side.

Long about the middle of the night, our coulee pickets were driven in by Indians firing and the coulee occupied by a mess of 'em, maybe several hundred. There was lots of other Sioux off on the other side set to cut us off 'case we decided to run that way. Both groups commenced firing on us and just riddled the camp. Several of 'em got in the picket holes by the coulee and commenced killing stock in our corral. They killed over twenty horses during the night. All night long the reds were hootin' like owls, howling like coyotes, and when a flock of geese came over camp, they changed their tune and started honkin' like geese. I remember some of the dogs ran out and the Sioux killed a couple of 'em and ate 'em right there in the coulee that night. One of the Sioux chiefs had a little bell, and when it would tinkle, we'd get a volley of fire from 'em. It happened most of the night and we soon learned to lie low when the bell rang.

Anyway, when morning light came, here was a red in one of our picket holes, been firing into us from about fifty yards or less. Bill Cameron elected to take a shot at him with the big gun. He cut the fuse short and depressed the piece. The redskin had put a large piece of driftwood in front of him, thinking he was behind cover. When the shell struck it, it exploded and later we found pieces of Indian all over. When the Bighorn gun fired, all of us yelled, and from that time on, the Indians never hardly uttered a sound during any fighting. It was a mind-turning thing, you see, and we put the jinx on 'em.

There was an ash grove about one hundred yards or more from the corral where some heavy firing was comin' from. Cameron gave it two doses of canister and cleared 'em out of there in jig time,

When it had lightened, the boys started doing some better shooting and it wasn't long before we had nine or ten Indians hit in the head, over the eyes. Then they'd hold a pistol over the bank of the coulee and shoot without aiming." He chuckled, "We shot the hands off a number of 'em on that trick.

The coulee was still full of reds so Matthew and I organized a charging party to clean it out, three parties to strike the coulee high, low and in the middle. When the big guns fired, all the men on the coulee side fired, too, to keep their heads down and the parties went running out.

In a few seconds, we reached the coulee and using our pistols, we dealt death to those reds, who were nearly paralyzed when they saw us come up over the rim. They dropped their guns and all and took out, leaving another thirteen dead. We gathered a quantity of robes, blankets, meat, guns and twenty-three horses, making up for the ones they killed in our corral. After the charge on the coulee, the boys charged the bluffs on the other side of the corral and drove 'em off there, killin' a couple more. I remember after this, a warrior with a fine warbonnet on and mounted on a beautiful horse, came out to make a bravo ride about five hundred yards from us on the bench. A dozen of the boys elected to fire a volley at him and the horse and rider both fell. We checked the horse later, not finding the rider, and counted nine bullet holes in it. Good shootin' at five hundred yards on a running horse!

The boys being boys, loaded some shells that we thought might fit their guns, putting dynamite in 'em in place of gunpowder. We threw these around where they would find 'em. They also dosed up the pemmican we'd captured with strychnine and left it there, too.

Next few days, despite some that wanted to go back to Bozeman, we traveled on up the Rosebud. We camped at the forks, then went up the middle fork to the divide between the Rosebud and the Little Horn River. Then we went on down to the Little Horn, fighting each and every day. Jack Bean, one of the outfit's finest shots, hit a bravo rider one of those days just after our artillery ran off a bunch of about six hundred braves. When a bunch of the boys went out to scalp him, Zack Yates got shot right in the heart. They brought him back to camp and later we buried him at night camp, running the stock and wagons over the grave to keep the Indians from finding it. At a camp later on Long Creek, we dug a hole and put our last shell from the big gun in it, along with a bunch of log chains, bolts, etc., and some more giant powder—piled it up like a grave and stuck up a head board. We learned afterward our nasty little tricks did for quite a few Indians.

Next morning, we crossed Lodge Grass Creek and just after getting across, here come, out of a cottonwood grove, a line of white shirted Cheyennes. We learned later that they'd come from the Agency, had their new white shirts on, which made it look like troops in uniform. There was three or four hundred of 'em and they'd bragged to the Sioux that they would ride right over us. Out on the left, we had a few flankers that were afoot. All but four of these ran in. These four, French Pete, Tom Rhea, Gillis and Hopkins, charged the Cheyenne all by theirselves.

The Cheyenne couldn't believe this, seeing the four run at 'em, stop and kneel down to shoot, then jump up and run at 'em again, and they swung away from the four to the front of the train, where our advance guard did the same as Pete and the others. The Cheyenne didn't like this either, so they went to cover. About this time, here come the Sioux behind us, four or five hundred of 'em, and they hit the rear of the train, then pulled back to a little coulee. We charged 'em out of that, killing one or two and wounding a few, and they scattered like sheep."

He looked at Howard, who sat pensively, contemplating the scene his imagination drew. Toby brought him a refill and he paused in his story as a wolf howled south of them toward the buttes.

"Next day, a couple Indians came out on a hill and fired at our horse corral. Jack Bean returned the compliment with his Sharps, a 45/120, and derned if he didn't drop one of the reds. The boys all thought it was nearly a mile shot. It was the last shot fired on the trip at an Indian, but I'd say we killed upwards of a hundred of 'em, which is maybe more than Custer did. And we did it with the loss of only one man, Zack Yates. Bostwick and Woods both healed up. Probably we were facing all told, about a 1000 reds in the last fight, as there were Cheyennes, Ogalallas and the UncPapa Sioux all in it. From flour sacks and guns we picked up, other gear and such, we concluded they were Fort Peck Indians. "

His story told, Frank sat back and sipped on his cooling coffee.

"Quite a story, Frank. I'm glad you told it to me," Howard said, getting up from his seat by the fire and stretching out the kinks.

"It reminds me of Stanley's trip through Africa, but his men had rifles against warriors that were armed with only spears and bows, while you men went against Indians as well armed nearly as yourselves."

"Yes, they were, but discipline, leadership and gun handling counted heavily in our favor," Frank drawled.

"And by leadership, I mean Matthew Grounds, for he was the guiding spirit. His judgment was always sound and there probably wasn't another man there who could have controlled those boys so well. I wish you'd come over when you can, to meet him." Frank stood to offer his hand to this young man, a good one, he felt, and a decent one to have for a neighbor.

"I will, Frank. I'd like to meet him. By the way, the outfit did live up to its name, alright," Howard said. Frank chuckled.

"I guess so!" Toby said, "You never told me all that before, Frank."

"Huh, Toby. You think that story was something, tomorrow night I'll tell you about the time I went with the Custer expedition to the Black Hills. We found the gold and Custer shot a grizzly bear ten feet tall!" Janey remarked, a little jealously.

"But, Janey," Toby protested, "the same Indians Frank fought killed Custer!"

"Well," she muttered, "maybe so, but most of Custer's men had never fought Indians, or anybody else much, as far as that goes. They were just young kids, raw recruits." She grumbled off to bed.

* * *

A month later, Matthew topped the bluff overlooking the spring and liked what he saw: over on the far bank of the creek on the north side of the spring was a long, well-built cabin with a red scoria dirt roof. Smoke came from its rock chimney. Down off the rise and closer to the creek on the south side of the cabin was a compact little barn and a good set of corrals. There were several horses in it, and he could see someone, Toby it looked like, coming from the barn door. The figure waved excitedly as he saw the large horse herd stream down over the rim and begin watering at the creek. Matthew spurred his horse on behind, "Hold 'em here, boys, we're home!"

He splashed on through the rivulet and up to the cabin. There was a hitch rail and he threw his reins over it as Frank came out the door. The two came together, looking in each other's eyes, and the handshake, despite themselves, was emotional, though an idle onlooker would perhaps not have so noted it.

"Good to see you, pard," Frank choked out.

"And you, old horse," Matthew answered, with a wide smile.

Toby came running up, then, and hugged Matthew when he held out his hand. Then he stepped back, half ashamed of himself. "We're sure glad you're back, Matthew. Me and Frank was getting worried. Man, that's sure some bunch of horses!"

"Yes, they are, aren't they?" Matthew's pride was evident in his voice. "I had hell's own time gathering them, but we made it." He turned back to the horse band still drinking at the creek. "Put 'em on in the corral, boys, and come on up. Toby, why don't you run down and open the gate?"

"Sure thing, Matthew." The boy turned and headed back down to the corral.

"He's filled out. Put some muscle on. You're looking good, too, Frank. I'm seeing work agrees with you," Matthew teased.

"Huh. Left us here to do all the work, as usual. Come on in, the coffee's on." He turned and went through the cabin door and Matthew followed. They stepped into a well-built cabin, Matthew saw, with a stout door and narrow shuttered windows for excellent defense, if necessary. The floor, like the roof above them, was two-by-six planking, but someone, he noted, had taken time to plane the floor to a nice smoothness. Chairs and benches surrounded the large rough table at its center and the fireplace at its end was crackling cheerily to a nice fire. A lantern hung above the table and another sat on the fireplace mantle. The walls were studded with pegs on which gear and weapons hung. Some fairly well built cabinets to one side housed their kitchen gear and Matthew saw a door on the hill side of the cabin, which he correctly guessed was a pantry root cellar. The other end of the cabin was given over to bunks.

"Pretty fancy quarters for a couple old hide hunters," Matthew commented with a pleased tone."You've done a good job here, I can see already!"

"We've put in our time, all right. Couldn't find any help right away and Janey Canary came over and chipped in. She's a fair hand with wood, Matthew, and worked hard. Did you see her at her diggins down east?"

"No, the cabin was empty, but we'd heard she was whooping it up in town. You paid her off, I suppose?"

"Yes, and I hated to. I knew she'd make a beeline for the bottle. She was doin' well here." Frank sighed, got down some more cups and poured two for Matthew and him. Matthew took a sip.

"Good to be back. The town was busier than ever. Drovers, freighters, —and that railroad is charging right for us. They'll be across the line this year and probably into Miles by next year. I could have sold this band of horses at a large profit right there." Matthew raised his eyebrows as Frank clumped a can of milk down on the table.

"Pretty fancy, huh?" he grinned, "Steamboats been comin' right by us and they've done most of our freighting for us. Hauled our lumber. Hauled up our mowing machine: Leighton sent us a Buckeye. And I got a horse rake cheap. Sent us a set of wheels and axles and we've been building a flat-bed haywagon. Buying by boat sure beats fightin' those cutbanks and coulee crossings."

Toby came in, followed by two men. Matthew stood up to introduce them.

"Boys, this is Frank Shannon and Toby, our son. These two riders are 'Syrup' Smith and Gil Reardon. Syrup told me he wouldn't work for an outfit that didn't stock the stuff." They laughed and Matthew told them to sit. Frank poured them out a cup and slid the cream can toward them.

He liked what he saw. Neither of the men were young. Smith wore a brushy mustache and had bushy eyebrows to match. A bent nose stuck out over the gray brush and snappy bright eyes peered from under the brows. He was small but solid built and bowlegged from years in the saddle. He wore a long barreled Colt on his right side that had seen hard use. Reardon was taller, more slender, and not as bowlegged, though he, too, showed his years in the saddle. He had a square face with curly brown hair topping it. A smaller, trimmed mustache tipped with gray sprung out from his upper lip. When he gathered his cup in, Frank saw his thumb was missing on his left hand. Both wore chaps and spurs.

"Real nice place you built here," Smith admired after he blew his coffee drinkable.

"Sure is," his riding partner agreed, "Been any Indians?"

"We've been lucky, had little bands of reds come by, but they've left us alone. Been quite a little travel going on by here. Fact is, we even had some sheep visit," Frank stated.

"Sheep?" Smith echoed, "Sheep already up here? The stinking things should be run out of the Territory! Hope the Indians get 'em."

"Wal, they just might. Young man that brought 'em in headed up the Rosebud with 'em." Frank lit his pipe. "Right nice, he was. He's been back through several times. Tells me his brother's coming up with another band this summer."

"Is that trouble for us, Frank?" Matthew questioned.

"Oh, I don't think so. Howard's a reasonable person. Wants to get along. 'Sides, he's further up the Rosebud by a good ways. We won't have any problem with them. Figgered we'd hold this side of the Rosebud to the Buttes and siding the Yellowstone, then on down to Janey's and over to the Buttes again. There's two more springs we've found and we've got good running water on two sides, three if Graveyard runs all year, which it won't."

Cappy strode in through the open door and both men at the table stared, "Jesus! Thought a bear was comin' in," Gil ventured.

"That's Cappy. He's harmless. Come over here, dog, and get acquainted," Toby said, steering the big dog over to the new men. After a few sniffs, he went and lay down by the fire.

Later, down at the corral, Matthew gazed at the log horse barn connected to it and said, "Pard, you couldn't have gotten all this handled with just Toby and Janey. You got too much done." They leaned companionably together on the top rail.

"You're right, Matthew. Leighton sent a couple men over several weeks ago. They were good hands and it went up fast, then. I make it 142 head. How did you come up with so many?"

"Most all the she-stuff is aged trolley mares from back east. I got them at auction, and even the best came pretty cheap. They're good for a couple, three colts, or more if we feed 'em good through the winter. The stud there is American Saddle bred out of Rex Peavine blood. He came out of Kentucky, though I didn't have to go that far to get him. He's got a good topline, doesn't he? Clean legs and a nice head. He'll throw some good colts. I looked hard for some Arabians but didn't find any. Maybe next time."

They were looking at a good sized blood-bay with a black mane and tail. The muscle development on his forelegs and the stifles of his hind legs indicated he had some speed to him. His smallish head and black, hard hooves showed intelligence and durability. Any cavalryman worth his salt would nearly kill for such a mount.

"I got as far back as Chicago to the market there and bought and sold 'til I got what you see here." Matthew said, rolling his shoulder a little.

"How's the shoulder? You're looking damn good," Frank remarked, seeing his gesture.

"Feeling pretty well now. Went to the doc once while I was back east and he said it was a good job. Wasn't sleeping too good, but he gave me some stuff and now I'm fine. Little sore, is all."

As a matter of fact, both men looked better than Toby had seen them for years. Matthew was rested, and Frank, though he'd gone at it hard, had paced himself and enjoyed the work much more than the dirty job of hide hunting. None of them missed that life.

"Bought a special horse for you, Frank, and another for Toby." Matthew indicated a big black gelding. "That's yours, the big black there with the white star on his forehead. Seller said he's Standard-bred and Thoroughbred. Got some Peter the Great blood on his sire's side. With that thoroughbred in him, he looks to be fast." Frank stared, the horseman in him flaring to life. Matthew pointed at a small deep-chested sorrel.

"Another American Saddle with some Peavine blood. Belonged to a rich family back there that lost their kids to typhoid fever. They sold it cheap when I said it was for a boy." He paused, "Lots of sickness back there. Too many people, I think. This country is looking good."

Frank assented absently, still looking at the black horse.

"Hell, with a start like this, we're set, Matthew."

"Yeah, there's twenty, thirty head there we can break out and sell quick. Smith's a good horse hand and'll be a lot of help. Reardon can herd, and you and I can take turnabout. We'll let Toby handle the horses much as we can, get him experience early."

Frank couldn't stand it any longer and got a lariat from the barn. With a flip, he roped the black. When the rope settled on its neck, it faced him and Frank walked up to it and stroked its nose. It stood with no fuss.

"Seems gentle and smart, pard. I like him. Think I'll throw the leather on and take a little ride." Matthew smiled. Toby was coming from the cabin after washing up, Cappy, as usual, trailing in his wake.

He was going to cherish the look on the boy's face when he saw the sorrel.

* * *

They got the hay wagon finished, and Smith, with Toby helping, started working out the geldings in the small round work corral off the big one. Matthew and Frank helped, turnabout, though Frank had too little patience to make the best kind of horse handler, and he knew it. Toby, though, was shaping up to be a great horseman.

Twice the steamboat stopped and they bought supplies. Once they went over to visit Janey Canary, but she wasn't home. Every week, travelers, prospectors usually, came by the spring but most went up the north side, following the old military road. The sheepman, Howard, came through on his way to Miles, and when he came back, his brother and their other band of sheep came with him. Matthew liked them both, as Frank had predicted, but he was glad they had located a distance away.

In September, Matthew, Smith and Toby drove twenty-eight head of broke geldings to Keogh.

When they reached Janey's cabin, she was there, but so were a couple sullen-faced drunken sots. When she went to introduce them, she couldn't remember their names, and even Toby knew that she was drunk, from the way she stumbled around trying to make coffee for them. It made him sad for her. He liked her and it hurt to see her in that condition. They didn't stay long.

They corralled the little herd in the afternoon at the Keogh army pens and Matthew went to see if the general was in. He returned with Captain Borden, who was glad to see them again. He commented on how Toby had grown and praised the quality of the boy's new horse, to his red-faced delight.

"Son, the Army's prepared to give you a good price for that charger of yours. What do you say? $150?" he teased, pulling off his white gauntlets to pet its neck.

"No, sir! Matthew bought him just for me. He wouldn't like me to sell him."

"Well, if you ever want to turn a profit," the captain said, more serious now, "I'll personally give you $250 for him. He really takes my fancy. Now, Matthew, let's see what you brought us." He bustled over to the corral and had Smith and his sergeant bring out the horses one by one, where he went over them carefully, checking their teeth, their feet, eyes and conformation. He eventually rejected three; each of which Matthew and Frank, Smith, too, had considered might be, but had thrown in to test the Quartermaster's buying style.

"Well, Matthew, sorry I had to turn those three down, but just doin' my job. The General would have given me hell if I'd taken 'em." Borden was apologetic.

"Hell, don't worry, Captain, we'll sell the three over in town, maybe." He was well pleased. They had gotten $165 average on twenty head and $180 for the others. A good start on their enterprise. He made it $4200. They'd gotten more than half their investment back already. A damn good start.

"I'll have to get the General to countersign the draft, Matthew. He's down at the rifle range. I'll work it up and have the sergeant bring it to you in town, if you don't want to wait here. You'll be at Leighton's?"

"That'll be fine, Captain. Thank you. What's the latest on the Indian situation?"

"Well, eighty lodges of Sioux came in around the middle of June. Rain-in-the-Face has been giving us fits lately, but we're expecting he and Black Moon to come in soon, too. Rain-in-the-Face's crew killed some Mounties up north, we heard. So, he's in a bind now. He knows we'll get 'em sooner or later. Black Moon will follow Rain-in-the-Face. What's keeping us busy now are all the little groups of Gros Ventres and Sioux running renegade, separate from the main bands. Your horses will see a lot of service, for sure, Matthew. Been bothered by horse thieves yet?"

"No, we've been lucky so far," Matthew replied.

"Well, not all of 'em are Indians, Matthew, remember that."

"I get your drift, Captain. We'll keep our eyes peeled,"

After selling all three rejects at the Livery, they pulled up at Leighton's and got an effusive greeting from the storekeeper. Smith picked up a few things and told Matthew he was heading over to Tate's for a drink. Toby was telling Joe about their place when they heard a shot, then two more, out in front of the store. Looking out, they saw Smith lying on his side in the street, his belt gun in his outflung hand. Standing over him were three men, one with a pistol still in his hand.

"Stay here, son." Matthew flung the words over his shoulder as he stepped through the door. Toby, caught by surprise, could only stare.

Matthew reached the edge of the boardwalk and stepped down. He tucked his coat back away from the yellowed grips of his Colt. The men turned, startled.

"Watch it, Brocky, it's the old timer. Stringer, that's the one killed Baker last year." The speaker was a wiry little man with a full beard.

"Old timer, me and him had an argument. He drew and I killed him. You'all got a quarrel with that?" Gallagher was belligerent, his pistol still out. On either side, spectators came edging up, taking in the scene but ready to duck.

"Yes. He was a friend of mine, besides working for me. I don't take kindly to my friends being killed by scum like you."

"Harsh words, Mr.," the one called Stringer ground out. His face was still and set. His hand rested close to his gun, too.

"I got those two covered, Matthew." Leighton called out from the store front. A rifle stuck out from the door jamb.

"That makes it you and me, Texas." Matthew's lisp was softer than usual.

Gallagher had never holstered his weapon. He deemed it a simple matter to bring it up and make his kill. He started his move.

Matthew's hand blurred and his pistol flamed. Gallagher, hit in the act of firing, was thrown sideways. He made an effort to turn back, bring the gun in his hand on line, then the world exploded in a flash of light. Matthew had fired again, a head shot. It dropped Gallagher in the dusty street, lying parallel to and almost touching the little puncher, Smith. The inexorable force and quickness of the old man paralyzed the men facing him.

"Now, Mr. Stringer Jack. You and I'll have it on." Matthew called out to Leighton. "Joe, back off on these two. I want them—both" Matthew holstered his gun.

"Hold it, you men!"

An authoritative voice bellowed at them from the side.

All of them looked to see Sheriff Tom Irvine and Deputy Jim Conley standing close by the corner of the store, shotguns pointed at them.

"I can't have my streets cluttered up with dead men. Raise your hands, boys." Irvine gestured with the ten gauge.

"Jim, get their gun belts."

130

Conley propped his shotgun against the store wall and moved out with his belt gun drawn to comply with Irvine's order.

"Now we'll take a little walk to the jail. Leighton," he hollered, "Would you send for the coroner? Watch these dead ones 'til he comes, all right?" Leighton assented and the group walked on down to the jail. Toby followed, miserable and shaking from the episode.

"Against the wall there, men. Now, Jim, search 'em down good," A search revealed a variety of weapons from all three, including Matthew. Irvine grunted.

"Now sit down by the table there. Keep your hands where we can see them. Jim, pour 'em some coffee and we'll have a little chat. What happened? You first, Grounds."

"I heard shots from inside Leighton's. I came to the door and the Texas puncher had killed my wrangler, Smith. So, I killed him." Matthew sipped his coffee but kept his eyes on Stringer, who stared back. Irvine waited, but Matthew had finished.

"Well, Stringer?"

"Just as he says, Sheriff. Smith called Gallagher a name and drew on him. Brocky killed him. Then, this man stepped out and called Brocky. Evidently, he thought we were backing Gallagher and called us, too. Then you showed up."

Stringer's voice was steady and his manner urbane, but the flat stare he directed at the old man opposite him was wild and deadly.

"Was it self-defense, an even break on both sides?" Irvine asked. Matthew was silent.

"I would say it was, Sheriff, on both sides," Stringer said smoothly.

"What do you say, McKenzie?" Irvine shot his finger at Stringer's companion.

"Nothin', Sheriff. I mean, it was like Stringer says." He replied nervously.

Irvine looked at both men. A steady, long look. McKenzie wouldn't meet his eyes.

"Alright, Stringer, you can leave. Jim, give 'em their gear."

Stringer, after a last, long look at Matthew, got up and strolled out, McKenzie scuttling after him. Irvine watched them go, then turned to Matthew. The older man picked up his cup with a steady hand and sipped the scalding liquid.

"Damn, Grounds, I'm sorry! We heard shots and came running. If I'd known it was you and Stringer, I'd of let you kill him. When we got there, I had to do something. The town expects it."

Matthew looked at him directly for the first time. He rubbed a hand over his face.

"All right, Sheriff. I understand what you're saying. It's just too bad you didn't let me finish it." Toby came in, then, and unobtrusively took a seat at the table, close to Matthew.

"How do, Toby." Irvine gave him a pat on the shoulder. "You still know how to make a good cup of coffee?"

"Sure do, Sheriff. You want me to make you a pot?" Toby was eager to do something for the man who had saved Matthew's life, he thought.

"If you would. The bucket's out back."

Toby went out for the water. Tom turned back to Matthew.

"Grounds, I said it to your pardner and now I'm saying it to you. Jack Stringer's a murdering killer. His crew's as bad, or worse. I'm sure they're responsible for the deaths of several hunters on the North Side, killed for their hides. They've tried to make it look like Indians, but we're sure it's them. And they've got it in for you and Shannon."

"Sheriff, appreciate your concern, you're a good man. I remember how you backed up Frank at the river. You didn't need to do that. We'll step light." Matthew held his hand out. Irvine took it. "Good luck. Say hello to Frank for me. I'm sorry as hell about your wrangler."

Matthew waited for Toby to make the coffee, then they left, going down to the coroner's office to make the arrangements to bury Smith.

They were headed out of town after concluding their business with Joe Leighton who'd bought their three reject mounts, when they heard a call behind them. Reuben was lumbering behind, trying to catch them.

"Mistuh Matthew, Mistuh Matthew! Ease up so's Reuben can talk wid you!" the big Negro puffed.

"Why, hello, Reuben. How've you been?"

Matthew leaned out of the saddle and grasped the big black paw that Reuben thrust at him.

"How you is, Mistuh Matthew? How's your shoulder? Course it mus' be fine, cause I saw you throw your gun today! Whoeee, you ain't lose your touch enny!"

"Yes, I'm fine, Reuben. How's your Missus?"

Reuben's big face sobered, "Well, sir, she been sick a while. Don' know what's wrong, she won't tell me. She stays in her bed mos' all day now. The doc, he keeps sayin' he too busy to come. Will you come see if you find out what's wrong wid her, Mistuh Matthew?" The black eyes filled with tears.

"Certainly, I will. Son, you go on back to Leighton's and wait for me."

"Yes, sir." Toby turned his horse around, pulling the lead on the pack horse they'd brought with them. Matthew went back down the street with Reuben walking close beside him.

"Why, Toby, back already? More trouble?" Leighton asked him anxiously.

"No, Mr. Leighton, Reuben came and got Matthew. Somebody's sick, I think."

"Oh." Leighton seemed troubled but said no more. His establishment was busy and he went to wait on a customer.

Toby roamed the store listlessly. He tried to avoid thinking or looking at the dark bloody spot where Smith's body had lain. They had become good friends and the little horseman had taught Toby a lot in the weeks they'd worked together. He couldn't quite grasp the fact that he was gone. He went out, finally, and fooled with his horse, which he'd named Beaver for no real reason, except that it threw its tail once in a while in a way that reminded him of one. It was a good-looking horse and he'd been neglecting his little buckskin and feeling some guilt about it. Its gait was harsh and choppy compared with the smoothness of the sorrel. Presently Matthew came back and Toby noticed he was looking grim.

"Let's shake the dust out, son." It was a silent trip home and they avoided Janey's.

* * *

At dusk, down at the barn, Frank met them with a puzzled frown.

"Say, pard, you got shut of 'em all. That's fine, but where's Smith?"

Reardon came from the barn after forking some hay down in the stalls. "S'pose that derned rim-rocker stayed in Miles and got a snoot full. You didn't fire him, did you, boss?" Reardon asked anxiously. Matthew swung stiffly off his horse.

"Syrup's dead, Gil. A man named Gallagher killed him."

Reardon looked stunned, then blazed angrily, "Brocky Gallagher! We rode together once, but Gallagher liked the easy life too much. I'll kill that son-of-a-bitch!"

"You won't have to, Gil," Toby said quietly. "Matthew did it for you." He turned away so they wouldn't see his tears.

Next morning Gil Reardon asked for his time. Matthew wrote a check for him on Miles' new bank, the First National. The fact they'd made Joe Leighton President had temporarily restored Frank's faith in the banking system and they had decided to try banking there.

"I'm sorry to be goin', Matthew, Frank. You men treated me fine. I'd stay but think I'd better go."

He shook hands and said to Toby, "Take care, kid, you got a couple good men behind you." They went to the porch and watched him ride across the creek.

"Well, old salt, that really puts the pinch on us. Any ideas?" Frank said to his partner.

"I told Joe to send us out a couple good men, if he could. Let's wait and see if he does." Matthew sighed and sat down on the cottonwood log bench along the porch. Cappy came and threw his big bulk down by his feet.

Three days later, two riders splashed through the creek and up to the cabin.

"Howdy the house! Anybody stirring?" Frank stepped to the door, his rifle across his arm. Inside, Toby was at the near window, peering out with his rifle beside him.

"How do, boys, what's your pleasure? Got time for a cup of brew or a feed?"

"Thank you. You'd be Frank Shannon?" The one who spoke was a whip-thin rider who rode a big rough buckskin.

Frank's eyes narrowed. He straightened and tensed a little.

"Know that horse you're on. Used to belong to a friend. Where'd you happen across it?"

The tall rider stayed relaxed. He chuckled, "Easy, now. The horse belonged to Tom Healey. I bought him from Irvine when Healey died. The money was part of what he said he gave that boy of yours. The feed bill on him was gettin' sky-high."

"Sorry. Seeing the horse surprised me." Frank motioned to them. "Step on down and come in."

"Thanks."

The men threw their reins around the hitching post and tied up their pack horses.

Inside, Toby racked the rifle he was holding and got down the cups. He poured for the men as they trooped in the door, spurs jingling. Frank likewise put his gun away.

"I'm hoping real strong that Leighton sent you."

"You're right there. My name's Chipper Bowe. Hail from Odessa, Texas. This's my pard, 'Slow' Bill Hollister." They shook hands all around. Matthew came in at that moment from the barn.

Hollister was a pock-faced, older man with a deeply cleft chin. His easy smile was pleasant and he revealed a slight stutter when he talked, which he seldom did.

Matthew spoke. "I remember you. Saw you with McLean last year on the north side. You were hunting some strayed horses. Ever find them?"

"By gosh, I remember you and the boy now, too!" Chipper exclaimed, "No, we never did get 'em back. McLean was hoppin' mad,"

Slow Bill looked around, "R-r-real nice place. D-D-Don't see a s-s-smooth wood floor in a cabin m-m-much."

"For sure. We're getting real prissified in our old age. Trouble with pretty things is you have to pamper 'em. Appreciate it if you boys wouldn't drag spur tracks on it, spit on it, things like that. Guess we'll try to keep it nice if we can." Frank was only half-joking. He and Janey had worked on it for days. Matthew snorted and the two cowhands looked confused. They self-consciously lifted their boots a little.

Bowe recovered first."Sheriff said you were ex-Rangers. He thought you might give us some jobs. Working horses sounds better than pushing cows up the trail again. Slow Bill and I thought we'd stay around the country, if we could,"

Matthew spoke up."Been some guns going off lately. Sheriff mention that?"

Bowe looked at Hollister."He told us. But we could use a job. We've heard it before. We'd like to stick around, "

"You boys are welcome to stay, long as you know up front that some of the trash element around here aren't very happy with Frank and me."

"Mind if we bring our gear in?" Bowe got up and his pard followed. Frank followed them out.

135

"How's that big buckskin for ridin'?" he inquired, as the two men began untying their packs.

"Well, have to admit he's a little rough. But I've always been partial to buckskins. 'Specially big ones. Actually this one here," he indicated the packhorse,"I call him Stonewall, is a better rider, but he doesn't have the toughness Titan does. He don't tire out. Got any buckskins in your herd?"

"Sorry to say we don't. Army's partial to solid colors, bays and duns, sorrels and browns, mostly, so we have to cater to their likin'."

Frank had noted, as he knew Matthew did, that Bowe and Hollister both wore their belt guns low and they looked well used. They seemed tough and competent, he thought with satisfaction, just what they needed. And they were Texas men.

* * *

In the coming weeks, both men proved to Frank and Matthew's satisfaction that they were handy with horses and weapons. Twice they had occasion to run small bunches of Sioux away from the horse band, wounding or killing at least three braves. Both men were good with horses, too, though Hollister was the more patient and methodical of the two. Bowe's smooth, freckled face and sandy hair, coupled with a slim nose and straight mouth, lent him a boyish look that belied his years served on the Texas border and the cattle trails north. Like Hollister, his legs were bowed from years in the saddle. Both wore the southern belled spurs, the jingle bobs that rang when they walked, which was as seldom as possible. They also wore the heavy chaps which were designed to turn the brambles and thorns of the Texas thicket country. Their stirrups had tapaderos, too, to protect their legs and feet. Both had thrown their sawbucks and gear in the barn's tack room when they'd first come, and Smith's tack being still there, had asked the inevitable questions. Toby had left while Frank explained what had happened to the little wrangler. The way they'd taken it, Frank knew they had heard it before, probably from Irvine. It heartened him. They most likely wouldn't quit if the going got a little rough.

The horse band had stirred the enthusiasm of the two hands. Though Bowe had decried the lack of buckskins in the bunch, he'd had to admit that Matthew had bought well. The stallion caught their eye

136

immediately and both sung its praises, to Matthew's intense satisfaction.

"Now, if he was just a buckskin," Chipper lamented, "he'd be perfect!"

* * *

Lycurgeous Smith, the woodhawk who'd settled east of the mouth of the Rosebud, came up to see them when the grass hay was getting ripe. He was a lean man, worn down by hard living and hard work in the cottonwood groves along the river, supplying the steamboats with their needed cords of wood. His boy, a heavily muscled, retarded youth of about twenty, came with him. They refused to come into the cabin but sat on the ground in front of the door, sipping their coffee.

"This's my kid, Zeb. He's a little slow but he's a hell of a worker. We'd like to know if you might buy some hay from us. Those mares of yours'll need feed through the winter, if it's a hard one."

"Sure," Matthew told him. "We're in the market for some. How much a ton?"

"Ten dollars a ton, same as the cordwood per cord,"

"That'd be fine. Bring us up five or six cords of wood, too." Matthew thought. "We'll be doing some haying ourselves, but you can start with fifty tons."

"Guess we could do that but we'd have to charge a little more for haulage, say two dollars a ton for delivery."

"Be all right if you do." They shook hands.

"Say, guess you boys knew the grading crews were coming in to get the track beds ready along the river?" Smith asked. It picked the ears up of all the men.

"What do you mean, Smith?" Frank asked.

"From what I heard from Marsh, Northern Pacific's making a hell of a push, trying to get up to the gold fields. They reached Glendive already and they're laying track west from there about a mile and a half a day. They're sending surveyors and grading crews along the river all the way up to Livingston. Should be in Miles town sometime this month."

He spit out his cud of tobacco and took another drink of coffee.

"Ain't progress somethin'?"

"Yeah," Frank said sourly. "It's real great."

"They already talked to me 'bout crossin' my land, fixin' to pay me $200.00 to do it. But I heard they was claimin' a lot of the ground along the right-of-way by pre-emption."

After Smith left, they held council and it was decided that Matthew should go to Miles City to the land office and see about getting a solid claim on their place. Bowe would go with him, along with eleven head that were ready to sell.

"Now, Matthew, try not to spill any blood while you boys're in there. We're gonna wear out our welcome."

Next day they cut the broke stock out from the band of geldings and the two headed for town. Frank stewed while they were gone, nervous as a cat on a skillet, until finally Toby turned the horse they were working out of the corral and into the holding pasture.

Exasperated, Frank asked him, "Why'd you do that, son?"

"'Cause all we were doing was stirring the poor thing up, we weren't getting anywhere with him." He hung up the halter. Frank was set back but finally decided the boy was right.

"Oh, well, in that case, let's go do some shootin'. I want to see you try killin' some rocks if I throw 'em." He paused in the door of the tack room.

"You're right, son, never mess with horses when your mind isn't on it."

Toby snorted, "My mind!"

* * *

Matthew and Chipper Bowe came back a little after dusk and Frank lit a lantern to give them some light in the barn. Far off in the northwest, a front of dark clouds threw streaks of lightning in irregular patterns. Thunder muttered. Sometimes, when the cloud layers were right they could hear the hide hunters still at work north of the river, the distant sound of their guns like far-off thunder. It hurt Frank to hear it, because he knew, they all knew, that it heralded the end of the buffalo. A bitter end.

"Damn fools gotta shoot, shoot, shoot, even with the hides not prime," he thought. "But, then, who am I to talk? When I started, I was just as bad," That made him feel worse.

Matthew had filed on their claim; luckily it was on ground not already claimed by the railroad. They'd had no trouble, seen nothing of Stringer Jack's crew.

The country that summer began to fill up. With Miles City the end of track, settlers were streaming in. The Howards had settled twelve miles up Rosebud Creek. They were bringing in their families next year, after their buildings were up and the hostiles thinned out. A hunter named Pete Jackson had taken up land on the north side at the mouth of the Little Porcupine Creek, on the flat below Table top Butte. Jackson, who was known by Frank and Matthew from Bozeman, was quite a hunter, having meat hunted for the miners in the west for years. East of him, a sheep man named A.M. Cree had brought several bands in to Horse Creek and was settling in. Another man named Albright had homesteaded across from Smith on the river's north side and started a little store in his house. Smith had brought the news of them when he'd come up with another load of hay. He seemed to know everything that transpired in a hundred mile radius.

"Country's filling up with people now the Army's gettin' the redskins under control. Have to hand it to the General, he's a stiff son-of-a-bitch, but he did the job when Crook, Custer and Terry couldn't handle it." He accepted a refill, sitting as usual on the ground in front of the door. "Hear he's gonna be leaving soon. They're shipping him back east to a desk job at Washington. Wonder who they'll bring in?"

* * *

That fall, Matthew took Toby down along the river bottom for some bird hunting. Frank wouldn't go, claiming it hurt his shoulder, which had been bothering him. The geese and ducks were flying up and down the river in dense flocks. Toby used one of Matthew's shotguns and the old man showed him how to put a correct lead on the swift flying feathered projectiles. They hid along the river bank and managed several braces of mallards and canvasbacks. Once in a while they'd down a big goose, the heavy body falling from the sky so hard it would split the breast when it smacked the ground. Cappy loved the outings, his whole body quivering with anticipation when he saw the two getting their gear together. Eventually he made a fair retriever, though his mouth was hard and they had to argue with him over the birds at times.

139

His coat was thin like a horse's and he wouldn't brave the cold water, no matter how much Toby coaxed and pleaded, so they made sure they dropped their prey on land.

Several times the three went southward to some of the chokecherry and wild plum coulees where the sharp-tail grouse liked to feed. The buff colored birds rose in whirring flocks when they flushed them and were good sport, much better eating than the tough, gamey sage hens that were numerous, also. Those birds, bigger and darker than the prairie chickens, were also more stupid, walking in front of them and sometimes refusing to fly until Cappy would grab one. Then they would raise on ponderous wings and glide off down into another coulee.

It was while they were down along the river one crisp fall day that Toby, idly waiting for a flock of ducks to pass his spot under the cottonwoods by the river, saw a flurry of insect activity in the air to his right, off at the edge of a little clearing. He watched for a while, then moved to the clearing's center and saw that the activity was bees, and that they were flying into a hole in a huge dead cottonwood way high up on its broad trunk. 'That's a bee tree,' he thought.'Bet the old thing is filled with honey.'

That evening Toby mentioned his find to the men at the supper meal and Frank got excited.

"Why, boys, we can get that honey this fall! We'll smoke 'em out and cut that old snag down, slick as you please! Ain't nothin' better than wild honey and we'll have barrels of it! Why, we can sell it in Miles this winter for a bunch 'cause every man I know has a sweet tooth for honey."

The others weren't that eager. In fact, Hollister claimed that bees made him swell up like a 'toad frog.' "No, sir. He hadn't signed on to corral any flying bugs, thank you."

"Well, hell, Bill, we can handle the tree without you, but just remember how good that honey is on buttered biscuits when we're eatin' it and you're not." Eventually, Frank talked them all into helping, even the reluctant Hollister.

Frank went about his preparations with all the care and tactical methodism of a wily general planning a campaign. He gathered up and washed all the containers around the place, cherishing especially the gallon kerosene containers, which had to be boiled. He stopped one of the steamboats and bought some more washtubs and pails. He also bought a bunch of burlap sacks. Getting some long sticks, he wrapped the ends in sacking.

"Come to the day, we'll dip these in kerosene. They'll make a good smudge for us," he explained to his dubious helpers.

They waited for a cold morning, then Frank gathered his cross-cut saw, smudge sticks, and containers and loaded the equipment in the wagon. Bill brought the horses and they hitched the team. Heading down to the river bottom, they noticed the trees had finished turning their fall colors and leaves were starting to drop from the branches. A jackrabbit bounced from beneath a sagebrush, its fur a blotchy brown and white, its color change a harbinger of the coming winter. A bunny or two peered from their little burrows as they passed by.

"Looks like Toby hasn't got all the rabbits close by with his little popgun, have you, son?" Frank chuckled. He was in high spirits, repeatedly telling them, "Wait 'til you taste that honey, boys!"

They pulled down close to the tree and dropped their gear off, then pulled the team off quite a ways to protect the horses.

"Alright, boys, pull these sacks over your hats and put your gloves on. Start the pots and the smudge sticks." They got the smudges going and Frank took his lariat, threw it over a high limb and then made a loop in its end.

"I'll stick my foot in, boys, and you pull me up there." He took one of the smoldering sticks and held on to the rope as they pulled on the other end, dragging him foot by foot up to the hole high in the bole of the tree. When they had just about gotten him there, several bees flew out of the tree and zeroed in on Frank. He ignored them and stuffed the smudge into the hole.

"Now let me down," he hollered.

Bowe chopped the kerf, the axe blows giving off a hollow sound. The cross-cut saw ate through the tree, Frank taking a turn with the rest. When the saw cut had nearly reached the kerf, the tree started leaning and Matthew shouted for them to clear away. Toby noticed that Hollister ran off a good distance before he turned to the tree's crash.

The big cottonwood hit and burst like a ripe melon, spilling honey and combs in the wreck, together with mad, bewildered but cold bees who sluggishly crawled over one another, some dropping from the heavy smoke.

"Damn, boys, she's busted on us! Get the pails and save what you can!" Frank ordered, waving the smoking sticks over the tree.

Toby grabbed a bucket and dipped honey into a tub 'til it was full, the others doing the same. The broken combs went in, also, along with dead bees and debris. Chopping open the trunk, they were able to get at the rest, saving quite a bit.

Finally Frank sent Bill off to get the team and wagon. They loaded the gear and the tubs in and headed home. Frank was exultant and they all were in good spirits, with the exception perhaps, of Toby, who had some regrets about the destroyed bee colony. Despite his early fears, none had been too badly bitten.

After Frank and his helpers had gotten done cleaning the honey, they ended up with over twenty gallons. To celebrate the occasion, Toby set in and made several dozen sourdough biscuits. They spread honey on warm bread and ate 'til they were stuffed. Even Matthew had to admit the idea had been a good one. Frank beamed.

Later on, they stopped a steamboat, the *F. Y. Batchelor* , and Bill and Frank took fifteen gallons aboard to trade to Leighton. They gave Captain Todd a gallon for the ride down river, leaving him well satisfied.

Getting off at the landing, they piled the gallons of honey on the wharf, where Frank left Bill to watch over them. He came back with a wagon from Leighton's and they loaded the honey aboard. At Leighton's store, Frank proceeded to buy a winter's supply of groceries: 300 pounds of sugar, 400 pounds of flour, 50 pounds of coffee, dried fruits, canned tomatoes, peaches, milk, sides of smoke bacon, 100 pounds of salt and some other assorted condiments. Then he brought plenty of 44/40 ammunition and .44 and .45 pistol caliber. He also bought some winter clothes and buffalo coats for the whole crew. Matthew had instructed him to gather all the reading material he could find, so Leighton obligingly gave him a bunch of back issue *Yellowstone Journals* and *Police Gazettes* he'd accumulated. Joe had tasted the honey and told him he'd go fifteen dollars a gallon. The honey money more than paid their winter supply bill, a fact which made Frank chortle, to Bill's growing irritation. The fact was that all the outfit had heard about enough of honey and bees, though they were happy about the good tasting sweet stuff stored in the root cellar.

Joe was inclined to visit.

"What'd you think of me and Irvine sending you a couple Texicans like Bill here and Chipper Bowe?"

"You done good, alright, Joe. Tell Irvine for me, too, if I don't see him. Only thing is, Bill here is a little spooky around bugs; has a downright hate for 'em, seems like. I figger it comes from somethin' that happened when he's a kid back in Texas. The bugs down there grow big as sage hens, you know. Sometimes you'd look up and see somethin' in the sky, comin' down at you, lookin' big as a turkey vulture. But it'd be a mud dauber wasp that you'd have to shoot. Now, up here in this cold country, I figger it stunts their growth by havin' to go through these winters and they can't even get a start on growin', but Bill's still feared of 'em."

Leighton and Bill just shook their heads.

"Speaking of cold, Frank, I just got something in back here you'd probably like. Let me show you."

They followed Joe to the rear of the store, threading their way through bales of blankets, wool underwear and piles of coats and wool shirts. Near the back, they came on some stoves. Joe stopped at a beautiful one with nickel hardware all over it and shining isinglass windows.

"This here is a new type of heater stove, comes with a coal grate, along with the regular grate. It's called a 'Smokeless Garland,' and it'd sure keep you warm in that big cabin of yours." He opened the door, adjusted grates, showed them its large capacity interior, which would hold a huge amount of wood or coal.

"What's the tariff on a stove like that?" Frank asked dubiously.

"Well, to you, I'll sell for a hundred even."

"Consider it bought. I like the idea of a warm cabin in my old age." Frank took five golden eagles out of his money belt and handed them over.

"Considering the 'honey money,' guess we're still ahead," he crowed.

Bill groaned and went up to look at the guns while the two old timers continued to look at the stove.

"The news? Well," Joe said, "the most of it you can read in the *Journals.* Knight seems to sniff out more than even I ever hear. Guess you know we got us a railroad now. No more can we merchants use the excuse, "It'll be up on the next boat or the first boat in the spring!" Joe chuckled, "Railroad coming in sure has dropped the freight prices on things, like your stove, for instance. But that's a rough crowd the railroad's got on their track gang. Several shootings and roughhouses between the soldiers and some of our resident toughs and the track layers. Things been even livelier around here lately."

"How's the hunting been? The buffalo about done?" Frank asked.

"It's been pretty good. Prices are up, plenty of buffalo out north, but some of the hunters don't know how to take care of the hides. Lots of 'em are rotting on the ground. I can't see another year of it, Frank."

"Nor can I, and maybe it's best to get it over with and done."

"I've made a lot of money out of the business, but I have to say I agree. I'll be glad myself, when it's done. It's a dirty business."

Keeping their belt guns handy and their eyes peeled, they walked down to Tate's, where Bill had several whiskies and Tate set up coffee for Frank. The bar was nearly full of soldiers, and O'Brien and his shadow, the red-haired corporal, came charging over to shake Frank's hand and have a drink.

"See you boys have adopted Tate here for your waterin' hole," Frank remarked after he'd introduced Bill.

"Yeah, Tate's been good to us. Loans the boys money 'til payday and such." O'Brien responded, "He doesn't cuss the army either, like some of the towners I could name."

Next day they caught the *Rosebud* on its last up-river run, their stove and supplies stowed on deck. At their landing, the steamboat hooted several times while they unloaded, and pretty soon, Chipper Bowe showed up with the wagon to cart the stuff up the draw.

"What the hell is that?" Matthew asked as they came puffing into the cabin with the heavy stove. "And how much did it cost? Good God, Frank, we can't even send you to town for supplies without you shooting someone or buying some contraption."

"This here is a 'Smokeless Garland' stove, and when you go sticking your feet out of your bedroll of a winter night when it's fifty below and the cabin's still warm from this big hunk of iron being stoked up, you'll thank your old pard time and again for being so smart as to buy it for us."

"How much did the damn thing cost?" Matthew persisted, peering at the big hunk of shining iron.

"Well, I got it cheap, a hundred dollars, but I traded honey for all our other supplies," Frank replied, "Pretty good, huh?"

"Hum. Well, I have to admit you made a good trade if you got our winter supplies with the honey, but please, please, can we get off the

144

honey subject, finally?" Matthew pleaded. The remark brought a chorus of amens from the others which made Frank glare.

When they got the stove set up, Frank pronounced, "We're set now, boys! Hay up, wood stacked, a good stove, supplies in. Weather turns a shade colder, we'll drop a couple buffalo and hang 'em by the spring here. We'll let Toby get a couple whitetails down on the river, too!"

* * *

The winter came with a rush. Overnight the temperature dropped to zero. Yet, always across the river they could hear the boom of the hunters' guns, a sound they, for the most part, tried to shut out. As the cold increased, the river began to freeze and the ducks and geese grew fewer along its banks. Bowe took Toby to the river, then, and they jumped whitetails in the brush 'til the boy got a shot at a big five-point buck. He downed it with one shot, but felt sad as he watched the big brown eyes glaze over in death. Bowe patted his shoulder. "Don't feel bad, kid. He had a good life heah on earth and he's going to deer heaven. We'll cut his tail off, see, and hang it in the tree, heah. The Indians say it frees the spirit of the deer on up there." They did that, and for some reason, Toby felt better.

He woke one day to look out the window and see all the brush, trees, even the grass and ground laced silvery with frost, while the cold air itself was crystal clear. Matthew and Frank were both at a loss to explain the phenomenon: some trick of nature that froze the moisture in the air and dropped it to the ground, Matthew thought. Whatever the reason, it looked like all the trees were wearing dresses, Toby thought, of purest white.

With the weather change, the amount of travelers passing by dwindled until only one or two a week were showing up. One of those who did come by, though, was Granville Stuart, traveling with a couple friends, Luther "Yellowstone" Kelley and Gene Lamphere.

"Get down, get down, boys," Frank hollered when he saw them ride up.

"We'll just stay for a cup or two, Frank. We want to get over to Fort Custer if we can, before dark. Wanted to see how you boys had made out with your horse outfit. Borden and the others told me you were doing fine and you had some pretty good stock. Any for sale?"

They trooped in and sat up to the table, after remarking enviously on Frank's pride and joy, the big heater stove doing its duty in the center of the cabin. Toby poured out the coffee and set out some biscuits and honey in a crock jar. The men's eyes lit up. Stuart threw off his big buffalo coat.

"Hey, bread and honey!" Kelley exclaimed, "You boys're feeding high on the hog!"

Frank told them about the honey tree while they pitched into the biscuits and sipped their coffee.

"Now, how's the horse business treating you, Frank?" Stuart asked, petting Cappy's big head as he came over, insisting on being noticed.

"Good, so far. Matthew went east and bought all the way to Chicago. Most of the horses came from there, at the auction yards. We been working the geldings out and taking 'em into the Army. What they reject, Leighton or Hubbell been taking off our hands. Sold a few to passers-by and outfits close around, too. In the spring, Matthew's gonna take another run to Chicago, if we can get him to go. He don't like all the people back there. We been talkin' Denver, too."

"What's chances of buying some geldings, preferably broke, but I'll take what I can get?" Stuart asked as he ladled honey on another fluffy biscuit.

"Well, we got about thirty head of geldings left. About half of 'em broke. I guess we could ride out there and you could take a look, see if you wanted them. I warn you, though, they won't be cheap."

Stuart rose, stuffing the last of the biscuit in his mouth, and the others got up, too. Frank threw on his coat and grabbed his spurs.

"Stay here, son, and we'll go on out. You might as well plan on 'em being here for dinner." He went out and the men were cinching up, climbing in the saddle, their bulky clothes making it awkward. He led them down to the barn where he had his big black, that he'd named Ben. Throwing his saddle on, he proceeded to cinch up and lead him out.

"There's a nice horse, Frank. Is he Thoroughbred?" Stuart said admiringly. "A big one."

"Yeah, I like 'em big and Matthew knows it. He bought him for me. We got some others left that look about as good. We were putting a little more time on 'em to sell for officers' horses."

He swung into the saddle and they rode out south where Bowe was holding the geldings in a long grassy draw. He'd started a little fire and had his own coffee going. Frank hailed the fire as they rode up, knowing Bowe was alert to their coming, anyway.

One of Stuart's men, Kelley, knew Bowe already and they visited back and forth while gathering the herd for Stuart to view. The horses were in good shape, snorting and playful in the snappy cold weather.

"We bring 'em out and herd 'em like sheep," Frank explained, "Then, nights, we bring 'em in closer to our holding pasture and water 'em. Haven't lost a one, so far!" Frank said proudly. "The snow gets too deep, we'll herd 'em close and feed 'em bluestem, the best horse hay there is."

Stuart rode back and forth through the loose bunch of horses 'til finally he rode over to the fire, where Frank was talking with Bowe.

"Believe I'll just try to take some off your hands, Frank, if we can do a deal," Stuart stated, getting down to warm his hands.

"Should have my number one dealer here to talk this high finance. He and Hollister are across the river, lookin' for buffalo. I can tell you what the army's been paying for top horses, but I'm betting you know already, from being friends with Borden and all." Frank hedged.

"Yes, I do know." Stuart's grave face cracked in a smile. "But I see a couple there that I couldn't pay that much for; that one dun, for instance." He pointed.

"Yeah, there's a couple, three that we were planning on selling to Hubbell, probably," Frank admitted, "And the boys all got a horse in there that they've had their eye on, too. Suppose you let us cut the herd and we'll see where we're at."

Stuart assented and the men held the little bunch while he and Bowe moved through and cut out several horses belonging to Toby and the rest of them. Then Frank cut out the dun and another horse that Stuart pointed to. Bowe kept this little bunch separate from the rest.

"There now, does that suit you a little better?" Frank asked.

"Well, I hated to see you cut that sorrel and the big buckskin back," Stuart replied. Frank laughed.

"The one's Toby's and the buckskin belongs to Chipper. Used to be Healey's, remember?"

"Now you mention it, I do," Stuart agreed, "Those left I could go $150 for, I guess."

"Don't believe we could let 'em go for that," Frank bargained, "I was thinking more in the $200 range."

"Well, I could go to the middle of those figures, I guess, to $180," Stuart came back.

"Make it $185, and we're in the middle, square," Frank countered.

"Should have talked with the easy end of the pardnership," Stuart groused, "I probably could have swung a better deal."

Frank chuckled, "I doubt it. Matthew's been set on getting $200 for this little bunch, just the way we cut 'em. We were gonna put a few more rides on 'em, though." He thought a little. "Fact is, he probably would go $180 for you, Stuart, so let's leave it at that."

Stuart protested, "Hell's bells, man. I'm well satisfied with $185." They shook hands and started the bunch to the barn.

They corralled the horses, then went up to eat Toby's meal, after which Stuart paid Frank with a check: which, coming from Stuart, Frank knew was good. Then Frank dictated a bill of sale that Toby wrote out and proudly signed. Frank put his X on it and Toby signed it for him, too.

"Guess you don't want to sell the sorrel, eh, Toby?" Stuart smiled, tucking the bill of sale in his vest pocket.

"No, sir. That horse and I are pardners, now. I couldn't do that," Toby resisted, "Tell you, though, sir, Frank might sell that big black of his," he retorted with a shy smile.

"Huh, fat chance in hell of that. Matthew'd shoot both of us." Frank snorted, "Wish you'd had time to go out and look at the stud we're using. He's a good one."

"Maybe next time, Frank. We'd better get on the trail with these before a blizzard catches us. You all take care. These stock thieves are getting more active as time goes by, and you know, they don't hold much love for you or Matthew." Stuart rose to leave.

"Appreciate your concern, and you can bet we're keeping a sharp eye out." Frank and Toby followed them out to the porch as Stuart swung into the saddle.

"See you in the spring, then. We'll have a herd coming up that should be here in July or August. Maybe I'll come down and meet it. If so, I'll see you then. Might be in the market for some more stock about that time, if you've got any left." He waved as Kelley and Lamphere started the horse band down the trail to the west, then turned and followed them over the rim of the hill.

* * *

A month went by. The river froze hard and Bowe went across on the ice to shoot a couple buffalo with his partner, Bill, taking the team with them. Neither Matthew nor Frank would go, and Toby wouldn't go without them. They didn't press him.

Toby had filled out and shot up, it seemed like overnight. His parents must have been of Scandinavian blood, the old men thought. His blonde head and blue eyes gave him the eagle look of a young Viking. His strength was coming to him also, in the widening of his wrists, the swelling of his arms and legs with muscle.

Matthew, observing him carefully, was concerned about his gentleness. He displayed a patience and kindness with the horses which usually got more done than the harsher methods employed by the others, but the gentleness was disturbing to both men, inured as they were to the vagaries of the frontier. Both knew a gentle person was not one who could long survive out there, life was too harsh.

Two days later, Chipper Bowe and Hollister came back with a buffalo cow, which they hung up and skinned. They pulled the quarters high into the trees to keep wolves and the ever-present coyotes from bothering it and tarped them to keep the magpies and crows off.

* * *

One night Toby woke to see Cappy gone from beside his bed and standing by the door. He got up to let him out and when he opened the door, Cappy stood in it, in an attitude of listening. Drowsily, Toby did the same. He heard it then, a muffled eerie thumping. It sounded down the draw, somewhere close by the west trail. He went back, thinking to waken the men, but Matthew rose up, putting a finger to his lips. Toby went to his bunk and pulled on his boots. Matthew swung out from his and did the same. Together, they followed Cappy as he padded down the draw, the night cool but not really cold. The moon was full and the reflected light shone blue from the snow on the ground. For some reason, neither spoke, just followed Cappy as he went along. Had he shown alarm they would have perhaps been more cautious. Indeed, Matthew, from force of habit, had slipped his gun belt on, but didn't tell Toby to do the same.

149

Over the hill, Cappy stopped and Toby and Matthew came up behind him. The thumping sound was louder and they saw its source, the sight raising the hair on the nape of both their necks. Several yards from them, but oblivious to them, was a ring of jackrabbits. The ring of animals was approximately ten yards across, and composed of about sixty or seventy of the large, white bunnies on a wind-swept bench. As they watched, one of the upright figures began thumping its hind leg on the frozen ground. Across the ring, another figure began, then several started in reply. It was a strange sight, a phenomenon of nature that even Matthew in his experience, had never seen and was at a loss to explain. Cappy, uncharacteristically, stayed close to his humans, and didn't try to chase the rabbits. The three watched for a while then went back to the cabin as quiet as they had come. The sight later was the source of much conversation, with the others testifying to its oddity. None had heard or seen such a thing but each could relate different strange freaks of nature they had witnessed.

* * *

All winter, they'd worked at times on their gear. Hollister was an expert braider, braiding halters, reins, hatbands, whatever he could with the material he had at hand. He'd worked the horse's tails hard fall and winter, cut up hides for rawhide, even cut up old clothing for making soft ropes to use on the horses. Each of the others had pieces of gear that Hollister had made. For Christmas, Hollister had given Toby a beautiful hackamore and reins he'd made.

Chipper Bowe was a leather worker. With his little kit of tools, he could repair, stitch and refashion harnesses, saddles, headstalls, even belts and chaps. When asked by Toby where he'd learned, he explained, "An old Mexican I used to hang around when I was a ranch kid taught me most of it. Rest of it I just picked up here and there." From Bowe, they had all gotten new belts, something Toby, growing like he was, badly needed.

The turkey dinner that day was a masterpiece of Toby's culinary art and all the men praised the meal, to the Boy's intense satisfaction. Matthew hadn't spoken again to him about his going to school back East, and he certainly wasn't going to bring it up. His life was right here.

In January, Irvine and a deputy, Jack Johnson, stopped in. The temperature was about twenty degrees with a light snowfall coming down and the men were stiff and frozen from their ride. Frank went out to wait with them as they put their horses in the barn.

"Did you boys stop at Janey's place?"

"Stopped, but she wasn't there. A couple whiskey bums were, though, and they said she was down in the gulch somewhere, at the railroad camp." Irvine replied.

He stripped off his saddle and bridle, and Frank forked some hay down for the saddle horses and the pack horse carrying their gear. "We went on down there, had a tip on a stolen horse, but we never found it." Frank closed the barn door and they headed back to the cabin. Irvine spoke again.

"This stock thieving is getting out of hand, Frank. We got stock being stolen in Montana and taken to the Black Hills to sell. Horses stolen in Wyoming and the Black Hills are coming up here and stuff getting stole elsewhere is going both ways. It seems well organized and there's a good mind or two behind it. Just now, I'm beginning to think the worst thing I did was to keep Matthew from killing Jack Stringer. I'm pretty sure he's one of the heads, if not *the* head of the gang up around here. Parrott was the head, I think, down in Wyoming, and I just got word they lynched him down at Rawlings. That's good news, at least, but it hasn't stopped the rustling."

They reached the cabin and went in to a hot meal, well appreciated by the two travelers. Bowe and Hollister were out with the horses and Matthew sent Toby out with their meal. Stumpy Jack, his leg shot off in the war, massaged his stump while they talked.

"From what we heard from Biedler, Teton Jackson's crew is operating out of Jackson Hole. Up north, around the Musselshell and across the North Side, we got Stringer Jack's outfit. They're buying horses from the Indians with whiskey and guns, taking 'em up into Canada to sell and bringing stolen Canadian horses back down here. The Mounties up north been having fits with the Sioux being in cahoots with 'em and doing a lot of their sneak work. Down south there, we got a lot of stock movement around the Hole-in-the-Wall country. Nate Champion runs a gang down on that end. He's a different kind of hardcase, a smart one like Stringer. They're all having a good time switching stock from one area to the next, egging on the Indians, and stealing a payroll or killing a miner or a hunter from time to time. Most of them run a sideline, like hide hunting or mining to explain their having money, if a lawman gets curious."

He looked around, then said quietly, "And that's another thing. There's a few lawmen around that aren't lined up on the right side, if you take my meaning. We're going to have to organize ourselves. I've talked to Stuart and some others about it, already. Keep it quiet, though. We'll get in touch."

He gave them all a long level look. "When we go to move on 'em, we'll need horses. Can we rely on fifteen or so from you boys?"

Matthew looked at Frank, then nodded without speaking. Frank said, "Hell yes, you can, and our guns, too, far's that goes."

* * *

In March, a chinook began that blew off the remaining snow and started all the streams and coulees running. Travel was difficult, if not downright impossible, in the gumbo hills and they laid off working the horses in the muddy corral. Toby and Frank were busy putting the finishing touches on a buffalo roast meal, complete with biscuits, frying pan bread and honey, when they heard a deep rumbling sound like thunder, from the direction of the river. Matthew went to the door and watched for a while, "The ice is going out on the river, looks like."

They all went to the porch to watch. Big chunks of ice were tipping up and bumping against each other. They could hear the grinding of the cakes rubbing against each other from their vantage point.

"Soon as it clears, we can expect the boats upriver to Custer and Coulson," Frank mentioned.

The first boat arrived four days later, and Frank and Toby met it at the landing. It was the *Batchelor.* Some deckhands ran out the plank and Frank went aboard to visit with Captain Todd. When he came back down the plank to shore, he saw Toby speaking with a bearded young man. He looked familiar and when he saw Frank, he held out his hand.

"Hello, Frank, how've you been?"

"Why, hells bells, if it isn't Jason!" Frank exclaimed. He grabbed the proffered hand.

"I'm fine, son, how's things with you?" Frank's keen eye took in the young man's shabby clothes and lack of gear. "Down on your luck, son?" he asked kindly. He'd been there himself.

152

"Oh, no. Been doing all right. Worked as a skinner for a while, then on the railroad. I've got a chance just now to hire on with the survey crew going west, but I need a horse. I heard you were raising horses, so I thought I might come out and see if I could buy one from you. They're scarce in town right now, and pretty dear." He grinned at Toby and stopped to pet Cappy, who appeared to remember him.

"What happened to Whitey?" Toby innocently asked. Jason's shamed look told volumes, and the boy didn't press it.

"We've got horses to sell, don't we, Frank? Especially to old friends," Toby added, "Why, I could sell him my little buckskin cheap. I never ride him like I should,"

"Well, son, you could do that, if you'd like to. Maybe we could throw Smith's saddle in on the deal," Frank told him cheerily.

They brought Jason up to the spring, where he showed an interest in everything they'd accomplished, met Bowe and Hollister, and exclaimed over the sorrel horse that Toby proudly showed him.

"I can't decide which I like best, Frank's black or that sorrel of yours, Toby," he stated, "Guess I'd have to pick your sorrel, I like his head a little better." The choice pleased Toby and made Frank snort.

The next morning he started off, headed back to the Gulch, riding Toby's little Indian buckskin, mounted on Smith's saddle. Toby had insisted he take no more than $80 for the deal, which Jason quickly paid, in gold double eagles. Something about the way he clinked them in his hand before handing them over to the boy made Matthew pause, but he dismissed the thought.

* * *

With the coming of spring, Frank brought up a sore subject. "Guess we'd better think about you heading for Chicago on a horse buying trip in a while or so, pard,"

"I suppose so, but I don't look forward to that again, by any means. Think I'll take Chipper and Toby with me, if you can handle it alright here with Bill."

"Me and Bill can do 'er, but it'll be a strain with just the two of us," Frank hedged, "Wonder if another hand wouldn't be a good idea through foaling time?" He winked.

"Or, you might leave Toby home."

Matthew smiled.

"Yes, maybe we could do that."

Toby had an anguished look on his face. "Aww, Frank, you're spoiling my trip. You and Matthew said I could go."

Frank relented with a grin.

"Well, son, we did at that. Guess Bill and I'll go into Miles before you boys take off. We'll pick up supplies and cast around a little for a man to help us while you're gone."

Daylight next morning found the men down at the barn hitching the team to the wagon. Bill drove it up to the cabin, then, with Frank following on his 'Ben' horse. They ate breakfast and, fortified by a couple last cups of coffee, were on their way to Miles City. The wagon path, too primitive yet to be called a road, was getting worn in now by travel. Most of the crossings of coulees and creeks had been worked on by those going through, flat sandstone rocks thrown in at strategic places being the most frequent and advantageous repair. The wagon, with Frank following horseback to provide extra pulling power if need be, made good time, and they pulled into Janey's in little over an hour. She came to the door and hailed them into the cabin.

She appeared to be in good spirits and health, though gaunt, Frank thought, probably from the winter's bout with the bottle. The cabin was neat appearing and she was alone. She bustled around, pouring the coffee.

"Frank, I just gotta tell you! Had quite an experience a little time back. One of the track layers came up, asking if I'd come down and take a look at his wife. She was real sick. She'd gotten a case of winter fever living in one of those damn dugouts down in the gulch, there. Damn poor quarters, especially for a woman, and her pregnant! So, I brought 'er up here and nursed her a while, and by God, she had 'er baby, a baby girl, right here! Probably the first white baby born around here. So I got to play nursemaid and babysitter. They're good people, name of Barley. He likes the country and he's gonna take up a homestead, other side of the river. They're tough people, both hard workers, should do real well." [Author's note: This is the story of my Grandmother's birth, as I got it from her.]

She sat down and chatted with them a while and they learned the grade crew had begun working around the bluffs west of the Rosebud.

"Yeah, we heard the work trains pulling past, down by the bluffs there," Frank mentioned, "They run the line that close to the river, they're gonna have to rip-rap their track bed awful heavy or the river'll take it. Probably will, anyway."

"They are, they're bringing granite in all the way from the Black Hills. The NP does it up right, for sure. They brought in a bridge, put it together, set it across the Rosebud and were laying track on the other side in three days! I'm thinkin' of moving on myself, on up the river."

They got into Miles in the afternoon, and pulled into Hubbell's to put up the team. The town was busier than ever. Leading his black horse, Frank walked with Bill down the street to Leighton's. The big sleek black drew several admiring looks from the numerous stockmen and drovers on the boardwalk. One individual, a square faced man, his hat back on his head, planted his bow legs in front of them as they started to pass by and stated, "Gentlemen, I sure admire a good horse, and there's one at the end of those reins. Might I ask if he'd be for sale?" The tanned face was split by a friendly grin, and Frank took no offense.

"Can't say that he is, but I can see you're a man who knows a good horse."

The other laughed, and replied.

"Yes, I've been afoot enough times to appreciate the four-legged animals that carry us around,"

The young man, evidently a drover himself, asked them in for a drink and they went into Tate's, leaving Ben at the hitch rail.

Tate, talking to a soldier at the end of the bar, came down when he saw Frank and shook hands with him and Bill.

"Good to see you boys. Looks like you wintered well. How's your pard?"

He set up a drink for Bill and the drover, poured coffee for Frank and himself. When the drover mentioned Frank's horse, Tate walked to the door and looked.

Coming back, he said, "Hell of a nice horse, alright, Frank. He's got a lot of leg under him. I'd say he'd show some speed, is that right?"

"Fact is, I've never had occasion yet to run him out. Matthew brought him back for me last fall," Frank replied.

"I'd like to see him run." The drover downed his whiskey and Tate set up another round.

"Plenty of good horses in town. What say we get up a race for tomorrow?" The cowboy, who'd introduced himself as Charlie Russell, urged.

"Well," Frank hedged, "should get back tomorrow. Told my pard we'd be there by evening."

"Well, hell, Frank. It won't take long to run a race. We could load up early tomorrow, run it, and still be home by sundown," Bill protested.

Frank gave in.

"Guess that might work. I'd like to run him, myself."

The drover left them, saying he was going over to the MacQueen House to drum up some business. "We'll charge a $50 entry. Tate can hold the stakes. Winner takes the pot. That alright with you boys?" he said, before leaving.

Frank agreed. Bill looked fidgety.

"Gettin' too damn old to be racing horses. Bill, why don't you ride for me?" Frank asked him, knowing what the trouble was.

Bill looked thoughtful for just a second, then assented, "Guess I could, if you want me to. I'll use my saddle, too. It's not as heavy as that Myers you ride."

"Tate, here's my fifty, then, and another $100 for you to bet." Frank dug in his money belt and pulled some gold coins out. "Matthew's death on me drinking but he never said anything 'bout me gamblin'. Guess I better hand some wages over, Bill, so's you can spend a little, too." Bill looked pleased as Frank clanked more gold coins on the bar and pushed them over to him.

"There, you're paid up to this month." Bill immediately gave Tate $100, also. Frank downed his coffee.

"Think I'll go down to Leighton's and buy supplies."

They ambled on down the street and went into Leighton's. Elmer, the clerk, met them and said Leighton was over at the bank.

"What can I do for you boys? You in town to do some stocking up? Been a long winter. You boys run short?"

Frank pulled his list out and gave it to Elmer, who immediately set off on a run to gather the supplies. Bill began gathering the things he wanted: new underwear, shirts, socks, pants, new kerchiefs. "I s'pose I should break down an get a new pair of boots, too," he remarked ruefully, looking at his cracked, separated old ones, victims of too much weather and horse manure.

"Well, I'll walk down to Boston's with you. Elmer says MacDonald's went out of business," Frank said, "I don't think we better travel around town alone."

They walked down the street, passing a Chinese wash house, a bakery, a couple saloons, Chinnick's being one, and a hardware store, Broadwater, Hubbell and Company at the corner of Fifth and Main. They went into a store advertised as the Boston Boot and Shoe Company, C. B. Tower, Proprietor. Next to it was Sipes Barber Shop, doing a brisk business.

"Let's get a shave and a haircut while we're here," Frank told Bill, gesturing to the place with his thumb as they went into Boston's.

They ate supper at MacQueen's and stayed there the night. Next morning at first light they ate a quick breakfast and went down to Hubbell's Livery, where they saddled Ben and hitched up the team. Sam was acting gloomy and Frank asked what was wrong.

"Damn railroad's running the company out of business. Won't be too long before I'll be looking for a job," he grumbled.

Frank looked at Bill.

"The hell you say. What are you making here, Sam?" Frank asked him.

"Forty a month and found. Gettin' too old to be cowboyin', but I guess I'm going to have to go lookin soon."

"Why don't you throw in your time, Sam, and come out to work for us?" Frank told him. "We need someone that's good with horses out at the ranch."

Sam looked startled, "You hiring?"

"Yeah, we could use a hand, for the summer and fall, anyway. Could probably use you even through the winter, if you wanted to stay."

"Thank you, Frank, I'll damn sure think about it."

"Think quick, because we're leaving this afternoon and we'll have to know before we do."

"I'll let you know. You'll be at Leighton's?"

"Sure will. Got a horse race to run at mid-day, then we're headin' back."

"You running this black?" Sam asked, interested.

"Now, Sam, thought I'd run one of the bay team here." Frank joshed. Bill laughed.

"Say, Frank, this here horse might win you some money. He looks pretty speedy," Sam told him, walking around Ben, ignoring the jibe. "Think I'll put a bet down on 'im."

Back at Leighton's, Frank hitched Ben to the rail, while Bill drove around to the back to load up. Joe bustled out as he stepped up on the boardwalk. "Frank!" He held out his hand.

"How do, Joe. Glad to see you!"

"I hear from Elmer that you're running this black today in a race. Is it pretty fast, Frank?" He stroked the black's silky nose.

"That's a good question, Joe. Guess we'll find out the answer today," Frank drawled.

After a visit, they loaded the wagon, then went down to Tate's. The place was full of soldiers and a few drovers, Russell among them. He got up from the table and came over when he saw them come in.

"Say there, boys, I've got quite a lineup for us. Daley's got a red roan he's goin' to run. Hutch has got a bay he thinks is fast, the LO's got a little buckskin, Whiskey Dick's gonna run his 'Little Pete' horse and Romer's got a thoroughbred he brought in from the N Bar. All fast horses, to hear their owners talk." They laughed. He stuck his thumbs in his cartridge belt. "Captain Borden heard about the race and the army's backin' a horse he put in, a big bay horse. The boys say it can run. Guess the '44 and Fannie French are both puttin' a horse up, too." He laughed.

"Wonder what they put up in the way of bets?"

"Hmmm." Frank looked thoughtful. Chances were they'd sold the horse to the army, but he wasn't sure which it was. They'd had a lot of bays in their bunch. Russell went on.

"We set it up for the usual, about a half mile right down the middle of town out to the big cottonwood with a flag on it and back again.

"Sounds like you got us a horse race, Russell," Frank said.

"Is our money covered?"

"You bet," the square faced young man rejoined, "Got any more you want up, I'm sure Tate could find someone to cover it, too."

"Well, a hundred's probably my limit. Sounds like the competition's pretty stiff."

"I'll put up another fifty," Bill said unexpectedly.

"Good man, Bill!" Frank said heartily. "Guess if you can, I will, too."

The racers assembled at noon in front of Tate's. Russell and a friend named Kid White got punchers to clear the street and watch the intersections so no drunks or pilgrims were run over.

Frank went with Tate to watch from the boardwalk with the rest.

Bill, stripped of his gun belt, hat and boots, his saddle minus lariat and taps, kneed the big black horse up to the line drawn in the street. Borden walked over to Frank and Tate, greeted them and at their request, pointed out the army's horse, a wiry little private aboard it. Frank's horse eyes noticed that, while there were some fine looking animals in the line, his Ben horse looked the best of them, he thought.

Another horse that took his eye especially, though, was the N Bar Thoroughbred, ridden by a little puncher stripped down like Bill was. The brown horse had the long topline, the small head, long legs of an animal bred for speed. The rest, with the exception of Borden's, were the shorter coupled, thicker muscled cow ponies, which, even so, couldn't be discounted. As the riders jockeyed for position up to the line, the crowd's attention was caught by another horse which was prancing up from behind the pack. Frank heard murmurs from the crowd.

"Fannie French's entry," Tate told him. "Sweet looking little mare, isn't it?"

"She's a beauty," Frank agreed. The horse was a small clean limbed gray Arabian mare with a young Negro riding. He brought it up to the line with effortless ease. His betting money suddenly seemed in danger, he thought. So be it. Like any Texan, he loved a horse race.

With nine excited horses and riders striving for position on the line across the street, it was inevitable that two or three would be edged out at the start, it seemed, but Charlie Brown, the starter, waited patiently for the lineup to sort itself out. At last, it did, and Brown's pistol blossomed flame.

The quick little mare jumped into an almost instant lead, the young Negro using the quirt with abandon on its rump. Borden's chestnut was hot on its heels and Frank saw with satisfaction that Bill and Ben were in third. The field drummed down the street, dirt flying and the crowd whooping and cheering. Though races were a fairly frequent affair in the horse-filled town, still they were always greeted with excited interest.

Just a few minutes later, a cry went up at the end of the street and all present knew that 'here they come'!

Frank craned out into the street and saw that the front runner was none of those who'd led the pack in the beginning. Rather, it was Romer's Thoroughbred, a beautiful dark bay, running strong. Then, with a thrill, he saw that Bill was crowding the Romer horse close behind, closing perhaps, the big black lunging furiously under Bill's urging. Close back of them came the little mare, still working hard, the Negro flat on the mare's short back, his arm still working the quirt. The rest, including Borden's horse, were strung out behind, Daley's roan perhaps a fourth.

Frank found himself yelling like a boy. 'Damn, Wish Toby and Matthew was here,' he thought. Beside him, Tate was hollering encouragement, too.

The horses came on, Romer's Thoroughbred making a gallant effort to keep its lead. Bill edging up, the little mare falling back. The Army horse coming strong.

Suddenly, Bill's hand came up and flashed down, striking the big black's rump. It leaped forward, bridging the gap. As they streaked by, Frank thought Ben about half a nose ahead, but he really wasn't sure. He yelled, anyway, happy the black had made a good showing. Tate, beside himself, jumped up, down and around. He grabbed Frank and they spun, nearly falling off the boardwalk as the other horses came strung out down the stretch.

"He got him, He got him! He damn sure got him!" Tate yelled. The rest of the horses streamed by, the little mare, Frank saw, beat at the finish by Daley's roan. Tate leaped down from the boardwalk to accost Brown and his judges.

"Charlie, the verdict! What's the decision?"

"Frank's black by a nose!" Brown replied with a grin.

"Hot damn!" Frank exploded, "Hot damn!"

He felt an excitement surge in him that was akin to the bottle fever he'd experienced so often. A reckless thrill that elevated his blood, brought sweat to his palms. "Hot damn!"

Bill trotted back to the front of Tate's. "Did we do it?" he yelled, knowing already that they had, hardly believing it.

"You sure did, you riding son-of-a-gun!" Frank drawled, striving to regain his calm, and grinning all over his face despite himself.

Bill stepped down and was immediately swept into Tate's, Frank along with him, despite his weak objections, by the yelling, gesturing crowd.

Reuben appeared at Frank's side. "I'll take care of the black, Mistuh Frank. Don't worry."

Frank gave himself up to the moment. Tate threw glasses on the bar, lined them up and ran the whiskey bottle up and down the row.

160

Hands grabbed the glasses and Russell, his face alight, threw up a toast. It was followed by another, then another.

* * *

Two days later, Frank awoke with a groan, uncertain of his surroundings. It was dark but dawn, he could feel, was not far off. He was sober, nearly, but weak, so damn weak. Dried vomit streaked his shirt and he noticed his pants and boots were off. He was in the livery, saddle blankets under him and over him.

A voice spoke from the darkness."I'se over here, Mistuh Frank. You all right? You were pretty sick last night."

"I think I died and went to Hell, Reuben. You been taking care of me?"

"I just followed you around, tried to cover your back a little."

"I got to thank you for that, I guess, but right now, I wish someone would've shot me." Frank moaned, "What about Bill?"

"He started back yesterday with the supplies. He couldn't get you to break loose. I said I'd get you lined out soon's I could,"

Frank groaned again.

"Is my horse all right?" he asked presently.

"He fine, Mistuh Frank. Ready to run again." Reuben's hand came out of the darkness with a cup of coffee in it that Frank grabbed with a trembling hand.

"What about you? Isn't Gertie going to be upset with you?" He groaned as the coffee started down, a wave of pain hitting his middle.

"She dead, Mistuh Frank."

"She's dead?" Frank asked sharply.

"She died a week ago. Put her under a week from yesterday."

"Shit. What'd she die of?"

"Some kind of female disease, I think they call it sypillisus or somethin'."

"Jesus Gertrude gone." Frank muttered.

A wave of nostalgia swept him. Another friend dead. They had gone back a long ways. He checked his money belt and found he still had more than he'd come with. He vaguely remembered collecting his winnings.

Later, cleaned up and presentable again and freshly shaved in clean new clothes, Frank went back with Reuben to the livery and saddled Ben. He led him out, Sam following.

"Well, Sam, what's your decision on the job?"

Sam looked down. "Guess I'll pass, Frank. Never was much good with a gun."

Frank looked at him sharply. "Didn't say we needed a shooter, Sam, just a horse handler."

"Just the same, think I'll pass. Thanks, though."

Frank's gaze shifted to Reuben. "All right, Reuben, that leaves me open to offer you a job. Same wages: forty dollars a month."

"'Preciate the offer, Mistuh Frank. I really does. But I'se a towner, like people around, not horses, so I guess I'se gonna pass, too. Mistuh Leighton offer me a job for now, guardin' his store nights."

"Can't make a nickel here, then, I see. Guess I'd better head for home."

He swung Ben around and down the street, waving to Tate as he looked from his saloon door.

'Matthew,' he thought with a sharp pang of guilt, 'What was he going to tell him this time?'

* * *

Soon as he topped the rim overlooking the creek, he could see things were bad. The smoke he'd taken for a cook fire was smoldering embers of the partially burned cabin. In front of the cabin lay a dark object he knew was a body, he'd seen too many of those to be mistaken.

With a catch in his throat and a sudden resurgence of the hangover headache which nearly made him sway in the saddle, he urged Ben down off the edge, and across the creek. Coming up to the figure he saw with relief that it wasn't Matthew, but did identify it nearly as quickly as Chipper Bowe.

He dismounted after a swift scrutiny for an ambush. Bowe had been hit twice in the chest. His gun and hat, spurs were missing. His face showed damage from the ever-present magpies, always alert to a scavenged meal. Frank saw his pockets had been turned out, too, evidently in a hurried search for money. He rose and looked around, fearful of what he'd find next. Figuring he'd check the wrecked cabin later, he walked to the barn, the black horse trailing him.

162

Like the cabin, it had been fired. With cured hay in the loft, it had caught and burned fiercely. Even some of the nearby posts of the corral had started afire and had partially burned. What he saw by the ruined barn, though, grabbed his soul and started to squeeze.

Matthew lay there, his seamed old face turned to the sky, his eye sockets empty from the swift work of the scavengers. White hair lay round his head like a snowy halo and one knee remained drawn up from the mortis of death. Like Bowe, his boots were gone, likewise his hat, watch and gun. His pockets, too, were turned out and empty, and his money belt was missing. Frank saw he'd been hit crosswise in the chest by a big caliber bullet, likely a Sharps, which had literally torn his lungs from his body. Death, at least, must have been immediate.

Slowly Frank sank down to his knees beside the body.

"Jesus, Jesus, Jesus, old pard. They finally put you under."

He stared at the cold carcass of his old friend and tears came, riding slowly down his lined face, dripping to the ground. Ben sidled forward and snuffled the body, then blew the dead smell out of his nostrils and backed away. Still Frank sat, his mind a numb thing which rode down the paths of all the years the two men had been together.

A sound brought him to awareness and the horror continued: several mares had been in the holding pasture with their young colts. He looked and saw that the mares were gone. Most all of the colts were down, lying as if dead. One, however, and Frank saw it was Lark, the little filly Toby had named, was still up but staggering, its head almost to the ground by the creek, as if wanting to drink. He rose and went to it. Coming up, he saw blood on its jaw, and worked the little things' mouth open. Someone, he saw, with gathering rage, had cut its tongue off, making it unable to suck, even had its mother been there for her. He examined the others, and saw that they also had been subjected to the inhumane torture, someone had pried the little jaws apart, grasped the tongue and sliced it off, leaving the animal to bleed to death. He drew his pistol and put the suffering creature out of its misery.

He went back up the slight grade to the house, the horse, Ben, following him with Matthew draped over the saddle. At Bowe's body, he reached up and pulled the thing that had once been his friend out of the saddle and laid it beside the other. Black thoughts of suicide winged their way through his mind, the first he'd had since the war.

As he straightened, he thought that he heard something. It came from the burned cabin. A muffled sound, like a thumping noise.

163

'The hideout?' Frank looked and then waded through the burned debris to what had been the root cellar door, saw it was still intact, though badly burned, and that it was blocked by burned timber which had fallen against it. There was hammering from behind the door.

"Hold up, I'm coming!" Frank hollered.

He couldn't move the roof logs by hand, so he went back and brought Ben in close as he could, and used the lariat and the horse to get the job done. The door fell open then and Toby, a scorched, blackened Toby, fell out, coughing and choking from the ash dust which enveloped them. Frank caught him and held him close, then led him out, too late thinking of the two bodies which lay there in front of them.

Toby saw them before Frank could block his view. He broke from Frank's grasp and went over to the bodies, staring down at them in anguish, tears streaking down through the black ash on his face.

Frank tugged gently at him, seeing as he did that the boy's left ear was sliced half off and the remainder swollen.

"Come on, son, let's go down to the creek for a wash-up."

Numbly, Toby let himself be led to the creek, where he nearly fell face forward into the water, gulping it down in great long droughts. Frank had to pull him up, make him ease off, lest he make himself sick.

He washed the boy as best he could, using his shirttail and plenty of water. The ear injury he could do little about. It evidently was quite painful as Toby flinched away from any touch near it. It would have to wait. Frank got him up and, after one more drink, led him to where the black horse waited. Again, the boy turned and looked at the two huddled shapes on the ground before the blackened embers of the cabin. Great sobs came then, rocking the boys' body. He came to Frank, seeking comfort and the old man's arms opened and enfolded the youngster. Frank spoke, his voice choked and low, "I shoulda been here, son. I shoulda been here."

When Frank finally tried to hoist Toby onto the big black's saddle, the boy resisted and said, "What about them, Frank? We can't just leave 'em out here."

"Well," Frank looked around, "We can put 'em in the root cellar for now, I guess."

Together, the boy helping as much as he could, they struggled the two bodies into the root cellar. When Frank started to close the door,

164

Toby stopped him and led Frank down to a spot by the barn where, in the weeds, they came on the body of the big pit dog.

The boy knelt down and stroked the brindle face. Frank saw the dog had been shot at least three times. From the cloth clutched in its jaws, Frank could see it had fought to the death.

Frank bent down and gathered the dog into his arms, Toby trying to help him. They took him up and put him in the cellar, also, closing the door and propping it shut as best they could. Something locked in Frank, then. His rage was complete and only death would bring satisfaction.

Frank walked the Ben horse back to Janey's where he thankfully saw a wisp of smoke trailing out of the cabin's chimney. He'd not stopped on his way back, in the mood he was in. Neither had talked on the way to Janey's and now the woman, coming to the door, saw immediately that something was wrong. She came out and helped Frank swing Toby off the horse, helped him half-carry the boy inside. They laid him on one of the bunks and Janey spoke, "Frank, there's coffee. Pour a slug of whiskey in some cups and we'll all have a drink."

Frank complied and they raised Toby up and got him to drink some of the mixture. Then he curled himself into a ball and faced the wall. She covered him with a blanket.

"I'm gonna heat some water and work on that ear a little. It needs stitches. How about you? Are you all right?" She looked at the old man facing her and was inwardly shocked by the pain that showed in his eyes, his face.

"Matthew and Bowe are dead, Janey. I got a feelin' Bill is too, but I didn't find him yet. They hit the place when I was in town. Matthew was shot with a big caliber Sharps. They must have fired the cabin and killed Bowe when he came out."

He shook his head.

"They killed the dog, too, and cut the tongues out of the colts before they left. Just out of pure orneriness."

The woman waited, but Frank said nothing more. She bustled around, then, getting a clean dishcloth out, some soap, a pan of warm water. Frank helped her and they cleaned the ear, which started bleeding again. The boy's pain hurt the old man further.

When they were done, Frank said, "Janey, I need your shovel, axe, some blankets, and a post bar. Guess I'll need your wagon. I want to go back and bury them right like I should,"

"I'd help you, but I better stay here with Toby," she said gently. She went with him to help hitch up and find the tools, then Frank returned to the spring.

He went to the top of the hill over the spring and dug three holes in the gravelly soil, cleaning off the cactus and sagebrush first with the axe. The work took him some hours and he was beginning to feel lightheaded from the effects of shock, too much booze and too little food.

Going back down and around to the burned cabin, he brought the wagon in close and loaded the bodies, having trouble with the heavy Bowe. The dead bodies, stiff from rigor mortis, seemed to have a mind of their own, and fought against being transported or buried. This was something that Frank, from his years of war service and ranger work, was accustomed to, ordinarily. This time, and in these circumstances, it was almost beyond his waning capabilities. He seemed to be fading in and out mentally and each task physically took enormous effort and produced tremendous strain.

At last, though, the job was done. Three graves, side by side, covered with rock, lay on the hill. To the west, the sun was sinking on the horizon behind scattered clouds of violet hue. Mourning doves cooed in the distance. Otherwise, the air was still. Wearily, he half sat, half collapsed beside the graves. Something should be said over them he felt, but his numb brain just wouldn't function. Maybe later, he finally decided, he and the boy could return. Yes, that was it, they would come back and pay their respects in a proper manner when they could.

He staggered when he got up, went to the wagon and threw the tools in.

Chapter 7

Miles City.

Three days later, the door of the Sheriff's office slammed open, an action which startled the sheriff and his deputy at their morning cribbage game.

"Irvine, Loan me your ten gauge!"

Coming out of their surprise, somewhat, Irvine replied, "Why, Frank. . . What's wrong?"

Frank stalked in, Leighton behind him. "He wants your ten gauge because he's going to brace Stringer's crew down at Chinnick's, the damn fool!" Joe burst out.

"What the hell's going on?" Irvine protested. By the look on Frank's set, pain-lined face, he knew that something bad had happened. Frank's answer proved him right.

"Matthew and Bowe are dead. Stringer Jack's crew paid 'em a little visit when I was in town boozing it up. They back shot Matthew and burned Bowe out, then killed him. They caught Hollister on the road and shot him from ambush. They were hoping to get me, too, then, I'm sure. They burned us out, Tom, cabin, barn, hay and corrals. They killed our dog, stole the mares and killed our colts by cutting their tongues out so they'd bleed to death." He scrubbed a hand over his face, then locked eyes with Irvine.

"I'm going to war, Irvine. I want your heavy artillery."

Leighton said, "Tom, don't let him go. He can't brace that whole bunch alone."

Irvine looked at Frank a moment longer, then replied, "Doesn't look like I can stop him, Joe. You can see he's got a mad on."

He went to the gun cabinet and unlocked it with a key from his vest, reached in and pulled out a heavy shotgun. Turning, he put it in Frank's hands. Going to a desk, he pulled open a drawer and took out a box of shells. He gave them to Frank, too. Frank opened it and filled the gun, then stuck some more into his vest pockets. He nodded and walked out.

He'd come in from Janey's to see Irvine and perhaps X. Biedler, the U. S. Marshal, if he was in town. Not that he wanted to push it off on them, but more to get information about Stringer's gang, who was in it, where they were holed up.

Toby, when he could talk, had told them that he'd been grabbed at the barn by a huge man who'd held a knife to his neck and shouted to Matthew to come out. Just then, Cappy had rushed in and grabbed the man by the leg, making him howl. Whether by accident or design, the man had sliced Toby's ear in the struggle.

At that time, Matthew had appeared, and sighting around Toby, had shot the man in the face. The same instant, a rifle shot had put Matthew down. Toby had run to Matthew but he was dead. Then he heard shots from the cabin. The boy was at a loss as to what to do. Then he saw, in the twilight, three men coming toward him from beside the barn, one of them with a Sharps rifle in his hands. He turned and ran, Cappy by his side. The men, two of them, ran after him and Cappy turned back to meet them. As he went over the hill to the west, Toby heard more shots. He ran as hard as he could to the west, then angled around to the creek and sneaked into the cabin, passing Bowe's dead form lying by the door as he did so. Running to the root cellar, he opened the door, lifted the trap in the floor and jumping down into the hole, pulled it back over him. The next he knew, he heard voices, then smelled smoke as they fired the cabin above him. The smoke and heat had nearly killed him. Later, when he'd tried to get out, he found out he was trapped.

After Frank had heard the story, he'd paced Janey's cabin for the rest of the day, uncertain as to what to do. Finally, Janey had convinced him to come to town. She'd ridden with Toby in the wagon. On the way they'd found Bill's body by the magpies feeding on it, which they'd brought in. When they'd gotten to town, they'd passed Chinnick's and a man had peered from the door. Frank noticed his sneering face but it wasn't until they'd pulled up at Leighton's that Toby had told him, fear in his voice, that he thought the man was one of those at the barn. Leighton had sworn in amazement when he heard the story but when Frank had asked for a ten gauge, had tried his best to talk him out of going back to Chinnick's.

168

"Frank, there's too many of them! Why, there's eighteen or twenty men in there, must be. You can't fight that many and Toby don't know for certain sure, even, that he really recognized the man!" Joe protested.

Frank's rage, ever present, surfaced and he'd stalked out, heading for the jail, Leighton following.

Toby and Janey had stayed at Leighton's, uncertain as to what they should do, when Toby, watching out the window for Frank's return, saw Granville Stuart and several men riding by. He ran from the store and intercepted the group, screaming the leader's name.

"Mr. Stuart, Mr. Stuart! Wait!" The riders pulled up. The men, Toby saw in passing, were nearly all mounted on horses that Stuart had bought from them.

"Why, hello, Toby, how's the young horse rancher?" Granville's stern face split by a grin that faded as he listened to the boy's story.

Frank reached Hubbell's store front, the shotgun resting easy over his arm, his belt gun matched with another short-barreled .44 Colt stuck inside his belt on his left side that he'd gotten from Leighton when Matthew had been sick out at Keogh's. Resting in its holster on his right was his own Colt. In his vest pocket was a .44 Remington two-shot derringer. 'If there was eighteen or twenty of the skunks in that den, he had just about enough armament,' he thought.

'Question was, could he stay on his feet long enough to use it all? Fear of dying didn't enter into it—-fear of not getting the job done was more the point,' he'd decided. 'And, if Stringer Jack was absent, he'd really thrown his life away, for it wasn't enough to just kill the Indians, the chief needed to die, as well,' he thought. But enough of the uncertainty he'd had raging in him. Action would stop it.

Chinnick's, as usual about dusk, was noisy, and even from right outside its entrance, Frank could smell the musty beer joint smell of a frontier bar—spilled beer, whiskey, cigar smoke, coal oil lanterns, unwashed bodies, it all came boiling out the doors of these places, hitting a person used to breathing the fresh outdoor air like a slosh of cold water from a bucket.

As he paused, mentally rehearsing his moves—the shotgun right, then left, discard it, then use his belt guns—he became aware of a form-up of men to either side of him on the busy street. He turned to meet what he perceived almost too late to be an attack, when suddenly Stuart and Irvine were standing in front of him. The men with them closed in.

"Frank, you need to come with us. This isn't the way to do it."

"They killed the best friend I'll ever have, Stuart," Frank choked out. "You want me to let 'em go now, you say? Go to hell!" He started forward, shouldered Stuart and Irvine aside, who must have given some signal to the men around them, for they reached with a multitude of hands and arms, smothering Frank's response almost before it began. Then, they hustled him away in the growing dusk.

PART II

STUART'S 'STRANGLERS'

Granville Stuart 1883
courtesy of Library of Congress

Chapter 8

In 1882, buffalo hunting and Indian chasing were the two main occupations in the Yellowstone country, with every other occupation of the whites in the country engaged in supporting these two. Two short years later, the Indians were subdued, the buffalo were nearly gone and $35,000,000 worth of cattle and horses were grazing in their stead, walking the trails the buffalo had carved in the country over eons, drinking from streams and rivers that, until then, had never seen the reflection of a longhorn. In 1882, the buffalo hunters rubbed elbows with each other at every shipping point in the territory. By 1884, their quarry was gone, and the drovers and stockmen were coming into their heyday.

To bring a herd up the trail to this huge pasture of northern grass was expensive. The general rule was: drive three thousand head of cattle three thousand miles for three thousand dollars. That was after the cattle had already been raised or purchased. Capital of that size was beyond the scope of most stockmen, but men like the Marquis De Mores, a wealthy French nobleman, Theodore Roosevelt, a wealthy Easterner and Stuart, Daley and Hauser, wealthy miners from the goldfields, comprised a cross-section of the type of entrepreneurs who saw an opportunity to make money in an adventurous undertaking and seized the chance Fate offered. The East was begging for beef to feed their growing post-war industrial expansion. The herds poured into the open country like a plague of locusts.

With stock scattered on the northern range worth millions of dollars, Indians pushed onto reserves who resented the loss of their liberty and their buffalo, white hunters who were unemployed but still armed and active, the pot suddenly boiled over and large scale cattle losses began showing up. In an attempt to deal with the rustling by legal means, a bill was introduced in the territorial legislature for brand inspecting and registering livestock. It was defeated, outraging the stockmen and filling the rustlers with glee.

The April meeting was, therefore, tumultuous, with the hotheads clamoring for direct action, but their president, Granville Stuart, counseling caution against taking the law into their own hands, warning that the rustlers were dangerous and well organized. The hotheads, lead by Roosevelt and De Mores, clamored for lynch law and accused Stuart of backing water, of being yellow. His call for caution nevertheless won out. The frustrated ranchers returned to their homes to find the outlaw organizations more active than ever.

The Rosebud Vigilantes

Chapter 9

DHS Ranch Headquarters

Day was just breaking and the cook had the breakfast fire going and the coffee pot steaming. When Stuart came into the cook shack from the main house, several of the others had already started on their second cup. The long table, flanked by benches on either side, was still scattered with the cups and can ash trays from last night's conference. Stuart poured himself a cup and sat down across from Frank and greeted him. The latter grunted.

"Morning." He got his pipe going and flicked the match into the can. "Few hours of sun and we can be moving, I'd say. Good rain."

Last night before dark had seen the sky clearing and the rain, which had come down steady for three days, begin tapering off. The storm had stopped travel for the time being.

Stuart sipped his coffee. The normal banter and morning talk was absent and the men seated at the table, like Stuart, were silent and contained. What they were about to do could very well brand them as outlaws. At the very least, some would probably be killed. Stuart, like Frank, seemed immune to the tension. He sipped his coffee, then spoke.

"For the last time, Frank, I think the boy should stay behind. He's too young for this."

"And I told you, Stuart, and this is the last time I'll mention it also, that he goes. Subject closed," Frank put down his cup and the two locked eyes. Stuart's dropped first.

"Have it your way, then. But, you know Frank, that he can stay here and welcome. He's a good boy and deserves a future without the taint this is probably going to bring down on the rest of us."

Frank's set face softened, "I know you're just thinking of him, Stuart, and I thank you for it. But he'll need to hold his head up when

174

he's grown, too. How could he do that if he stayed out of it?" Stuart said nothing. Clearly, Frank's mind would not be changed.

Two hours later, breakfast finished, the horses saddled and others packed, Frank swung into the leather and the others followed, Toby among them. Stuart and some of the other men watched them go as they rode off to Fort Maginnis.

This post, with its army detachment, and the lowly collection of squalid cabins and whiskey joints near it, nestled on the east flank of the Judith Mountains. The party from the DHS reached it a little before noon the next day, the creek crossings and muddy trail impeding their travel.

"McKenzie's shack is the third one there," one of the cowboys, Butch Starley, pointed out. The other four reined up and Frank looked the situation over. The little sod roofed cabin showed no smoke and looked deserted.

"Toby, you stay here with the packs. Come on, boys, we'll pay him a little visit. Butch, you and Charley go around back. While you're there, check those horses. Jack and I'll see to the front." Jack Ludich, a short compact, dark haired DHS hand who perpetually wore a rolled cigarette in his mouth and chaps on his bowed legs, merely nodded. Like the others, with the exception of Toby, he was an older mature man who'd been through hard, rough times that had tempered him into steel and taken the back-up out of him. Left-handed, he carried his Colt in a cross/draw holster on his right side and Stuart had recommended him as a 'quick, crack shot with a pistol and iron nerves.'

With Toby holding the pack horses back, the men surrounded the cabin. Though noon, there was little activity on the outskirts of the village, most of the inhabitants either up at the saloon, or sleeping their last night's drunk off. Frank, watching close, did see movement at the window of the cabin next to McKenzie's and told Ludich to handle that one."

The 'Ben' horse stopped in front of the cabin and Frank stepped down. He called.

"Hey, McKenzie, come on out."

A sleep-groggy voice answered him.

"Who the hell is it?"

"Come on out, McKenzie," Frank repeated. The door swung open and Sam McKenzie, hair tousled, stocking footed, his pants open and unbelted, stood in the doorway, a pistol in his hand. He lowered it when he saw Frank's leveled Colt staring at him eyeball-to-barrel.

"Uncock and hand it over!" the old man grated. The little horse thief, mesmerized by Frank's steely eyes and unwavering pistol, complied with alacrity.

"Stand still," Frank commanded, stepping down.

He pulled a thin pigging string from over his saddle horn and quickly tied the man's hands behind him.

Starley and Pettit appeared from behind the cabin.

"Four horses there, Frank, two of 'em are N. Looks like they've been changed to an M. The other two are ours. The brands are blotted so you can't read 'em anymore," Starley said.

McKenzie started to whine in a wheedling tone.

"Now boys, I bought those horses from some Blackfeet over at Benton. I didn't know they was stolen but you can sure take 'em if that's your bent."

Frank took another rope from his saddle, this one with a hangman's noose tied in its end, and flipped the loop over the tied man's head. Grinning like a snarling wolf, he jerked it, making the little thief stumble forward.

"Why thanks, friend. I believe we'll do just that!" He stepped into the leather and took a couple dallies around his horn.

"Come on, boys, let's find a tree with a good limb. Charlie, turn those horses out and bring 'em along." He swung around and stepped the horse out, back towards the pack horses waiting by the boy. "Come on, Jack, and we'll go decorate a tree," he called.

Jack Ludich, still facing the cabin he'd been instructed to watch, began backing his roan horse, the animal taking deliberate steps with no apparent urging from its rider. At a hundred yards, he turned and spurred, jumping the roan into a gallop that brought him up to the others, with McKenzie stumbling along in his socked feet, behind. When they reached Toby, Frank asked him, "This one of them, son, or can you tell?"

The boy, white faced and trembling, answered in a quavery voice that he attempted to steady. "I don't know for sure, Frank."

"Don't matter none, now, I guess." He flipped the rope over a branch and the big horse walked away.

* * *

176

Back at the DHS headquarters the next day, the horses were turned into the corral. Stuart and a man he introduced as Gus Cramer inspected the brands the four stolen ones carried. A message was sent to the N ranch concerning the two with the blotched M.

Cramer, it turned out, was a stock detective employed by the Association. He seemed to have an intimate knowledge of who the outlaws were and where they were located, a fact which made Frank suspicious of him. No one, not even Stuart himself, knew all those associated with the rustler organization. Even the Territorial Legislature was apparently infiltrated with their members. Yet this Cramer set himself up as an expert at the outlaw business!! Frank wondered greatly but withheld judgment. Future events would tell.

Entering the DHS cook shack, a long sod-roofed cabin like most other frontier structures, Frank sat up to the table and the cook, a stove-up old cowboy with a bad hip named Leaky Pete, poured him a cup of coffee. Stuart, Cramer and the others trooped in, Toby with them, and all sat down to coffee up.

Stuart commented, "Our horses, alright, but the brands are so blotted you can't read them. Looks like they're making the S into an 8. Charlie says you hung him?"

Frank nodded, "We did,"

"He was alone?"

"He was, far as we could see."

Stuart's gray bearded face nodded seriously.

"Did Toby recognize him?"

"Nope." Frank sipped his coffee and got his pipe out. Seeing he was likely to get little more information out of Frank, Stuart turned to Cramer.

"Gus Marsh, over at Rocky Point, has been sending us information as he can. We've been paying him fifty dollars a month for whatever he can find out. The rustlers been stopping at his saloon there on their stealing trips up and down the Missouri. I just got word from him that Red Mike, Louis Meyers, and a couple others brought some horses through that they stole from Power Brothers over in the Moccasins. One of them was that new Thoroughbred stallion they just brought in from Colorado. Marsh says they dared Powers' foreman, the Dutchman, to try to come down there and get them back. I sent Brother

James and Andrew Fergus with a couple men to try and catch them." He put his cup down. "We'll wait a while and see how they make out."

Frank puffed his pipe. "Like I said before, you wait too long, they'll all do a fade on us and we'll never get 'em."

"Just the same, let's wait a couple days."

Toby went back down to the corral to be with the horses. He was miserable. Since the killings, Frank had been a different man, no longer the cheerful, joking storyteller, but a man obsessed with revenge. He had told Stuart that Toby wanted to ride with him. It wasn't the truth. The truth was Toby was sickened by the killings, sickened by the hanging of McKenzie, and he wanted no more of it. What he'd like to do, wanted to do, was to stay at the DHS with the Stuarts for a while. Not forever, maybe, just until Frank had turned back into his old self again. The DHS, with Stuart running it, was a secure haven.

For all his stern manner, Toby liked Granville Stuart. His character and good-heartedness shone through. He also liked Aubony, Stuart's Snake Indian wife, and he got along with the kids, all the boys and the three girls. Plus, there were the Anderson girls, whom he was getting to know, too. Granville had evidently told them Toby's story, for they all went out of their way to treat him nice, except for Lizzie, the youngest of Stuart's girls. She was jealous of Toby's attention to Mary, the middle Stuart girl, who was a bright, pretty little thing Toby's age. Though Toby was physically and mentally down when they'd arrived at the DHS weeks before, the close proximity of the other kids, their cheerfulness and constant skylarking had started to bring him out of his depression. They had raced horses, helped with the cattle, played tricks on each other and generally let off their childish steam. Toby's life seemed to be mending, though he still grieved for Matthew and Cappy.

Frank, though, had remained morose and unreachable. Although a Texan and a stockman, he didn't really fit in with the DHS crew, and he made no effort to, where in times past he would have been a favorite of the cowpunchers. He had no interest now, it seemed, in anything except killing rustlers. He took no hand in the work, preferring instead, to ride out on his black horse and practice his shooting. Sometimes he'd return with meat his Henry had taken, sometimes he brought word of this cow or that horse needing help, but rarely did he turn to and lend a hand.

The other men, with the exception of Reece Anderson, Stuart's partner and foreman, left him alone. Anderson himself hated a horse thief and sympathized with Frank's single-mindedness. Stuart, knowing that they were in a fight to the absolute finish with the well-organized rustlers, recognized the value of the two older men and had promised them leadership roles in the coming conflict. It had sufficed to stay Frank's hand, for the moment. Together, the men had planned their campaign. Stuart, from his role of leadership in the Stockgrowers Association, had taken the reins and started the wagon of destiny rolling.

Granville Stuart was Montana Territory. He had participated in the first gold strike at Gold Creek in '57. It had started a run that eventually populated the western Rockies with mining communities. He prospered, owning mining properties, stores, lumber mills. Early on, he'd ranched in the Deer Lodge Valley, raising horses, cattle and crops to feed the miners. He had participated in the Vigilante sweep of Virginia City and Bannack, being well acquainted with all the players of that drama, including Plummer. Some said/whispered that he was the brains behind the Vigilantes. During that time, in 1862, he'd married a Snake Indian, Aubony. Later, when many white men had no longer felt it fashionable to keep their Indian wives, he'd continued to cherish her.

In 1880, he'd looked the country over and settled there east of the Judiths in the best cattle country in Montana. He and his pardners, Sam Hauser of Helena, A. J. Davis of Butte, and Reece Anderson, his longtime mining pardner and friend, had formed the DHS Cattle Company. They'd brought 5,000 cattle in, built headquarters, bunkhouses, stables and corrals. Built like forts, all the buildings had portholes to fight from. The big bunkhouse and stable had a sixty foot stockade built between them. The first year the Blackfeet had pestered them continually, sniping, trying to steal horses and butchering beef, 'til finally Stuart and his men had ridden over to the Blackfoot encampment and told them to pack their teepees and pull out across the Missouri. And stay there."

Although the buffalo at that time were plentiful and the tribe had the whole area north of the river to hunt and raid, they'd come south for their fun, all twelve hundred of them, and the army wouldn't do anything. When Stuart had given them his ultimatum, they'd looked at the gray bearded stern visage, the cocked Winchesters of his crew, and decided they would listen. Incredibly, he'd made his warning stick. Now he faced a different foe.

Frank and Toby had stayed behind at the ranch when Stuart had gone to the Stockgrowers meeting, but they knew what had transpired. The stockmen in the 'know' had voted against a war on the rustlers. That was the public vote, so as not to alarm the outlaws. But, in executive session, after the regular meeting, a vigilante organization was set up, with Granville Stuart at its head. 'Executive Committees' would carry out the action against the rustlers. Stuart had returned from the meeting with anguish in his heart at the course that was to be taken but was determined to follow it to the bitter end. Plans were made and it was decided to let the rustlers, in each case, make their move so they might be caught red-handed. That way, it was hoped that public censure would be less. Immediately, some stockmen found they had business out of state when this action began, not wanting to get their hands dirty or endanger themselves. Others sat back and were satisfied to let Stuart and his men do the dirty work. To do that work, he gathered a hard riding crew, borrowing in some cases from other ranches, those men with hard reputations and a penchant for closed mouths.

* * *

On the twenty-sixth of June, a rider had come into the ranch on a foam-sweated horse. When the men saw him, they came to the cook shack on a high lope, knowing something was up. The rider was Bill Thompson. When Frank came in, he was already into his story.

"I ran 'em down and shot Varner, then made the mistake of taking Lavardure alive. I should have killed him, too, but I didn't recognize him right away. I tied him up and brought him back to Wells' camp. They've got him in a stable over there right now, but I wouldn't be surprised if they let him go. He's talking big about Stringer Jack's bunch coming down to get him out and make it hot for me and anyone else that tries to stop them."

"What happened?" Frank asked, impatiently.

Reece replied, "Thompson here caught Lavardure and Joe Varner stealing horses from Wells' horse band. He caught 'em coming up Eagle Creek and recognized the horses so he took out after them. They shot at him, so he shot back."

"He killed Varner," Ludich added, with satisfaction.

"Stuart," Frank started in,"let me and Reece go over there and gather up Lavardure."

Stuart thought a while, the men fidgety but quiet, respecting the boss they had a great deal of loyalty and affection for. At last, he spoke.

"We'll all go. You boys saddle up. Gather your war plunder, we might run into Stringer's outfit. If so, there'll most likely be a fight."

The men scattered.

Riding through the night, the Vigilantes rode up to Wells' camp at 2:00 a.m. The night herder came out to meet them.

"Hold it up, there!" he shouted, "Who are you?"

Stuart replied, "Vigilance Committee, come to get a man called Weepy Lavardure for horse stealing."

"Pass, friends!" The herder stepped his horse aside.

Lavardure was tied hand and foot in a stable stall. When he saw the men, though it was dark and he couldn't recognize features, he instinctively knew his time was up. Hibbs and Pettit reached in and brought him out, untied his feet, and hoisted him on a horse. Frank flipped a noose over his head and they led him away from camp.

"You boys don't want to kill me. I'll get out of the country, you let me go. Please! And I can tell you where 'bouts the others are hiding. Please, boys, please!" A low whine came from his throat. No one answered him.

A quarter mile from camp, a suitable tree was found and the rope was thrown over a protruding limb, then tied to the trunk.

Frank broke his silence then, asking him, "One thing, you son-of-a-bitch, before you swing. Were you one of them killed my partner over on the Rosebud?"

"I heard about it, but I sure never was in on it." Lavardure's voice quavered, "You know he killed Paddy Rose. Shot him right in the eye as he was holding some kid," He tried to swallow, the stiff rope making it hard to speak.

"I sure wasn't in on it, though."

"Who shot him in the back?" Frank spat out. "Who was it, damn you?"

"I'll tell you if you let me go. Please!"

"No deals with horse thieves. You ride with 'em, you die with 'em," Frank answered.

"Then, you Ranger bastard, you ain't gonna find out from me!" Lavardure kicked his horse and began a convulsive midair dance.

A few days later had come news that McKenzie had returned to Fort Maginnis with four horses in his possession, most probably not his own. McKenzie was a half-breed Scotchman from north of the border whose many Indian friends had so far kept him from harm. His luck had run out on July third when Frank and his crew had caught and hanged him.

Chapter 10

Mouth of the Musselshell.

Where the Musselshell River runs into the Missouri, the bluffs widen out and make a flat with lots of room for grazing. The Indians, particularly the Sioux, had preferred it as a camping area, being especially happy with the ford at the spot. They were not happy with the whites' decision to build a fort there, and the locale was the scene of many conflicts between white and red until the Indians were defeated. The fort was deserted and fell into disrepair.

Billy Downs and a couple others had occupied the old post, moving into the big two room store, taking the corrals and stockade for their use. For a while, they'd traded with the Indians, cut wood for the steamboats, sold whiskey to the hunters. Most of the boats had quit when the buffalo had run out. The Indians were mostly on their reservations. Now, Downs and his helpers sold to the wolfers and trappers—and horse thieves.

On the night of July 4th, Reece Anderson, Frank, and the rest of the 'Executive Committee' arrived at the fort. They gathered at the corral.

"Come on out, Downs, and tell us about the horses here," Reece called.

The men had ridden straight to the corral and checked the stock there. All the horses bore brands of known stock raisers of the area.

Downs called back from inside the store, his voice muffled, "We can talk from right here. What do you fellahs want, eh?"

Frank hollered, then. "We're after horse thieves and killers, Downs. Remember me?"

"Yeah. You're the old ranger killed Dyer and Lopez in Miles City. You've got no call to come at us. I've got my wife in here, too."

Reece replied.

"We know that, Billy, but you're just putting her in danger if you hold out in there. Those old logs'll burn like tinder with a little coal oil, and we've got some along!" He held up a can of the flammable liquid they'd had the foresight to throw on a pack.

The men could hear a heated argument going on inside, then Downs yelled, "Hold fire, then, we're coming out to talk."

Presently he came out, another man with him.

"California Ed Lowney." Cramer whispered to Frank. "He's a damn horse thief, too."

When the men had ventured a little further from the store, the vigilantes surrounded them, then disarmed and tied their hands. Some of the men went inside to search the house.

"Now boys, tell us about them horses." Reece instructed them as they stood there.

Downs looked at Frank, roved his eyes around the stern, still group, then muttered, "We didn't steal 'em. We bought 'em from the Indians."

"What about this?" Ludich thrust some jerked meat he'd found in the store room in Down's face.

"Buffalo meat."

"Hell, Downs, ain't been any buffalo around for a year or more." Ludich smelled it.

"Beef!"

A yell from the stable brought forth two other men, Hibbs and Pettit, who carried some fresh, salted beef hides, branded Fergus Stock Company. Downs and Lowney hung their heads.

"Let's go, boys."

A little ways out from the fort was a grove of trees. The men were walked to a suitable tree and their legs tied.

"'Fore you boys swing, I got a question to ask you all."

Frank drawled, "Who was it killed my pardner?"

California Ed spoke for the first time."You mean the white-haired old bastard? The one shot Baker and Rose?"

"That's the one."

"Shut up, you sack of shit." Downs whispered, then gagged an instant later, as he was swung in the air on a signal from Frank.

"There, now we won't have no interruptions."

Frank offered a rolled cigarette to the other outlaw, courtesy of Ludich's making. He stuck it in the man's mouth, then lit it, the glow of the tiny ember a spot of starry fire in the summer night. Lowney drew in a great puff and coughed a little.

"Now tell me who killed my pardner," Frank asked again.

"One that pulled the trigger was Stringer Jack. From ambush. I wasn't there, but Downs talked about it. Don't bother me to tell you. Stringer killed a pardner of mine last winter, for no reason at all. Maybe this'll get him back for it." He puffed on the cigarette, calm in what he knew were his last moments on this earth.

"Much obliged, California, for what it's worth, you've got my thanks. You ready?"

"Let 'er rip, boys."

They swung him up to kick beside the now quiet Downs. From the fort, the men could hear a woman wailing.

If Toby had been miserable before, it was a certainty that he was twice as miserable now. Riding back to the DHS with the 'Executive Committee,' he never spoke a word. Not that the others talked all that much. 'Stringer Jack!' The name ran through all their minds.

Toby had tried to stay back this time, had even told Frank he was sick. It hadn't mattered. Frank had swung his saddle on the horse Stuart had given him and ordered him on it. When Downs and his helper were about to hang, the boy had closed his eyes, stopped his ears in the darkness to shut out the grunting, grisly sounds of death. The wailing of the woman had further unnerved him. He swore to himself he wasn't going out again. He'd run away first.

* * *

Into the DHS headquarters came another rider, this one from Lewistown. Another 'Executive Committee' had followed two notorious rustlers and killers into Lewistown, where the Fourth of July celebration was in full swing. Knowing they'd been followed and probably aware they were doomed, the two decided to go out fighting. They'd taken on the whole town, right on main street, killing one man and wounding several others before being put under by a swelling cross-fire from the town's enraged citizens. Stuart crossed the names of Fallon and Owens off his lengthy list.

On the sixth of July, a man rode in and asked to speak with Granville Stuart. Pettit had gone up to the house and fetched the boss. The man identified himself as Buck Hawkins, from over by Pease

Bottom on the Yellowstone. To his silent listeners, he related that he had been robbed of fifty head of horses, had trailed them all the way to the Missouri River and with field glasses, had watched five men working over their brands. All those present looked to Stuart, who nodded, then said, "Frank, you take some men and go with Hawkins here and get his horses back. We'll continue to wait for word from James and Fergus."'

Frank turned to the waiting group.

"Come on, Reece, Adams, you, too, Patterson. Hibbs, you and Jack and Starley. Toby, you saddle up, too." The men hurried off to throw the leather on their horses and get the packs ready. The boy went, too. Despite his promise to himself, no ready excuse had come to him to stay behind.

Hard riding brought them to the Missouri, just a mile or two from where they had lately hung McKenzie. They camped for the night and Toby, at least, found it impossible to sleep. Early the next morning, about 4:30, Frank got them up and into the saddle, with only jerky and water for breakfast.

As they rode close to the site where Hawkins had said the horses were being held, the men saw, in the growing light of the dawn, a horseman riding hard away from them, evidently to give the alarm. Immediately, Frank hollered at Patterson and Hibbs, both well mounted, to give chase.

"Hurry, you boys, and catch him before he throws the game for us!"

The two men so designated as chasers quirted their horses and jumped into a run. As the watchers looked on, the chasers closed on the fleeing man, until in the distance, Toby saw him throw up his arms. As the group rode up, Hibbs and young Patterson were off their horses, tying the man hand and foot. Ludich grabbed the tied man's horse.

"This horse is a Pioneer Cattle Company one, by the brand," Ludich called to Frank.

Gus Cramer turned the man over and exclaimed, "Hell, boys, this here is Jack Perkins. He's got a $500 reward on his head for murder and robbery back east! Hot damn!"

They left him lying on the ground to come back for later, then went on in to the cabin. Toby could see that, over behind the cabin, there was a corral full of horses. Hawkins whispered excitedly that they were his. "My horses, I know 'em all!" They dismounted and crept forward.

Frank signaled with his arms, both hands being full of pistols, for them to split and take either side of the long structure. He motioned to Reece then, and the two older men, their guns ready, jumped through the partially open door. If the other thought the two were going to hold up the cabin full of men, they were mistaken. Shots, muffled by the cabin walls, resounded, their whip crack echoing in the little clearing. Toby and the rest stood transfixed. The shooting quit, then a last shot and both men, Frank and Reece stumbled from the smoke filled interior. Reece was clutching an arm that dripped blood.

The others crowded to the doorway and saw four men lying in various attitudes of death inside. Ludich stepped inside and collected their guns, prying a pistol from the dead hands of one, a rifle from under another. Toby, his stomach shaky again, turned aside.

Frank tied up Reece's arm. The two men seemed indifferent to the mayhem they had just dealt. Reece smoked while Frank tended the wound.

"No bones broke. It went through clean. You'll heal up fine, I think." Frank commented.

Hibbs turned the horses out and the men started Hawkins back on his way. "I'll ride a ways with him, Frank, and get 'em lined out," Charley called.

They went back to the tied horse thief and Ludich untied his feet and got him up. When Frank took a hanging noose from his saddle horn and dropped it over the man's head, Cramer protested.

"Frank, boys, that there man's worth a lot of money! You boys don't need to bother with him, I'll take him if you want and split with you, later."

Frank ignored him, pulled the rope taut and started the man walking toward the trees.

Cramer called out, "Goddammit, hold up, Shannon. Hold up!"

Frank turned then, in the saddle, the man at the end of the rope stumbling to his knees, a low choking sound coming from him.

"I'm holdin,' Cramer."

The stock detective looked around, seeking support.

"I said I want that man to hand over to the law, damn it!" His hand went to his belt gun.

"And I'm goin' to hang him, Mr. Stock Detective. Make your play if you don't like it," Frank said mildly.

Cramer looked around. Ludich was off to one side, Anderson, his arm in a kerchief sling, on his other side. Hibbs and Patterson behind him. To Cramer, seeking support, they all looked hostile. He caved in.

"Oh, the hell with it, Frank. Go ahead if you're set on it. I'll write a letter and see if that's enough. Maybe, can I get you boys to sign it." The tension eased.

Frank walked the black to a large nut pine, tossed the rope over a limb and dallied.

"One question before we swing you. Were you in on the killings over on the Rosebud?" He reached over and knocked the man's hat off, which had fallen over his face.

"I don't even know who you are, old man. I don't know anything." His eyes glared. The black walked away.

* * *

They headed back to the DHS and on the way a rider intercepted them. He was a tall, muscled man with a drooping long mustache like Frank and Reece Anderson. He told them his name was Bill Cantrell and that he wanted to visit with Stuart. Cramer, edging up, looked at him and said that he was a woodhawk from up river and that he could be in with the thieves. Frank pulled his belt gun.

"Throw 'em up, Cantrell, and we'll relieve you of your hardware, then we can ride along peaceable." Cantrell did so and Starley took his pistol and rifle, a big one, Frank noticed, a .50/95 Winchester.

"Pretty big hardware, Cantrell. Stuart shoots one of them, too," Reece observed.

"I like to throw a lot of lead in the air." The man grinned, apparently unconcerned.

At the ranch, Stuart told them that Meyers and Red Mike had gotten away from Fergus and the others. The men were eating a late lunch in the cookshack.

"We recovered the stock and some harness they'd stolen, though," Fergus said, "They got word of us coming, damn it." He was a fiery, hot-tempered younger brother of James Fergus, owner of Fergus Livestock Company from the Moccasin Stockman's Association. Frank had been against using him and suspected Stuart felt the same way, but the families were friends, and Stuart probably hesitated to offend. Stuart consoled him,

"Never mind. We're bound to miss some. We'll get them if they come back in the country."

Cantrell was brought in. He looked around, sensing the hostile atmosphere but stood straight and without fear. He held out his hand to Stuart and they shook.

"Stuart, I'm not a stock thief, but I know about them. They've been after me to join them. It was either leave the country, join their thieving gang, or come here and ask to join you. Doin' the last seemed the best course for me to take."

Stuart, impressed at his straightforwardness, poured him a cup of coffee. "All right, Cantrell. Saying we let you in, what can you tell us?"

Cantrell sat up to the table with the rest and leaned forward. The others, sensing he possessed information of importance, did likewise.

"Sir, I can tell you straight that about twelve of Stringer's gang is at the James Wood yard over at Bates Point and they've just got there with over a hundred head of stolen horses!"

Stuart looked at Frank, then Reece, who spoke.

"Bates Point is right down amongst them, the middle of their country. It could be a trap, Granville."

Stuart looked hard at Cantrell, who told him, "I know you don't trust me but I'm telling you the truth. Come with me and I'll show you."

Stuart put him off.

"Did you see the brands, Cantrell? What ranch did they come from?"

"That's why I came here, Stuart. Most of 'em are your horses!" He grinned a likable grin. "At least, all I saw were."

Toby, listening at the window with Charlie Stuart, one of Granville's sons, began trembling. He knew that it meant another round of killing. Charlie looked at him in sympathy. All the kids felt bad for Toby and gave him as much comfort and understanding as they could.

Chapter 11

Bates Point, deep in the Missouri River Breaks

The whole outfit, sixteen strong, headed out the next day. Toby brought up the rear with the pack horses. Bates Point was located twenty miles below the mouth of the Musselshell on the north side of the river. The James Wood yard, a sod-roofed cabin and a stable with a corral connecting the two, was located in a beautiful bottom covered with cottonwoods, willows and rye grass. The James boys were cousins of the Jesse James clan in Missouri. Like them, they had a wild outlaw streak and the folks back there had finally gotten fed up with their criminal activities. The family particularly liked horses: usually belonging to someone else.

Stuart, his big Winchester .50/95, a twin of the one Cantrell carried, across his saddle, led his band through the river ford at the mouth of the Musselshell on the night of the sixteenth. They moved in darkness to within five miles of the point, then Stuart ordered camp made. They laid up the next day and Stuart sent Frank, Cantrell and Ludich downriver at dusk to scout.

The middle of the night Toby heard the guard softly challenge, then dimly saw the scouting party return. Hibbs threw some wood on the fire and Toby saw Stuart and Gus Cramer get up and put the coffee on. The talk was low and the boy could hear little that was said. He turned over and went back to trying to sleep.

The next night, after another day of lay-up, they moved into position, avoiding the two guards that the scout party had located. They left Toby with the horses and Frank cautioned him to keep his pistol out and ready."

When the sun rose, the two guards came in, heading for breakfast, and bumped into the vigilantes. Frank saw that they were two older boys, dark haired, one limping from some kind of wound. When they saw him and the others, they pulled their guns and began to shoot, screaming at the same time.

"Pa, Stringer! The stranglers are here! They got us surrounded,"

Frank, behind a big cottonwood, leaned out and shot, hitting the limping one in the good leg, putting him down, but still he kept shooting and yelling. The other pulled him into cover behind a large stump. Stuart called out.

"You men inside, come on out or we'll burn you out!"

"Come on in, you strangler sonsabitches, and we'll make it hot for you!" was the reply.

The firing grew heavy.

Off to one side and slightly behind the cabin was a wall tent. Stuart had put five men, Hibbs, Proctor, Headley, Starley, and Bill Clark, to take the tent under fire. They put some bullets through it and were startled to see it erupt with men, who ran in all directions, most getting under cover by a large woodpile.

Ludich and Frank crawled off to either side of the boys stump, flanking them. The uninjured youngster, seeing their danger, stood up to try and get his brother away. Ludich shot him in the chest and he fell across the other's leg, causing him to scream in pain. As he raised partly up, his pistol still in his hand, a heavy caliber shot sounded, Cantrell's big rifle. The boy slumped beside his brother.

Patterson and Jack Tabor, a daring DHS hand, crawled up behind the cabin and sloshed some coal oil on its log walls, then lit it. The flames shot up the side, crackling in quick intensity. The firing from the cabin slackened, then 'Old Man' James and Baker jumped from the door, shooting. Stuart's big rifle boomed, as did Frank's Henry and the Winchesters of the other men.

As James and Baker went down, another pair of men took their places, Dutch Henry and a weasel faced little man who worked pistols with both hands while Henry used his Winchester. The booming weapons in the hands of the vigilantes put them down beside the other two. A pause, then a dirty shirt flopped from the door and Stuart yelled, "Throw out your guns, then come out with your hands in the air!"

Jason Wheeler slunk out, holding his shoulder, which dripped blood.

* * *

Toby heard all the shooting and had his hands full calming the horses. The shots masked the noise behind him and the first he knew, two men stood in front of him, chests heaving, their guns out. Then he recognized the younger one, a boy, really, little older than he.

"Shoot him, Dee, and let's get out of here," the older man hissed.

Dee Nickerson, his eyes wild, had to make an effort to focus his eyes and mind.

"But, Dad, he's just a kid, like me!"

"Shoot him, I said!"

Toby saw then that the man's left arm was streaming red, he'd been hit there, also down low on the left side. He clamped his arm against his body and breathed hoarsely through his mouth. Dee raised his pistol, his hand trembling and Toby, in pure reflex, raised his own to ward off the bullet and found the gun in it.

They shot at the same time and both fell.

Nickerson slumped down, looking at his son. The boy was dead, shot in the head. He sighed, scrabbled the gun from his son's hand and stuck it in his waistband. He limped to the tied horses, picking out a sleek big black that looked like a runner. He pulled himself up, then, and was about to turn aside, when the brush moved and Stringer Jack lunged out, his green eyes flashing and his face bloody. He'd been shot in the right cheekbone, the bullet tearing away the flesh and bone, then glancing off to tear a jagged wound channel in his face and ear. He lurched and staggered to Nickerson's side. Silas saw that he'd been hit in the thigh, too.

"Nickerson, help me! I don't think I can mount with this leg!"

"Help yourself! I made it up and I'm all shot to hell, myself!"

Stringer turned, surveyed the horse string, then swung back and without a pause, shot Nickerson off the black horse, causing it to shy. He went over, swinging his leg, stepping over both boys' forms as he did so, with scarcely a glance. He caught the black's reins and clambered painfully aboard, then jumped him into a swift gallop north.

Chapter 12

DHS Ranch headquarters

Toby finally came awake enough to open his eyes, which action just about exhausted him. He was lying in bed: there were curtains on a window, pictures on the whitewashed log wall, a dresser with a round little mirror above it. Sunshine was coming through the panes and he guessed that it was a morning sun. He tilted his head a little to look at the sunbeams and saw with surprise that someone was sitting by his bed. A female, with hair haloed by the sun, dark hair. It was Katie, Stuart's oldest girl, he saw. She, seeing perhaps the movement of his head out of the corner of her eye, looked up from her knitting and exclaimed,

"Oh, you're awake, finally!" She put down her knitting and stood, "I'll call Ma. How do you feel? Mary'll be mad you didn't wake up when she was here." She chuckled.

Toby tried to speak but his mouth was dry and he merely croaked a little. He looked toward the china pitcher. "Some water?" Katy asked. He blinked his eyes and she poured a glass and helped him to drink, then left to summon her mother, who bustled in. Aubony, the mother of the Stuart clan, had been raised like a white girl and was perhaps more prim and proper even than her white counterpart. She pulled the covers down and examined something that hurt Toby. Suddenly his body feeling came back and he was aware of a fiery ache in his left side. He croaked out a question and she responded.

"Oh, you were shot, alright, sonny. A bullet that nearly killed you, but now you're mending pretty well." She pulled the covers back up to his chin. "It broke some ribs and touched a lung, I think. Maybe even the heart sack. Oh, it was a near thing. The men all thought you'd probably die, but we women sometimes know better about things like that." She got up from the bed.

"Some soup, maybe?" He nodded.

Next day, he felt a little stronger and Mary and Charlie came in to visit a while.

"Most all the men are gone," they told him. "They're still after horse thieves down along the river."

"How'd I get here?"

Charlie replied with a grin. "Frank carried you in all the way. He wouldn't let any of the rest of them pack you."

"How long I been here?"

"Oh, it's a good week or more, now. The men all thought you were gonna be a corpse, but Ma and the girls just kept on nursing you, and you kept on abreathin'."

Toby was quiet for a while, then asked, "What about Dee?"

Charlie and Mary were puzzled.

"Dee?"

"Dee Nickerson. I shot him, I think." He remembered the scene now, the father with blood dripping down his arm, telling Dee, the boy, to shoot.

Charlie spoke up. "I heard the hands talking and they said that someone had shot another kid where they found you. Is that who you mean? Your gun was out but they said it was fired only once and they found a man dead there, too, and thought maybe you'd shot him. Which one was Dee?"

But Toby had closed his eyes, exhausted. The two Stuarts shushed each other and crept out.

Later Toby learned that both Nickersons had died there and that several other outlaws had gotten away. Charlie was an eager informant.

"I heard 'em talking. Dutch Henry and another one weren't dead and they went ahead and hanged 'em anyway. The ones that got away stole the packs so Pa stopped a steamboat and got some grub for 'em. Then they brought you back here."

"Where's Frank and the rest of the men?" Toby wanted to know.

Charlie looked around and then whispered.

"When they came back, they was all mad because so many had got away. Pa sent some messages around on the telegraph asking people to keep their eyes peeled for 'em and he got word some of 'em were over at Poplar. The Indian Police picked 'em up, and Anderson, Jim Hibbs and Charlie Pettit went over there to bring 'em back. They'd got Swift Bill, Orvil Edwards and a couple others. Then, Pa sent Frank,

Gus Adams and Cantrell and some of the rest to meet 'em when they was coming back."

Charlie winked and Toby solemnly nodded, then asked,

"Well, where are they at now, then?"

"They all went south to the railroad and caught a train to go hang some more rustlers!" Charlie said triumphantly.

"They're gonna clean 'em up, once an' for all."

Chapter 13

North of the Missouri River

The big black horse lunged into a gallop with a swiftness that made the wounded man on his back gasp with pain. The charging speed and apparent endurance confirmed Jack Stringer's instinctive guess that the animal would be the best that he'd ever thrown a leg over. The fact that he'd killed a man to get it caused him no remorse. The men he had led on countless stock raids and killings had never had his loyalty or his affection. He'd saved all that for himself and survival was his only concern at the moment.

The surprise raid by the crew of the DHS had at first thrown him into a blind panic so deep he had trouble firing his weapon or reloading. As the battle wore on, though, his funk wore off and reason took over. Until then, he'd cared little before as to whether he lived or died. He'd thought of his present life as a dream. This time, for some reason, he did care but he didn't have the time to figure out just why. As his head had cleared, the desperate situation they were in became evident. The vigilantes had moved in under dark and pinpointed the positions of the two guards Stringer had set, then killed them both when they sounded the alarm at daylight. Now they were trying their best to kill him.

He'd bedded down the night before in the large tent, a little irritated that the others had crowded into the cabin so that he himself, their chief, was forced to settle for the leaky tent, made out of an old wagon tarp. It shortly was to save his life, for the cabin became a death trap to those inside.

At the sound of the shots which killed the two James youngsters, Stringer had raised up in his blankets and taken a bullet in the face that knocked him back down. Then came a volley which whistled through the tent, flapping and tearing the canvas. From one of the men beside him came a groan which shortly turned into the gargle of death.

Stringer passed out. When he came to, the firing was heavy and he was alone in the tent beside a corpse. Panic set in and he went stumbling from the sieved tent out into the swirling smoke of the battle.

"Stringer, Over here, dammit!"

Quick hands reached out and pulled him down by the woodpile, where several men, in various attitudes of crouching down or jumping up to shoot, had barricaded themselves for a stand.

"Here, get to pullin' a trigger!"

The same hands, Orvil Edwards' he saw now, shoved a gun at him. Still he sat, his face throbbing, his mind numb, the gun unfired in his lifeless fingers, until, with a seeming jerk, he was pulled back to reality by another bullet slapping into his leg.

His bloody face swiveled in the direction of the shot and he reacted instinctively, seeing they'd been flanked by a man in the trees off on their right. He shot then and missed, caught the hammer on the gun's familiar recoil, then put a bullet into the crouched figure that knocked it back and down. After that, his face still throbbing and his leg numb, he fired until his pistol was empty, then searched his pockets for shells. Finding none, he dragged himself back into the tent and located his gun belt. At that moment, with a whoosh, the back of the nearby cabin went up in flames.

"They fired the cabin, the sonsabitches!" one of the men crouched by the woodpile screeched.

The reek of coal oil told them that some one of the opposing group had daringly sneaked his way to the back of the old log structure and soaked it with the volatile liquid, then set it ablaze.

The cabin burned fiercely. Suddenly, from the cabin door jumped two men, their guns working. Their desperate move centered the vigilantes' attention on them and inadvertently gave the men behind the woodpile a moment's respite. Of one accord, this group saw its chance, and, each alone in his terror, they began to skulk away. Stringer attempted to rise, then fell back with a groan. Edwards knelt over him, blood from an arm wound dripping nearly in Stringer's face.

"You better get your ass up off that ground, or you'll be swinging from a cottonwood limb. C'mon!"

He reached down and grabbed a hand that Stringer raised, then pulled him to his feet with a powerful jerk.

Once there, he tugged him limping along beside him and they reached the dubious cover of the trees. Back of them sounded another fusillade of shots, greeting more men who tumbled from the door of the burning cabin. The first two, Stringer saw with a backwards glance, were down and not moving. They hurried forward, Edwards propelling them along at a rapid pace.

Presently Stringer stumbled to a stop. "You're heading for the river," he panted.

Edwards yanked at him, trying to get him moving again. "Damn right I am. C'mon, we're about there."

Stringer looked at him through blood rimmed eyes. "I can't swim."

"We'll find a tree limb or somethin'. You'll make it!' Edwards hissed, looking back at the smoke rising behind them.

Stringer held back. "I can't do it, Orvil. Me and water don't mix. I'm going to try for the horses."

Edwards backed off, shaking his head, "Suit yourself. I say you're crazy to try to ride with that leg." He turned then and scuttled into the willows lining the bank. Stringer heard him call back, a low 'Good luck.'

Stringer turned then and began limping along upstream, listening to the firing, sporadic now. He was nearly at the end of his strength when he'd literally fallen into the hollow where the Vigilantes horses were being held. Two lifeless forms lay on the ground, and Nickerson, streaming blood was already up on the black.

At a glance, Stringer saw that Nickerson was atop the best horse in the bunch, and with hardly a pause in his limping advance, shot the man out of the saddle. To catch the skittish horse, then, and climb aboard took just about all the strength he had left.

* * *

Back at the river, Frank lay cussing on his side behind a mossy stump, his rifle thrust out beside it. It had been hit by a bullet and his hands were still stinging from the blow. It had also twisted the magazine so that he couldn't jack shells through it and had now to feed it single shot through the breech. He put it aside and drew his belt gun. At that instant, a dirty white shirt waved from the burning cabin and Frank, seeing it, hollered.

"Hold your fire, they had enough! Come on out, horse thieves!"

He wasn't really surprised when Jason Wheeler, shot in the left shoulder with blood dripping from between his fingers, stepped warily out.

"Any more in there, Wheeler?" Frank shouted. The young man shook his head.

"No, none alive at least, the rest are all dead,"

Around the clearing, men began to appear. Bill Clark came up on the run. "There was a pile of 'em back there in the tent!! They got behind the woodpile and gave us hell. Proctor and Headley're dead. Starley's hit hard. A bunch of 'em got away."

He slumped panting down onto a stump, then jumped up and led Stuart and Cramer back to where the little puncher lay. A ragged hole in his middle, just over his gunbelt, pulsed dark blood. Stuart knelt down by him. He opened the bloody shirt and took a long look, then turned him gently over and checked the exit wound. A stifled groan escaped the hurt man's lips. Then Stuart, Adams helping, returned him to his back.

"It isn't good, Butch." Stuart said gravely.

"I know, Boss. My guts are leaking, I can smell them. Prop me up and roll me a smoke. I want to see the show." The men surrounding him complied.

Frank, meanwhile, with Hibbs helping, began checking the bodies lying in front of the burning cabin.

"Well, boys, here's one that ain't gone under."Hibbs called, stepping back and drawing his gun.

Dutch Henry, when turned over, had opened his eyes and fixed them on Hibbs with a baleful stare. He'd been shot three times, once through the neck, twice in the upper body. They rolled him over again, and heedless of his groans, tied his hands.

"Get some rope, Cantrell, and we'll finish the job." Frank directed.

Cantrell had found some rope. Sight of it brought young Wheeler over, hands tied behind his back, the one arm still dripping blood. His face was white and strained. He leaned toward Frank, his stocky frame quivering.

"Frank, for Christ's sake, you're not going to let them hang me, are you?" He tried to jerk away from Cantrell's grasp and fell to his knees. Bill pulled him back to his feet and Frank leaned over him, poking his chest with a bony forefinger.

"Son, you ride with 'em, you die with 'em. Besides, I'm thinkin' you tipped 'em to our layout over on the Rosebud. Am I right?" Fierce old gray eyes bored into the young Englishman's blue ones. Under their impact, Wheeler's wavered and looked away.

"Find a good limb, boys!"

The last swinging figure had just ceased its kicking air dance when Ludich burst from the surrounding trees.

"Hell, boys, they got to our horses," he panted out. The grim dark face worked as he turned to Frank. "I hate to tell you —Toby's shot bad, Frank. Some of the horses are gone, too."

Frank blinked and turned away, picking up his battered Henry. Without a backward glance at the figures swinging silently from the cottonwood, he began striding back toward the deadly hollow.

"Frank! Send." Stuart's shout was drowned out by a pistol shot. Starley had made sure that he wouldn't slow them down. Frank broke into a shambling run.

* * *

Many hours later, the worn-out band of vigilantes trotted into the DHS, minus those who'd stayed back to bring in the stolen horses. A challenge rang out and was answered as most of the men turned into the barn. They dismounted wearily and began unsaddling. Three burdens, though, they eased off and gently lay to one side.

Meanwhile, a light shone in the main cabin as Stuart helped Frank carry a limp form through the narrow doorway. An interval later Frank reappeared and headed his halting steps toward the cookshack, where lantern light was shining through a greasy, flyspecked window. He entered the low doorway where Leaky Pete, the gimpy cook, thrust a steaming mug of coffee into his hands. Then he dropped down on the low bench flanking the scarred, rough table. The eyes of the several men along its length watched him sympathetically but no one ventured to open his mouth. All of them knew the boy had taken a .45 slug in the chest, close to the heart. It was a wound that would kill most men. Hell, all of them had killed men or big game, even bear, with chest shots from their belt guns. The boy had almost no chance to come through. They knew it and they knew Frank, old hand that he was, knew it, too. No matter that he'd said, all the way from Bates' Point that the boy would make it.

Because of that, none of them could meet his eyes. They were all surprised then, when the silent old cook spoke.

"Well, you got 'im here alive, Frank. Miz Stuart can save him if anyone can. She's a real hand at doctorin'." He shuffled over behind the stove and drew forth a half empty quart whiskey bottle. Then he further astounded the group by walking the length of the table, pouring a stout shot into each cup. Frank made as though to wave him off.

The old cook misunderstood his hesitation.

"Hell, the boss won't mind us havin' a short one just now."

* * *

After they'd returned from the battle at Bate's Point, Stuart had straight away ridden in to Fort Maginnis. From there, he'd sent telegrams to all points of the territory to watch for the outlaws who'd escaped from the fight. The Army, victims of several horse raids themselves, had just lost a payroll to thieves and were willing to help all they could.

When Stuart returned to the DHS, the boy, to his surprise, was still alive. His wife, a woman with a gift in healing, had worked on him all night. The stolen horses had come in, ninety-one head. The men were all down at the corrals checking brands or working over their gear. Stuart, worn out from so many hours in the saddle, was still so keyed up he couldn't sleep.

He walked down to the cookshack to get some coffee. When he entered, Frank was sitting at the table. He looked up as Stuart sat down facing him.

"He's holding his own."

Frank passed a hand over his eyes. "My fault, Stuart, you told me not to take him along, but I had to think I knew best."

"Well, Frank, The Bible says, 'To each of us, there is a time.' Matthew's time came, just as it will to each of us—to you, to me, to Toby. You can't blame yourself about the turns Fate takes. When it comes, we all, no matter how young, how old, how tough, will lay down our earthly burden and shuffle off into the Hereafter. How many times have we both seen it? Don't give up on Toby yet. Maybe there's a pattern but it isn't given to us mortals to understand it. It's too deep a subject for such as us." Blinking with fatigue, he brought the cup to his lips.

"It would'na been for Matthew. He wasn't a big talker but he thought deep."

"Yes, I heard he was an educated man. Harvard, wasn't it? I heard too, that Jack Stringer had gone to Yale. Curious."

Frank looked out the cloudy window. "Stringer killed Matthew. He was the one I wanted."

"Young Patterson will bring word from Fort Maginnis if any comes."

Frank grunted and took another sip of coffee. Then he spoke in a low, flat voice.

"First my pardner and our hands shot, then our boy. Now my horse stolen, the one Matthew give me. I swear, Stuart, that son-of-a-bitch's day is coming and I'm the one to bring it to him." Their eyes locked.

"I believe you will, Frank. You know I'll do what I can. Take my gray. He's the equal of your Ben horse." He reached out in a rare display of emotion for him, and patted Frank's arm.

Frank nodded, "Thanks, Granville."

Stuart looked at the man facing him. He sighed, thinking how blessed he'd been in his own pardner, Reece, and his brother, James. Both men were very close to him. What a loss if he should lose either of them.

Like himself, Reece had a family to think about, though he rarely did. Ludich had told him how Reece and Frank had killed the cabin full of outlaws, Reece being wounded in the arm.

These men they were up against were kin to the buffalo wolves. Like them, they had until recently preyed upon the herds. But with the buffalo gone, the wolves and many of the hunters had turned to the cattle and horse herds flooding in to take the buffalo's place on the Montana and Wyoming plains. Now it was war for survival, pure and simple. But however it came out, the death of men like Matthew Grounds, Butch Starley, Headley and Pete Proctor would haunt him the rest of his life. And it wasn't over by any means. The breaks along the Missouri were full of nests like Bate's Point, all loosely connected. If he couldn't gain the approval and backing of the general membership of the Montana Livestock Association this month at the Miles City meeting, he'd better start thinking seriously about pulling out. The rustlers would have won. The problem would be talking Reece into it. The man was as stubborn as the one sitting across from him. He sipped again at his coffee, the thoughts tumbling around in his head, like swirling mist.

Patterson rode in that evening, bringing the news that Marshal Fischall and some Indian Police had taken five prisoners at Poplar that answered the descriptions Stuart had given over the telegraph. A little later, Anderson, Hibbs and Pettit headed east.

At dawn, the barn door opened and Frank appeared leading a big gray horse, followed by Ludich, Cramer and Cantrell with their saddled horses and four pack horses. They swung into the leather and headed over to the main cabin where Stuart stood on the porch, waiting.

"Mornin', Stuart. How's the boy?" Frank asked, anxiously.

"He had a good night, Aubony tells me."

Frank swung down and tightened his cinch a notch. "Told you he'll make it. With your good wife's care and the girls there to help her, he's gonna be fine."

"Long as infection doesn't set in." Stuart stepped off the porch and handed Frank a rifle.

"Here's my big Winchester and a couple of boxes of shells." he waved off Frank's protest.

"Your's is wrecked and you'll need a rifle." Except for a couple of the outlaws' pistols, in their hurry they'd taken nothing away from Bate's Point and rifles were in short supply.

"Your horse, now your rifle. Appreciate it, Granville. I'll try to bring 'em back in one piece." Frank pulled the mangled Henry out of its scabbard and, extending it to Stuart, pushed the heavy lever action repeater down in its place.

"No matter, Frank. You boys be careful."

He stepped back and raised his hand as the little group swung their horses around and headed east, into the rising sun.

Chapter 14

Poplar, Montana Territory

Marshal Bill Fischall was having a good week. First, the telegram from Granville Stuart had arrived. Then, his Indian police had heard of several white men, most of them wounded and exhausted, who'd been taken in by the Assiniboines on the reservation. His men had brought him the news and they all had gone out in the early morning darkness to surround the teepees where the men were holed up. He'd gained a lot of respect, then, by walking right in and demanding their surrender. His Indian policemen had backed him and he'd pulled it off, taking a gun right out of the hand of one of the gang, an individual named Orvil Edwards. Not a shot had been fired, somewhat to the disappointment of his men, who wouldn't have minded killing some whites.

Leg irons and handcuffs were roughly put on each of them, despite some visible wounds. The wagons were brought up, and with the whole camp watching, the poor wretches were bundled in and they were off to town. The town was alerted and all turned out when they came triumphantly riding in, to his great satisfaction. The crowd had formed as they unloaded the chained men. Curious saloon loafers, cowpunchers, Indians, kids, everybody had to see what was going on. Of course, when the talking had started, he was the focus of attention. And it felt good. That had started him thinking, dreaming. Territorial Marshal, maybe, with politics next, Senator, perhaps, with Governor somewhere in the future. When Daniel Drake, the Poplar Post's editor, said he just had to see him to get the story, Fischall had said,

"Sure, but not right now, Dan, I have to get these boys on the line." 'Let him stew a while,' he thought. 'It would give him a chance to decide how to tell it just right.'

The line was a heavy cable strung between two cottonwood trees. The neck chains were attached to the cable and the men were leashed like dogs there on the bare ground. With leg irons and wrist manacles, they weren't going anywhere, even if the town didn't have a proper jail, yet. He left two guards with them and sent the rest off to dinner, then went home to eat, himself. Drake had come, then and the story he'd gotten had been a good one. Around dusk the next day, three men had shown up in response to the telegram he'd sent Granville Stuart. Their leader, Reece Anderson, Stuart's partner, wanted to take the men back to Fort Maginnis to face charges ranging from stock rustling to payroll theft.

Letting the men out of his custody so soon wasn't exactly how he'd pictured the affair ending, but thinking on it, he'd decided maybe some good might come of it—if he took the men he'd captured over to Maginnis himself. Anderson didn't argue. In fact, Anderson declared it to be a good idea, to Fischall's relief. Certainly, it would mean his name in another story. And he'd probably have to testify, tell how he'd captured them. More good publicity.

They left town much like they'd come in—with everyone turning out to see the spectacle. He'd sat tall in the wagon seat, looking neither right nor left, with his two men, Kills Twice and Bad Wound, along with Anderson and his two cowhands following behind. The morning, so bright and summer fresh, was a fine one for traveling because there'd been a light rain just before dawn, soaking in enough to keep down the dust but not so bad as to make the roads too muddy. The outlaws, sprawled in the box, were still wet and shivering. One, named Swift Bill, was only semi-conscious. He kept up a soft, monotonous moaning despite the fact that his friends, tired of listening to him, had slapped him and threatened to beat his head off if he didn't quit.

Doc Tinedale, after looking them all over before they left, had said the hip wound Swift Bill had was rotten with gangrene already and his dying was just a matter of time. The others were little better off. Only Phelps was unhit. Edwards was shot in the forearm, Dixie Burr had taken a bullet in the butt, through both cheeks, and another in the upper right arm. Johnnie Owens had a nasty looking thigh wound. All of them had been in the river for a long time and all of them except Burr had lost their boots. He'd tied his around his neck. None of them had rifles when they'd been caught, only pistols. And the bullets were no good from being in the river so long. That and their wounds explained the lack of fight they'd shown. Of course, no one needed to know that.

All the day long, with just a short noon break, the wagon and riders had threaded their way through the pine-covered breaks and sagebrush flats, taking a meandering westward direction that paralleled the big Missouri River. The road was really just a few wheel tracks going in the same direction, now coming together at a creek or coulee crossing, now back tracking to head a deep cut.

Several times, to get the wagon across, he'd had to climb down, get out a couple shovels, and with some others helping, fill in with dirt and rocks or level off a steep spot where water had cut out the trail. He'd been graining his team and they were in pretty good shape. The dun horse that he'd gotten on a trade last fall from the tribe was finally getting over his damn balking. Lord knew, he'd worn out a club or two on the sonofabitch. He called him Rocky for what was between his mule-like ears. For all that, he was a pretty good puller when he worked, just as good as the white horse, Whitey. They made good time until almost dark, when they'd pulled off at Cedar Springs to camp for the night.

He had the other prisoners lift the moaner out and try to make him comfortable if they could, so they maybe wouldn't have to listen to it all night, too. He got out a bucket and dunked it into the ice-cold water, then carried it and a dipper over to the wounded men, who drank with feverish thirst. His two Indians were busy building a fire while one cowboy took to snaking in some firewood with his horse. The others went to taking care of the stock. Himself, he started getting out the cookpans and grub.

In no time, they had a good fire going, which he allowed to die down before he set in cooking the spuds and venison off the fresh haunch he'd brought along, wrapped in a piece of tarp. The coffee was hot and black, with enough in the big blue stoneware pot to go around. Even the moaner had managed a little of it, and some of the food before he lay back.

The cowboys had been in a storytelling mood that evening. They brewed up some more coffee after the big meal they'd eaten and Anderson surprised him by bringing out a bottle to 'touch up their cups with'. Then the stories really flew. Anderson told a couple about the gold camp days with Stuart. The cowboys chimed in with some about trailing herds up from Texas, the Indian fights, the stampedes, crossing the treacherous rivers, water horses they'd had, or runners. 'Course, then he had to tell a few, himself, like the one where he'd faced down the saloon full of Hat X boys when they were causing a ruckus, and how he'd nearly single-handedly rounded up this motley gang they were bringing back to justice. The two Indians sat and listened, contributing nothing to the white men's talk beyond the slurping of the whiskeyed coffee, which Anderson had poured for them, over his weak objections. Really, his men and he were on duty, being they were transporting prisoners. Nobody'd know, though, and if they did, so what? No harm done.

It was late before they turned in, and they'd killed two bottles. And, sure enough, you might know it, the damned moaner started in. He was grateful when Anderson finally got yet another bottle out of his packs and gave the noisy bastard a stiff jolt. It settled him down. But then the others, seeing him get a drink, started in, and Anderson, cussing, finally just gave the whole bottle over to them, to shut 'em up.

He got an hour or two of sleep, maybe, then it was time to roll out and hitch up. He had a blinding headache, which the black coffee helped some, but it did little to make up for his bleary-eyed lack of sleep. Still, the cowhands didn't look too much the worse for wear, so he tried to buck up, himself.

Like the day before, things went along pretty well. Once up on Antelope Flats they made good time, snaking their way through the tall sage and grease wood. The moaner had passed out, so they heard little from him. The others though, were suffering and muttering, especially Burr. The bright sun accentuated his headache, making it throb so bad he kept his eyes shut as much as he could. He didn't notice therefore, for quite a while, that the cowboy, Pettit, was not with them. When he did, he pulled Whitey and Rocky to a stop.

"Where'd your other man go, Reece?" he hollered back, for the riders were loafing a ways in the rear. Anderson rode up to the wagon.

"No problem, Marshal, he just stayed back a ways to take a shit. We saw some prairie chickens, too, and he wanted to get some for supper."

Fischall squinted his eyes against the headache and the sun, peering down their back-trail, but the rider was nowhere in sight.

"Okay, just wondered where he was, is all. Guess some birds would go good tonight." He slapped the reins on the butts of his team and the wagon jerked forward. The moaner moaned, awake again.

Dusk of that day, Fischall was so drowsy and headachy he knew he was going to have to stop soon. He'd tried to turn off a couple times but Anderson had urged him to try to make another mile or two. The missing hand, Pettit, had shown up hours before, throwing some gutted birds into the back of the wagon. The moaner, out for a while, had come to again and started up, so they'd stopped and watered up from the big bag hanging on the side of the wagon. They went on, Fischall nodding over the reins.

It was nearly dark when, Fischall, alerted, raised his head and saw horses standing on either side of the road. At a shouted command to "Hold up" an instant later, he rose to his feet and muscled his team to a stop.

"Who's there?" he shouted when the team had quieted. Then, from the pines on the right and left of him came several dark figures. Behind him, he heard Edwards say, 'Well, boys, looks like this is the end of our little wagon ride." The moaner moaned.

Marshal Fischall started down for his belt gun, but with a click of the hammer, a big rifle was thrust right up against his chest. Instantly, he raised his arms and a hand came out and took his pistol.

"Climb down and stand by your team, Marshal. We need to visit with that wagon load of manure you're haulin'."

He complied, wondering what had happened to his Indians. They were nowhere about. Anderson and his two cowhands were disarmed by another dark figure who came up from behind them. They were ordered to stand by the Marshal, then the wagon tailgate was dropped.

"Get down, boys, and we'll have a little visit." There was steel in the voice coming from under the handkerchief mask and reluctantly the chained men complied. Carrying the moaner, they were led away into the darkness.

Fischall started to move. "Hold on, those men are my prisoners!"

Anderson grabbed his arm. "Shut up, damn you, or they'll kill us all!"

Thinking on it, he allowed Anderson to hold onto him. Without his men to back him, and if Anderson wasn't going to, he was better off not to make a fuss. If Anderson was scared, he could excuse the fear in himself. Back in the pines there, he could hear the mutter of a harsh voice but he couldn't get what was said. He slumped against the wagon. It looked like his week was going to Hell,—and from what he could hear back in the pines, it was going to have company.

That morning, Pettit had split off from the group and ridden a big fast circle around in front of the wagon, figuring that he would run into Frank not too far to the west. The two horses tied to either side of the trail alerted him just before he was hailed.

"Hey Charlie, whoa up!"

Frank appeared from the trees, Stuart's big rifle over his arm. Pettit leaned on his horse's neck while they talked. Ludich came slouching from behind his horse on the right. He waved but didn't come closer.

"They're quite a ways back, Frank, but they'll get here before dark. You better pull back a mile or two unless you want to hit us in the daylight."

"No, we'll go back some, and hold up right before Timber Creek. There's a good spot there that I saw. If we do it in daylight he's apt to tie us together. Let's try to keep that from happenin'."

"He's got a couple tribal police along. One of 'em looks pretty handy."

"Tell Reece to talk to 'em. Tell them it's a 'white man' matter and they should stay out of it."

"I'll do that. We can turn 'em back, I think. If we can't, it'll be two dead Indians." Frank chuckled.

"How'd it go last night?

"Real good," Pettit likewise chuckled, "The Marshal's got him a terrific headache today. He didn't get much shuteye, either. A couple of those men, it'll be a mercy to hang 'em."

"Well, head on back, then."

Frank waved and Ludich came over with a string of gutted prairie chickens. He handed them up to Pettit, who tied them on his saddle. Then he swung his horse around and sent him down his back-trail.

That evening, with the Indian Police doing a fade, the Marshal off the wagon and disarmed, the outlaws were brought into the pines to a little clearing. A large tree stood there with a big overhanging branch which jutted out. Two of the masked men threw ropes over it with nooses already tied in them. Then the one carrying the big Winchester spoke.

"Now I just would like to know one thing, boys, before you swing. Does any of you know where your boss got off to?"

Silence ensued, broken only by the moaning of Swift Bill. Then Edwards broke it, saying in an even, sullen voice,

"I know who you are, old man. The buffalo hunter from over on the Rosebud. We killed your pardner, didn't we? And some of your hands, too. That bowlegged Texas boy for one. Sure was too bad we missed you that day. But your partner got his guts blowed out."

The big rifle came around off Frank's arm and cracked Edwards across the face. Unconscious, he slumped to the ground.

"Pull 'em up!!"

In succession, each of the men, including Swift Bill and Edwards, swung up into the night air. The heavy branch creaked but held through the gyrations of the strangling, kicking bodies.

The Marshal and Anderson, along with his men, were directed to stay where they were. In a little while, hearing hoofbeats fading, Anderson said, "Come on, Bill!" Together, they rushed through the trees, coming in an instant to the little clearing. The heavy branch, with its gruesome burden, had bent down to where one of the hanged men's feet almost touched the ground. He was, however, as still as the rest.

"Well, Goddam, they swung 'em all!" Anderson exclaimed. The Marshal looked at him then, a light dawning in his fatigued mind.

"You! Anderson! You were in on this all the time, weren't you?" he nearly screamed, "I'll lose my job for this, God damn you!"

"I don't think so, Bill." Reece came smoothly back. "Why, I seen you was about to jump them and held you back from getting shot. I'll damn sure tell them you did everything you could," He turned to Pettit, standing back of him.

"C'mon, Charlie, let's give him a hand. Got your knife?"

Chapter 15

North side of the Missouri River

John Stringer had ridden the Ben horse until he'd passed out and fallen off. When he awoke, his face felt as if it were on fire, and his leg, twisted under him, was numb and useless. He was weak as a baby and he knew it was from loss of blood and lack of food. He wasn't feverish but he knew that likely would come later. He raised his head.

It was nearly dark. He didn't expect to see the horse. However, it nickered lightly and looking over, Stringer could just make out the black shape against the dim horizon. He crawled to the animal, softly thanking him out loud for being a gentle horse, not a bronc who wasn't ground broke. The black horse, in fact, was so gentle it didn't mind when he attempted several times to get back in the saddle and failed. He could only tie the reins to a bush and then lie back and wait for daylight.

Finally streaks of light shone to the east, the sun rising through pearl colored clouds tinged with darker rose. He was on a sagebrush ridge, he saw, with cedar breaks falling off to either side. A game trail followed the ridge, with elk and deer tracks clearly imprinted there in the dust. He crawled to where he could see his back trail and it looked clear so far of any pursuit.

Water was the thing he had to have, both for himself and his horse. Following the game trail would maybe take him to some, if he could just get back into the saddle. He looked around for a way. Not too far from him was a steep break which cut off to a deeper, sandstone sided canyon. He might just be able to position the horse down below him, then work his way off the ledge and onto its back: if, and it was a big if, the horse would cooperate. He damn sure couldn't stay where he was, and he couldn't walk. Dragging his leg, he crawled to the horse and untied the reins.

The horse did cooperate. A range horse would likely have scattered him all over the ridge, Stringer knew. It caused him to look even more closely at the animal. Someone had taken more than usual care of it, trimming the mane, the tail and its fetlocks. And, it was shod. Clearly, it was more than a cowpony to someone.

Once in the saddle, his leg pain nearly causing him to pass out again, he started the horse down the trail at a slow walk. It followed the bottom of the wooded canyon.

Coming around some trees, he spooked back a little bunch of elk. A raghorn bull was in the lead and he twirled and chased his little harem of four cows back along the trail. It made Stringer think with some hope that they must be coming up from water.

Sure enough, some few hundred yards farther down, he came onto a little creek. It fell, he saw, from a spring up on the cliff side of the canyon wall. The elk had been watering there. He looked around and reined the horse to a tree limb which he used to pull himself off the back of the horse, then let himself down as easily as he could on his good leg. The short ride had loosened him up some and he was able to hobble, leading the horse, to a small pool of water. Man and horse drank thirstily.

An hour or so later, Stringer had the black horse over by a rock and was struggling to get on again from the off side when it threw its head up, looking up the canyon.

Stringer, wriggling back, fell from the rock onto his injured leg. The pain caused him to black out again.

When he came to, it was nearly dark. He could smell woodsmoke. Feeling his face, he found it bound with a buckskin rag. It felt better, numb. His leg was likewise bound and numb. He was under a lean-to, lying on a springy bed of pine and cedar boughs overlaid with a buffalo robe. Another robe, a smoky elk hide, was covering him. He gave himself up to exhausted sleep.

* * *

As soon as Frank and his crew arrived back at the DHS, he went immediately to the main cabin where Aubony Stuart was waiting on the porch, having seen the men ride in.

"He's still alive and fighting, Mr. Shannon. But he hasn't really come to, yet." She crossed her arms primly, a stiff, starchy little lady. Behind her, one of the little girls peered through the screen door.

Frank stood by the bottom of the steps, the late morning sun shining off the graying brown hair capping the lean head. His old high crowned Stetson was in his hands and he gripped it by the brim, turning it round and round in a nervous gesture. He made a striking figure. Tall, his long legs showed the slight horseman's bow, covered by pin striped California leather trimmed riding pants touching the ground over handmade boots, held up behind by large roweled silver inlaid spurs. Round his waist was a heavy cartridge studded gun belt with a Colt revolver hanging low on his right side. A brown wool vest covered a soiled white shirt, but there hung no watch chain or fob from it, as was the custom of most men of the day to carry.

"Well, Ma'am, we're headin' out directly. Will you let the boy know, when he wakes up, that I hope to make it back for him?"

The hat went round and round in his hands. Mrs. Stuart's assurances seemed to allay his anxiety and he turned for the cookshack, the jinglebobs on his spurs a musical accompaniment to his strides.

When he entered, Leaky Pete poured him a tin cup full of coffee and he went to lean on the wall outside, easing his stiff legs after the hard riding they'd been doing. The men were grouped around Reece Anderson, who stood on the porch step.

"But we've got them on the run around here." Reece was saying. "What we need to do now is head down East and give Irvine a hand down at Miles."

"That's so, He could sure use some help with the Chinnick bunch down there," Cramer offered.

"Just running the town is keeping his hands full now, what with all the riffraff comin' in."

The other men looked grave. "I don't know," Ludich spoke up. "I'll fight for the brand I'm workin' for, on the range they're runnin' their stock on. But I think maybe we're overstepping our bounds if we go beyond the Association's ground here. Will Irvine deputize us if we go down there, or are we on our own?"

The rest of the cowboys were silent. Jack Ludich had expressed most of the other hands' feelings on the issue. None were really gunmen, though some had killed before, just handy men with a lifetime of hard living under their belts. And none had a personal feud going such as Frank had, just the universal range prejudice against stock thieves. They'd just buried their comrades in a growing cemetery behind the ranch headquarters. A funeral for three men was a sobering spectacle.

Reece Anderson's harsh voice broke the silence. "You tellin' us that you're showing yellow now that we got a good start on these bastards?" He spit a stream of brown tobacco juice. "Come on, Jack. Do we treat you bad? Pay you less? Feed poor? Why, we even let you boys run your own stock on the range, if you want. Do you see any other brands doin' that? I ask you!"

Ludich looked around before replying. "The things you're sayin' is all true, Boss. And there's none of us goin' to dispute it. But we're all just worried about how we're goin' to be looked at if we go off our range. You tell us the law will cover us and we'll be behind you." The others said nothing, but nodded their heads. Anderson threw up his hands.

"Boys, I'll get a telegram to Irvine right away, telling him we'll come help, but we'll need deputy badges. If he says yes, we go. If not, we don't. How's that sound?" Reece graveled.

Frank snorted.

Ludich answered, "Boss, that's all we ask. Thank you." He got up to put his cup in the washpan and the others followed, their spurs dragging musically as they stepped off the rough planks. Frank stayed back, along with Cantrell and Adams.

"Sounds like the boys are getting cold feet, Reece. I wouldn't have thought it of Ludich."

"Don't worry, Frank, they'll back us. We got some good men there."

"I am worrying. What if Irvine says 'No, he can't do it?'

Reece grinned his wolfish grin. "Then, old horse, it's up to us."

"The three" Cantrell started to speak.

"No, by God. I'm in this, too." Cramer broke in. "And Stuart'll be with us. You can't count him out."

Frank looked at each in turn. "It's settled, then, that we're going through with it?"

"Damn right!" Reece agreed. The others all nodded.

"Fine. Then send your telegram. While you're at it, maybe you can send a couple riders across the river to look for sign in that direction. How's that?"

"I better make it four. They may run into a hornet's nest over there."

"They gonna balk at this, too, wantin' a tin star from Irvine before they cross the river?" Frank asked sarcastically. A silence ensued that Reece finally broke.

"Frank, you got the boys wrong. They're willin'. They showed that at Bate's Point and our little sojourn to Plentywood. And don't forget Mackenzie and Billy Downes. They're behind us and you're just letting your poison over your dead pardner and the kid get the best of you. Besides, we need them and you know it." Two pairs of eyes locked and held. Frank finally looked away.

"Mebbe so, Reece, but it doesn't sit easy. I remember times years back when Matthew and I. Like you and me, when we took on that bunch in the cabin a couple weeks ago. These youngsters today don't have the kind of iron backbone we had to grow to survive. 'Course, they didn't have our advantages, I guess, the war, the Comanches, the guerrillas and all." A faint grin creased his face.

"Yeah, Frank, that's so Leaky, you got that bottle hid somewheres about?"

Reece raised his voice and the old cook shuffled over and poured a splash in each of their cups from the bottle he had stashed behind the stove. Frank looked away, then eyed the cup. Leaky, as he turned, raised the bottle and took a long, gurgling drink before he replaced it in its hiding place by the ash bucket. Frank brought the cup up and took a hesitating sip, then downed it in a gulp.

* * *

In April, 1884, the Montana Stockgrowers Association came together for their annual meeting in Miles City, a group that two years before had been non-existent.

Reece went off to Fort Maginnis to send his telegram after asking Frank to pick a crew to send north of the river. Frank found he was unable to just sit idle, waiting for Toby to regain consciousness, so he decided to Hell with it, he'd go himself to look for sign. As he was throwing the leather on Stuart's big gray, Jack Ludich came into the barn. A pack horse was already loaded with Frank's trail gear. He pulled his cinch tight, dropped the stirrup and shoved the big loaded Winchester down into its scabbard, ignoring the puncher standing by the door. From the back of the barn, the door swung back and Cantrell came through it with his sorrel horse following him. Without a word, he stepped into the tack room, gathered his gear and began saddling up.

"Where you goin'?" Frank inquired, glancing at him.

"With you. Stuart said I was to trail you." Cantrell retorted. Without a word, Frank turned, and looking straight through Ludich, who stepped out of his way, he led the gray through the door. A moment later Cantrell followed. Ludich, folding his arms, watched them go, biting his lip.

A beautiful morning greeted them. Off in the sagebrush, the meadowlarks were trilling a discordant cadence. To the south two eagles floated high above the foothills. For a time, they trotted single-file, each leading a pack horse, over a narrow trail to the north. Presently though, after a stretch of a couple miles, the trail widened out onto a big flat.

Frank dropped back to a walk and Cantrell's sorrel came abreast of Stuart's big gray.

"How's the action on that big plow horse, Frank?" Bill inquired, half-jokingly, hoping to penetrate the other man's silence.

Frank snorted, "This ain't no plow horse. He's got some nice moves to him. Be interestin' to try him and Ben for a mile or so."

"Hope we can get him back for you. He's probably into Canada by now, though." He reached out a calloused hand and petted the neck of his own blaze-faced sorrel. The muscled animal was a magnificent one in its own right, though it had some age on it. Cantrell had stolen him years back from the Sioux.

At the time, he'd been wood-hawking along the Missouri, selling cord wood to the boats supplying the mines. An outlaw Sioux band had come through on their way to the Canadian border after their battle with Custer on the Rosebud. They'd surprised Cantrell and shot him but he'd escaped into the willows lining the river. After a desultory search for him, they had then taken his Indian wife, a young Pawnee, and all his horses. A steamboat had pulled in to his signal the next day and taken him to Fort Benton, more dead than alive.

He'd pulled through, gone after the band but had never caught up with them. He thought at times maybe they had killed her. She'd been a kind of contrary thing but he'd been fond of her. Pawnee and Sioux hated each other, and both hated a white man's squaw. If she had fought them enough, they'd have just cut her throat. He and a friend, Pike Landusky, had gone up there and killed some of them and got a few horses back, but he'd never managed to find out anything about his Pawnee girl. Among the horses was the big sorrel that he'd ridden when they fled back over the line, a jump ahead of forty warriors raring for their scalps. They had to leave back some of the slower horses that day but the sorrel had done great duty, probably saving his life.

'Wild Plum, his little Pawnee girl. . .' He sighed. He'd paid five horses and couple boxes of rifle shells for her. He'd thought that he'd made a good bargain. They had gotten along pretty good. For some reason, he still missed her.

'The hell with it, thinking about it just made him gloomy.'

"What was that, Shannon?" Frank had asked him something, but it hadn't registered.

"I said, where you from? I can hear the South in your lingo, but it isn't Texas."

"No. I'm from Arkansas. My father and me rode with Cantrell's Raiders during the war. He was our famous cousin, a bloody bastard. Dad was killed in one of the raids and I cut loose from 'em just before the war ended. I joined up with the regulars and fought with Bragg at Stone River and Perryville, then with Lee at the Wilderness. You?"

"With Hood and the Texas Brigade through most all of it. Me'n Matthew." He spurred the gray.

For the best part of three days, they traveled a circular route, seeing little but occasional bands of elk and deer. Once though, through his battered old spy glass, Frank saw mounted riders far out on the prairie—Indians, it looked like. He watched them disappear in a deep cut, still heading west. "War party. Probably Sioux," he grunted, snapping the glass shut and stowing it back in his saddlebag. Cantrell dismounted and began tightening his cinch.

"Well, let's go after the bastards!" he grated. Frank shook his head.

"Nope, I'm after Stringer just now. The Indians aren't my meat. 'Sides, I don't want to get killed before I get that bastard," He turned his horse east again. Cantrell cursed but followed.

Chapter 16

Indian camp north of the river

Stringer came back to consciousness mid-morning the next day. He felt better, rested, but hungry. His face, though swollen so that he could barely open his jaw, didn't pain him so much. His leg, though, ached like a real bad tooth. Smelling food, he raised up and looked out the lean-to, towards a small fire close to the stream. A small figure, a tiny woman, was bending over the fire, cooking something. Another woman, an old one, was playing with a young child. She would roll stones and the boy would scramble after them, trying to catch them before they reached the creek. Two scrubby horses were standing under the pines beside the unsaddled black he'd been riding. The saddle lay under the trees. Stringer saw that travois poles made up the sloped sides of the lean-to he was under. Skin packs lay under the canopy beside him.

"Hey," His voice was weak and muffled from his swollen face. Both women turned at the sound.

"He awakes!" the old one cackled. Stringer, not understanding the language, thought they might be Sioux. The young one got up and came to him, so little that she didn't have to stoop under the lean-to's ridgepole.

She wore a beautifully beaded buckskin dress, he noticed, off-white and long, fringed on the bottom, with tiny moccasins peeping out from beneath it. Her black hair was braided and twined around her head with two bone somethings to hold it in place. Her face, though high-cheekboned, still was slender, in keeping with the rest of her. She really was quite miniature, Stringer saw. Like an elf, he thought with surprise, an Indian elf. He would have laughed out loud had not his face wound prevented him. He made the drink sign instead, and she turned away to get a tin cup that lay just outside the lean-to.

"Who are you?" he croaked, after she had brought him water. He pointed to her.

"Cha'pa, me." she replied shyly, looking down from where she kneeled by his side.

"Where'd you come from?" He handed the cup back and watched as her tiny hand came out and grasped it, then saw with a shock that it was missing two fingers. They had been cut off—and quite recently. Yet she showed no apparent pain. She turned away, putting the utensil back in its place outside the lean-to.

"What tribe?" he persisted, "What people?" Damn it, the sign for it escaped him.

She turned back, facing him in the entrance."Dacotah, me. Billy Downs' squaw. The stranglers kill him," she intoned in a piping sing-song voice. She made a jerking motion alongside her head that Stringer immediately understood.

"They killed Billy?"

"Yah. The sons-a-bitches kill him. With rope. 'Nother man, too," she replied, "Billy good man. Much meat, much horses." she pointed at the child scampering after another rock. "Him baby." She turned away.

An elf, he thought again. He'd read *Gulliver's Travels* as a lad, being fascinated with Swift's account of the Lilliputians. Later he'd read of the Norse "*Hudufolk*", meaning the secret people. Like England's pixies, and Ireland's leprechauns, Hudufolk had magic powers and often behaved mischievously. Nearly every country's literature, he'd found, had a common thread of secret little people in their folklore. And the notion evidently appeared in societies that had no written language. Since he'd been West, he'd heard the Indians had such legends, too. The Crows, in particular, told stories of a race of Indian elves who lived in the Pryor Mountains south of the Yellowstone.

This young squaw, in her tininess, reminded him again of the legends and folklore that as a child he'd read and so enjoyed. What was the fairy queen's name in *Romeo and Juliet*? Mab. He chuckled. Fairies often aided people in various ways. He'd call his little nurse, Mab, after the queen in the famous love story, and her young one, Puck. The old crone, who looked like a fanciful version of one of *Hamlet's* witches, would be just that, Witch. He went to sleep with a lighter heart.

The wrinkled old gal, he found later the next day, was the young one's grandmother. She mostly helped with the child, Wahpe-popa, who was about three years old and of normal size. He was a good little boy, never crying, never fussy. For a time, he was stand-offish with Stringer, but the man found something, finally, that enticed him into the lean-to. He pulled his watch out of his vest pocket, and opening the case, dangled it in front of him. The shiny gold caught the light and sparkled as it revolved. He whistled softly through his teeth and the breech-clothed tyke turned in the old grandmother's lap out in front of the lean-to. Stringer went on playing with the watch until presently the boy, curious as any child, was in at his side, reaching for the shiny object. Then Stringer turned the hands to twelve and let the boy listen to the soft chimes coming from the watch. He was entranced, sitting quietly, as the man ran the hands around to twelve again and let the chimes ring. This time even Cha'pa and the crone came to the bed and begged to hear it again. He obliged, getting a kick out of their spellbound attention. He let each in turn hold the watch, then, and noticed how closely they studied it, awe in their faces.

* * *

Mab, the little fairy queen, was busy giving her son his daily bath in the spring creek. He squirmed like a large trout, shiny brown in the early morning's light. The old grandmother he called the 'Witch' was stirring her eternal cook pot, Stringer saw, as he threw aside the elk robe. He gingerly drew his wounded leg over and stood erect. He could hobble now without too much difficulty and he headed upstream for a morning drink and a wash-up. He'd been here a week. Cha 'pa and the old woman had brewed a concoction out of some flowers they called "Tezinga-maka" and had used it on his wounds. It, along with another something they brewed up and had him drink, had largely taken away his pain and much of the swelling. He was definitely on the mend.

Sure of it, because last night Cha'pa, his Mab, had crept under the lean-to and knelt by his bed. When he'd awakened and looked at her, she had pointed silently. He'd nodded, suddenly excited. She then had pulled her buckskin dress over her shiny hair and folded it daintily beside the robes. The fire, dying, still gave off a rosy glow that made her small body shine in the reflected light. She paused, as, about to turn the cover robe back, their eyes met. Her calmness struck him. He thought of the women he'd had, the raping of the southern women, even some of the slave women during the war. Then later, the whores and the Indian girls they'd either bought or stolen. Downs himself had sold some of these to his gang. Never had he felt anything like the excitement and anticipation he felt now. Downs had apparently kept this little morsel for himself back at his post and he could certainly see why.

She came to him beneath the robe and he couldn't wait to get his hands on her. She was careful of his leg and knowing in the way she enticed and teased, seeking with her birdlike tiny hands. Asking nothing but that he enjoy her, the elfin Indian girl wove her magic spell around him. For the first time, Stringer felt something for another person, this Indian elf, his Mab. Exhausted from the sexual struggle, he fell asleep with his arms around her.

Now, in the early morning, he relieved himself and hobbled to the fire. Witch handed him his wooden bowl and he dipped into the pot and sipped the nutritious soup she'd made. There was a rabbit in the pot, he knew, but what else, other than some pemmican she'd thrown in from the parfletche bags, he wasn't sure. Some plants, also. Whatever, it had a wild tangy taste he liked. To please her, he smacked his lips and grinned.

The old gal giggled and said something that, of course, he didn't get. Cha'pa and the boy came to the cook fire, she chasing behind the laughing child in growling play. Stringer noticed that before they took the bowls of food, they offered up some prayer or other to what they called "the One Above." They each in turn took a little piece of meat from their bowl with a tiny wooden skewer and carried it to a round brushed patch of earth away from the fire, where they reverently laid it. As they started to eat, Stringer put aside his own bowl and took out the watch. The others looked as he spun it and it caught the sunlight, sparkling and reflecting the beams.

"It gathers the power of the Sun." Cha'pa exclaimed. The crone nodded. An idea struck her. She hissed in Sioux.

"Do you care for this Washichu (white man), Little Plum? I heard you go to his bed last night."

Cha'pa looked down at her mutilated hand. She nodded slowly.

"Then I will give him a present — his life." She went to her parfletche. From it, she took an assortment of articles, then returned to the fire. In the tribe she had been known for many years as a medicine

222

woman of considerable talent. She spread out a small circle of old white buckskin and arranged a strangely colored stone, an owl's tailfeather, a string of many finger bones, a small whitetail antler and a buckskin bag.

She then asked Cha'pa to bring the watch, and after receiving it from a puzzled Stringer, placed it reverently in the center of the white leather. Then she faced the east, took up the little bag and sprinkled some of its contents on the fire. She began a chant that continued for some minutes. Then she touched the watch with each of the articles on the leather. After this, she fanned the smoke so that it passed over the leather and its objects. One by one, then, she replaced everything back in her bag. The watch she gave back to Stringer.

"I have given it a helper, who will live in the gold thing. Now it will protect its owner from harm. Tell the Washichu to keep it always with him," the old woman muttered to her granddaughter. Cha'pa carried it back to Stringer in both hands and offered it to him, saying, "Keep, keep. You have. Long, long." Her limited English kept her from the explanation she wanted to give him, but she tried. He slipped it back in his vest pocket wondering what that had all been about. He limped back to the lean-to and laid down. Presently, he fell asleep.

When he first heard the coarse laughter, he thought perhaps he was back in the winter dugout with his old gang. He came up out of sleep and looked out of the lean-to. What he saw gave him a chill. Several Indian braves stood across the creek, just yards away. Already they had the black horse untied and were evidently wrangling among themselves as to whose it was. Cha'pa, the boy and the old grandmother stood by the fire, both women in violent argument with two of the heavily painted warriors. In a swift, reflexive movement, he grabbed his gunbelt and swung its reassuring weight around his middle. As he came out from under the lean-to, he saw the bigger brave at the fire swing up his war club. Thinking he was about to brain Cha'pa, he drew and shot. It was probably the one and only selfless act in his life. As soon as he shot, he was horrified at what he'd done. For sure he was a dead man, seeing the odds. Almost calmly, he flipped the loading gate on his pistol open, popped out the empty and stuck in a loaded round. With a full cylinder, he'd at least put out the lights on a few of 'em before they killed him.

Old Witch saved him. With a high-pitched screech, and waving her talon-like hands, she transfixed the group of braves with a torrent of Indian gibberish that Stringer could only wonder at. Whether cussing, cajoling, or threatening, he didn't know. However, it was effective. The others picked up the fallen brave, bleeding from a side wound, slung him on a horse and pulled out, with many a backward, baleful stare. The old crone seemed to grow in stature as she followed along, screaming and pointing at the sullen, demoralized warriors. Stringer held his pistol ready, not daring to believe his luck, bitterly wishing he had his rifle. Cha'pa and the boy came to his side.

Unconsciously, he put his arm around her and she came willingly against him. The boy clung to her skirt.

"Your tribe?" he asked her.

"No. Gros Ventres. My tribe Sioux. Friends."

"Didn't seem like friends to me," he replied wryly.

"Want horses. Grandmother medicine woman. Spirit woman. Scare 'em." she told him, looking up. What he saw in those black eyes made his heart turn over.

* * *

The shot, when it came, was so soft with distance that Cantrell almost discounted that he'd heard it. But it was a shot, far away, and in the direction the Indians had been going—westerly. He turned in the saddle to call to Frank.

"Hear that?" he asked.

"Hear what?" Frank rejoined. He was feeling his age and his shoulder ached.

"I thought I heard a shot back there," Cantrell told him, reining in. Frank pulled up, too.

"So what? One of 'em probably shot some meat," Frank said. He started on.

Cantrell gazed fixedly to the west." Nope. Think it was a pistol."

Frank stopped again. "A pistol? Still, it coulda been a meat shot," he said dubiously.

Cantrell swung his horse around, and pulling his pack horse behind, he started toward the west.

* * *

Stringer was uneasy. Had the war party really gone or were they still skulking around yet? He'd feel better if he were on the black horse they could never catch him then. He needed to see if they really had gone. He went to the black and succeeded in getting Cha'pa to help him saddle up and mount the gentle animal. His leg was painful but should loosen up with a little riding.

He looked down at the three small figures on the ground. Cha'pa showed in her eyes an apprehension that he was leaving them.

"I'll be back in a little while. Just want to do some scouting is all," he reassured her

He smiled. Despite a face full of whiskers and his soiled, bedraggled appearance, he was a handsome, intelligent looking man. He'd lost his hat at the Bates Point fight and his auburn hair hung long over his ears and down to his shoulders. As he looked down at Cha'pa, he realized that he cared for this small woman in a way that he'd never felt for anyone in his life before up to now. She was to him erotic in her tininess, yet kind and simple, a hardworking mother. He wanted to stay with her. He felt suddenly vulnerable. It was a feeling he didn't like. Never had he worried about anybody besides himself.

He reined the horse around, headed it up the canyon on the trail of the warriors. As it had before, the animal impressed him mightily with its action and its easy way of traveling. Even despite his pain, it was a joy to ride.

After a ways, the trail took a turn and divided. One path led up and out on top. From the sign, the war party had continued on the other, on down the bottom, possibly because the left one was steep and rough. He took it in the hope of getting to a viewpoint that would show the country around. The big horse took the grade with no trouble at all.

* * *

"See that? Cantrell called back to Frank, who was slightly behind him. He pointed.

"Yeah." He swung down and got out his spotting glass from its case behind his saddle. He pulled his horse around and, opening the old telescope, he rested it on his saddle. "Hold still, damn it," he growled at the gray. Far off, they had both caught a twinkle of sunlight flashing off something. Frank's glass brought it up close. He stiffened.

"By Gawdamighy! It's the black! And I think it's Stringer on him!" He handed the glass to Cantrell.

"Here. Your eyes are younger'n mine. Take a look."

225

Cantrell complied, but he sat down and rested his elbows on his knees, the big glass out in front of him.

"It's him, alright! He exclaimed, "And your Ben horse."

Frank swung up and Cantrell handed up the glass. Frank stowed it away in its case with trembling hands. They started down off the ridge.

* * *

When Stringer topped out above the canyon, he beheld a wonderful panorama. The sun, still in the eastern sky, shone with a mid-morning warmth upon the land, its slanting rays visible through a series of thin, puffy clouds passing overhead. As far as the eye could see, brown ridges were criss-crossed with coulees in which scrub cedar and pine grew, interspersed here and there with gumbo knobs rising up from sagebrush flats and prairie. The buffalo were gone but the antelope and mule deer were present, little bands of both showing at intervals in the wild natural scene. He looked to the west but saw no sign of the war party. He swung to the east. There, far out, he saw antelope running. They seemed spooked by something. Then, as he stared, two larger dots and two smaller became visible. Horses and riders! They were heading for the canyon. No! They were heading straight for him! He cursed. His fervent swearing and jerks at the bridle made the black nervous. It danced a few steps there on the edge of the canyon.

The Stranglers had followed him and all he had was his six-gun— and the black. Almost certainly they would have rifles. But with the black, he was sure to be able to outrun them. A sudden thought struck him. Cha'pa! He looked again. Right now, they were still heading right for him. The earlier shot might have alerted them. Whatever, he had to lead them away from her. Anyone out here could well be a threat to an Indian woman. In his rush of fear and anger, he didn't stop to think that others might have a higher regard for Indians and women than he or his men had, only that she would be in danger.

He started the black along the canyon wall, following the line of it off to the north, quartering away from his pursuers. As he rode, he tried to think of a plan. All that came to mind was that if he could get ahead of the war party to his front, maybe by a long circle northerly, it might run his pursuers into the group of Indians. With luck, the two parties would finish each other and allow him to circle back to Cha'pa.

Frank, ahead, hollered back. "He's seen us—he's on the run!"

Suddenly he pulled up and swung down. Cantrell almost thundered into him, but managed to avoid a collision. He pulled his sorrel to a halt, the pack horses crowding him.

"What the hell you doing?" he shouted.

Frank grabbed the lead ropes from him.

"Get down and throw your leather on a pack horse! We've been riding ours right along and they need a breather. We'll cache the packs here and one of us run 'im and one lead the other horses. Make sure you got plenty shells."

They swiftly stripped the packs off the bay and the buckskin, then threw on their saddles. Halters were traded for bridles. Coats, ropes and saddlebags came off the saddles and were tossed on the packs piled there on the ground, to lighten the loads.

"I'll run him first, Bill. You follow with the horses on a lope. I'll push him hard, then slack off and change horses while you run him." He tightened his cinch, dropped his stirrup and swung aboard.

"He'll kill your black if we push him that way, Frank!" Cantrell stated, working furiously.

"Can't be helped. We gotta get the sonuvabitch!"

Frank settled the big rifle in its scabbard and jumped the buckskin into a gallop. Cantrell shook his head but prepared to follow.

Stringer, far ahead, let the black run. The horse was fresh and once he got his head, it was all Stringer could do to guide him. His leg ached. Looking back, he at first couldn't see any pursuit. He skirted the canyon, looking into it when he could, wondering where the war party had gotten to. Probably they had stopped somewhere to doctor the wounded one. He scanned the horizon ahead. The country was big— and it was empty. Since the buffalo had been shot out and the tribes mostly contained, there were vast open stretches like these with nothing really in them. The antelope and deer, even the small game, were all getting scarce as the wolves, having lost their chief food source, turned to the other animals. The cattlemen, coming north with their vast herds, had not yet penetrated this far. None of that though, concerned Stringer as he assessed his situation. He'd been in other scrapes as serious, he thought, but never had he a horse under him like this one now. It encouraged him to realize that. He urged it on with a slap of the reins. The black responded willingly.

With a clatter of hooves, he jumped the horse down off a rock ledge and onto soft ground, headed for the end of the long canyon. Rounding a low hill, he and the black nearly collided with some horses held, he saw, by two of the war party. The others were grouped around a small fire. Near it was lying the wounded brave.

'What the hell,' he thought. 'Let's stir up the hornets' nest.' He pulled out his pistol and swerved toward the fire, the warriors clustered around it jumping aside. He leveled his gun along his horse's neck and shot twice before he was through them. The first took a stocky warrior in the throat. The other was a clear miss on a brave painted in black and white stripes from head to foot. He seemed to shimmer aside just as Stringer shot. Then he was past and by them as they leaped for horses and guns.

'The black is showing us his heels!' Frank saw with mingled pride and dismay. The buckskin he was riding was a horse with some bottom but slow, so slow! Each animal has a favorite gait. This horse liked to trot but he was a jarring runner. Frank kept him at it, though he kept trying to drop back into his trot. He wished now that he'd grabbed the bay, instead.

Ahead he heard two shots. It puzzled him for an instant until he remembered the war party they'd seen before. Had Stringer maybe run into that bunch? He looked back to see that Cantrell was coming steadily behind. The two saddle horses he was leading were evidently cooperating. He followed the black's trail down off a rocky ledge, then onto softer ground.

Quite a ways up ahead he glimpsed Stringer and the black disappearing over a ridge. Between them was the head of the canyon. He came around a small hill and saw what he feared: the war party. Some were gathered around a couple forms lying by a small fire. The rest were up on horses, milling about.

'He must have run right through them,' Frank thought. Knowing that, with them ready, it wouldn't work for him, he yanked the buckskin in, swung down and shot the horse behind the ear. It dropped like a cut sack and Frank pulled his rifle free as it went down. He holstered his Colt, and using the rifle, knelt in back of the still kicking animal and shot a warrior coming in at him that had stripes all over his body. The

228

big Winchester took the Indian high in the chest and flipped him neatly off his horse with the impact.

Frank ducked down as he saw the other braves get into action and the dead carcass in front of him shook as bullets jarred into it. He fed a cigar-sized shell into his rifle magazine and popped up over the horse's belly. Two of the horseback braves were charging straight at him, one with his coup stick extended. Frank's weapon flamed and the foremost Indian spun from his horse. The other fired a pistol at him and the bullet furrowed a red line on the side of Frank's neck. He levered the rifle and shot the stocky brave in the stomach as he came on. Then he dropped back behind the dead horse as the warrior slammed into the dust in front of him.

Cantrell, clattering behind, didn't hear Stringer's pistol shots, but the solid boom of the big Winchester got through the noise of the hoofbeats and alerted him to trouble ahead. Instinctively, he swerved off the trail and reined in the bay. He undallied the lead ropes and dropping them, pulled his own rifle out of the scabbard under his leg, a twin to Granville Stuart's big .50/95 Winchester. He cranked a shell in the chamber and let the hammer down to half-cock, fed another into the magazine. Pausing for an instant to pinpoint the firing, he jumped the bay off at an angle to come in on the side. He pounded over a slight rise and into a defile.

There were two forms by a little fire, lying motionless. Dead braves. Off some fifty yards to the left was the buckskin Frank had been riding. Frank's rifle protruded over its dead carcass. In front of him lay three more dead warriors, their horses heading away from the firing and the bodies. As Cantrell appeared, the warriors left alive sheared off and both Frank and he pumped lead at them as they beat their horses away over the ridge. Cantrell galloped behind them to the top and sped them on with two more shots, better aimed. He thought he saw one slump over his horse's neck and a hit was confirmed when another brave circled back to help the wounded one. Cantrell turned then, and headed back to Frank, who stood up from behind his dead horse and propped his rifle against its butt. He loosened the cinch and pulled his saddle free.

"You okay?" Cantrell could see blood seeping from the old man's neck.

"Yeah. One of 'em burned me a little, is all. Where'd the other ones go?" He reached up and touched the wound gingerly.

"They're gone. Looked like a bunch of young ones. I doubt they'll be back for a while. Want me to catch you a horse?"

"Get me that pinto over there, then gather up another one that looks good. We're burning daylight."

Cantrell stuck his rifle back in its scabbard, and with some effort, caught the pinto and brought him over to Frank, who began saddling him. Curious, he rode over to the fire and viewed the two bodies lying there. One was sporting reddish and black splotches of paint over his chest. They were both dead, one shot in the throat, and the other lying by him, a young brave with a low chest wound. The ones in front of Frank's dead horse all were dead before they hit the ground, the big bullet blowing a fist-size hole through them.

When he returned, Frank was just throwing a leg over the paint horse. It crow-hopped a couple times until Frank pulled its head up, then stood trembling. Like most Indian horses, it didn't like the white man's smell or his habit of mounting on the left. While Cantrell went back to gather his string, Frank took off on a hard run to make up time. Out on the flat, he flogged the paint hard and kept a sharp eye peeled as he galloped on the black's trail north.

Some miles on, the country began breaking into rough areas again. The tracks ahead led down into a small dry creek bed, with a narrow but deep little cut at its bottom. He expected the paint to jump it, giving it little thought. Instead, the horse balked, nearly unseating him. The saddle horn jabbed him painfully in the abdomen and that brought suddenly a greater pain, a shooting star of pain in his stomach that felt like he'd been shot. He reached and felt the place but, looking at his hand, saw no blood. He doubled over the horse's neck with the shock of it, then straightened with a supreme effort and walked the horse to a spot where it would cross.

* * *

With the black on level ground, Stringer risked a look back over his shoulder. Behind him the prairie was empty except for a coyote whose head was peeking over the sagebrush, watching the horseman thundering by. After several miles with little lessening of speed, Stringer had reined the black down to a distance-eating gallop that the big, muscular horse took to and stuck with. Never had the man been aboard a horse such as this. The black's pace was a durable charge that melted the miles away under its pounding hooves. White foamy sweat was just beginning to appear on the shiny hide, whipped off by the passing wind. Coming down into a little round bowl, a huge flock of sage hens got up around them. The big ungainly birds fluttered away in every direction before settling back into the buffalo grass and sagebrush, to cluck indignantly at the sudden interruption to their daily routine.

Sometime later, up ahead he could see a line of green three or four miles away. The Milk River. He'd rustled enough stock and driven them north of the Milk to sell that he could recognize its tree-lined banks, even coming into it from this angle. The black had been at the gallop for hours, a running machine. His leg was an agonizing soreness, each jolt sending a wave of pain through his body. Something in the way he had to straddle the horse and put weight on it for balance worked against the wound just right and hammered the pain home with the rhythm of the running horse. It was bleeding again and he could feel the wetness gathering in his boot. He was getting weak and starting to feel dizzy.

Another mile and he looked back. As he did so, the black's left front leg reached out in its stride and came down on a small rock in just the wrong way. It popped a shoe nail. Another half mile and the shoe was loose. Immediately the horse's gait was altered and Stringer, horseman that he was, divined the problem.

* * *

Back on the canyon rim, Cha'pa was jubilant as she rummaged through the packs she had found. Sugar, salt, bacon—even coffee and some canned fruit! She knew what they were by the pictures on the cans. After Downs had been killed by the Vigilantes, Cha'pa, the boy and her old grandmother had eaten most of the store goods up before they'd left. Tonight they would feast again!

After waiting for Stringer to come back from his scout trip, she had finally gone looking for him, half afraid that the war party had circled back and caught him. If that had happened, she knew what she would find. His mutilated remains. Her liking for the auburn haired man was strong and her concern had grown until finally, she had saddled up one of the ragged little ponies and rode out to look for him.

She saw where the big black horse's shod tracks had turned off to the path going up on the canyon rim and followed them.

Like him, she had stopped under the trees and taken a careful look around. The prairie off to the west where his tracks led was empty. To the east, though, something white was laying out in the sagebrush. Curious, she rode out the mile or so to it. As she went, trotting the scrawny buckskin, she crossed the tracks of a bunch of horses, all of them shod, and realized then what must have occurred. When Stringer had shown himself above the canyon, a group of white men, probably Vigilantes on his trail, had sighted him and chased him. She was even more sure when she came to the patch of white she'd seen. It was a pile of canvas covered packs and gear strewn on the ground, thrown off in an evident hurry.

Before dismounting, she steadied the horse and stood up on its rump, scanning the country around her with care. These men would return, unless they had the bad luck to run into the war party. Then, maybe they wouldn't. If they did come back and she had made it seem like animals had been at the packs, maybe they wouldn't come looking. She became a little whirlwind then, going carefully through the gear, scattering the grub pack around, ripping canvas with her knife and her tiny maimed but strong hands. She made up a sack of things, tied it on her horse, and hurried on her back-trail to the canyon path. Under the trees she tied the animal, then tearing off a couple branches for brooms, she ran back out to the packs and carefully swept her tracks out. Using her knuckles, she cleverly substituted some coyote tracks in their stead. Always she watched the horizon to the west.

* * *

Stringer cursed. The shoe would have to be removed, then the other shoe removed, so the balance in the front legs could be kept. Otherwise the horse was sure to go lame. A lame horse meant he might as well make a stand right here. He cussed again. He didn't have anything to pull it with, he didn't think. Or did he? He looked back as he pulled the horse down to a trot, then finally a walk. No pursuit yet. Glancing down, he saw a small tool scabbard hanging on the saddle skirt. Opening it, it revealed a pair of hoof pliers. He rejoiced. Most cowhands didn't shoe their horses. It was too expensive and too much trouble, if they weren't in rocky country. Having a string of horses to switch on a more or less daily basis was easier, so they didn't get ridden down. However, the owner of this one had taken special pains to make sure he could be ridden day after day, proof again he wasn't just a cow pony.

He stopped and eased himself to the ground, almost falling. Favoring his leg, he got the pliers out, lifted the foot and pulled the shoe. The horse gave him absolutely no trouble, seeming to know what needed to be done. Getting the other shoe loose and off, though, took much of his precious strength and time. When it finally came, he dropped the heavy hoof back into the dust, straightened and was hit by a wave of dizziness. He leaned on the horse and peered down his back trail. In the gathering heat of the afternoon, he could see a speck on the horizon. Someone coming. He tried to focus on the object. Just one. He turned and made a supreme effort, pulling himself into the saddle again, the pliers falling on the trail. The black, its blood up, wanted to go again, but Stringer held him in a little to see how the leg was. After a ways, he could tell the horse was favoring it a little, a bad sign. His own leg was a thundering mass of pain.

Ahead, the trail went into a grove of young cottonwoods before coming to the ford. As Stringer reached the trees, he threw another look back. The speck had turned into a rider, discernible in the distance. The hat was proof he wasn't an Indian. Stringer cursed again. What to do? His leg and the black's couldn't stand another long run just now. And how had that bastard caught up to him? There was only one rider that he could see. An ambush here at the ford could take him out, with a little luck. He'd have a chance to rest, maybe even circle back to Cha'pa.

Luck. Somehow that thought reminded him of the old witch muttering over the watch. He pulled it out, looked around, then starting forward, hung it carefully over a tree limb close to the trail where it would be seen. He reined the black into the water, pulling its head up viciously when it attempted to drink, then turned upstream a few yards and back up the bank. He tied the black's reins to a nearby tree, after he'd slid stiffly off him. Then he hobbled back and hid behind the trunk of a large older cottonwood. His position afforded him a clear view of the trail and the watch dangling there in the sun. He pulled his pistol, checked his loads and waited, trying to quiet his furiously beating heart.

* * *

Frank had conquered his stomach pain, finally. The fire of it had doubled him over for several minutes before he was able to bring it to bay. Probing with his fingers, he was able to feel something inside him that was foreign—solid, unyielding and painful to his pushing. He had a horrified suspicion that it was some kind of tumor. He fought against passing out by strength of will. Finally, savagely, he spurred the paint horse on.

Half an hour later, Cantrell came upon him. By then, Frank had stripped his gear off the little pinto. It was standing spraddle legged and spent on the trail.

"Never killed it, I see." Cantrell remarked, throwing the gray horse's halter rope to Frank.

"Nope." Frank ground out, his teeth tight-clamped against the pain that was making him sweaty and pale. Cantrell noticed his distress.

"Hey, you get hit back there?" he exclaimed.

Frank didn't reply. He bridled the gray, threw his blanket over its back and tried twice to pick up the heavy saddle. Cantrell, alarmed, swung down and helped him throw it on the horse.

"Frank, what's wrong?" he asked again.

"Don't know. Something inside my guts." Frank managed to choke out. He rested his head on the leather.

"Frank, you stay here! I'll get him for you." Cantrell offered eagerly. He began stripping his own gear off the sweaty, trembling bay and putting it on his sorrel. Though warmed up, neither the sorrel nor the gray were leg weary like the two who'd been packing a heavy saddle and a rider's weight.

Frank came to, marshaling his force like a weary fighter for the last round.

"No! Goddammit. He's mine. If it's the last thing I do!" He reached in a small saddle pouch and withdrew a flask. Unscrewing its cap, he tipped it up and swallowed several times, then handed it to Cantrell, who obligingly took a swig. It was strong whiskey and it seemed to revitalize the old man. He slipped the flask back in its pocket and pulled his cinch tight, dropped his stirrup and stepped aboard with an agonized effort.

"You keep up close as you can. The black can run the legs off us, if we aren't careful. And you still might be the one to have to take him on." He reined the gray around and spurred him into a run.

"He isn't going to make it." Cantrell thought out loud as he finished saddling the sorrel. Pulling his rifle, he filled its magazine with shells, then, taking a last glance at the exhausted pinto, he swung himself aboard and prepared to follow.

The smooth gait of the gray eased Frank's pain, along with the warming glow of the gulps of whiskey he'd downed. It stilled his quivering legs and gave them strength. He quirted the reins across the gray's butt and it lunged forward, stretching out.

* * *

Hours later, the gray horse blown and trembly on its legs, Frank, half-drunk from repeated pulls on the flask, peered ahead and saw the ribbon of green that he guessed marked the Milk River. He was getting close now. He'd seen the pliers lying in the trail and saw by the tracks what had happened. He pulled the Stuart horse down into a trot and jerked out his rifle.

"You sonofabitch, your time is about to come!" he thought exultantly. The surge of anticipation brought a measure of swift relief to his fatigue. For now, the stomach pain had retreated into an ever-present ache that he could handle. He trotted the gray into the cottonwoods. It was cooler in their shade and now he could smell the river, a moist smell of mud and leaves that reminded him it had been hours since he'd drank or eaten.

Ahead, he could see the shine of the water—and something else, a twinkle of sunlight reflecting off an object swinging on a limb. Curious, his dulled mind screaming an alarm, he shifted the rifle to his left hand and reached for what he saw now was a watch, hanging there in the sun. He rested the buttstock on his leg as he examined the timepiece. Must have been pulled loose by the limb as the rider had passed. Suddenly, he heard a horse nicker close by, there on his left. He'd partially turned the gray to the sound when a shot blasted at him. The bullet struck the rifle stock, knocking it back into his side, but he hung on to it. He brought it around, and with the watch still in his trigger hand, sent a bullet toward the man he saw standing there by a tree. Caught in the action of aiming, the figure threw up an arm and stumbled back, then went down.

Frank knew the other had heard the slap of the bullet into the stock and figured wrongly that he'd made a killing shot. Eager, his error had caused him to come out from behind the tree. Cautiously, Frank threw a leg over the horse and stumbled to the ground, nearly falling as his stiff muscles refused to respond. He absently stuck the watch in his vest pocket, knowing it had been a decoy that had nearly gotten him killed. He walked forward, leaving the gray head-down and exhausted.

There in the trees he found Stringer Jack, his arm out-flung to the Colt revolver lying a foot out of his reach. Frank stooped and picked it up. The man on the ground, shot in the chest, opened his green eyes. He recognized Frank, but the words that came were, "Cha'pa, I wish…"

His eyes closed forever. Frank, looking down, felt nothing except relief. It was over. He'd lasted to the finish.

When Cantrell came up, Frank was down by the river, watering the black and the gray, side by side.

Chapter 17

Milk River, Montana Territory

Worn out though Frank was, and sick too, Cantrell noticed that he took special pains to cool the two horses down after their hard run. He'd torn the ragged shirt off the dead man lying back in the trees and used it to wash down the backs and the legs on both of them.

Bill helped with the horses a while, taking special care with his own sorrel, then gathered wood and built a roaring fire. The war party survivors crossed his mind briefly, but he said the hell with it, they needed some comfort after their trying day. Taking his rifle, he sneaked along the river looking for meat. Now that the run was over, he was ravenously hungry.

Just before dusk, he jumped two whitetail does and was about to shoot the smaller, when a little spike buck walked out and joined them by the bank. He dropped it with a neck shot and the does scampered away. Pulling his knife, he laid the hide back and took the loins, the liver and the tongue. Then he hung the quarters in a tree high as he could get them.

By the time he'd returned, the fire had burned down and he rigged some roasting sticks around it with meat impaled on them. The smell of the roasting venison dripping on the fire brought Frank awake. He'd been lying against his saddle, facing the fire, and had dozed off, exhausted. Together, they devoured most of the half-raw meat.

They camped there two days before Frank felt well enough to begin the ride back. That next day, Bill saw that the older man was in no shape to travel and convinced him to lay over, using the black's leg as an excuse. Frank didn't argue much. He lay under his saddle blanket looking like a corpse. The first day, Cantrell threw a lead rope around Stringer's dead body and pulled him back into the woods a ways, under a big cottonwood, then he went through the dead man's pockets. He found a crude money belt under the gun belt and pulled it off. It contained over $2000 in currency and gold coins. He took the gun belt, too. He chipped away some of the heavy bark and carved "Here lays a Horsethief—Stringer Jack" on the tree above the body. Coming back to the fire, he picked up the pistol Stringer had carried, a .44 Colt single action revolver, its wooden grips showing much use. The initials JS were carved in them. It had one fired cylinder and the hammer was eared back. He eased it down. He stuck the weapon in the gun belt's holster and turned to Frank, watching him over the fire.

"How you feelin'?"

"Better." Frank grunted. He handed the flask he had in his hand to Cantrell. "One swig left, go on."

"No thanks, Frank. We'll save it for you, for later." The younger man returned it. Frank grunted again and stowed the container back in its pocket.

"Sure could use a pot of Toby's fine coffee right now. Wonder how the boy's doin'," he commented idly, leaning back.

"He's a tough lad, he'll be fine, I'm bettin'." Bill said, kneeling down to feed the fire.

"Yep, I think so, too." Frank rejoined thoughtfully. His whisker stubbled face was reflective with his concern as he pondered.

Presently Bill spoke up. "Frank, I took a bundle of money off Stringer back there. Here it is. His gun belt, too. Thought you'd want it."

Frank looked up. "How much'd that rustler have on 'im?" he asked.

"Looks like about $2000. Little over." Cantrell remarked. He spread the currency and coin out to show the older man. Frank looked at it a while, then reached out and divided it in three piles. "Here ya go. You, me and Toby. I'll tuck his and mine in my saddle pocket here. You see he gets it if anything happens to me. Likewise what's in my own belt". He tapped his middle.

"Can I count on you?" He glanced at Bill, who nodded his head.

"Sure, Frank." He took the money offered him and held it in his hand, "Say, Frank, I'd sure like to have Stringer's gun. Can I buy it or trade you out of it?" he asked hesitantly.

Frank waved a hand, "Sure as hell, go ahead and take it. I got his watch here, come to think it." He pulled it out and opened it, then offered it silently to Cantrell for inspection. He told the other how he came by it.

Bill read the inscription engraved on the inside of the hunter case. "Looks like somebody loved the bastard once."

* * *

On the way back, they found the hoof pliers lying in the trail. Later, they ran onto the paint horse close to where they'd left him, grazing in the bottom. Cantrell noticed that Frank was weaving in the saddle again, but he kept silent. Before, when he'd asked if he was all right, Frank had barked at him to tend to himself.

When they finally drew up to the spot on the plain where they had dumped their packs, Cantrell saw with dismay that what he'd feared would happen apparently had. Their gear was scattered from hell to breakfast. It looked like coyotes, from the marks he saw when he dismounted. While Frank half stepped, half fell from his horse, Cantrell roamed through the brush and started throwing stuff back to the pile, to be repacked. Frank weakly tried to help.

"Let's pull those back shoes off Ben before we put a pack on him. He's not reaching right with his front ones off and them others still on."

Bill agreed, and took on the task, while Frank finished gathering what he could find of their supplies.

"Damn coyotes!" he exclaimed, bending down in the sagebrush for yet another piece of gear. Suddenly he stopped, grabbed the piece of canvas at his feet and drew it up closely to his eyes. "Looks like knife cuts, more like." he muttered. He started a circle, looking down at the ground. When Cantrell finished with Ben, he looked around to find Frank four or five hundred yards out on the flat, head down like an old hound following a scent.

Cantrell found the hoof rasp and smoothed Ben's feet, then packed the buckskin and the little paint as best he could. That done, he left them and, leading the gray, rode out to where Frank was still working out some sort of trail.

"What're you following, Frank?"

"Looks like a single pony track. Tried to rub their tracks out from our gear." He looked up. "Trail goes on down into the canyon." He struggled onto his horse and straightened up painfully.

"Go get the horses and we'll follow up this 'coyote' that plundered our outfit."

When Cantrell returned, together they pulled their rifles and rode down into the canyon. On the canyon floor, Frank, in the lead, pulled up the gray, and when Cantrell rode up alongside, whispered, "I smell smoke!"

Cantrell drew in some air. He nodded, "Yeah. Me, too."

They quietly stepped down and tied their horses, then went on afoot.

The old mother sensed their coming and hissed to Cha'pa at the fire. As she turned to look, Frank and Cantrell came from the trees. The women noticed the younger man turn and help the older one. Cha'pa called out to them.

"Come. Eat."

She waved to them to come to the fire. 'Strangler sonsabitches.' she thought.

As they came up, the older man collapsed and the young one eased him down to the ground.

* * *

When Frank opened his eyes, they were looking almost directly into the dark black ones of Cha'pa, bending over to spoon a concoction into his open mouth. He closed it with a snap and sputtered. It tasted like dirt and something else. He raised his hand up and weakly pushed it away. The Indian woman chattered something in Sioux, then said, "You take," in English. She brought it to his mouth again and he gave in, nearly choking.

"What is that stuff?" he grumbled. She forced some more down him.

"I said, what is that you're poking down me?"

"Good you." was all she said.

She turned away with a swirl of buckskins and Frank saw then how small she was. He checked himself. He did feel a little better. He looked out of the same lean-to Stringer had slept in, saw the hobbled horses across the same stream. They were unsaddled, the gear piled by the creek. He could tell by the manure they'd been there a while. A shadow darkened the lean-to's entrance.

240

Cantrell said, "So. How're you feelin' today, Frank?" There was concern in his voice.

"Better. How long we been here?"

"Couple days. The horses have had a good rest. So did I." Cantrell chuckled, "Cha'pa here is a good cook."

Beside him a small form wriggled its way in beside Cantrell. "Her kid. She was Billy Down"s squaw. Tells me the Stranglers got him."

He picked up the willing infant and joggled him in his arms. The boy squealed with pleasure. Cha'pa came with a tin cup of water. She handed it over to Frank. Looking in her eyes again, Frank thought he detected a knowledge of who he was, and a subsequent dislike. He saw she was looking at his vest, at the watch fob hanging from the pocket. He pulled it out and the watch dangled in the sun, catching the light. Then it was that Frank saw a flash of pure hate in the dark eyes of the tiny Indian woman before her face closed in typical Indian fashion and she turned away. Thoughtfully, Frank stuck the watch back in his vest.

Cantrell was puzzled. Cha'pa, the little Sioux maiden he'd come to have a regard for in the short time he'd known her, had grabbed the boy from his arms and called to the old woman. Together they had begun striking camp, packing their gear in beaded leather bags, rigging their horses with their Indian saddles, filling the waterskins, all in a sense of sullen urgency.

He went to her and she shrugged him off, continued her furious rush and he heard her mutter, "Strangler sonsabitches," as she went to tying packs on the ponies. In no time at all, despite Cantrell's protests and unanswered questions, the women were horseback and headed down the canyon.

"Hell's Bells!" He swore and kicked a rock in the creek. 'Damn, he'd been getting along so well with them—her— until Frank had come to. Why, then, had she suddenly gotten so furious?'

He strode back to the lean-to and found Frank in the act of pulling on his boots.

"They pulled out, Frank. Damn if I know why."

Frank buckled on his gun belt.

"Sounds like you and her was getting pretty friendly, Bill." Frank chuckled.

"Was. Sure didn't last long, though." Cantrell muttered.

"Wonder what happened."

241

"She saw Stringer's watch." Frank stated, "Seemed to piss her off." He handed the younger man some gold coins.

"Ride after 'em and give it to her."

Cantrell hurriedly saddled his sorrel and took off down the trail. The women had gotten further than he'd reckoned but he soon came up to them.

"Cha'pa! Hold up!"

Face forward, the woman neither stopped nor acknowledged him.

"Cha'pa! What's wrong, damn it?" He pulled his horse in front of the plodding ponies.

"STRANGLER SONSABITCHES!!" She reined her horse around him and struck at him with her quirt as she passed. He ducked away. The old woman, though, was not so full of venom. She laughed as she went by and Cantrell held out the coins to her. She, when she saw the gold, drew up and stuck out her hand. Cantrell dropped the coins in it and she bobbed her head in thanks. He reflected as he rode on back to the camp that she would probably just throw the money away, not knowing its value. But, maybe not. She was a shrewd old bird. The Hell with it.

Back at the fire, Cantrell saw evidence that Frank was feeling better— he had the saddle on his Ben horse and the packs ready to throw on the other horses. Bill got down and threw some water on the fire.

"Well? Did she take the money?"

"Not much! She tried to hit me with her quirt! The old one took it, though."

"She did, huh?" Frank laughed. The first laugh Cantrell had ever heard from the old man. It was a rich satisfying sound that Cantrell hungered to hear again. He realized suddenly that he liked and respected Frank very much. It was a strange feeling for him. He was a loner who went his own way in the world, caring little for any man or what he thought, ever since the war, since his father's death. Right up until the day that he had to make a choice: go outside the law for the easy money to be made there or declare himself with those being victimized by the stock thieves. It was a choice he had made almost casually, now he thought about it, a choice made more because of his personal dislike for Paddy Rose, Lavadure, Stringer Jack and most of the rest of those killers and robbers that infested the country. They disgusted him. They were a blot on mankind, on the word 'Man,' and what he had come to believe it stood for.

His father and his dear mother, both dead these many years now, had brought him up to fear God and respect life. During the war, many, including himself, had forgotten those precepts. Some had never regained them. Maybe he'd never be a churchgoer again, but he thanked God now that he'd made the choice he had and gone to Stuart when he did. Though he had never told Frank or Granville, it had been the news that Matthew Grounds had killed Paddy Rose over on the Rosebud that had given him the incentive to make the decision.

Rose had been the worst of the bunch, a perverted child molester and killer, a vicious hulking bully. Cantrell had made the mistake of fighting him bare handed at Fort Benton and Rose had nearly killed him. Later, he had determined to kill the man but had never found an opportunity to carry out his intent. That Grounds had done so made his friends Cantrell's.

The ride that day was a leisurely one. And the Frank Shannon he rode with was a different man altogether than the one he'd known on Stringer's trail. This one talked and laughed. Had Toby heard him, he would have called him 'the old Frank'.

The next day they reached the Missouri. The river was low and they crossed at the mouth of the Musselshell, at the old ford. The old Fort buildings that Downs had inhabited and used as a trading post were deserted and bleak.

"The black's a little stiff, Frank, but I don't think his wind's broke. Doesn't seem to have strained anything either, that I can see. He's walked that bit of lameness out of him." Cantrell remarked. Frank leaned in the saddle and patted the horse on the neck.

"No, can't see that he suffered any. That was quite a run. You saw, Bill, in an equal race he'd of put the gray right under. Tell Stuart that when we get back, will you?"

Frank grinned, and Cantrell, happy to see the old man's spirits so lifted, grinned back.

"Guess I'll have to tell him, but the way he loves that horse, he'll probably fire me."

They laughed.

"Aw, I doubt it. Maybe at that we'd better break it to him easy. Say, did I ever tell you about the black's race at Miles City? He beat some hellish horses that day! Fannie French had a beautiful little mare there that could run with the wind. Had a little black boy ridin' that was sure a jockey. And the N Bar had a thoroughbred horse that nearly took Ben to camp, but he ended up beatin' it by a nose at the finish. Won me some money that day!" Frank was enthused, remembering the black's triumph. Then his face darkened.

"Stringer's bunch hit the ranch over on the Rosebud while I was sleepin' off a drunk there in town the next day. Won some money and lost a pardner. What a piss-poor trade."

Cantrell, seeing he was about to slip back into his familiar black mood again, hurried to divert him.

"You know, I think I remember seeing that mare race over in Helena. They run her short, about five hundred yards. She was a real quick starter, took the field by a length or more. She could run like a streak, all right."

He looked to the horizon. Out to the southeast he could see a dust cloud rising. In the clear air, it showed as a large hazy spot.

"See that? Looks like buffalo," he remarked. Frank looked where he pointed.

"Trail herd, I would imagine. Wonder if it's stolen? Be our luck to run into a bunch more rustlers'n we can handle." He pulled his pistol, checked its loads, did the same with his rifle, then pulled another pistol out of his saddle bag and checked it. That one he stowed in his belt.

Cantrell, meanwhile, did likewise, even to pulling Stringer's pistol and, after checking it, stowing it where he could get to it quick. Then they rode on.

"What was the slickest race you ever saw, Frank?"

The old man chuckled, a low sound.

"Guess it'd be the time my cousin Bert and I ran the two bay mares. Bert had him a real fast mare that I came up with a match to. Looked like they were twins. Couldn't tell 'em apart, hardly. But one was a runner and one wasn't much. We took the slow one down to Radford that summer and lost some money on her at the Fourth of July races. Then we moped around the saloons a while and Bert got drunk and set us up a quarter mile race with some of the big talkin' winners. Those boys had a couple of good horses, I'll give them that. One of 'em was a sorrel that yours reminds me of. They was pretty proud of them and, since they'd seen our little mare eat dust that day, they drank hard and bet heavy. The night before the race, I brought the fast one in and pulled the switch with no one noticin'." He smiled, remembering back to that day.

"Had ourselves a fright when the gun sounded. Our little mare stumbled. First time she'd ever done it. I thought we'd lost it right there. But she caught herself and came back. She ended up winning it by a short nose. Took a bunch of money off some long faces that day!" He laughed outright at the memory, at the astonishment of those men who'd lost.

"What happened to her?" Cantrell asked.

"Bert died ridin' her at Brandy Station in '63. Reckon some one of Pleasanton's Cavalry got her."

For a while they rode in silence, the war a shadow on their minds. Then Frank spoke with a sigh, "Seems like every good memory I have is bound up in some bad ones."

The younger man spat and cussed, "The damned war hurt us all, Frank. The whole country is a festering wound that don't seem to heal. It's even reached all the way out here." Cantrell, as he spoke, was watching the dust cloud to their front growing larger.

An east wind was coming up, cool and refreshing. The sky was marbled with fast moving clouds. Overhead a huge flock of sandhill cranes was flying, heading west, their shrill cries audible in the clear air for miles after they passed. It was a lonely land, but a clean one. He couldn't think of another place he'd rather be— or another person he'd rather be with, now that he thought on it. Well, maybe the tiny Sioux gal, Cha'pa. She'd been a welcome distraction.

"Wonder if I'll ever see her again," he thought.

Over south, the dust cloud had disintegrated into individual shapes of riders and cattle, a dust haze hanging over them. Frank altered their direction to intercept the point of the herd and they saw a couple riders coming out on a lope toward them.

Frank and Bill pulled their rifles, and when the riders came into range, both parties stopped, eying each other. Frank hollered, "Where you boys trailing to?"

The rider in the white shirt and dark Stetson, astride a deep-chested sorrel almost a twin of Cantrell's, shouted back, "Headin' up to the Missouri. Seen any Injun sign? Let's talk, we're peaceful."

Frank started forward and Cantrell followed, dallying the lead ropes so his hands were able to use his rifle, if need be. The two riders sat passively, waiting for them to come up.

Frank, as he approached, was reassured by the looks of the two. 'Texas boys,' he thought, riding good horses with the same brand, N. The cattle, as they began streaming by with a big steer in the lead, were also branded with the N, and Frank knew they were seeing a legitimate trail herd and its outfit. The chuckwagon and remuda of seventy or eighty horses came in sight, flanking the herd upwind of the dust. The two riders were joined by two more flankers, all riding horses branded the same.

Frank put away his rifle. "I take it this is a Bar N trail herd up from Texas. You boys are a long ways off your range," he drawled.

The white shirted rider, a sunburnt freckled young man, sidled his horse up to Frank and stuck out his hand, "The farthest north of any herd so far. Your drawl tells me you're off that same range back home, sir. Sure good to see another Texas brush-buster!"

Frank chuckled and shook the offered hand.

The young man continued, "I'm Johnnie Burgess and this's Dallas Lund. These others are Luke White and Buster Bell." The others were also young men, like the first two.

Frank introduced himself and Cantrell and they shook hands all around.

"Just so you boys will know we're not rustlers, I'll tell you that we were sent out from the DHS ranch by Granville Stuart, the President of the Stockgrower's Association, after a horse thief." The men, at ease now that they'd taken the measure of the two riders confronting them, brought out tobacco and either bit off a chew or rolled a cigarette. Frank accepted a chew but Cantrell declined, rolling a cigarette himself.

"Did you-all come up to him?" one of the men, Luke White, inquired.

"We did. Left him on the bank of the Milk for the wolves," Frank stated. The other men nodded, alike in their hatred of a stock thief.

"Heard in Miles there was some trouble up this way," Burgess said.

"That there is. This whole country's needin' the scum shook out of it," Frank told them.

"What's the country like over on the Milk?" Luke inquired, evidently the gabby one.

"Well, it's good grass, about like here. Lots of feed right now, with the buffalo gone. Country's open but the wolves are bad and there's some war parties, both Gros Ventres and Sioux, moving through. Keep a sharp lookout and you'll be all right, I should imagine," Frank answered. Cantrell, who'd kept quiet, nodded. As the drag of the herd passed, the men relaxed, exchanging bits of information.

The chuckwagon angled up and Burgess, evidently the foreman, directed it to a likely camp spot. "We'll make a dry camp here. There'll be water ahead of us in the morning, from what Shannon says." The others rode away to pull the herd up and bed it down.

Frank and Cantrell pulled off their saddles and packs and a cowboy ran their horses into the remuda. Another swung down and helped unhitch the team. The harness was hung on the side of the wagon and the team likewise turned into the horse herd.

Bill, unrolling his bed, saw that the horse wrangler was a Mexican boy. He was well mounted on the only animal Cantrell had seen that wasn't branded with an N. It was certainly a horse that caught the eye, a dark palomino with the lighter mane and tail that showed some grooming. It had the small, fine featured and alert Arab head, with small ears and large, intelligent eyes. Cantrell had seen only a few before and they had never failed to impress him. Most times they had come up, he'd found, from deep in Mexico, off one of the old estancios that had kept the bloodlines pure down through the centuries. Never had he found one for sale, though once he'd tried very hard to pry one loose from its owner. Cantrell poked Frank and pointed the horse out to him and together they sat on their bedrolls and watched the horse and boy work the herd. The big animal was quick and agile, with heavily muscled hindquarters, an excellent topline and the long, clean legs of a thoroughbred. Its hooves were small and dark and it carried them almost daintily. The more Cantrell looked, the more impressed he became. He noticed, too, it was a stallion, rare on the range.

"There's a horse, Frank, that I think would give Ben quite a run. What do you think?"

Frank grunted, then grudgingly admitted, "Hate to say it, but you're right. That's quite a horse. I'd make a bet that it has a bloodline longer'n your arm."

They lay there at their ease, discussing similar horses they had seen in the past, until Cantrell finally roused himself, and finding the cleaning gear, began working their weapons over. Presently the cook, whom they'd heard the men call Rollie, brought over the steaming coffee pot and a couple cups. They thanked him and sipped the scalding liquid gingerly.

Some of the riders came loping in, then, and swinging down, were soon sipping coffee and joshing each other. All of them, Cantrell saw, were young men, men either in their teens or scarcely out of them. They were a boisterous bunch, full of fun, and he thought a little wistfully of his own youth, gone with the war. They were fed, and after their night horses were caught up, several rode out to relieve the others at the herd.

Each time the Mexican lad had cast a flawless loop with his rawhide riata to catch the horse the cowboy called for. It was an impressive display of dexterity but no one who witnessed it thought anything of it. Good ropers were common in that day and time, and usually the Mexicans, with their long riatas and little loops, were the best of the lot. Frank and Bill came to the fire and accepted in turn their plate of beans, biscuits and barbecue beef, spicy hot as the Texans liked it.

The second crew came in and to the fire. Like the others, they were young, with one exception—an older man about Cantrell's age. Dark haired like Cantrell, he had a full black beard and a stocky, burly build to him that bespoke strength. The others, Cantrell noted, kept apart from him a little. For his part, he was indifferent to them, calling loudly to the cook to give him more barbecue, then later hollering loudly to the wrangler to bring out his night horse. He was saddling up when Rollie called out, "Billie Juan, come on in and eat now."

The boy came flashing up and stepped gracefully to the ground. Cantrell took note of the huge silver mounted spurs, a silver studded bridle and the gleaming saddle decked with more silver. The boy was slight of stature, straight and erect, with a royal profile that showed as much good breeding as that of his horse. He dropped the reins and the animal stood still as stone. It was a picture to capture the heart of any horseman.

Cantrell had crawled in his bed and was nearly asleep when he heard a shout. He raised up in time to see the older bearded rider leap forward and dash a pan of water out of the Mexican lad's hands. The older rider grabbed the boy's shirt and brought him close to his angry face, spitting out, "You little greaser bastard! I'm tired of seeing you pamper that pet of yours. The rest of the stock can't water, so it damn sure isn't gettin' any, either."

The boy protested, squirming in the strong grasp of the other.

"Senor, he worked hard today! The water barrel is nearly full and the others will water tomorrow."

"You little Greaser, if my horse isn't drinkin', neither is yours."
He threw the boy back in a sprawl of legs and spurs.

One of the other trail hands muttered, "Oh, Hell, Grafford, what's a little water?"

Cantrell then saw what he feared—Frank, his shirt off and his hair wet, showing he'd been washing up, strode into the firelight. "Leave the boy alone. The cook says your water's not a problem." His easy manner was conciliatory but the other took it as a weakness. Grafford turned, his hand significantly close to his gun.

"Get out of here, old man, this is Bar N business!"

Frank drawled, "Seems like everybody has an opinion 'bout my age. Even a bearded butt-head like you."

"I warned you" The man started a draw that, even as the pistol came clear of the holster, was interrupted by Frank's shot. Cantrell, his rifle up, saw Grafford's gun go spinning off and thought at first that Frank had hit it, but saw then that he'd hit the arm at the elbow. Grafford clutched it in agony. Cantrell had meanwhile covered the rest of the crew and noticed that Frank squared away and did the same. They needn't have bothered, for the other hands were not interested in mixing in, rather they seemed embarrassed at what had happened. The injured man sank slowly down to his knees, still holding his arm. The beat of hooves came with the rush of a horse into the firelight and Burgess flung himself from his saddle. His eyes riveted on the kneeling figure, he rasped out," I heard the shot. What happened?"

Rollie, the cook, came forward, still holding a ladle in his hand.

"Grafford was cussing Billie Juan again. Shannon called him on it and they shot it out—or anyway, Grafford started to pull on Shannon and got a bullet in the arm. Served him right, the sonofabitch."

Several of the crew nodded or spoke assent as Burgess looked around the group. Frank remained in the shadows, a significant and menacing figure.

Rollie went over and pulled Grafford up by the other arm and led him to the wagon, where he and Burgess examined the wound. The injured man, when they peeled the blood soaked shirt away, fell back in a faint. While the others held the arm still, Rollie washed the blood off.

"Looks like it broke through the elbow joint and out again,"

The majority of the young cowboys came clustering in to stare in morbid fascination. Cantrell, who'd seen plenty enough wounds to last a lifetime, lay back in his bedroll, uncocking his rifle. The explosive suddenness of the incident and the murmurs of the men at the wagon didn't keep him awake for long. He did remember noticing the young Mexican swing onto his horse and ride out into the darkness. He slept.

Working together almost like a team, the two men cleaned up the wound as best they could, poured some whiskey on it and bound it up with a clean dish towel, the cook grumbling all the while about its loss, that the injured man wasn't hardly worth it.

"Tole you in Miles that we shouldna hired him, Johnnie. Just a would-be gun thrower lookin' for trouble, is all he is."

"Go on now, Rollie," Burgess drawled, "We needed riders. You know that. What else was I to do?"

Together, they got the unconscious man into the wagon and covered him with his bedroll. Then they returned to the fire, where Rollie poured coffee. The foreman spoke apologetically. "I'm sorry, Shannon, that you-all did what I or one of my crew should have done. Lord knows he's been askin' for it."

Frank waved the apology away.

"Maybe I should have killed him, but this wasn't a killing matter, I didn't think. At that, he might die anyway—or lose his arm."

"Dunno." The foreman took a sip from his cup. "But I'd bet he never uses that wing to pull a gun again."

Next morning the camp came alive in the early light to Rollie banging on a pan. Cantrell, rising late, wasn't surprised to see Frank at the fire, sipping coffee and visiting with the young cowpunchers. Bill observed that, in their talk and the looks they gave the old man, he had made a hit with the crew. Frank noticed him stirring and came over with a cup of steaming hot coffee. He took it with thanks and noticed then that his sorrel was already tied to the wagon, waiting to be saddled. From the wagon he heard a muffled groaning.

They pulled away from the trail herd with the sun well above the horizon and the prairie alive with colors and the early morning sounds.

"Lots of meadowlarks this year. I sure like to hear 'em," Frank remarked, feeling his smooth face. He had borrowed some hot water from the cook and shaved and cleaned up. Cantrell thought he looked and sounded better than he had since they had crossed the river. He'd also curried the Ben horse and it was looking as good as its rider. He glanced back and saw the rest of the herd trailing over a distant hill, the drag partially obscured by dust, with the chuck wagon rolling along upwind. The remuda was out of sight.

They traveled southwest for three or four hours, not hurrying. Like the day before, Frank was in a talkative mood, regaling Cantrell with Texas Ranger tales. His dead partner, Matthew, was usually the principal character of the stories.

"You know, Bill, he was about the fastest and most accurate pistol shot I even seen, and I seen a few, let me tell you."

Cantrell felt impelled to speak. "Seems to me you've a pretty quick hand yourself, Frank. Your partner was in good company."

Frank gave a careless flick of his wrist, disparagingly. "Oh, I could always handle myself, if it come to that."

They pulled up in the late morning by a small creek where a gnarled old cottonwood spread a little shade with what green branches it had left. Bill gathered a few pieces of dead wood from around its trunk and they started a fire and put the coffee on. The pot was simmering when Frank looked to the south and stood up.

"We got riders comin', two of 'em," he said.

Cantrell glanced up from pouring their cups full and shaded his eyes with his free hand, "That one sits a horse like Ludich. Don't recognize the other."

The riders came in and it was indeed Jack Ludich, on his blue roan, and another DHS hand, the young Bill Clark. They dismounted at the fire and rummaged in their gear for their cups.

"Glad we met up with you, Frank. Stuart sent us out to find you. He"

"Tell me how the boy is, first!" Frank interrupted harshly.

"Your boy woke up. He's mending fine, Mrs. Stuart says. Sleeps a lot, but that's natural with a bad wound," Ludich sipped his coffee, and, avoiding Frank's eyes, stared at the Ben horse.

"Good. That's good!" Frank exclaimed joyously. Any bad humor he'd evidenced at Ludich's arrival was swept away with the easing of the guilt burden he had been packing over Toby's injury.

"Stuart told us to find you and ask you if you and Cantrell would head down to Miles City. Cramer is already on his way. They got the deputy business all straightened out with Irvine down there and they could use some help. He said he'd gladly deputize us all." He paused, "I'm supposed to trail along with you. Stuart said to find some extra horses if we could, and bring 'em to Miles."

Frank looked over at Cantrell. "Miles City, huh?"

"See you got your horse back, Frank. Did you get Stringer?" Ludich asked.

"He's feeding the wolves over on the Milk River," Frank rejoined shortly.

Ludich gave a nervous laugh. "The gray ran him down for you, huh?

Cantrell spoke. "Frank relayed him down. At that, the black threw a shoe or we'd probably never have caught him. He was running away from the gray."

Ludich shook his head admiringly. "Is that a fact?" His eyes ran over the beautiful animal again. "Sure don't seem to be any the worse for wear."

"No. Didn't hurt him none that we can tell," Cantrell replied. Frank said nothing.

Ludich, a dark suntanned puncher of medium height, showed the outward characteristics of most of the region's hands. He hailed from the Southwest, having come up with a Mill-iron trail herd. His somewhat square face was showing several day's stubble. His bowed rider's legs were perched on small feet cased in fancy high topped, high heeled boots carrying a pair of inlaid gold and silver Mexican spurs. Like many Texas drovers, he carried his life's wealth with him, his gun belt studded with silver conchos and a beautiful engraved buckle, his saddle and bridle likewise brilliantly reflecting the sun's rays. Some punchers, and Ludich was one, were pretty sights to see on the range. Mostly they were excellent stockmen, masters of their trade who knew the horse and cow as few men could. They made their living horseback by the rough code they had developed and Cantrell knew that Ludich was one of this breed, a man to be respected. He was known to have killed at least three men with the ivory gripped .45 he carried, yet, curiously, Cantrell detected a nervousness in the man as he watched him facing Frank. Did the old man spook this hard faced rider that much or was there something else? He listened closely to their talk. Ludich spoke hesitantly. "Frank, maybe you-all don't want me trailin' along with you boys to Miles?"

Frank reached over and poured the other's cup full and looked him in the eye.

"Well, I don't know, Jack. Are we gonna look around the next time we get in a tight spot and not find you?"

Ludich raised his head then and stared defiantly into Frank's faded blue eyes. "That'll never happen. It didn't before——and it won't in the future, if you'll have me." He tore his gaze from Frank.

"It's just that I had some hopes of maybe settling later around Lewistown, and I didn't want any law problems following me. That's why, you know." He trailed off.

The other looked away, all of them surprised as his emotion became evident. After a pause, Frank put his hand on Ludich's shoulder and spoke kindly.

"Hell, Jack. Come along then, and welcome — and thanks for the news about Toby."

The puncher gave a grateful nod. It was evident that he cared very much about Frank's opinion of him, Cantrell saw.

They presently gathered and stored the coffee gear, snuffed out the fire and parted with Clark. Along with the gray, Frank sent the big .50/95 Winchester rifle to return to Stuart.

"Tell Granville both of 'em served me well and I'm grateful. The bullet in the stock is compliments of Stringer Jack."

They watched him go, then turned southeast on the trail to Miles City. It was well defined, as the recent herd's passing was very evident in the hoof-churned earth.

photograph by L.A. Huffman

Chapter 18

Miles City

Mid-morning of the fourth day saw them on the yellow bluffs above the Yellowstone River overlooking the mouth of the Tongue River. On the east side of the Tongue was the town, on the west was the military reservation, Fort Keogh. Both were clearly visible from the bluff, as were two steamboats tied a few hundred yards up the Tongue from its mouth, but Frank noted that the Nez Perce lodges which had dotted the flats out by the rifle range to the south of the Fort were gone. He wondered where they had been sent. Poor damned people.

The trip across country from the Musselshell had been almost incredible. From the time they had crossed the north fork of Lodge Pole Creek they had encountered cattle, thousands of them. Longhorned Texas steers they were, mostly two and three and year olds, nearly as wild as the buffalo had been whose bones they walked among. They saw that the brands were mainly T4 and 79, although as they got closer to Big Dry creek, they started running into N-N land.   .

The first night they camped with an N-N trail outfit that had just finished the drive up from the South. Like the N crew, it was mostly composed of Texas boys, southern in their talk and manner. Frank and Ludich were kindred spirits, even to knowing several of their families. The cook was one an outfit could be proud of. He fed a supper of beefsteak, potatoes, cornpone and a dessert of raisin duff with canned milk to nineteen men in half an hour. The men sat mostly under a spread wagon tarp staked out and tied down to give them some shade.

"We'll be heading on over to the Musselshell to build a headquarters," the foreman told them as they ate.

"Probably build a camp on the Little Dry, too. The boss bought out Captain Lake's scrip holdings over there, along with his brand,"

With Frank and an old hand, "Porky" Bill Stouder, telling stories, the group was late getting to their blankets that night. Breakfast was almost a repetition of the night before—a heavy meal that included beefsteak, biscuits and gravy. Frank, though, drank only coffee.

In response to Frank's inquiry, the foreman had mentioned a man named Bill Hunter, who had moved in on Big Dry and would probably have some horses to sell. They rode in that direction consequently, amazed by the influx of cattle and people into the country. Several times they passed wagons with men, women and kids out picking up buffalo bones. Once they even passed a creek crossing that sported a dugout saloon, a whiskey seller out trying to peddle some of his home brew to passing trail drivers. And always there were more cattle—a Circle C herd and one branded HT that they passed before they came to Hunter's camp on the Dry.

They began seeing horses on the open range, mainly short backed, deep chested bays and sorrels, fairly long legged and showing some Morgan breeding. Those carried an H3 brand on their left hip, but there were quite a few others that showed miscellaneous trail brands, indicating Hunter had bought up stock from outfits that had closed out their holdings, probably at Miles City, their point of destination, and sold to another brand.

"The man has a nice bunch of horses. Wonder how he's kept 'em, with all the stock thieves around?" Ludich remarked. Frank snorted.

They continued on and found the camp where Quarles, the N-N foreman, had told them it was. A dugout had been built into the side of a hill above the creek, facing a little flat where a set of round corrals had been built out of cedar posts and lodgepole railings, evidently freighted in from the Bull Mountains. The dugout had been front-walled with chisel-squared sandstone. Rifle ports had been cut into the rock and the place looked solid as a fort. They hailed as they came in sight and a man appeared in the doorway holding a rifle. Behind him, a dog barked, then appeared between his legs, peering out at them.

"Help you boys?" the man hollered.

Frank grinned and called back.

"Wanta see a man about a horse, Mr. Hunter. We're in the market to buy."

The man, a portly round-faced individual with a drooping black and silver mustache that bristled all over his upper lip, turned to someone inside and said something, then called to them to come ahead. The men rode up and swung down. After a lightening swift scrutiny, the man invited them to come in, swinging the heavy planked door wide.

"The wife's got the coffee on, boys. Come on in."

In front of the dugout was a hitching post to which they tied their horses. Inside was a surprisingly neat abode. A table, chairs, some packing box shelving and some rough bunks comprised the furniture but there were miscellaneous weapons and tack hanging from the walls and the supporting roof posts. The one small window had been made with four clear liquor bottles set in a row with their necks broken off. A wood stove was set in the corner. A woman, a tanned, rugged looking white woman, was busy stoking its fire. She smiled a gap-toothed grin and said a cheery hello. She put out cups from a packing box shelf lined with wax paper. The portly man introduced himself and they shook hands around. He looked at Frank with a piercing blue eye when he heard his name

"Frank Shannon," he repeated, "Rides a big black horse with a white patch on its forehead. Sit down, boys, and the wife'll have the coffee on in just a minute."

As they sat to the table, Hunter spoke again. "I remember O'Malley telling about a horse race there in Miles. All the top horses roundabouts there got beat by a big black, owned by a man name of Shannon."

Frank laughed, "Guess I'll have to plead guilty."

"Wouldn't want to sell or trade him, would you? I've got some horses you might like." Hunter's eyes held a horsetrader's gleam.

"Nope. The black ain't for sale or trade. Had too much trouble keepin' him. What we got in mind, though, is some cash buyin'. Ours been seeing some long riding, lately."

Hunter nodded his round head wisely. "Heard the DHS was pullin' some long circles, all right. Now, if you like, you can borrow some of my best and use 'em long as you need to. I want one and all to know I'm with you boys on this."

Frank nodded, "That's real decent of you, Hunter, but I'd just as soon buy, if I can. You never know what might happen to 'em."

"Suit yourself. I'll price them low as I can, and buy 'em back later, if you want."

The woman brought the coffeepot, a large enamelware pot, to the table and poured out cups for all. They smiled at her in thanks and she placed a jar of cream on the table. Frank's bushy eyebrows rose.

256

"By gosh, Hunter. You got a cow?"

It was the horseman's turn to laugh. "Nope, Got it from some bonepickers happened by. They had a cow comin' fresh."

Taking turns, all of the men dipped into the jar and spooned the precious rich liquid into their cups. Presently, Ludich and Cantrell went out to run in the horse herd.

Hunter spoke, "I hear that the rustlers and such are getting pretty thinned down over on the Missouri. It's sure put the spook in a bunch of 'em. Been a steady stream of riders goin' by, usually at night. Guess most of 'em got a case of rope fever and think the night riding might relieve it."

Frank gave the man across the table a hard look.

"Hasn't been hard so far to catch the man who makes no bones of being a thief, Hunter. The real trick is trying to figure out who the men are that's behind them, putting up the money for the stolen stock."

The portly man's face blanched, "Hey now. You're way off the mark if you're aiming at me. I'm an honest stockman, and I've got a good bill of sale for every horse I own". He spread his hands in a placating gesture. "It's true, Shannon, and I won't deny it, that I have sold stock to men whose money I maybe wondered where it came from. But sellin' ain't a crime. No businessman can know what all his customers been up to. But I never traded horses with those men, or took in an animal whose ownership I wasn't sure of. Go out and take a look for yourself."

"I intend to do that, but maybe in the meantime, you'll bring out the sale bills for me. Mind you, I don't have a badge. It might be a help to you, later, though, if anyone asks you, that you can tell 'em we were here and looked over your herd and your waybills."

Hunter got up from the table and started angrily for a corner of the dugout, but his wife had anticipated him, handing a tin box over. He flung it open and, pulling the sheaf of papers from within, started to throw them on the table, then thinking the better of it, laid them in front of Frank. "You're right, Shannon, and I've got nothing to hide. Take a gander at each and every one of 'em." He pulled out his chair and sat back down at the table. Frank sipped his coffee and shuffled through the papers half-heartedly, concealing the fact that he couldn't read. Hunter and his wife waited anxiously until he reached the end of the pile. Presently Frank handed them back to Hunter.

"All of 'em seem okay to me. Well, I hear the boys bringing 'em in. Let's go do some horse trading." With a relieved look, Hunter gave them to his wife.

Together, they headed for the corral, from which a cloud of dust arose. Once there, the two men leaned on the top bar of the corral, Hunter having to stretch a little to accomplish it. He offered a chew of tobacco to Frank, who took it, while they watched the horses mill in the enclosure.

So you need some war horses, huh? These'll do you good enough. They got some body to 'em, good, deep lungs makes 'em stayers down the stretch, like that black of yours. Good legs, too, especially those that have my breedin'. Top of that, they're all broke. Just to show there ain't any hard feelin's, I want to take your pick of 'em. First one's free, on me." He gestured at the full corral with a wave of his hand.

Frank chuckled, "Hope you don't figure to get the price of it back on the rest. I'm goin' to drive a hard bargain with you. I'll just take your offer, though. I'm never one to look a gift horse in the mouth. Ha!" He stretched a finger at a mouse colored dun horse with a dished face that was showing some extra quickness in the turns the milling herd was making around the enclosure. Immediately Ludich, who had been standing by with coiled rope and a ready loop, strode out and made a catch of its front feet as it sped by him. The horse came to a sliding stop and turned to face him.

"Good pick." Hunter commented, "Not one of my breedin, but I'm partial to it, just the same." Frank grunted. Then in rapid succession, he picked three other horses from the herd, Ludich catching each as he pointed him out and leading them over to Cantrell, who put a halter on and snubbed the horse to the corral.

"Go ahead, boys, and make your pick." Frank then called. When the two men had made and caught their choices, Hunter groaned, "You men just managed to top my herd. I'm going to have to put the price at $110 a head,"

"That's a mite steep. Believe we'd be about right at $90."

They settled at $100 a head, both sides satisfied. Frank paid the total out of his money belt and got a receipt that he carefully folded and stuck back in his belt, along with the waybills of each of the horses. Hunter asked them to stay and eat.

"Appreciate the hospitality, but we've got to be headin' for Miles." The two men shook hands and Frank swung aboard the horse Ludich had saddled for him, the dun horse he had first picked out. The man and wife stood waving by the door of the dugout as they swung back into the trail again, each mounted on their pick and chowsing the other saddle horses in front of them.

Now, they stood on the bank of the Yellowstone, attempting to catch the attention of the ferry man on the south side. Finally Frank drew his pistol and fired a shot in the air. That drew the man from his shack on the gravel bar. He yawned hugely and stretched, then yelled over, "Ferry prices just went up: two bits fer the loose horses and four bits a man. Still wanta keep your boots dry?"

Frank started to answer him, then clutched his middle, drawing his right leg out the stirrup with the pain. Cantrell edged in and took his arm, steadying him in the saddle. He shouted, "C'mon! Bring the damn boat and make it snappy. We got a sick man here!" By the time the planked contrivance touched the north shore, Frank was down off his horse, stretched on the ground, with Bill and Jack bending over him.

"So, how's business been, Doc?" Frank weakly greeted the Major as the stocky big surgeon strode into the examination room from his office. Frank rose with some effort from the cane back chair where he'd been sitting and the two shook hands.

"The Indian fighter returns. You've been busy, I hear, but not with redskins." Girard's piercing eyes met Frank's. "What's a tough old bird like you need with a doctor? Didn't you hear there a pretty good one now over in town?"

"It's my gut, Major, been hurtin' me."

"What'd you do, swallow your chew?" The Major grinned.

Frank chuckled, "Not that I know of, Doc, but I wanted you to look at it, not some stranger."

"Hmm. Well, take your shirt off." He reached in a drawer and pulled out a stethoscope. Expertly, he ran it over the stringy lean old body, front and back. Then he began poking here and there with stiff fingers, finally drawing an agonized grunt from his patient as he zeroed in on the source of Frank's pain, low in the abdomen. Finally Girard sat back, drew a couple cigars from his vest pocket and offered one to Frank. For a short time, neither spoke as they enjoyed the bite of the nicotine.

The doctor broke the silence.

"It's a tumor. A big one. Probably growing on the stomach wall. Back East now, they're sometimes going in the body cavity and taking them out, successfully. "

"Figured so. You see 'em once in a while on horses and such. An operation like that, goin' in and rooting around in a man's insides, how many survive it? Seems to me, rememberin' the war, you were most as good as dead with a wound that went inside of you." Frank drew pensively on his cigar, looking out the window at the sun setting red over the bluffs of the Yellowstone.

"Well, it's true that with the septic conditions of the war, many men died of surgery. But things have changed some since then in the field of medicine. However, throwing all the odds in the pot, I'd say it's around 10 to 1 that you wouldn't make it. Maybe more, given your age. A tumor that big will have roots like a sagebrush that go awful deep." He paused, looking at his cigar ash. "Sorry, Frank"

The older man snorted, "No need to be, Major. I've lived out my life and she's been a good one. No Regrets do I have—except maybe one."

When the stocky doctor came out of his examination room wearing a stern, sober face, Cantrell expected the worst.

"How is he, Major?"

The tired surgeon collapsed in a chair behind his desk. "How is He? Exhausted. Malnourished. Old and tired out. And he's got a tumor in his stomach as big as a plate that's going to kill him, sooner if not later." He struck a match and brought it to the end of his dead cigar, blew out a cloud of evil smelling smoke. Then he looked out the window to avoid meeting Cantrell's stricken eyes.

"Nuthin you can do?"

"Someday, maybe surgery will get to the point to where we can open the abdominal cavity, take out a big tumor like that and successfully sew it back up without killing the patient. We haven't reached that point yet, and probably won't in my lifetime." He shook his head, "No, there's nothing we can do—except help make the end as painless as possible."

Cantrell studied his boots.

"Well, how long's he got?"

"He asked me that question, too, and I had to tell him that I really didn't know—a month, three? I can't be sure enough to nail a time down, but it can't be long, as quick as it must have grown in him."

"What should I do?"

"Leave him here for now. He's worn out. Come back tomorrow and take him into town. Get a room at the MacQueen for him to headquarter in. I'll stop by from time to time with some painkiller. Beyond that, I can't think of anything."

* * *

The room at the MacQueen House was light and spacious, letting out onto the upstairs sun porch overlooking the street and facing north into Riverside Park. Cantrell would wake in the light of early dawn and, looking over, see that Frank had already slipped his blankets and parked himself with a cup of coffee out on the porch, his feet up on the railing, watching the sun come up. Without saying much, he took a great interest in the comings and goings in the dusty street. After a light breakfast which the cook down in the dining room sent up to the room, a knock would sound and it was usually an old-timer come to visit with Frank, sometimes with a bottle in his hand. Cantrell often made himself scarce, then, walking down to check on the horses at Broadwater and Hubbell's Livery on the corner of Fifth and Main. Frank had sent Ludich back to the DHS several days before and had tried to do the same with Cantrell, to no avail. Bill had insisted on sticking around. That first day, he'd gone in and had a drink at Charlie Brown's, feeling old alongside of the young cowboys bellied up there on the either side of him. He'd listened to their boisterous talk for a while, mostly about nothing that interested him, then went out and headed for a barber shop. The hot towels and ministrations of the barber's dexterous fingers lulled him to sleep in the chair. When the man shook him awake and turned him toward the mirror, he was startled to see the lean, tanned dark face that stared back. He'd asked the barber to leave the mustache, and in its black silkiness, he could see some gray coming in. Also in the dark hair at his temples did some gray show up.

At 36, his life had already been a hard one. The war, losing both his parents early, his wife and son, numerous wounds, all these combined to make him a man who, although not bitter, certainly was cynical and fatalistic. The lines reflecting this were beginning to show up in his face.

He paid, and clumped down the wooden boardwalk, stopping occasionally to peer into some of the more interesting doors and windows facing the street. Music came from several of them, with stomping men and twirling skirts of the hall girls within. He ignored it all.

* * *

Charlie Brown stopped wiping the beer mug he was holding and gave his complete attention to what had just rode up to the front of his saloon. The rider just stepping down from one of the prettiest palominos he'd ever seen was a young Mexican boy, big hatted and spurred. The horse was magnificent, although almost too heavily muscled in the forequarters.

"Say, men, look here! Quite a horse, eh?" Several of the loungers in the front of the saloon had already gotten to their feet and surrounded the horse, who stood quietly, tolerating their inspection. Others in the saloon's dark interior came to the window or the door to better see the lines of the beautiful animal. Charlie broke through their ranks as the young rider stepped to the boardwalk and confronted him.

"That's quite a horse you got there. Want to trade or sell him, Amigo?"

"No, Sen'or. My 'orse is no for sale." the slight Mexican shook his head for emphasis, leaving Charlie with the impression the boy had answered that question many times before. "But could you tell me if you have seen three men, one of them a man called Frank Shannon?"

"Frank Shannon?" Charlie looked again at the boy before him and could see no danger in telling him where he could find Frank. "Sure. He's down at the MacQueen House." He pointed down the street. He dearly wanted to ask what business the young man had with Frank, but didn't.

"Thank you, Sen'or."

The boy turned and waded through the group crowded about his horse, mounted with a fluid ease and cantered off in the direction of MacQueen's.

"Hell of a horse, huh, Charlie?" one of the cowhands, a squarefaced individual, said.

"Surely is. Wisht I coulda bought 'im." the saloon owner responded absently, returning to his daily chores. The horse looked like it had speed, and they hadn't had a really good race since Frank's black had taken the field around Miles. Outside of some poker games and a couple bare knuckle matches, things had gotten boring.

Down the street, at MacQueen's hitching rail, Billy Juan halted El Tigre and swung down again. His big spurs jangling musically, he strode in to the hotel.

Frank was seated out on the veranda of his room, and had watched the boy as he rode down the street toward him. He recognized the horse and rider immediately and wondered idly what the boy had deserted the herd for. He was alone at the moment. Cantrell was off down to Hubbell's and Light Sam, a friend from Kansas days, had not shown up as yet. He sipped his coffee and felt his middle. It was a little tender to the touch but he was learning to get along with it some. As long as he didn't strain the stomach muscles or eat or drink very much, it mostly just ached, like a throbbing bad tooth. It was when he irritated it, that it flared and acted like it was chomping on his insides. It made sense then, to send Cantrell back to Stuart to report their inactivity, but Cantrell, stubborn as he was, just wouldn't go.

No, it was going to end for him right here in Miles and he had some regrets, chiefly about his pard, Matthew, and Toby, but that was the way of it. No help for it now. However, if he could take some of Chinnick's crew down with him, it would be a last pay-back to vindicate himself in his own mind.

He stood stiffly, pushing himself up from the chair and went into the room, hearing a knock at the hall door. He pulled his revolver and checked the loads as he called.

"Who is it?" Knowing what the answer would be.

"It's me, Sen'or, Billy Juan, from the N Bar."

Frank strode to the door and unlocked it, then pulled it open, the gun out of sight in his right hand. With his left, he reached out and propelled the youngster into the room, then quickly surveyed the hallway to see if they were being watched.

No one was there. He turned, then, and examined the boy standing before him.

"Now, Son, what do you want with me?"

For answer, Billy Juan swung off his large sombrero and holding it to his front, began what was a carefully memorized statement of thanks for Frank's shooting of Grafford. Frank halted him in mid-sentence, gesturing with his right hand, which, holding his pistol, frightened the boy momentarily.

"No need for that, boy. A man like him wouldn't last out here anyways. If I hadn't done it, one of the other riders, maybe even yourself, would have eventually."

"Maybe, Sen'or. But you did it. Not the others. I am thankful for what you did."

"Leave it at that, then." Frank said, surveying the lad in front of him. He liked what he saw. Billy Juan, slim as he was, stood ramrod straight and wore his rider's clothes with a style that rivaled his horse for natural elegance. It affected him and reminded him of great Mexican riders he had known in his young days. He gestured to a chair by the foot of the bed. He himself laid his old frame down on the creaking mattress and put his hands behind his head, the pistol lying by his side.

"Sit down, Son. Tell me how the herd is doin'."

The boy sat obediently.

"The herd we scattered along the breaks of the Musselshell, Sen'or. I asked for my time, then, and came along to find you and thank you."

"And now you've done it, what's your plans?"

"Find another job, Sen'or. We cannot return to Texas."

"And why is that, my young friend?"

The lad bit his lip, hesitated, then answered with the assurance that the old man <u>was</u> his friend and could be confided in. "It concerns a killing, Sen'or," he said gravely.

"I see. Well, stayin' around here may present a problem for thin blooded hosses and men from the South when the Northers begin to blow. The winters can be vicious and I wouldn't recommend them if you got someplace else to go."

"That I have heard, Sen'or. Perhaps a man like yourself might give a young man some advice from the wisdom of your years."

"Well now, kinda nice to hear a young'un ask for some advice. Mebbe there's some merit in living so long, after all," Frank rejoined with a grin showing under his long mustache.

Their conversation was interrupted by a soft knock on the door. Frank swung off the bed to his feet, bringing the revolver up. He padded silently to the door and queried in a low voice.

"Who is it?"

"Sam."

Frank shot the bolt and cracked the door as he had before, holding the revolver behind him down by his leg. Then he swung the door open for a man to enter.

"H'lo, Frank. Company, I see," The one who'd entered observed amiably. He was a grizzled, white bearded unkempt appearing man, short of stature but standing on stocky legs cased to the knees in boots and affecting the red sash of the French Canadiens one sometimes saw along the frontier. The butt of a pistol protruded from above it on the right side, and the boy saw the hilt of a knife tucked in the top of the right boot. He looked to be the efficient buffalo skinner that the boy guessed he had been. He set a bottle of whiskey on the wooden soda cracker box which served as a night table by the bed.

"Here's yore cough medicine'", he announced.

"Now, Sam, I thank you. Feel a cough comin' right now, as a matter of fact. Grab those glasses over there and we'll take a shot or two of this medicine, see if it helps any." Frank reached and grabbed the amber filled bottle, twisting the cork out of its neck. "By the way, this here's Billy Juan, an ex-N Bar rider. He n' his crew brought a herd up over on the Musselshell lately. That ugly piece of coyote-kill out there in front of the hotel is his. He was just tellin' me he'd sell 'im to me for a double eagle. Look out the window there and tell me if you think he might be worth it," Frank chuckled.

"Sen'or." the boy protested.

"Saw the horse when I came up." Sam laughed, "He's a beauty. I might have to bid on him myself."

265

"Sen'ors! The Tiger is not for sale!" The lad got up, clearly about to leave. Sam put a meaty hand on his shoulder, pushing him back down on the hard chair.

"Simmer down, Son, Frank and me is just funning you. That horse is a beautiful animal, but like a beautiful woman, they can be a source of considerable trouble."

He winked at Frank, who nodded his head.

"Beautiful horses and beautiful women—somebody always wants 'em." He sipped his medicine thoughtfully. "Stay around here in Miles, Son, and you probably won't have it long. Horse thieves in these parts are a dime a dozen." He put his pistol in its holster hanging on the bedstead, then paused, thinking."You know, that gives me an idea is that horse as fast as it looks?"

"Sen'or, El Tigre has never been beaten at any distance—no other horse can do it—or so I believe!"

"Hmmm. What do you think of horse thieves, Billy?"

"They all should be hanged, Sen'or. It is only justice that they be."

"You wouldn't mind helping me'n Sam here, then, and a few others to see that some of the horse thieves cluttering up the country right now gets the justice they deserve?"

"If it is helping you, Sen'or, I will do it. Anything." The boy was earnest in his offer, Frank could see.

* * *

Cantrell stepped cautiously out and away from the Hubbell Livery barn where he'd been checking on the horses—and incidentally watching the comings and goings at Chinnick's Saloon. Some of them he'd recognized from his time there in the Missouri Breaks. Outlaws, all. Cantrell had been within an ace of becoming one of them. But he just couldn't reconcile his conscience with some of their doings—- like the attack on Frank's place there on the Rosebud. He'd been asked to go on that raid by Stringer himself, and had nearly gone, knowing that if he didn't, it was a declaration on his part that he wasn't going to align himself with the Missouri Breaks crew, but would be against them. He was glad now, down to the depths of his soul, that he had gone the other way. Knowing Frank, Reece Anderson and Granville Stuart, he would most probably now be a dead man—and deserving of his fate, he thought.

The walk back to the MacQueen House along the streets of Miles City just at dusk was one of interest. The section crews had returned from their hard days' work of track laying and the hurdy-gurdies were cranking up. Likewise the saloons were getting noisy and crowded. Off-duty soldiers from Keogh, cowhands, steamboat men and freighters made up most of the groups, but here and there on the street was the odd Indian, gambler and merchant. All men, as the few women of the area were either whores in their cribs, readying themselves for the nights work or officer's wives safe in their homes out at the fort. Those made sure they came to town in company, with their husbands or with an escort. There were few others, and it was a good thing. He'd seen the country settle up, though, in the Mid-West, as the merchants and ranchers brought their wives from the east. A woman, a respectable woman, should never walk a street like this, full of saloons, dancehalls and whorehouses. But it would soon change, as even Dodge City had.

Passing the Three Jacks Saloon, a drunk came crashing through the swing doors and careened into him. Without pausing, Cantrell swung his left arm like a sledge, hammering the man away from him and into the wall, where he slammed with a resounding crash that shook the structure and slumped the man down on the boardwalk. A few men looked around but most never broke stride. Cantrell kept going. For some reason, he felt better.

At Leighton's store, he turned in and went idly to the section. Behind the counter was a great assortment of weapons, including a wide variety of used and new rifles and shotguns. The counter itself contained a conglomeration of used and new pistols.

Frank had told him to watch for Matthew's guns and his, Frank's buffalo rifle, taken when the Stringer bunch had raided their ranch. He didn't see what looked like them. He bought some more pistol shells from the clerk and was about to go out, when Leighton called out to him from the back of the store.

"You're Cantrell, is that right? You rode in with Frank this trip?"

"Yes, that's right." The two men shook hands. Leighton shook his head.

"Frank. Now there's a tail twister for you. Nearly every time he's come to town, a body's gone out to Boothill. Know what he was goin' to do the last time? Take on the whole of Stringer Jack's band there in

Chinnnick's all by himself. I got Stuart's crew to talk him out of that, believe me. That gang was hell on wheels—killed Frank's partner, Matthew, and their hired hands over on the Rosebud this last winter. Burned them out. Why, I told Frank he'd just get himself killed, too. But he wouldn't listen to me. No Sir!! Took Irvine and Stuart's whole crew to put him off the notion. And they caught him just as he was about to brace 'em all. Damn good man, just like his partner was, but stubborn as hell. Come here, I want to show you somethin' I just got in."

Cantrell turned and went back to where Leighton kept a crowded and cluttered office.

The storekeeper was spinning the dial on his great big safe. He swung the door open and reached in, pulling out a Sharps rifle.

"That look familiar?" He asked, handing the heavy gun to Cantrell.

"Sharps .45/120 Old Reliable. Same caliber as Frank's. Could be his, alright. Who brought it in?" Cantrell asked.

"One of that crowd from over at Chinnick's. Traded for a Winchester. I was almost sure it's Frank's." Leighton said"I could point him out."

"I'll leave it with you and get Frank over to look at it this afternoon. Thanks, Leighton. I'd better get back and tell him." As Leighton put the big rifle back into the huge safe, Cantrell headed out of the store. He'd thought of telling Frank's friend about his illness, but decided it was Frank's business.

When he returned to the room, the atmosphere was convivial and He noticed that a new bottle was half-empty. The two men were regaling Billy Juan with stories of Kansas days. Cantrell greeted the young Mexican and turned to Frank.

"Leighton's got your Sharps over at the store, we think, Frank."

Frank's eyes turned hard, "That so?"

"Yeah. I thought you might like to go over this afternoon and take a look at it."

"I'll need to do that. Who'd he get it from?"

"Some drifter from Chinnick's. He says he can point him out."

"Good. He get any other guns? Matthew's Colt?"

"Nope. I brought us back some pistol ammo."

Frank grunted.

That afternoon, Frank walked into Leighton's store, through it and into the office.

Leighton was seated at his desk, a scarred rolltop that had seen better days.

"Frank!" How are you?"

"Dyin'. How 'bout yourself?"

Leighton looked away. He'd heard the verdict from another acquaintance.

"Oh, don't be so touchy, Joe. We all gotta go sometime." Frank sat down. "Hear you got my rifle from one of Chinnick's bunch."

Leighton got up and began spinning the dial on his safe. "Yeah. Bill and I looked at it and thought it might be yours. .45/120. Sonofabitch traded it for a Winchester." He pulled it from the safe and handed it to Frank, who examined it, rubbing a hand over its familiar scarred buttstock.

"Yeah, it's mine, alright. He bring any others?"

"No, just this one."

"What do I owe you?"

"Frank, you don't owe me a damn thing. You tryin' to hurt my feelings?"

"Well, much obliged, but there's no sense you bein' out for our misfortune."

"I want to be. Leave it at that."

"Joe, we got some of them, but there's still a few was in on Matthew's killin' that I need to attend to. I might meet 'em in Hell, but I want the privilege of sendin' 'em on before me." Frank spat in the cuspidor by the desk.

"What about Toby, Don't you care about him anymore?" Leighton said, "He's gonna need you, Frank."

"Like I said, I'm dyin'. Besides, he'll understand,"

"Maybe. But you're just throwing' your life away on scum, is what I think."

"Some of 'em were in on the raid on our ranch, Leighton. Will you help?"

"Haven't I always?" In a rare gesture of affection, the pugnacious little man put his hand out and patted Frank's arm.

"Yes, you have, Joe. You've been a true friend. Matthew would damn sure say the same."

269

The light of late morning saw Frank and Cantrell in the dining room of MacQueen's, lingering over coffee. Cantrell had just finished writing on his napkin. Frank spoke up in his lazy drawl.

"That should do it, have the printer run off a hundred or so and scatter them all over. Gaines over at the stage office'll send 'em toward Deadwood for you, if you ask him, and drop 'em off at Volberg, Alzada and Belle Fourche along the way. Get someone on the huffer-puffer to spread 'em on the rail line toward Glendive and parts east."

Art James, the editor, was curious about the upcoming race.

"Wasn't that 'Ben' horse the one beat Fanny's mare last year about this time?"

"Yeah. Belongs to Frank Shannon." Cantrell replied.

"Should be a hell of a race, then. I saw that Mex kid's horse at the livery barn. What an animal that is!" Art said in admiration.

After he'd pounded the posters up on just about every corner and cottonwood tree on Main street, Cantrell decided he'd step in to Leighton's and look at a used Sharp's rifle he'd spotted there earlier. It was a .45/120 caliber"Old Reliable," like Frank's, heavy enough of weight and caliber that many men would shy away from it. Evidently the previous owner had felt that way also, since it was just like new. Set off with an octagonal tapered barrel, figured walnut stock, long range sights and set triggers, it was a rifleman's dream and Cantrell, seeing it, had decided for some reason that he needed another long gun. It wasn't that his big Winchester wasn't adequate—the price of the Sharp's at $35.00 was just too good to pass up. So what if the buffalo were nearly gone and the gun was deprived of the work for which it had been made? Did a man always need a good reason to buy a gun? Leighton stepped around the counter, his old merchant's nose sensing a sale.

"One hell of a price for this gun, Bill. I'll even throw the cleaning and loading tools in."

He stretched the big gun over the scratched counter to Cantrell's waiting hands like a mama handing her baby over to a stranger. Cantrell took it and brought it up to his burly shoulder, automatically sighting down the barrel at a fly on the ceiling. It fit him so well he hated to bring it down. He levered down the breech, looking inside the barrel.

The button rifling was clean and shone in the afternoon sun. He rubbed his hand over the smooth walnut. Yup, he needed this gun.

"Take $25.00?" he asked hopefully. It never hurt to ask.

Leighton shook his head regretfully."Tell you though, I'll throw some new brass in— got a couple hundred back here from another trade." He rummaged around under the counter and came up with a canvas pouch that jingled when he threw it on the boards in front of Cantrell.

"All right. You got yourself a deal, though I don't know why. These big Sharps are a thing of the past, I'm thinkin'." Cantrell pulled a roll of bills from his vest pocket and peeled off five $10 dollar bills from it, handing them over."Give me some powder, lead and a scabbard for it, while you're at it, Sam."

Heavily weighed down, with the scabbarded rifle over his shoulder, he headed back to the MacQueen House to deposit his load.

As expected, Frank gave him a ration of talk against his purchase.

"Why in the Hell didn't you say you wanted an old Sharps, son. I'da give you mine." he exploded, "One rifle's enough for a man to carry 'round, anyway. 'Specially a different caliber. What we need right now is repeaters."

"Now, Frank, nobody said you had to carry it. I'll maybe leave it with Leighton. I just always wanted a big Sharps and this one fits me like my saddle." Bill's saddle was a fairly new Hamley and he was as proud of it as he was of his old sorrel horse.

Frank's hands, always ready to be doing something, took up the reloading tools and began working them expertly.

"Anyway, might's well work up some cartridges since you got the makin's here," he said.

Bill started the totally unnecessary cleaning ritual that most all men go through when they purchase a new gun. The loud knock on the door, though, made both men quietly draw their pistols.

"Come in!' Frank called.

Sheriff Irvine stepped through the doorway. The sheriff looked around the room, taking in the piled gear and guns in the corner.

"Hello, Frank, Bill. Came to tell you that Stuart and his men'll be in tomorrow night on the 8:20. He sent me a code wire from Fort Maginnis."

Frank snorted, "the 8:20 what?"

"Why, the work train from the west. They'll meet it at Coulson's Landing. He wants you boys and the horses to be ready to go with him down east to hit some of the rustler nests that direction." Irvine eased himself down into a straight-backed chair by window."Course, Stuart didn't know you were laid up." Frank scratched his jaw.

"We had plans already to get 'em all up here to Miles."

"That why you got them racing posters up around town? So you could get 'em all gathered here? Figured as much. But you would have had to have help —and I don't appreciate havin' my town all shot up. Stuart's way is the right one. Listen to him. The town'll take care of Chinnick's by itself."

All Frank's grumbling was to no avail, but in any case, it didn't matter. That next day at breakfast they overheard some cowpunchers talking in Josey's Cafe.

"You hear about Chinnick? Seems some of the local citizenry gave him notice to get out of town yesterday. He got in an argument with his wife about going or stayin' and she shot him in the guts. Died this morning. Sheriff locked the place up."

"Holy hell. His own wife shootin' him. Damn women, ya can't trust a one of 'em." his table friend replied, "I had me a wife once that come close to doing the same for me." He let loose a long belch, and wiped his fuzzy face on a coat sleeve. Frank and Bill looked at each other.

"Looks like we go with Stuart, like it or not." Bill spoke quietly under the hubbub of the cafe.

"Looks that way. Ever been on a train?" Frank rejoined.

"Nope. Always wanted to, though. They're big machines, ain't they?"

They walked by Chinnick's and saw that the place was shuttered and locked, with a sign hung on the doors saying that," By order of the Sheriff, This establishment is closed for business."

"Wonder if Irvine knew this was comin' down?" Frank pondered.

Walking back to MacQueen's on the dusty street, Bill approached a touchy subject with what he thought was some tact.

"Frank, your gut is goin' to slow you down. Why don't you stay here this round?

"Son, I've gone this far after those bastards and I owe it to Matthew's memory to see it to the end. I'll make it fine. Just don't you tell Stuart." Bill, knowing he was going to be stonewalled, dropped the subject.

At Hubbell's, they looked over the horses. The two men compared the points of each, trying to decide which ones to take, for they had decided on three horses for each of them—one to wear a light pack, another to be ridden, and another as a spare. The remainder would go to Stuart for his bunch to use.

Heading back to MacQueen's, Frank slipped into the apothecary's and when Bill came in behind him, he heard Frank ask the clerk for a pint of laudanum. Stepping away from the counter, Frank wouldn't meet Bill's accusing eyes.

"Just in case, son, just in case."

Back at the room, they proceeded to gather their gear.

"Wonder what happened to Billy Juan, he said he'd be by this morning, but he never showed, " Frank commented.

"Come to think, I didn't see his horse at the livery."

An hour later, their question was answered at Hubbell's when they were saddling up and packing their outfit. At the livery entrance they heard a muffled step, then Billy appeared, staggering through the doorway.

"Frank!"

The sobbing cry brought them to the young man's side as he dropped to the floor.

Seeing blood on his shirtfront, Bill opened it to see an oozing bullet wound low down on the brown skin of the boy's left side. His face showed a great bruise on that side, too, closing his eye to a mere slit. Bill turned him on the littered floor to ascertain if the bullet had gone through. It had. Frank bent over him to ask:

"Who did it, boy?" His voice came in a fierce whisper.

Billy's arm came up in a mute appeal to the men who'd befriended him.

"They took him, Senors, took El Tigre from me. One hit me, the other shot me after I stabbed him!"

"Who did it, boy?" Frank grabbed the bloody hand and held it close.

"Two men. Down by the ferry. I was riding along the river. They were friendly at first. We talked about horses. Then the one the other called Mick accused me of stealing El Tigre. He knocked me off and grabbed El Tigre's rein. I stabbed him in the leg trying to get the rein

273

out of his hand and he kicked me, then the other man shot me. When I came to, the ferry man was pouring water on me. He called me a greaser, told me to get away from his ferry. I came looking for you."

Bill had been padding a torn shirt onto the boy's lean side. He took another shirt from his pack and tore strips that he wound around the light frame and tied as Frank held him up.

"We need to get him to Doc Girard as quick's we can, Frank."

"I think I can hand him up to you. Swing up and let's see."

As Bill swung into the saddle, Frank gathered the slight form and straightened up with it, lifting it higher so that Bill, leaning down from above, could grasp it. He did, adjusting the burden, hearing Frank gasp at the pain.

"I'm going!" The sorrel stepped out into the sunlight.

"Go ahead. I'll follow you in a minute." Frank grunted.

Bill, looking back, could see Frank doubled up in a knot. He straightened painfully as Bill rode from the livery, his sorrel horse breaking into a trot, then a lope as he sensed his master's urgency.

Major Girard came into the waiting room, looking around as he wiped his bloody hands. Frank and Bill were seated, sided by side.

"Frank. What are you doing up and around?"

"I'm not in the ground, yet." Frank answered testily. "How's the boy?"

"Not good. He lost quite a bit of blood, internal bleeding, I think it tore a chunk off his liver. Who shot him?"

"That's what we'd like to know. Evidently a couple rustlers. They took his horse." Frank answered.

"That beautiful animal? He loved that horse. That alone might kill him." Girard looked around the room at the perennial crowd staring back at him. He gestured to the one who looked the sickest, a small private clutching his shoulder in pain.

"Well, come on, Murphy, I better put that shoulder back in for you so you can get back to work." He turned and addressed the two men. "We'll know by morning."

Back at the livery, the two men somberly completed their packing and then choused the loose horses down to the railroad corrals at the edge of town. Without any talk, Frank kept the bunch closed up while Bill rode around and opened a gate that let them into a small enclosure with a water trough. Bill swung down and slipped the handle catch on the windmill. Creakily, it turned, caught a whiff of air and began pumping. Some of the horses, smelling water, crowded around the trough. Then Bill loosened his cinch as Frank slid off and did likewise. They had a two hour wait--If the train came in on time.

Settling back against a post, Bill rolled a cigarette. Frank brought out his scarred old pipe and began stoking it. Bill waited until he'd done so, then struck a match that lit both their smokes.

"Wonder how many men he'll bring with him." Bill commented, mainly to get Frank talking.

"I'd guess about fifteen. Reece'll be one of 'em, if he has any say-so. That arm of his should be healed up by now."

"First stop..?" Bill queried.

"Cahn's Coulee, I s'pect. Heard there's a hold-up outfit there hanging 'round the trail waitin' for any unsuspectin' pilgrims with heavy pockets. They'll get a surprise if they're still there."

Frank shifted his bulk heavily, seeking unsuccessfully to find a comfortable way to sit. "Son, I got a money belt on me with quite a bit in it. If I go under, keep half of it. You been a good pardner to an old man. Give the other half to Toby, if he makes it. If he doesn't, keep it all. Maybe it'll give you a new start."

"I 'preciate it, Frank, but Toby'll make it and he'll need it. I've got some put by, with that you gave me from Stringer's belt. I don't know what I'd do with it anyway. Lost my desire to have my own place when my woman got took. Maybe I'll stay on with Stuart if he'll keep me."

"You're way too young to think that way. Just do what I say."

"Suit yourself. Let's wait and see what happens. Maybe I'll go under first. If I do, give Toby my money. I left it back with Leighton along with the rest of my gear."

They smoked in silence a while.

"Leighton, now there's a scrapper." Frank chuckled, "Shoulda seen him last year, he and his clerk, takin' on some pilgrims right out in the street in front of his place." He chuckled again at the memory. Bill settled back, his cigarette going, listening again as Frank spun out his tale. Around the horse trough, one of the loose horses playfully bit another's rear, then turned away to nibble at some grass along the edge of the corral.

Later, Bill came out of a doze to hear the sound of a faraway train whistling for a crossing on the flat. Frank was over by the far side of the corral, looking carefully back at the town. "There's a rider coming out this way, looks like it might be Irvine."

The rider proved to be Tom Irvine, who arrived at the same time the train chuffed into a stop. No passenger cars showed in its short length, only freight cars, the middle one of which the door slid open and Granville Stuart and Reece Anderson dropped to the ground. Anderson gestured at the engineer and he pulled slowly forward, stopping the train again with an empty car at the corral's loading chute. Men dropped from the cars behind. Stuart came forward to the men grouped in the corral, his hand out to Irvine.

"How do, Tom, See you were able to round up Frank and Cantrell. Good to see you, men. Ludich tells me you caught up with Stringer. That right?" Bill glanced at Frank, who nodded without speaking.

"Yes, that's so, Mr. Stuart. Frank ran him down over on the Milk River with your gray. He's just another good rustler now."

"I knew my gray would go the distance for you!" Stuart glanced keenly at Frank."You can ride? Hear you're not feelin' so good,"

Frank snorted, "Good enough to see this through. You can't keep me out of this, Stuart."

"No, I know better than to try. We'll be needin' some fire breathers like you and Reece with us on this one." He turned to Tom Irvine."What about Chinnick, Tom?"

"All taken care of, Granville."

"Good. These the horses you got from Hunter, Frank? Some good lookin' stock. We can use them. Let's get 'em aboard, boys!"

That job in hand, Stuart turned to Irvine. "We'll be goin'. See you on the return, Tom." The two friends shook hands and Stuart swung up.

* * *

Inside the second car's dark interior, Frank and Bill at first could just make out shapes of men sitting along the sides, some sleeping, some talking above the clatter of the wheels. Finding empty spots, they plumped their gear down and sat as the train began to gather speed, disdaining to stop at the depot in the town's mid-section.

Frank, looking around, counted fourteen men including himself and Bill. He caught Reece's wink and nodded, seeing Cramer lounging on the opposite side of the car. He gave a casual wave. Ludich was sitting beside him and grinned in the dimness.

When Stuart settled beside him, he commented, "Kind of a small posse, ain't it?"

Granville was slow in his reply. "We wanted to keep this stunt to ourselves. I brought the absolute most that I thought could be trusted to do the job and keep still about it afterwards. I knew, though, if I didn't include you, Frank, you'd probably come gunning for me later." He didn't smile as he said it.

Twenty minutes later, the train slowed for a siding known as Cahn's Coulee after that worthy had $30,000 stolen from him there in a stage hold-up. The men were ready and all swung to the ground as the train ground to a stop. The first men down went to the other cars, opened doors and pulled out heavy ribbed planking that allowed the horses access down to the ground. All were saddled and their cinches were quickly tightened and the outfit climbed aboard. Quietly, without talk, the men walked their horses around the front of the train and south toward a cluster of cabins, one with a sign proclaiming it to be "The Star Saloon." Horses were bunched at the hitch rack, and Frank took a second look and pointed, catching Cantrell's eye. There in the middle of the tied bunch was Billy Juan's El Tigre. Frank swung the Ben horse over to Stuart's gray.

"The boy that owns that horse just got shot for it this afternoon. I want the S.O.B. that did it."

"Your play then, Frank. The boys and I will back you." At his gesture, the others spread out and swung down.

Frank, with Bill following close at his heels, caught the bat wing doors and crashed them open with his elbows. Cantrell came behind, taking a stride to the left. In back of him, Stuart's men filed through the doorway and spread out on either side.

The bar interior was smoky and strong smelling. Men sat or sprawled at the rough tables, most watching a card game in the far center of the room. All heads turned at the violent entrance.

"I'm lookin' for the bastard who stole that horse out there and shot its owner." Frank's voice was hard and his eyes turned alertly about the room. "Which one of you is called 'Mick?'" Several eyes swung to a man at the main card game, his upper leg showing a crude bandage. His face shaded white as he felt the room's attention center on him. The others around him began to edge away.

"That's my horse. The kid stole him from me. I just took him back." He began to bluster, then his hand dropped below the table and

Frank drew and shot him twice, the two shots coming as one, knocking him from his chair.

"Who'd he come in with?" Frank called out.

Bill, watching the bar, saw the bartender's eyes swing to another figure at the far end of the counter. Seeing he'd been spotted, the man brought a pistol up and leveled it at Frank, who didn't see the motion. Cantrell shot as the other's gun went off. Frank swiveled but the man had already dropped to the floor. He turned back again to the group around the table.

"All you men stand up and get against the wall there. You, too, bartender." Frank ordered, waving his pistol at the laggards.

"You hit, Frank?"

"No, didn't touch me but I felt the wind of it." Frank replied, "Thanks."

Granville Stuart and Cramer came forward and scrutinized the men lined up as for inspection. Under their gaze, more than one man hung his head.

"That one. And that one." Cramer pointed to a pair of men whose faces blanched when they were designated. Neither, however, said a word. The one, a man with a saber cut on his cheek that had destroyed his eye, stared at Adams with hatred out of the remaining orb. He made as if to wheel in flight, only to see his escape route blocked by Jack Ludich and another puncher coming in from the rear exit of the bar. Both men designated were grabbed and disarmed, their hands tied.

"Outside with them." Stuart ordered. He looked around the bar. "The rest of you men stay quiet and inside."

The Stuart crew pushed the men onto their horses. They all mounted and all rode back to the train, where ropes were thrown from the car. Cantrell saw that they already had hanging knots tied in them. Ludich and Cramer flipped them over the heads of the two and pulled the hemp tight. Their horses were led to the telegraph line and the ropes tossed over the crossbar of a pole and snubbed to its bottom.

"Any last words, rustlers?" Stuart asked in a tight voice.

"Nothin' you'd wanta hear, you Strangler bastids!" came from the scarred one. The other remained silent and Cantrell observed he was far gone in drink or terror, for he reeled in the saddle.

"Just as well," Cantrell thought.

With a snap of his quirt, Stuart started the horses and the bodies of the two men swung kicking in the air. Silently the men loaded their mounts back into the train, including El Tigre.

Chapter 19

Northern Pacific Rail line—East of Miles City

At Savage, thirty miles out of Glendive, the train pulled into a siding and ground to a halt. Stuart got stiffly to his feet and looked out the partly open door. Another cluster of rough cabins and a single store front faced the tracks. They'd made several stops, been shot at twice, shot three and hung a number of others, all men identified by Cramer. It had been a long two days.

"Let's walk over to the cafe and circle up some grub." he announced. The men were unanimous in murmuring agreement to the suggestion. The doors were pushed back and all swung to the ground. Suddenly, a rifle shot sounded, and a man doubled up and went to the ground. The others scattered, seeking cover. Some dove under the car and from the other side, another rifle spoke and another man grunted with the shock of a bullet slamming into him.

Stuart jumped back into the train car, hollering, "Jump back aboard, boys, it's an ambush!" He pumped his arm frantically, trying to get the train moving.

The rest of the men came scrambling through the open doorway as yet more shots banged out, both front and rear. The men worked hurriedly at piling saddles, beds and gear along the sides of the car for protection.

"Anybody help Currie back in? He was hit." Stuart asked. He was engaged in pushing the door part way shut. No one spoke.

"So was Johnson. In the guts, it looked like." Ludich offered. He crawled to the door and peered out, his pistol ready. What he saw was Frank calmly attempting to get Currie up and into the doorway.

"Here, boys, give me a hand," Ludich called, grabbing hold of the wounded man's arm, Frank flopped over the rail for him to pull on. Out at two hundred yards, toward a rack of poles and a small set of buildings, the rifle spoke again and splinters flew from the door frame. Then Stuart's big .50/95 boomed out over their heads, nearly deafening them. Beside them, another rifle got into action. Several willing hands grabbed the hit man and pulled him to shelter. Frank, instead of hopping up into the car, then proceeded around to the back of the train, which was beginning to move as the engineer grasped the predicament. Cantrell cursed, and scrambling over, started opening the back door to help Frank get the other man in. Frank was firing his pistol in spaced shots, keeping the rifleman's head down. Reece Anderson and Cantrell rolled out of the car and, grasping the gutshot man, threw him bodily into the now moving car. They both swung aboard and reached back to grab Frank in. He sprawled on the floor with his pistol still in his hand.

A couple of miles out from the ambush site, Stuart leaned out and got the engineer's attention with a wave of his arm. The train slowed and came to a stop. Stuart turned to the car interior.

"We'll pile off here and go back after 'em. It might be long range work, so be sure and grab your rifles." With that, he swung down and strode to the back cars to unload the horses. He was burning in fury at the ambush. Somehow, knowledge of the raid along the right-of-way had gotten out and ahead of them. It could only mean crooked telegraphers along the tracks, something that would have to be explored further later. Right now, it had cost him two men, as both were dead. Up to now, things had been going smoothly. They had struck again and again, surprise each time a factor that won the situation and had cost them no casualties. Loss of this element would increase the danger to them immeasurably.

Moving swiftly on their back trail, the group of riders split as Stuart directed them, some, with him, heading back to check out the ambush site, others going north and south to cut off any riders fleeing from the retribution they knew might soon strike.

Frank and Cantrell were motioned north, along with Ludich who rode at their heels. Moving at a lope, they soon lost sight of the main party. None of the men had eaten much in the last two days, partly from lack of food, partly from lack of time, but mostly because of the upsetting nature of their grisly task. Presently, reaching back into his saddlebags, Ludich drew some jerky out and, spurring his horse alongside of the two front riders, he handed both several pieces. Chewing as they rode, they topped a long ridge and Cantrell pointed ahead at several riders just going into a cut about a mile away. Without speaking, they swerved to intersect them.

"Looked like four. Did you see 'em?" Cantrell called to Frank riding the Ben horse slightly behind him.

"Looked like four of 'em, alright."

However, the men in front never topped the cut before the pursuers gained its edge. When they did, they saw it opened into a series of sprawling coulees, the sides and bottoms of each covered with low scrub cedars and sage brush. They drew up and Ludich stepped down to read the tracks when the crack of a shot came to them and Ludich spun down. Frank and Cantrell spurred their horses back from the edge, jumped down and helped Ludich. He clutched his right leg, where a hole through his chaps and blood gushing told the story of his wound. The other men laid him down, pulled his chaps off and split his pants to get at the gunshot.

"I don't think it's broke but all that blood don't look good," Frank commented in a whisper to Cantrell. Bill, without answering, jumped off the rim of the cut to catch Jack's horse and drag it back. Shots sounded but he was successful in getting the mount to safety. Frank was wrapping a tourniquet around the upper leg, a piece of rope with Ludich's pistol through it. Jack raised up, then lay back as the blood continued to pump swiftly from the bloody hole. Bill and Frank looked at each other in consternation. Frank drew the rope even tighter but the blood still flowed and ebbed with the pumping of Ludich's heart. He eyed them weakly, seeing in their faces his probable fate.

"Hell, I knew when I came on this party I wasn't going to make it back. Had a feelin' about it from the start. Roll me a cigarette, will you, Bill?"

Scant minutes later, despite even Frank's last ditch attempt to stem the blood flow by packing it with dirt, the head of their friend lay back and a quiver ran through the wiry figure, then he relaxed.

"Sonofabitch!" Frank exploded, "A damn leg wound and he's dead," The grizzled head hung for a moment, looking down at the dead man, then came up with a fire burning fiercely in the deep-set eyes. He gained his feet and strode to the black horse and pulled out his long Sharps from its scabbard.

"Had a hunch I'd need this." From a saddlebag he drew a rolled belt full of .45/120 cartridges.

"Grab your rifle and let's open the ball."

Bill pulled his Winchester from the scabbard, wishing he'd done as Frank had, and brought his new Sharps along. The big guns had no equal in a long range fight. 'Oh hell,' he thought. 'The big lever-action had always served him well.' He pulled a sack of shells out of his saddle bag and started a sneak around the rim of the drop-off that would put him into position while Frank kept their attention to the front.

Frank, meanwhile, squirmed to the edge and peered over just in time to catch sight of a puff of powder smoke way out at the extreme range of his vision. He ducked his head as a shot plowed dirt off to his right and howled off. The marksman had evidently caught a glimpse of Cantrell as he bobbed away and snapped a shot off, giving away his position. Frank peered through rheumy eyes that watered with concentration, estimating distance, bullet drop and a slight breeze from the west. He flipped up the long range back sight and set it for 400 yards. He levered down the breech and slid a big fat brass cartridge in the chamber, then pulled the lever back, causing the breech to slip smoothly shut. He grimaced, hating to fire the big weapon prone, as it kicked like hell, always hurting his war-damaged shoulder. Trying not to think about it and so flinch, ruining the shot, he wriggled his old carcass around and brought the front sight up to the spot where'd he'd seen the smoke eddy, and waited. Down there something flickered in his view, a hat or head sticking up. He set the trigger and drew steadily back, the rifle firing. The recoil slammed him, pushing him back on the rocky ground. He rolled sideways and jacked the empty out, sliding in a new cartridge and closing the breech. As he did so, he heard the rifle speak again, pushing him flat as another bullet whined over him. 'Close,' he thought. 'The bastard's got the range.'

The rifle sounded like a Sharps, but maybe a smaller caliber, he thought. Possibly a .40/65 or some such. The sound was more a crack than a boom. He carefully rolled and crawled a few yards to his right, watchful for cactus, and set up again for a shot. He was in time to see movement and fired again. This time, he saw the bullet throw up dirt a foot or more low. He re-set the sight, re-loaded and settled in again, waiting for another target to show. When it did, he was ready and the Sharps spoke with authority. On its echo came a shot from Cantrell's Winchester, the deep boom sounding far to the right and to Frank's front. Almost immediately came another shot, again from Cantrell's weapon. Frank hissed in satisfaction. The youngster was turning out to be a solid man, one that Matthew would have liked and been drawn to, he knew.

Pistol shots flared, then another rifle, a different one, possibly the same rifle that had helped bracket them back at the siding, for it had the sound of a Henry to Frank."Just the two rifles, maybe" he thought. He peered over cautiously but no shot came back at him.

To his right then, he saw Cantrell break from cover and make a short run before dipping down out of sight. An instant later came two pistol shots, then the pounding slam of Cantrell's rifle—once, twice. Frank hunkered over his Sharp's and watched the far coulee for movement but could discern nothing. Presently, he saw Cantrell stand and wave him on. Cautious as ever, though he wondered why, he backed away from the edge, then stood and scabbarded his rifle. Mounting, he gathered Cantrell's horse and made his way around where the younger man had gone, skirting a couple cuts and finally drawing up as Bill, sweating from exertion, came up to him. He raised a rifle in his left hand and Frank took it. It had blood on its breech and barrel, a .40/65 Business Model Sharps, as Frank had thought. He handed it back.

"They're dead, Frank. You blew the head off one. The others.." he gestured down into the coulee where the men lay sprawled. Frank rode over closer to the cut and looked down.

"Know any of 'em, Bill?"

"The one using the Sharps was a hunter out of Miles for Miles Burns down south on Pumpkin Creek, named Roger something. I saw him hanging around Chinnick's one time. He was the only one could shoot. Damn near got me. The others I don't remember seeing before."

He drew his kerchief and mopped his face, then shoved his own rifle in its scabbard and the two men rode down into the draw, where they began gathering the dead men's horses and gear together. The Sharps went into a scabbard on a buckskin. They pulled off bridles and started the cluster of horses back up to the ridge where Ludich's body lay.

* * *

Three days later, the train slowed down and chuffed to a stop at the corrals at Miles City. The door slid open on the freight car and Cantrell dropped to the ground. Anderson helped a weak and hurting Frank down into Bill's waiting hands. Frank had made it to the train but had collapsed in the car as it had pulled out of Savage. He'd missed the rest of the trip, resting in a bedroll that Bill had made up for him in the car. At Medora and several other stops, the posse had off-loaded and made short, hard rides into the countryside, coming back grim and in two cases, bloody from wounds. Bill had escaped injury, though, and had at times stayed behind to tend Frank.

It was while waiting for the others to return of an afternoon that he, for want of something do while Frank moaned and restlessly slept, went through the pile of rustler gear thrown haphazardly in one end of the car after each raid. The guns took his interest and he closely examined each of them to escape his boredom. Most of them were Colts and Winchesters, but there was a Remington pistol, with several Sharps in the heap, including the one that they had taken from those killed in the coulee. A short barreled Colt .45 took his eye and he picked it up. The front sight was worn down and the weapon's stag grips were likewise nearly smooth from wear and use. Idly, he turned it over and there on one grip end were the nearly illegible initials "MG". For an instant, the marks didn't register in his drowsy brain, then, with a surge of adrenaline, he came awake and examined the gun closely. He looked toward the other end of the boxcar where Frank was, on the verge of calling to him. He didn't, however, when he saw that his eyes were closed and he'd fallen away again into a semi-conscious state. The laudanum was gone and low moans escaped the old man's lips from time to time. Bill took the revolver to the door of the car and, after looking it over again, decided to go through the pile and re-examine each of the other guns for any telltale marks that might show ownership. Though several did, none were the"MG" that the .45 pistol had on its butt. Eventually, he cleaned the gun carefully and stowed it away in his own bedroll.

Upon returning to MacQueen's with Frank, Bill went straight away for the army doctor out at the Fort. The Major, on hearing of Frank's collapse, returned with Bill to the hotel. After examining Frank, who came partially awake but remained silent, Girard prescribed more laudanum for the pain. He shook his head as he left, refusing the gold eagle that Bill tried to get him to take. He had bad news, too, about Billy Juan. The boy had died the next day without regaining consciousness. Bill walked him to the door, then turned back to the sick man's bed.

"I'm going to head down and get your medicine, Frank. I'll be back directly."

Frank nodded weakly. "Take your time, son, I'm not going anywhere."

Bill remembered his find as he started out the door. He turned back and pulled the pistol from his gear and laid it on Frank's bed, "Just remembered this. I found it 'mongst the rustler's gear we'd gathered. Is it Matthew's?" Frank reached for it, almost too weak to pick it up. He turned it in his hand and saw the marks on its butt. His hand dropped and a tear squeezed from his closed eyes. "Yes, it was his, alright. Thanks, son."

* * *

In the ensuing days, Frank recuperated somewhat, mainly due to the heavy use of laudanum, which numbed his pain and gave him a measure of relief. He began leaving the room, visiting the saloons during the day, doing a little drinking and card playing in Brown's at night. Bill stayed with him, uncertain in his mind as to what course to chart for himself, reluctant to leave Frank in his illness. He'd never been a hard drinker and basically disliked people in groups, especially drunk ones. Frank, on the other hand, was a gregarious person at heart, even sick as he was. He enjoyed talking and visiting with anyone. Bill's increasing restlessness didn't escape his notice, however.

Chapter 20

DHS Ranch

In August, Granville Stuart returned to the ranch, along with some of the other men. He was surprised and pleased to see Toby sitting on the porch, on the mend.

"Where's Frank, Mr. Stuart?" Toby asked, "When's he coming back for me?" The old cowman's reply was evasive.

By September, Toby was well enough to get out and do some walking. Though weak at first, and awkward, he soon was working the horse corral again and enjoying, as always, his association with the horses. He met Stuart alone one beautiful fall day, as the older man was riding back from one of his numerous meetings, and, taking up his courage, reined in front of Stuart's horse, pulling him up.

"Sir, I don't mean to be disrespectful, I owe your family for taking care of me, but I need to know about Frank. Is he dead?" The thought had been forming in his mind that death was the reason for Stuart's evasiveness.

The tired, gray bearded man looked at him from over his high bridged, aristocratic nose, with piercing eyes grown softer from the summer's deadly work, not harder.

"Son, come to the ranch, we got a train to catch."

Chapter 21

Miles City

The cowtown was even busier and dustier than Toby remembered. They rode the train over a nice, new bridge across the Tongue and took rooms at the MacQueen House. On every hand, Stuart was greeted with respect and absolute courtesy, almost, Toby felt, as if he was a conquering general home from the war. If, however, it had changed the older man's demeanor, Toby could not see it.

After they'd eaten a late supper, Reece Anderson, who'd come with them, excused himself.

"Aren't you going to tell me what this is about, sir?" Toby asked, over coffee.

"Son, I could tell you things, but I think it's better to let Frank," the other replied.

Anderson came back in and whispered to Stuart, who rose. Toby got up, too, and they left the crowded dining room, several customers staring and whispering as they recognized Stuart.

They walked down the boardwalk, now lit by gas street lights, to Brown's Saloon. Anderson went in while the others waited. Presently, he reappeared, with Frank dragging behind him.

"Frank!" The boy flew at the old man and he, his face, working convulsively, half opened his arms when he saw the boy, then made as if, undecided, to turn away. The boy grabbed his arm. He could smell whiskey.

"Frank, why didn't you come for me?"

Stuart, with a look at Reece, walked off a ways, to give the two some privacy.

Toby pulled at the man in front of him.

"Frank, I waited for you. I knew you had business, but Mr. Stuart came back and you never did,"

Twice the old man started to speak. Finally, he said,

"Son, I figured it was best to leave you right there where you was. Stuarts and Andersons are good people and they'll take you in like you was their own. You know, Reece doesn't have any boys and he's taken a real shine to you."

The boy stuttered in his bewilderment.

"But, but, Frank, don't you want me anymore? Have I done something to make you 'shamed of me?" He thought a second, "Dee was going to shoot me, and I shot first, just like you told me to."

Tears coursed their way down his face and he wiped them angrily away. Frank awkwardly patted his shoulder.

"Not that at all, son. You did fine. You'll always do fine. It's me, boy, that's outlived my time." He looked around.

"Here, son, feel this." He took Toby's hand and brought it to his stomach, pressed it in.

"Feel that? It's a tumor, boy, a big one eatin' me up inside. Girard says it'll take me before long." The boy pulled his hand away in horror.

"But, Frank, can't he do something, cut it out of you?"

"Nope, nobody's cuttin' on my insides. These things happen, is all."

"But, Frank!"

The old man gripped his shoulders.

"Now, Toby, you and me, we've been like father and son. Matthew and I, we've loved you that much. You were good for us old-timers. Now my string's about run out but yours, why, it has a long way to go."

The boy sobbed.

"I want to be with you, Frank. You're gonna need me! I make the best coffee. I can cook for you, just like before!"

"Now, I said the way it has to be, Toby. You go 'long with Stuart and Reece." He half-pushed Toby, then turned him and pulled him in for a last hug.

"Son, let's make it a clean parting." He turned to the hitch rail, and Toby saw, for the first time, the sleek black horse tethered there. Frank stepped to him and deftly pulled the saddle off. He jerked the reins loose and handed them to the boy.

"Want you to take Ben, son. He needs to go with you." He reached inside his shirt and unbuckled a money belt. He took out some, then dropped it over the boy's shoulder.

"About six thousand there. I never did trust banks."

Toby shook his head, tears still streaming down his face.

"Frank!"

Frank patted him once more, then pulled out an object from his vest.

"One more little memento, son. You'll use it more than I will." He put it in the boy's hand, pressed his shoulder with a clawed old hand, looked in the boy's eyes, then turned back to the saloon. At the door, he paused and turned, his fierce old face in profile for an instant in the light of the moth-ridden gas street lamp, then he disappeared inside.

Toby turned the object over and saw it was a watch and fob. He opened the hunter case and read the inscription inside.

* * *

Two weeks dragged by, the weather ever hotter as late summer took hold along the Yellowstone. The cottonwoods released their seeds and the streets and sagebrush were decorated with wispy rolls of white cotton blowing with the warm winds that presaged the afternoon thunderstorms which came up from the west. The air was full of the hum of mosquitoes and at night the moths gathered thick around the yellow lamp poles which lined the streets now. Bill was at the livery after a lonesome supper, currying down his old sorrel and generally pampering the other horses in their string when Tom Irvine stepped in the door of the barn, closely followed by Stuart and Reece Anderson.

"Friends to see you, Bill," Tom's voice was low and he scrutinized the dim interior carefully for any other occupants as they came forward. Stuart's hand came up and gripped Bill's outstretched one firmly as he stepped away from his horse. Anderson shook briefly with him, also.

"Anyone else around?" Tom asked, his eyes still trying to adjust to the darkness.

"No, Elmer's stepped over to the cafe for a cup of coffee. I told him I'd watch the livery for him" Bill rejoined. He set his curry brush into the apple box nailed on the wall.

"I heard Frank is up and around, doing some drinkin' and gambling. Has he been talking any about our recent run east?" Stuart inquired.

"No. And I'm sure he won't, either. Whiskey don't affect him much, anymore." Bill said shortly. Stuart and the others noted his unspoken defense of his friend.

"Good. Bill, I wanted to talk to you about what you're going to do with yourself now. We'd all like you to stick with us. The Stockmen's Association has voted to hire another hard riding stock detective to keep a lid on the start we've made on a clean-up. We want you and Gus Cramer to carry on for us. You'll be wearing a badge as one of Tom's deputies, too, to give you some legal grounds for whatever you have to do. Will you consider such an offer? It could be a long term thing for you." Stuart's voice was placating and persuading at the same time.

Bill was silent, reviewing his bleak options. He'd taken no money for his involvement in the clean-up, preferring to clear his name and align himself with the side of inevitable right and trust to his future luck, but he did have his little cache from Stringer's pile. This could be a step further towards respectability. He didn't know what to do with himself, anyway.

"I guess it's a job I could do. Maybe I should ask who I would report to and what it pays?"

"$100 a month and expenses. A month's bonus for every rustler you catch. You'd report to me, Irvine or Reece. You and Gus would work separately most of the time. And there's a chance that you'd have a couple other men to help you as we find them."

"I'll take it—but what about Frank?" Bill was hesitant to leave him, though Frank had repeatedly urged him to do so.

"Stay by him until . . . he doesn't need you anymore. It can't be long from what Girard says. You're on the payroll as of now. It won't hurt for you to keep your eyes and ears open while you're here in Miles. Here's a $100. I'm counting it as money you've earned from your time with us already. No, we want you to take it!" He urged, as Bill made an attempt to deny the gold eagles Stuart offered. He finally allowed himself to be persuaded, to the others evident satisfaction. Then their heads came closer together and plans began to form as Bill's sorrel shifted his feet on the livery's straw-strewn floor.

Three nights later, Cantrell came awake to a low moaning from the other bed. He slipped out from under the flannel sheet he'd thrown over himself and lit the lamp. Under its soft light, the face of the old man shone with running sweat. He stepped to the side of the bed, then pulled a high backed chair to him.

"Gettin' worse, Frank?"

Silence for a while. Bill thought that the man on the bed maybe hadn't heard him. Then Frank muttered.

"Always thought I'd go quick—gun fight, arrow—mebbe drowned, even. Not this. Got a notion to use a gun right now, the way it hurts. Anythin' left of the laudanum?" Bill padded over to the dresser. The medicine bottle atop it was empty but there was a half-full whiskey bottle next to it. He took it to the bed.

"Just the whiskey. Want a glass?"

"Nope. This'll do."

He raised the bottle and took a long swig, then another. It seemed to suffice for the moment. He lay back with a sigh.

"You know, Son, I 'preciate you stickin' with me like this. You've been a pard."

"Nada. You'd done the same for me."

"Yeah. You know, I feel some easy now that we got most all of Stringer's bunch. We did clean up on 'em, didn't we?" He took another long drink that was interrupted by a tearing spasm, nearly causing him to drop the bottle.

Bill took it from the floor and set it on the box that did duty as a nightstand. When his eyes returned to the form on the bed, some sixth sense told him Frank was gone. He rose and brought the lamp close.

Yes, the fierce old eyes were open but unseeing. He gently brushed his hand over them and then pulled the blanket up and over the gray head. It was finished.

Despite himself, he felt a flood of relief.

END

LLOYD'S MONTANA SAGA

BOOK ONE – THE REBELS

Two confederates meet on the battlefield and become friends during the Civil War. After the conflict is over, the men go west to make a new start. War-weary and restless, they find it hard to settle down.

Their journey takes them to Texas where they find work as rangers, then to Kansas, hunting buffalo, and finally to Montana, to see and experience the gold camps there.

BOOK TWO – PARDNERS

The early 1880's finds Frank and Matthew, with their adopted son, Toby, working to make a stake hunting buffalo on the Montana Plains. They run afoul of Stringer Jack's band of horse thieves as they attempt to start a horse ranch on the Yellowstone River, hoping to sell mounts to Fort Keogh's cavalry.

BOOK THREE – T.S. GROUNDS

Toby Grounds, the adopted boy, starts out on his own. He finds work with Theodore Roosevelt on his ranch in North Dakota, and follows him to Cuba into the maelstrom of the Spanish-American War. Later, he participates in the Philippines Campaign, battling the fierce Insurrectos.

Home again, a bitter love affair causes him to respond to Roosevelt's request for help with the plight of American missionaries in China, as they become engulfed in the Boxer Rebellion.

Toby comes home to take up ranching again, only to succumb to his need for money, which drives him into a bounty chase for outlaws in Montana's south country.

BOOK FOUR – HOME RANCH

Last in the series, this book continues the family saga into the 1960s where Toby's son, Matthew, struggles to build a ranch, pursuing his father's dream. He passes on his love of the land and strong will to survive to his son, Gable, who endures the Korean War to find his own destiny.

Throughout the entire series, the reader will anxiously turn pages until the very end.

ABOUT THE AUTHOR

Dave Lloyd is a 4th generation Montanan whose great-grandmother traveled up the Yellowstone on a steamboat to the head-of-track outside Miles City. She knew and told her family stories of the men and the women who lived at the time. Dave grew up listening to her and his grandmother, the first white baby born in the county, as they reminisced of that era's rowdy times.

Later, Dave was a working cowboy and became assistant ranch-manager on one of the largest ranches in the state. Western Cattle Company, with hundreds of sections of land and cattle numbering in the thousands. He researches his books, and tries to make them historically accurate with their characters true to the times.

Lloyd has always been a gun, hunting and shooting enthusiast, and his readers are delighted by the old Sharps, Winchesters and other vintage rifles and pistols throughout Lloyd's novels.

The author lives in Helena, Montana with his wife, Donna and continues to write of the early beginnings of the state he loves.

For more about the author visit www.lloydsbooks.com